W9-BLI-912

DARK DESIRE

The moon was bright, the sands soft where the tide had not reached them. The wind had dropped and the air was warm, redolent, now that we had left the smell of fish far behind, of the scent of flowers escaping from unseen village gardens. It was a night for love and I was walking by the side of the man I loved. I felt exhilarated and could no more conquer the feeling than I could fly to the moon. Though he was indifferent to me, yet could I dream.

"Deborah," he said softly and I turned to him. "We must go back."

"Oh, not yet," I cried, not wishing to relinquish my dream. "This is so wonderful. I've never walked like this before . . . so late . . . at night."

My words limped to a halt as a look came into his eye that seemed to sap the breath from my body, and then his lips came down on mine, hard, urgent, demanding, awakening a blaze of desire in me, and I answered him kiss for kiss like an abandoned woman and could not help myself . . .

**TIME-TRAVEL ROMANCE
BY CONSTANCE O'DAY-FLANNERY**
*Discover the sensuous magic of passions
that know no boundaries, with
Constance O'Day-Flannery's captivating
time-travel romances!*

TIME-KISSED DESTINY   (2223, $3.95)
Brought together by the allure of sunken treasure and the
mysteries of time travel, neither 1980s beauty Kate Walker
nor 1860s shipping magnate Michael Sheridan dared believe
the other was real. But with one enchanting kiss, the destiny
that had joined them across the barriers of time could no
longer be denied!

TIME-SWEPT LOVERS   (2057, $3.95)
Somewhere during the course of her cross-country train
ride, beautiful corporate executive Jenna Weldon had fallen
backward through time! Now, in the arms of Morgan Tra-
hern—the original Marlboro man—the astonished Jenna
would experience a night of passion she would never forget!

TIMELESS PASSION   (1837, $3.95)
Brianne Quinlin awoke after the accident to find everything
gone: her car, the highway—even the tall buildings that had
lined the road. And when she gazed into the eyes of planta-
tion owner Ryan Barrington, the most handsome man
Brianne had ever seen, the enraptured lovely was certain she
had died and gone to heaven!

*Available wherever paperbacks are sold, or order direct from the
Publisher. Send cover price plus 50¢ per copy for mailing and handling to Zebra Books, Dept. 2562, 475 Park Avenue South, New
York, N.Y. 10016. Residents of New York, New Jersey and Penn-
sylvania must include sales tax. DO NOT SEND CASH.*

THE PERIWINKLE BROOCH

KATE FREDERICK

ZEBRA BOOKS
KENSINGTON PUBLISHING CORP.

ZEBRA BOOKS

are published by

Kensington Publishing Corp.
475 Park Avenue South
New York, NY 10016

Copyright © 1989 by Kate Frederick

All rights reserved. No part of this book may be reproduced in any form or by any means without the prior written consent of the Publisher, excepting brief quotes used in reviews.

First printing: January, 1989

Printed in the United States of America

Chapter One

The house came into view suddenly and unexpectedly. A turn in the road brought it to my sight. Of rose pink brick, set on a rise in the ground, I knew at once it was Rosemont.

Intricately carved chimneys, tall and fascinating, pierced the blue April sky; leaded casements, reflecting a thousand tiny suns, glittered like a jewelled necklace round a fine lady's throat. My heart leapt with delight and my enraptured gaze was held suspended while a love within me, long suppressed, awoke to renewed life in a sudden blaze of energy.

I had always loved painting and sketching, but since my father's death I had lost all interest in the art and laid aside my brushes and paints and charcoal sticks, thinking never to use them again. Now, on this bright morning in spring, at the turn of the nineteenth century, my fingers itched to hold them again and capture the sight that so entranced me. How long would it be, I wondered in a state of breathless excitement, before I could search out the best spot from which to make my first sketch? I felt I could hardly wait.

Yet I had not wanted to come to Rosemont.

We rumbled over a wooden bridge straddling a dry moat, passed under an archway topped by a crenellated tower, crossed a cobbled courtyard, and drew to a halt outside a massive nail-studded oakwood door.

The door swung open, and as I stepped down from the carriage my feeling of delight evaporated. My spirits had been lifted on the other side of the bridge and I had forgotten why I had come. Now they plunged downwards and all the brightness of the day seemed to vanish and only darkness loom ahead, and though I had never considered myself unduly sensitive to atmosphere, I became acutely aware that day of a menacing presence lurking within that shadowy interior. I knew that something . . . awesome . . . was lying in wait for me behind the butler's back, and I wanted nothing so much as to climb back into the carriage and order the coachman's immediate return to Hunt Park.

But of course I could not.

And there was nothing frightening about the smiling butler welcoming me in, nor about the footmen unloading my luggage. Nevertheless, I entered the lofty hall, with its hammerbeam roof and vast array of ancient weaponry arranged upon its stone walls, with a feeling of grave disquiet, and eyed uneasily suits of armour that looked for all the world as if still inhabited by their warlike owners awaiting the signal for attack.

I was escorted up a magnificent oaken staircase, along richly carpeted corridors, seemingly endless stretches of less finely carpeted stone passageways, up another staircase (cut out of stone and spiralling narrowly), and deposited with my baggage in a darkly furnished bedchamber.

Left alone, prey to all kinds of doubts and fears, I looked about me. The carpet beneath my feet was faded and worn. I could feel the chill of the stone floor rising up through its thinning weave and penetrating the soles of my soft kid boots. The furniture was of the Tudor period, dark and heavy. The curtains draping the four-poster bed and shutting out most of the light from the windows were of thick brocade. They might have been a bright golden yellow at one time, but age had robbed them of their glow and turned them the color of straw. Graying tapestries barely covered the walls. The impression the room gave was one of deep, dark gloom. It found an echo in my heart.

But a fire had been lit in the wide stone hearth and drew me towards it. Miniature flames licking at the base of the logs as yet offered no warmth, and while I waited for them to leap higher, I ventured to the windows, and parting the curtains as far as they would go, looked out through the diamond-paned casements upon the scene below.

Wide sloping lawns; trees and bushes burgeoning with fresh green leaf; a rhododendron walk, thickly budded, leading to a little rustic summerhouse; a meandering river sparkling in the April sunlight; a pair of snow white swans skimming the bright water and trailing a family of gray-brown cygnets behind them.

A peaceful panorama.

Why then, did I shudder and turn away?

Because I feared the menacing presence that I had sensed waiting for me in the hall now lurked outside — among the trees, down by the river, in the little rustic summerhouse.

Because I believed that wherever I went, inside or outside this house, there it would be, waiting for me, biding its time before . . .

Oh, stop it! I admonished myself forcibly and went back to the fireplace and the comforting sight of expanding yellow flame. Such foolish notions probably sprang from my bitter disappointment at having to come to Rosemont after praying so hard not to. Perhaps . . .

A knock at the door startled me, turning me from the path which would inevitably lead to increased misery and despair.

"Come in," I called and a young housemaid entered.

Bobbing a curtsey she said, "If you please miss, Miss Selina will see you now, in her boudoir."

Desperately seeking to delay this first meeting with Miss Selina, I withdrew my hands from my gloves and removed my hat and coat as slowly as I could. Then I went to stand in front of the long mirror I spied in a corner of the room, the only piece of furniture not of Tudor origin, and made a pretence of tidying my hair, smoothing out the creases from my slate gray skirt with my hands, ensuring all the buttons on the matching jacket were done up, that the fall of frill on my white blouse cascaded neatly.

I was surprised by my reflection in the mirror, surprised to see I looked exactly the same as I had always done, for I had felt certain there must be a change in me since setting out from Hunt Park two days ago. Yet there I was, small and slight, with the same brown hair, the same lips, the same chin, the same gray-green eyes. If a change had occurred in me, it did not show on the surface.

But it would—I knew it would—as the years passed.

The mirror misted over. The hot trickle of tears scalded my cheeks. Tears of self-pity. I banished them angrily. I had shed more than enough of them. I would shed no more. Life had dealt me a series of devastating blows over the last few months. I had survived them. I would survive this.

"Please, miss," the little maid burst out anxiously, "the mistress doesn't like to be kept waiting."

My footsteps lagged as I followed her neat little figure down the spiral staircase and along the silent passages, my reluctance to meet Miss Selina, Lord Denton's aunt, as great as my reluctance to meet Miss Alicia, his sister, for with those meetings I should cease to be Miss Deborah Conway of Conway Place and become the someone I had been trying to accustom myself to becoming for many days past—a lady's companion. I set no store by Lord Denton's promise that I should be treated like one of the family. Lady's companions, even when relatives of the family employing them, held no real status within the household and were treated like some kind of superior servant, tolerated above-stairs, unwelcome below. They existed in a kind of no-man's land—and that would be my fate, if I did not do something about it.

But I did intend to do something about it. I was going to fight it every inch of the way. I had a plan.

Lord Denton had agreed to pay me a monthly salary of generous proportions, and I did not think it would take me too long to save up enough money to enable me to take the shorthand and typewriting course I had begged Mrs. Morrison to allow me to take, only to be told caustically that such courses cost money — and I hadn't any. Whereas I was fully equipped without the need of expensive training to be a lady's companion, which was a much more genteel occupation for a young lady of breeding.

I had no idea how much such a course would cost, but no matter how much it was, no matter how long it took me to save for it, I was determined to join that growing band of forward-looking women eager to prove themselves in the business world of men. It might be hard work, difficult to achieve, but better by far to make the effort than to accept without demur the path Mrs. Morrison had mapped out for me.

Lost in my thoughts I was brought to awareness by a sudden seeping of ice into my bones. It might have been the chill of the stone emanating from the walls and floor — only I noted we were traversing one of the richly carpeted corridors and the walls were panelled with good strong English oak.

I found I had come to a halt outside a door at the head of the stairs, plain of itself but guarded two grotesquely carved pilasters. I stared with revulsion upon a strange creature — half man, half beast — writhing in agony as an army of small unnamable "things" gnawed away at every part of its body; a lion and a leopard locked together in combat, entwined about with fork-tongued snakes, while strange birds with evil grinning human faces hovered above, watching and waiting for a result that would never come.

Every instinct urged me to get away, as far away as possible, from the pilasters and the door they guarded, and

9

yet . . . and yet . . . My hand reached out to grasp the knob, turn it, and push the door. There was no yielding. The door was locked.

I tried to draw my hand away and to my horror found I was stuck. I tugged and pulled, but the knob had glued itself to my hand. Unable to retreat, I was suddenly under attack by the beasts who leapt down from the guardian pilasters to claw at me, rend me to pieces. I screamed.

"This way, miss, *please*."

As from the other side of a nightmare, the maid's voice reached me. Suddenly I was free. My hands were by my sides. The animals were back in their places. Had I screamed? The maid was not reacting as if I had. So had I imagined the whole thing? Common sense told me I must have done. Yet it had all seemed so real.

"Are you all right, Miss? You do look pale. You're not going to faint, are you?"

"No. No. I'm fine."

I quieted the girl's fears, but not my own. I could not quite convince myself that the bizarre occurrence had taken place in my imagination. And yet, how could it be otherwise? I had been prone to fretful imaginings ever since crossing the bridge and entering the confines of Rosemont. Was it because I was tired and hungry? I had eaten next to nothing since leaving Hunt Park and I had not slept well since Lord Denton's appearance on the scene. Had the lack of food and sleep combined to make me light-headed, overimaginative? Had I not heard sometime it could have that effect?

The maid stopped, knocked on a door, and ushered me into a room full of light. No Tudor darkness here. Only white paint gilt and pale satin met my eye.

"Good morning, Miss Conway. Please sit down."

A lady of indeterminate age, superbly gowned in dark blue moire silk, with diamonds at her ears and surrounding the little fob watch on her bosom, sat in the window embrasure motioning me toward a chair placed opposite her. As I drew near it struck me that she must at one time have been a great beauty. Evidence of it still showed in her fine bone structure, the regularity of feature, and clear blue of her eye, though her hair was laced with silver and a fine network of lines marred her skin.

I sat down, and with one pale long-fingered hand resting lightly on the top of the little rosewood table by her side, she regarded me speculatively.

"How young you are," she murmured sadly. Regretting her own lost youth?

"I'm eighteen," I declared.

She smiled, still wearing the same sad expression, then brightening, said, "Tell me about yourself."

What could I tell her that she did not already know?

I could tell you about Elizabeth, I said within myself, my friend since childhood, daughter of my father's best friend, Mr. Reginald Morrison of Hunt Park in Hertfordshire. I could tell you how, on their return from a protracted tour of the Continent, the Morrisons had sought me out and rescued me from a life of penury.

I could tell you how I came to be in that sorry state; about Conway Place, the house I grew up in — and how it was taken away from me after my father's death; how Aunt Susie and I had perforce to move into lodgings, and how I had to learn to wash and cook and clean, unable to afford even a scullery maid out of Aunt Susie's meagre savings, all we had left to live on. I could tell you about Aunt Susie, my father's only sister, who had brought me up from infancy. I could tell you about the seizure she sustained shortly after my father's death, and how unutterably bereft I felt after she passed away.

I could tell you all this, but I never shall. The telling would be too great a misery.

Nor shall I tell you of how happily I settled in at Hunt Park playing the role of second daughter to my benefactors, sister to Elizabeth and William, because that happiness had been too short-lived and was too precious to talk about.

If only William had not begun taking more than a brotherly interest in me, I might still be there. But he had, and his mother had not been slow to notice. And whereas she might have looked with favour on an alliance with the daughter of Sir Raymond Conway, heiress to Conway Place, a pauper living on charity was a different proposition altogether.

As soon as William returned to Oxford after the Christmas vacation, she set about enquiring amongst friends and acquaintances for a suitable post for me, brushing aside my protestations that to be employed by any family that had previously welcomed me as a guest was anathema to me. "Tut, miss," she had said. "You cannot afford to be so nice. Not now. Not in your present situation. You can't wish to impose on your friends indefinitely."

Impose! The word struck at my heart. For three months I had been encouraged to look upon myself as Mr. Morrison's ward and had been treated with every respect due to me as such. If it had been left to Mr. Morrison, I knew it would have continued so, but Mrs. Morrison ruled the roost at Hunt Park and his wishes were constantly being overridden.

"We can't turn her out, my love." I could hear him now, pleading with her in his gentle manner. "She's the daughter of my oldest friend. I went to school with him. Surely we have a duty to . . ."

"Our duty is to our son," was his wife's response, not noticing or not caring that I was in the vicinity. "She's a charity case and as such no fit mate for William. Of course we will not turn her out. But she must go. Just as soon as something turns up."

And something did turn up, (just when Elizabeth and I had begun to think it never would) in the shape of Baron Denton of Rosemont in the strange and remote county of East Anglia.

We both hated him on sight — as much for his cold superior manner and dark saturnine appearance as for his reason for coming to Hunt Park. He had heard, he said, addressing Mrs. Morrison in the drawing room where the three of us sat together, that she was seeking a genteel post for her ward, and had called in the hope of finding Miss Conway a suitable candidate for the position of companion to his young sister, Alicia.

Suitable! Suitable! Such lofty arrogance! Naively, I expected Mrs. Morrison to take exception to his words, as I did, and send him packing — she always said she could not abide proud and haughty people — but . . .

"I'm sure you will find her so," she said ingratiatingly. "She's gently born and has all the accomplishments. Admirably suited to be the companion of any young lady of quality."

Her voice flowed on while Lord Denton stared at me with narrowed eyes, considering my quality, assessing my worth. There was no warmth in his glance, only cold calculation which chilled my blood, and I knew I could not accept the position he offered. I could not place myself in a position where I should be beholden to him. Without understanding why, I felt threatened by him; afraid of the power he exuded without so much as moving an eyelid or saying a word.

I glared at him resentfully, head high, endeavouring to intimate I was not the malleable girl Mrs. Morrison was making me out to be, prompting him to think twice about his offer and withdraw it.

But aghast, I heard him say, "Then if Miss Conway is willing, I shall be most happy to welcome her into my household."

"No!" I cried out before I could stop myself. "I can't . . . I have no wish for the position."

Mrs. Morrison bestowed on me a look designed to wither further defiance in me. "Nonsense, child! How can you be so ungrateful? Excuse her, Lord Denton. She's overcome by the honor you do her, that's all. But after a little thought, I

13

can assure you, she will be glad to accept."

"But if she has no wish . . ."

"She's an orphan, living on charity, and must do as she is told," she interrupted him with some asperity, then aware that she had given offence, lapsed back into her ingratiating manner. "Besides, the dear child insists on earning her own living, expressing the view that she cannot go on being dependent on her friends' generosity. Though, of course, we are perfectly willing . . . It is a sad case, but the death of her father left her penniless. If it had not been for us, I do not know what would have happened to her. We found her in the most appalling state, you know. Dirty gowns, jagged finger-nails, hands roughened by the work she had to do—cook and clean and wash with no help at all, and a sick aunt to nurse. How she managed I'll never know."

Silently I beseeched her, "Don't. Don't. Don't shame me so before this man," but she was impervious to my plea, busy trying to set herself right in the eyes of his imperious lordship.

And now he turned to me. "Can you be ready to travel in two days' time, Miss Conway?"

I held my breath. I wanted to cry No! No, no, no!

"Certainly she can." I heard Mrs. Morrison answer for me.

And so it was arranged that he would call for me in his carriage on Tuesday morning. "It will take the best part of two days to accomplish our journey," he said, "so the earlier we leave, the better." But his person had been absent from the carriage when it arrived and a note of apology was delivered into my hands. Relief had surged through me as I read that something of great urgency had necessitated his immediate return to London, for the thought of being cooped up in his company for almost two days had worn my nerves to shreds.

I could tell Miss Selina nothing of all this, however. Yet she was patiently wanting to be told something. The bare

14

facts, then, unembellished. "As Lord Denton would have told you . . ."

Her eyes flashed. "Lord Denton has told me nothing. Why do you think we are having this interview? Apart from your name, and that you are to be Alicia's companion, I have no idea who you are or where you come from."

I thought it incredible that her nephew should have given her no information about me, and it crossed my mind that she was lying. But why should she lie? What could she gain by it?

"Ah well, never mind just now," she said. "You'd better meet Alicia," and she tugged at the bell rope close by her chair. A cryptic smile began playing about her mouth. A secretive expression entered her blue eyes. I shivered as I caught her glance. There was something about it that . . . I could not decide what it was. Or if I had imagined it.'

A footman arrived in answer to the summons and was directed to request Miss Alicia's immediate presence.

Miss Selina sat looking at me as if she were a cat and I a bowl of cream. Disconcerted, I looked away and tried to think about Alicia whom I was soon to meet. What was she like? Could we become friends? It was possible we could, two lonely girls together—Lord Denton had said Alicia was lonely. But my eyes kept returning to Miss Selina whose glance never wavered from my face. It unnerved me. And I wished she wouldn't smile like that.

It came as a great relief to me when a knock came at the door and it opened to reveal a ruddy-faced woman in black bombazine, with a little black lace cap perched atop her mass of frizzy hair, as brightly ginger as any I had ever seen. She entered with a reluctant young girl at her side.

I had thought never to see the girl who could rival Elizabeth's russet and cream beauty, but I saw her now, a vision of breathtaking loveliness with dark, dark eyes, long raven tresses, pale milky skin, and carmine-tinted cheeks. She was tall, inches taller than I who had risen automatically at her

15

entrance, and appeared to me, in her gown of ice-blue silk with matching ribbon tying back her glossy locks, to be a magical, ethereal being, not quite of this world—and my breath caught in my throat with an odd feeling of panic.

Selina Denton rose, revealing herself to be even taller than her niece. "Ah, Alicia." She brought the girl forward. "Come and meet your new companion, Miss Deborah Conway."

I held out my hand and it was left hanging in midair as Alicia stood before me in all her imperious height, unsmiling, unmoving, remote. In sudden consternation I wondered if she expected me to curtsey to her. Oh, no! That would be expecting too much of me. I still had my pride and did not intend to relinquish it for anything or anybody.

I gazed levelly into her eyes. Dark eyes they were, dark and shiny and—my heart started thumping dramatically— completely expressionless. My own eyes flew to meet Miss Selina's in voiceless questioning.

"Yes, Miss Conway," she said, smiling sweetly, "Alicia is blind. I do hope it has not come as too much of a shock to you."

But it had. I was shocked to the core. Blind! I had come to be companion to a blind girl! It was something I had never envisaged. The prospect appalled me.

"I thought my nephew would not have told you. That is his way, I'm afraid. He would have made no mention of Alicia's grievous affliction in case it should deter you from coming. And you would not have come, I warrant, if you had known. Indeed you would not."

Miss Selina's face wore the expression of one who knew herself to be right. And she was right. I should not have come if I had known—if I had had any say in the matter— which I had not.

I gazed angrily at Alicia, and gradually my heart began to melt. She looked so young, so vulnerable. And after all, it was not her fault I was here. I could not hold her to blame

16

for Mrs. Morrison's desire to be rid of me. I understood now why she had not taken my hand. She had no way of knowing it had been held out to her.

It suddenly smote me what her life must be like, how terrible it must be for her never to be able to see a sunset. Never see the moon and stars at night. Never to see a flower or a tree. Never to see her brother or her aunt or any of the people she came into contact with. Seized by compassion I reached for her hand and held it in mine. My voice was husky and I said, "I so hope we can become friends, Alicia."

But she withdrew her hand from mine quickly and moved away from me to stand at a distance, joined by the woman in black bombazine. So what should I do now? What else could I say? I turned to Miss Selina for guidance.

Miss Selina smiled. I was beginning to fear that smile.

"She won't answer you," she said softly. "She can't. She's dumb."

Chapter Two

"My nephew tells me you are an orphan, Miss Conway."

"Yes," I said, somewhat surprised, for only a short time ago she had complained he had told her nothing.

"And that your father died quite recently?"

"Yes."

"And your mother?"

"She died when I was a baby. I never knew her. My Aunt Susie brought me up."

"And she's dead, too, now, is she not?"

"Yes."

Why was she questioning me this way if she knew all the answers? She was dredging to the surface all the pain I had thought subdued with her probing.

"And after her death you went to live with the Morrisons?"

So she knew about that, too. She had been lying earlier on, as I had half-suspected. But why? To what purpose?

"At Hunt Park."

"Yes."

"How did they die?"

I choked on a sudden uprush of pain and was saved from answering the question that disturbed me so by a sudden change of mood on Miss Selina's part. She turned on her niece.

"Stop fiddling with your food, Alicia. Eat properly or not at all."

Alicia flinched and colored up. I was shocked and surprised, completely at a loss to understand Miss Selina's anger over so small an offence — if offence it was. But as fast as her mood had changed, it changed back again.

"Well?" She was looking at me with an almost ghoulish anticipation. "How did they die?"

"Don't you know?" I responded with some asperity.

Maybe it was ill-mannered of me, but I excused myself with the thought that her avid inquiry into a subject she must know was painful to me, was equally so.

"Would I be asking, if I did?" she retaliated.

"My — my father f-fell to his death," I stammered, my resistance crumbling as ice splintered from her eye and fell on me.

"When? Where? How?"

"He was ballooning. Attempting a record flight from France to England and . . . and . . ."

"The balloon ruptured and plunged into the sea." She came in quickly as my voice broke. "Yes, I remember reading about it in the newspapers. About a year ago."

She positively beamed at the remembrance and viewed me pensively, recalling, I did not doubt, further newspaper reports connected with the tragic event that had changed my life from one of carefree happiness to sorrowing despair. The newspapers had had a field day commenting on how heavily mortgaged Conway House was, and how Aunt Susie and I were left destitute. I did not want to think or talk about that time, but Miss Selina had not done with me yet.

"And your Aunt Susie — how did she . . . ?" With a hiss of exasperation she turned to admonish her niece again after the poor girl had accidentally knocked over her water glass. "If you cannot behave yourself, Alicia, I shall have you removed from the table. What Miss Conway thinks of you, I can't possibly imagine. I trust patience is one of your vir-

19

tues, my dear," to me again, sweetly, "for you'll need every ounce you can muster in your dealings with Alicia. As you will have noticed, she is not the brightest of creatures and, I am afraid, can be quite a handful one way and another. She has had more governesses than you can count on two hands. Not one stayed for any length of time, finding the task of contending with her moods more than they could bear."

I listened with growing concern and embarrassment to Miss Selina. Had she forgotten that though blind and dumb, Alicia was not deaf?

"I trust you will not be in such a hurry to leave us, but I do not count on it. She's such a troublesome, unmanageable child."

Troublesome! Unmanageable! I considered the silent girl sitting opposite me at the luncheon table and thought she did not appear to be either of these things. Quite the opposite, in fact. She looked as docile as a lamb. But then I noticed her lips tighten across her teeth and her breathing grow labored, and I wondered if her docility was only a surface thing, ready to break at any moment.

"Tell me about Hunt Park," Miss Selina said suddenly, and thankful that she had not returned to questioning me about my aunt, I replied cheerfully.

"Oh, it's a lovely house. Exceptionally fine. With beautiful gardens and an ornamental lake." I was glad to see Alicia's tension slacken as the spotlight was taken off her, and I continued to praise Hunt Park. "It was built in the Eighteenth Century in the Palladian style and is noted for its avenue of linden trees leading from the wrought iron gates to the front door."

"Rosemont dates back to Norman times." Selina tilted her head proudly, placing Hunt Park firmly in the role of modern upstart. "It wasn't called Rosemont then of course. It wasn't till the Great Change"—she capitalized the words—"of 1589 when the Elizabethan facade changed the look of the place forever, that it took that name. Up till then it was called Castle Humphrey after my ancestor, Humphrey d'Enton, one of the Conqueror's strongest baron knights, who played a big part in defeating Hereward the Wake and was awarded vast tracts of East Anglia as a result.

"Mind you, the land was not like it is now. Before Vermuyden's drains it was a conglomeration of islands floating amidst swampy marshland. So you may imagine the difficulties Humphrey encountered keeping the belligerent natives in check. It could not have been an easy task. They were a stubborn lot — they still are — and the last to bend the knee to Norman Will."

I listened to Miss Selina with growing interest. The history of East Anglia had hitherto been a closed book to me. Now it had been opened, I wished to learn more. I vaguely remembered hearing something about Hereward the Wake during my schoolroom lessons. It could not have been much. He had never attained a place on my list of historical heroes. But now he came alive for me. I saw him, a great leader of courageous Fenmen, defying the might of the invading Norman army, and I applauded him for it.

Selina, however, saw him in an altogether different light, which was natural enough, I supposed, since she was descended from the Normans whom he opposed. I listened to her extolling the virtues of her ruthless ancestors and vilifying the great East Anglian hero, and kept my thoughts to myself.

She told me how Rosemont had changed over the years from keep to castle to Elizabethan country house. Of its turbulent history. How it had withstood siege and Cromwell's cannon. How Capability Brown, set to landscape the grounds in the eighteenth century, had been thwarted in his wish to do away with the tower and drawbridge in order to lay out a sweeping driveway between an avenue of trees, ". . . something on the lines of your Hunt Park," she said with an air of disparagement.

"But the tower's crumbling all the time and will not

21

survive for much longer, if something is not done about it soon. I keep telling Charles it will be lamentable if such historical remains were lost for want of upkeep. But he doesn't take the interest he should. If I had my way . . . But I'm only a woman, and women do not inherit at Rosemont."

She made a vicious stab at the food on her plate, angry that the fate of Rosemont did not lie in her hands. It found an echo in my heart. I believed our historical buildings, our great cathedrals and castles, should be preserved for coming generations to admire and enjoy, and could not understand those who showed no feeling for such things.

"I've told him! It will finish up a ruin! Just one more pile of stones!"

"Surely he will not allow that to happen," I submitted.

"I shall see that he does not," she grated, stabbing again at her food, and I felt a sudden qualm for her nephew, disagreeable though he might be.

As she lapsed into silence I turned to Alicia—I had observed her listening to the conversation between her aunt and myself with keen attention—and asked, "Perhaps you wouldn't mind showing me round the house and grounds sometime, Alicia? I should be most interested."

Her eyelids flickered and fell, and her gleaming white teeth came out to bite deep into her lower lip. I could have kicked myself for my crass thoughtlessness. How could she, a blind girl, show me round?

"I can do that," Miss Selina said, with her sly secret smile. "I shall make you a better guide than she."

I could not restrain a frown of disapproval. What a thing to say! I had been insensitive. I had spoken without thinking and said the wrong thing—but in all innocence. It was a new experience for me, talking to a blind girl. It was not to Miss Selina, and again I was surprised at the underlying cruelty of her words.

I did not answer her, but to make amends for my stupid thoughtlessness, said to Alicia, "Do you like walking, Alicia?" At least there was no danger in that. You did not need to be able to see in order to enjoy walking. The exercise was pleasant enough in itself. "I'm extremely fond of it, myself. unable to recognize the danger signs. "What a fine sight it of Hunt Park. Perhaps you and I could do the same at Rosemont?"

"You are wasting your time," Miss Selina murmured softly. "She doesn't like walking — or indeed any kind of activity. Sitting around doing nothing is what she likes best."

Again there was that underlying cruelty about her words. I could not understand it. I did not think she intended to be deliberately cruel, but could she not see how the carelessness of expression could hurt?

"Then we could sit together in the gardens and talk," I said without pause. "Or in the little rustic summerhouse at the end of the rhododendron walk." I should have listened to what I was saying and held my tongue, but I rushed on unable to recognise the danger signs. "What a fine sight it will be in a week or two's time, when the fat buds open and the flowers appear in all their radiance and . . ."

Too late my voice gave out. Alicia rose from the table. Her chair rocketed backwards and fell with a crash. My skin began to crawl as I saw her body sway from side to side, her hands clasp together beneath her chin, her unseeing gaze fix itself on to me, her mouth work desperately — yet make no sound at all.

"I wonder how long you will last," murmured Miss Selina.

I threw her a mortified glance. I had blamed her earlier in my heart for her careless disregard of Alicia's feelings, yet it was I, with my prattle about gardens and flowers, who had brought on this terrible anguish. I had suggested we could sit in the gardens and talk. Alicia could neither see nor talk. The enormity of the situation I found myself in rose up to display the difficulties I should encounter in my role of companion to one who was both blind and dumb. I realized the deal of tact and diplomacy that would be required of me.

A nod from Miss Selina to Croft standing by the sideboard resulted in the swift despatch of a footman from the room. No one else moved. No one said a word. No one went to Alicia's aid, though she continued to sway from side to side mouthing her silent anguish.

Longing to help her, I remained seated, too afraid to move. Besides, what could I do to ease her? Such behavior was outside my experience. I might do more harm than good by interfering in something that, judging by the calm way all were taking it, was quite a usual occurrence. If anything was to be done, surely Miss Selina was the one to do it. And she had done it. A footman had been despatched — to bring help presumably. But help was a long time coming. How much longer could I sit here doing nothing?

So I debated within myself for what seemed like hours, till at last the door burst open and in rushed the ruddy-faced woman in black bombazine to enfold Alicia in her arms and croon soothingly, "There, there, my pretty. It's all right now. Murkett's here." And Alicia at once relaxed.

Murkett led her away, docile as a lamb now, and in going let fall on me a look of such malevolence it quite took my breath away. In a sudden panic, I thought, "She's a witch and she's put a curse on me, blaming me for what has just occurred."

"Tell me about your friends at Hunt Park."

Miss Selina was applying herself to her food again and addressing me as if nothing untoward had happened. I could only stare at her in amazement. Maybe Alicia's strange behavior had not surprised her, but had she not noticed how it had frightened me? And had she not seen the look the woman in black bombazine had bestowed on me?

"You will miss them greatly, I think. Especially Elizabeth,

24

with whom you seem to have a great deal in common."

Struggling to put the previous event behind me, as I was clearly expected to, I replied somewhat hesitantly, "She's my best friend. I've known her all my life."

"Is she very beautiful?"

Rich chestnut hair, thick and glossy, sherry-gold eyes, a Junoesque figure, and happy-go-lucky personality ousted the last vestiges of black bombazine from my mind.

"Oh, yes," I owned fervently. "Very beautiful."

Elizabeth had only to enter a room and every man's eyes were on her. Within seconds she would be surrounded by adoring males. Yet I never met a woman with a bad word to say about her. Not only was she lovely to look at, but she had a nature to match. Sweet-tempered, full of fun, she was never cruel, and no woman feared she would poach on her preserves.

I told Miss Selina this.

"You make her sound like a paragon of all the virtues," she said.

"I believe she is," I declared.

Miss Selina fell silent, and I became aware that she was weighing me up. A strange light shone from out her narrowed blue eyes, which had yet grown veiled and secretive again, and as before I was unnerved by her glance.

"You're not bad-looking, yourself, are you?" she said at length. "Quite a little beauty, in fact."

"Oh, no!" I shook my head vigorously. I might be passably good-looking, but beside Elizabeth, beside Alicia, I paled into insignificance.

"You don't agree? Then I suggest you observe yourself in the mirror sometime," she commented drily. And with the color high in my cheeks as I squirmed beneath her critical scrutiny, she went on to tell me that my features were good. My nose was small and straight, my eyes were an interesting color and sparkled with health, and though my mouth was a shade on the generous side, that was not necessarily a fault.

25

In fact some men preferred it.

Then, just when I thought she had done, she added something that set me trembling in every limb.

"I fear for you," she said. "There is a quality about you. It shines from your eyes. Innocence. You must take care. Innocence allied to beauty is a danger. A snare. A temptation for the unscrupulous. It courts evil. So keep your wits about you, my dear. Gird your loins. Don't say I didn't warn you."

I would have given anything to be able to pack my bags and leave Rosemont. I even got as far as taking my portmanteau from the cupboard it had been relegated to, by the someone unknown who had unpacked for me whilst I was at the luncheon table, and placing it on the bed. But even as I opened it, I knew it for a useless exercise. I could not leave. Where would I go? Back to Hunt Park? Back to Mrs. Morrison's scathing comments? I should only be sent back with a flea in my ear.

But what sort of a household had I come into?

I slumped back onto the counterpane with Miss Selina's dark words ringing in my ears. *Don't say I didn't warn you. Don't say I didn't warn you.*

Warn me against what?

She seemed to think some sort of evil threatened me, and mindful of the look of hatred served to me by the woman in black, my frightening experience outside the pilastered door, the strange forebodings that had gripped me since my arrival at Rosemont, I was inclined to think she might be right.

Or was I reading too much into Miss Selina's words? Had she only been cautioning me to be wary of men — as my Aunt Susie had often done — though not in quite the same way? Whatever the answer, all my earlier unease had returned and I lifted my head and scanned the room half-expecting to see someone — or some*thing* menacing me from the shadows, and could not keep up my judicious outlook, nor keep panic at bay.

My uneasy eye fell upon a table by the far wall. On it were placed my sketching tablet and my charcoal, unused for so long, but kept — just in case; and I blessed whoever had unpacked for me for leaving them where I could find them when I needed them most. They would bring ease to my troubled soul.

Scooping them up I ran from the house into the clear East Anglian air and lifted my face to the breeze. It was a cool breeze, a brisk breeze, but I welcomed it. It would blow away the tangled webs from my mind.

Making my way round the house, looking for the lawns leading down to the river — it was from the river bank I intended to make my first sketch of Rosemont — I stopped to gaze up at the crenellated gate tower standing bastion in the courtyard. It housed, I supposed, the heavy machinery needed for raising and lowering the drawbridge.

When was it last used? I wondered.

When the moat was deep and wide. Deeper than it was now and filled with water, dark and green and slimy. When there were marauding enemies to keep out — and hapless victims to keep in.

I shuddered as I thought of those times, of the violence prevalent then, and thankful I lived in a more enlightened age, hurried on to the river's edge.

I sat down on a mound of stone, part of the old castle walls I learned later, with my pad on my knees, and faced Rosemont. The old, gracious, lady of a house, with her necklace of sparkling diamonds, entranced me afresh, and the panic that had engulfed me within her walls subsided. I began to draw, working quickly and well, my fingers seeming to have only to trace something already outlined on the paper. When I sat back, the sketch at arm's length, a thrill of pleasure coursed through my veins. It was perfect.

My pleasure did not last long, however, for as I made my way back to the house, unease stirred in me again as the sun dipped behind gathering clouds so that Rosemont grew dark and hushed and secret, harbouring . . . What? Ghosts of the past? Ghoulish spectres that haunted its silent corridors when all was still? My feeling that something awesome lurked within the walls of Rosemont was only fancy. I knew that. But I could not rid myself of it. Nor of the sudden feeling that I was being watched from behind its darkened windows.

And if I were, I gave myself an angry little shake, what was so significant about that? I had been looking out of the window on to these very lawns myself not so long ago. Supposing I had seen someone and that person had been aware of my observance, would he or she have placed a sinister connotation upon it. Of course not! I had been extremely foolish to do so.

I quickened my footsteps into the house as drops of rain began to fall. The moment I entered the impressive hall, I was accosted by the maid who had earlier shown me to Miss Selina's boudoir.

"Oh, miss, where have you been? I've been looking all over for you. Miss Selina wants to see you at once."

A feeling of defiance came over me. I was not ready to relinquish my freedom and kowtow to Miss Selina, or anybody. I should have to eventually. Like this little servant girl I should have to jump when bidden. But now, just now, I would hold on to my freedom a little bit longer.

"I'll just take my things up to my room," I said.

"I'll do that, miss," the maid said quickly. "Miss Selina is waiting for you."

I looked at her closely as she relieved me of my things. She seemed to be in a permanent state of anxiety, and whenever she mentioned Miss Selina's name, an undertone of fear crept into her voice. Why? Did Miss Selina beat her if she did not attend to her wishes quickly enough?

"You'd better hurry, Miss. She's in her boudoir. Shall I show you . . . ?"

"No, I can remember the way," I said.

I went thoughtfully to Miss Selina's boudoir. Was she really the dragon the girl seemed to think her? The girl was plainly in awe of her, maybe even terrified. I was a little apprehensive of her myself, having witnessed how carelessly hurtful she could be—with words. But did she beat her servants? Some mistresses did. Would she? No! I did not think so. I could not see so dignified a lady as Miss Selina using physical violence upon anyone.

I knocked on her door and entered on her command. A tremor ran through me as I saw her standing at her window, her back to me, and I wondered if it had been she watching me as I came up to the house—but her room overlooked the courtyard at the front of the house, not the lawns at the back.

"You wished to see me, Miss Selina?"

"At last!" she snapped. "You have taken your time."

"I'm sorry. I was out walking. I've only just this minute come in."

"You should have left word where you could be reached."

"I'm sorry, Miss Selina." So I was to account for my every move from now on.

"I've been waiting to see you for over two hours."

"I'm sorry. I didn't know."

"You should have made it your business to know." She turned to face me now, blue eyes glacial, her words splinters of ice. "If this is an example of the service you will give, I can tell you at once, it will not do."

"I agree. I think I had better leave," I said with more bravado than I felt, for if she took me at my word, what should I do? Where should I go? Yet I refused to apologize a fourth time.

"That will not be necessary," she said with one of her swift changes of mood. "Come and sit down. I do not mean to be hard on you. I realize I must give you time to adjust to your new role of companion."

Indeed you must, I thought, for it is going to be very difficult. I was not by nature submissive and had always been allowed a great deal of licence by my indulgent father and gentle aunt, but here was Miss Selina making it abundantly clear I could no longer do as I pleased, that my will must henceforth be subordinate to her will—and Alicia's. It was what I had been trying to condition my mind to for days. I very much feared it would be beyond my powers.

Yet I must make the effort. I had little choice in the matter. And it was all down to the odious Lord Denton for turning up when he did. A little longer and I should have been able to persuade Mrs. Morrison she need not fear an alliance between William and me.

At the thought of Lord Denton my heart gave a jump of anxiety. Soon his urgent business in London would have been dealt with, and he would return to Rosemont, and that was something I did not look forward to. Not one little bit.

"So you've been out walking," Miss Selina spoke conversationally, yet with an underlying interrogative note that was strangely disturbing.

"Yes," I replied.

"Where did you go?"

"Down to the river."

"Just that? Nowhere else?"

"No. I stayed by the river. I made a sketch of the house from there."

"So we have an artist in our midst."

"I make no claim to being an artist. I just like drawing for my own pleasure."

"May I see the sketch?"

"Certainly. The maid took it to my room. I'll go and get it."

"Sit down, Miss Conway." She rebuked me sharply. "Are you a servant to be running errands? Ring the bell and ask the footman to bring it to you."

I rang the bell and sat down again obediently. My status might not be that of a servant, yet I must do her bidding.

While we waited for the sketch to arrive, she asked, "How long have you been acquainted with my nephew, Lord Denton?"

"I met him for the first time less than a week ago."

"Really?" My answer seemed to have surprised her. "So you are not in love with him?"

"Good heavens, no!" I imagined myself in love with Lord Denton and shuddered. Lord Denton was the last man I should fall in love with.

"Good," said Miss Selina. "Keep it that way. He is not the man to entertain tender feelings for. Many a foolish young chit has been taken in by him, to her cost. Don't add yourself to them. Jonathan, now, he's a different proposition altogether." Her face softened appreciably when she spoke of Jonathan and she handed me a silver-framed photograph to look at. "That's him. Handsome, isn't he? He's Charles's younger brother. And as different from him as chalk from cheese."

I guessed he was her favorite nephew, and as I looked at the young man in the photograph, I could understand why, and agreed he was handsome. He looked to be about twenty-four and very different from Lord Denton, whose good looks were spoiled by a stern forbidding expression. Jonathan's mouth was gentler, more relaxed—and he had laughing eyes. I could like him.

"He runs the estate for Ch—. Ah! Here comes your sketch."

She drew a deep sharp breath inwards as she took it into her hands and looked at it for a long time without speaking. Then, softly, whispered, "Beautiful. Beautiful. Why, it *is* Rosemont." She looked up eagerly. "May I keep it?"

"Certainly. I'm glad you like it."

"Thank you. I shall treasure it. Rosemont's been sketched many times before. Painted too. You have no doubt noticed the Allott hanging in the corridor outside. It's considered a masterpiece. But even he has not captured the spirit of the house as you have."

Feeling a bit of a fraud, recollecting how my fingers had seemed to be guided by something outside myself, I deemed such praise was not due to me and said so.

Miss Selina made a moue with her mouth. "My, we are modest, aren't we? Won't admit to being a beauty. Won't admit to being an artist. Yet both are markedly apparent. Modesty is a virtue, Miss Conway. But please don't overdo it. It can become tedious."

A belated smile took the edge off her words, but they were cutting, nonetheless. I began to appreciate how Alicia must feel and excused her earlier outbreak of what I had come to think of as a show of temperament. She had been on the receiving end of Miss Selina's biting tongue for, what? Years? How long before I lost patience and allowed ill-temper to show through? But I knew I must not allow myself such an indulgence. I was a paid employee in the household of which she was mistress. She could turn me out if she so wished, and what would I do then? I had nothing, no one, to fall back on.

She set aside the sketch and continued in a friendly way.

"I'm so glad you've come to Rosemont. I look forward to many pleasurable hours with you in the days — weeks — to come. We can draw together. I used to be considered quite good when I was — much younger. But I haven't done any sketching for years. You have inspired me to start again. Oh, I know you are supposed to be Alicia's companion, but the truth is, I need a companion more than she. She has Murkett. I have nobody."

A whine had crept into her voice and suddenly it became much stronger.

"I never go out these days. Never see anyone. I have a heart murmur, you see. I have to take pills."

She inclined her head in the direction of the small circular

32

rosewood table at which she sat. On it was set a small silver tray bearing a carafe of water, a crystal tumbler, and a pretty enamelled pill box. I had wondered about it earlier. Now I knew its purpose and sympathized with Miss Selina.

"The doctors say I am not to overexert myself," she said confidentially. "So you see, I must pursue only gentle diversions. We shall . . ."

She broke off as the chuntering of an automobile reached our ears and a look of revulsion crossed her face.

"Charles!" she spat angrily, rising to twitch back the curtains and look down on the courtyard below. "In that disgusting machine of his!"

Gray eyes, hard as sea pebbles, flashed across my mind's eye.

"Nasty smelly thing! Why he insists on using it is beyond me. Says it is the quickest way of getting to and from the station and saves having to call Rogers out with the carriage. But what's Rogers here for, if it's not to take the carriage out whenever it is required?"

Eyes that had looked me over coldly, dispassionately, assessingly.

"He knows it offends me!" She swung away from the window to glare at me resentfully. "That's probably why he insists on using it."

Suddenly I did not want to face those eyes again.

"I'd better go," I said rising swiftly.

Miss Selina flapped her hand at me. "No, no. Sit down. It will be you he has come to see. You — and Alicia. I'd better send for her."

But she made no move towards the bell rope, nor did she request me to do so.

"He'll want to make sure you've arrived," she said tetchily. "He could quite easily have telephoned. But oh, no! He has to come himself. Does he not trust me? Am I not capable?"

"Perhaps he was coming home, anyway," I said, trying to calm her, for I could see she was working herself up into a state over Lord Denton's insensitivity. She appeared to believe he was going out of his way to offend her. And she was probably right. *I* would not put anything beyond such a man. But to get so worked up about it could not be good for her heart. "He's probably finished his business in London and . . ."

"Do you think my nephew *lives* at Rosemont, child?" she intoned grandly, peering at me as if I were akin to an idiot.

"Why—yes." Hope sprang within me. "Doesn't he?"

"Pshaw!" Miss Selina tossed her head. "He forsook Rosemont years ago. He's not interested in Rosemont. Rosemont means nothing to him. Since his Uncle James took him on a voyage to the West Indies while he was still a lad, only ships and the sea have held any interest for him.

"I told my brother how it would be. 'Samuel,' I said, 'you'll never keep the boy at home if you let him go on this voyage.'—The sea is in his blood, you see, on his mother's side." She gave a disparaging sniff. "The Lockharts have a long tradition of seafaring behind them.—I said, 'Look how many hours he spends down at the estuary, going out with the wherrymen in defiance of your wishes.' But he wouldn't listen. 'Let the boy get it out of his system,' he said. 'He'll soon settle down.'

"Well, he was wrong, and I have been proved right. After that first voyage he went on another and another. Now he captains his own ship. And when he's not at sea, he lives in London with his Uncle James who retired a few years ago and now runs the Lockhart Shipping Company. We hardly ever see him at Rosemont. If it weren't for Alicia, we'd never see him. But he'll do anything for her—his beloved sister. Buy her anything. Give her anything. He spoils her. I've cautioned him about it. He takes no notice. I have taken on the responsibility of running this house for him, but my wishes count for nothing."

She ran out of steam for a moment, her heart heaving behind the dark blue bodice of her gown, and I grew concerned for her again. Then she regained momentum.

"Only a few weeks ago he gave her a kitten. Just because he found her nursing a doll. A doll! At her age! Never mind that I have a particular distaste for cats. Oh, no! He said it showed her need for something to love. I got rid of it, of course, the moment he returned to London."

She gave me a triumphant smile—expecting me to commend her act? I could not. I thought it mean and cruel. To deprive a lonely young girl of her pet for no reason seemed spiteful in the extreme. The fact that Miss Selina did not like cats could not provide sufficient reason. It would not have been too difficult to keep it out of her way in a house this size. I wondered if there could be another reason. What? Jealousy? Did she resent Lord Denton's kindness towards Alicia, feeling she did not receive enough of it herself? From all she said, he did not show much thought for her comfort and happiness.

A sudden knock at the door sent my heart frantically scuddering like a little mouse for a place to hide. I wanted to find a hiding place for my whole body. A hole in the floor to slide through or something. Anything, rather than face the man I knew was about to enter the room. But it was a meeting that could not be avoided.

The door was flung open with an expansive gesture, as if all its width were needed to accommodate Lord Charles Denton's stature. A wave of fresh air came in with him—sea air? It had clung to him on the first occasion of our meeting. I had not been able to give it its due worth then, but I knew now it was the air of a man who spent most of his life on the deck of a ship.

"Good evening, Aunt Selina. Oh!" He stopped and looked startled when he saw me. "Excuse me. I didn't know you had a visitor."

"Visitor, Charles? Surely you recognize Miss Conway."

"Miss Conway?" He evinced surprise. "But of course." He bowed, and managing one of his tight-lipped smiles asked, "How are you, Miss Conway? Settling in, I hope?"

"Yes, thank you, my lord," I replied politely, though I could tell from his manner he did not really care. Already he was turning back to Miss Selina, preparing to speak to her.

Miss Selina forestalled him. "She arrived safely this morning. A telephone call would have elicited the information for you and saved you a journey."

"A telephone call would not have done for the news I have to impart, Aunt. Bad news, I'm afraid."

As he spoke I caught sight of the broad band of black ribbon round the upper left sleeve of his jacket. Then I noticed the signs of strain around his eyes and mouth. His aunt noticed, too.

The blood drained from her face and she staggered backwards, clutching wildly for her chair as she breathed the name, "Jonathan . . ."

"No, Aunt, it's not Jonathan." Lord Denton was across the room in two strides steadying her and helping her into her chair. He glanced urgently at me. "Her pills. Where are her pills?"

I flew to take a pill from the enamelled pill box, poured water into the tumbler, and handed them to him as fast as I could, terrified Miss Selina was going to die. Her lips were turning a frightening blue—like Aunt Susie's before she died.

"Here, Aunt, take this." He was on his knees beside her. "Nothing's happened to Jonathan, I promise you."

"He's all right?" The color was returning to her cheeks.

"Yes. It's Uncle James who . . . Uncle James is dead."

"Oh, thank God! Thank God!" she cried, recovering remarkably quickly now.

The muscles of her nephew's face tightened at her words and he rose quickly from her side, crossed to the fireplace, and gripped the mantelpiece, staring down into the flames. I saw his knuckles turn white as his grip tried to bite into the marble. His aunt had spoken without thinking, but her words had sounded callous and, I could see, had wounded him deeply. For a brief moment I felt sorry for him. But then he turned round, fully restored to his usual cold, distant self.

"I came home in order to acquaint you with the news in person," he said unemotionally, "and to give you time to prepare yourself for the journey to Witchet Towers."

"Witchet Towers!" He might have said Hades from the way she reacted.

"Uncle James expressed the wish to be buried in Witchet churchyard. Not in the family vault inside the church. In the open. Facing the sea. He always said that if his last resting place could be where the salt winds of Devon swept over him, he would die a happy man. I intend his wish shall be carried out."

"But you can't expect me to travel all that way! Not with my heart!"

"It's the least you can do," was his pitiless response. "We leave first thing in the morning."

Miss Selina glared at her nephew with compressed lips, and it struck me that there was not much love lost between the two of them. Not that I was surprised. They were two such different personalities with different priorities. Her first priority was Rosemont. His was the sea. It was not his fault if the sea and his ships meant more to him than Rosemont and its lands—she had said the sea was in his blood—but it was plain she could never forgive him for it.

"Where is Jonathan?" he asked before she could venture to defy him as I felt certain she would have liked to do; only it would take a very brave heart to defy so authoritarian a gentleman.

"In Italy, I expect," was her truculent reply.

"Italy! What's he doing there?"

"What do you think? He's holidaying there."

"Holiday—! And what does he think is happening to Rosemont while he's away enjoying himself?"

"It's being well taken care of. Benson's looking after things."

"Benson!" Lord Denton looked ready to explode. "It's spring, dammit! Benson's got enough on hand at this time of the year without having Jonathan's responsibilities thrust on his shoulders."

"He's perfectly capable. Jonathan has great faith in him. And please don't use coarse language in my boudoir, Charles."

Selina's glance was all pained sweetness as she chastised her nephew, and with a choking sound that could have been an apology or another oath, he swung away to clutch at the mantelpiece again, knuckles white, shoulders tensed, endeavoring to keep a mounting anger in check.

All this time I had been dithering, wondering if I ought to excuse myself from what was a deeply personal conversation and nothing to do with me, waiting for an opportunity to depart. I thought that opportunity had now offered itself.

I opened my mouth, but before I could speak Miss Selina turned to me and said, "Jonathan's in Italy with a friend. Taking photographs. He's very keen on photography. Most of the photographs in this room were taken by him."

"He spends more time taking photographs than he does managing the estate," Lord Denton rasped from the fireplace.

His aunt rounded on him. "You've always begrudged him his hobby. Just as you begrudge him his leisure time."

"I don't begrudge him anything, but when it interferes with his job of running the estate . . ."

"He works very hard managing the estate—a job which should rightfully be yours, I may add. A week off here and there . . ."

"Here and there!" he scoffed. "As far as I can see, it's more often there than here. He's always away, coming back or just going, *whenever* I come to Rosemont. Is he ever here, I wonder?" Then suddenly, as if wearied of talking about

38

Jonathan, he hurled an abrupt question at me across the room. "Where is my sister, Miss Conway?"

"I . . . I . . . She . . . She . . ." I began stammering in my confusion. How could I confess to this flint-hearted man that I had not the least idea where his sister was? I searched vainly for a convincing excuse.

"Alicia is resting." Miss Selina came to my rescue and I turned to her in gratitude.

"She's not unwell?" Lord Denton asked anxiously.

"No, no," she said calmly. "She's just a little tired, that's all. Miss Conway and I . . ." She tutted impatiently. "No. Deborah. I shall call you Deborah since we are to become friends. Deborah and I were making arrangements to draw and maybe paint together."

"We agreed it was Alicia who needed a companion, Aunt Selina, not you," he scowled, anxiety giving way to annoyance.

"Oh, Alicia! Alicia!" she cried petulently. "It's always Alicia! No one else counts with you, do they? Not me. Not Jonathan. Not anyone."

"That's not true, Aunt Selina, and you know it. But Alicia is a special case. A young girl unable to fend for herself. Growing up in darkness. She needs a friend, companionship of someone her own age. I thought you understood that."

"I do. But what about my needs? You take no account of them." As she spoke, the whine I was becoming familiar with crept back into her voice. "Don't berate me, Charles. Of course I understand Deborah has come to be Alicia's companion, but you cannot deny me a little of her company, too. *I* need companionship just as much as Alicia does. *I* get very lonely, particularly when Jonathan is away. You never seem to understand *my* needs, Charles."

"I have never denied you anything, Aunt Selina," Lord Denton relaxed his stern manner in the face of her pitiful expression. "If you wish for a companion, I shall arrange for you to have one."

"I want Deborah," she cried, quick as a flash and with a spoilt child's impertinence.

"Deborah," he snapped, anger erupting again, "belongs to Alicia."

Chapter Three

I gazed at the door closing upon his departing back scarlet-cheeked and fuming with rage. He had made my position at Rosemont perfectly plain. I was less than a servant; I was a slave. Less than a slave, a commodity, a thing, an expensive present acquired by him for his spoilt sister's use.

I turned passionately to face Miss Selina.

"I don't belong to Alicia! I don't belong to anybody! I'm not a thing to be bought and given away!"

"Of course you are not," she agreed enthusiastically. 'But that is his way, I am afraid. He considers no one's feelings other than his own and Alicia's. You have seen how he treats me. How he insists on dragging me all the way across England to attend the funeral of a man I hardly knew and never cared for. How can you, an orphan with nobody to speak up for you, expect to be treated any differently? He has bought you for Alicia, just as he buys everything for Alicia. You're a gift for her amusement, just like the cat."

"Which you had removed," I scowled, half on her side now.

"Which I had removed. And if you have any sense, you will remove yourself. Leave Rosemont. Go back to your friends at Hunt Park. I shall be sorry to lose you. I think

41

we could have become friends. But for your own sake, I feel I must advise you to leave at once."

If only I could, how gladly I should take her advice, but I had been along that road already and realized I could not leave. There was nowhere for me to go. Without funds in my pocket to enable me to rent lodgings and feed myself til I found a job, I must stay where I was and make the best of things.

The best of things. In the quiet of my own room far from the main part of the house and where the chill of the stone all around me reminded me of Rosemont's earlier status as a Norman castle, I flung myself down on the big four-poster and thrashed about from side to side in a paroxysm of anger and despair. What was I doing here, Deborah Conway, only daughter of Sir Raymond Conway of Conway Place in Radnorshire, dependent on an unfeeling monster for my livelihood? I had thought I had scraped the bottom of the barrel, but it seemed the barrel was deeper than I had believed.

The best of things. Yes, I would have to make the best of things. But I would not bow to Lord Denton's definition of me. He would not turn me out if I failed to live up to it. He would have Mr. Morrison to answer to if he did, and Mr. Morrison would not stand idly by and see the daughter of his best friend so badly treated. But that would mean standing up against his wife, and I could not see him doing that. He was as weak as water where she was concerned. And Mrs. Morrison having got rid of me would not want me back in close proximity to her son again.

I was here at Rosemont and here I must stay. I could not tell myself that often enough. But the day would come, if I bided my time, when money in my pocket would give me the independence to stand up to his lordship and tell him exactly what I thought of him and his arrogant assumption that I would accept his estimation of my worth.

But that day, at this moment, seemed as far away as

Mount Olympus, and my fighting spirit was submerged beneath the weight of reality.

"Miss Conway. Miss Conway."

Exhausted by my tears and the events of the day, I had fallen asleep. I woke to my name being called and candle-light shining on my face.

I raised myself on my elbow and looked up into the face of the anxious little maid I was getting to know. "Hello," I smiled. "What time is it?"

"Time to dress for dinner, Miss," she said, adding with a touch of pleasure, "Miss Selina says I'm to look after you while you're here."

"Oh, how nice. I'm so glad." She was fast acquiring the status of a friend—and I didn't even know her name.

"What's your name?" I asked.

"Wicks, Miss."

"No. I mean your Christian name."

"Doreen, Miss." She set the candle down and crossed to the wardrobe. "What shall I put out for you to wear?"

"My black silk, I think, Doreen."

"Begging your pardon, Miss, you mustn't call me that. Wicks is what I'm known as." She eyed me unhappily, all anxiety again. "Miss Selina is very strict about such things."

"Very well," I promised, rising and going to the wash-stand, "in public I shall call you Wicks, but in private it will be Doreen."

She sighed. "Yes, Miss Conway, if you say so." She still sounded anxious, but I thought she was pleased.

"Deborah," I said gently.

"Miss Deborah," she smiled shyly, and with that I had to be content.

But a relationship had been cemented between us and I no longer felt so alone at Rosemont. I had found a friend.

"You'll need a necklace or a brooch to relieve this, Miss Deborah," my new friend said holding up my black silk gown. "I didn't come across your jewelry case when I un-packed for you. If you could tell me where it is . . ."

"I have no jewelry," I said sharply, splashing my tear-stained face with renewed vigour. Every piece I had pos-sessed had been sold off along with Aunt Susie's to help pay my father's debts.

If she was surprised at my lack of jewelry she made no comment, but proceeded to help me out of my now crum-pled and creased gray suit and into my black silk. As it fell in dark folds to the ground, I thought back with longing to all the pretty colorful gowns I used to own—all gone now the way of my jewelry. I had Mr. Morrison to thank for this black silk and the other decent clothes he had insisted on buying for me after finding me clad in a greasy dirty gown, one of only two still in my possession at the time. And I sighed for the shopping spree he had hinted at for Eliza-beth and myself only a week prior to Lord Denton's fateful visit. A spree that would never take place now. At least, not for me.

Doreen lit a separate candle for me and I wended my way by its flickering light down the narrow stone stair and along the stone passages, more than a little afraid of the silence and unseen watching eyes. I could not shake off this feeling of being watched, no matter how hard I tried. But once I turned into the thickly carpeted corridors where lamps blazed, eliminating shadows, my nervousness departed. I blew out my candle, set it down on a marble-topped side table to await my return, and ran swiftly down the fine oaken staircase—averting my eyes from the pilastered door dominating its head.

Lord Denton and his aunt were waiting in the drawing room dressed in mourning black, as I was. But Miss Selina, regally beautiful in a close-fitting gown of satin overlaid with the finest lace, had wound ropes of pearls round her neck to relieve the funereal effect and Lord Denton's som-bre garb was offset by a dazzling white shirt. With his dark

44

hair, strong nose, firm chin, his fine physique shown off to perfection by the superb cut of his suit, I thought, as I looked at him, What a fine and handsome man.

Handsome is as handsome does. Words that had frequently fallen from Aunt Susie's lips leapt into my mind and as I looked at him again, I thought, How could I have thought him handsome? Devilish would be a more appropriate word for a man as unfeeling as he, with his thin, cruel mouth, his hard cold eyes.

"Is something wrong, Miss Conway?" he asked abruptly, a puzzled light springing to his cold gray eyes.

Aware that I had been staring, I looked away quickly. "No. No. Nothing."

But I felt he was not satisfied with my answer and would have pressed me further if Alicia had not walked in, escorted as usual by the woman in black bombazine.

I watched the woman make a curtsey and depart without so much as a glance at me, for which I gave silent thanks. The last look she had given me was enough to last me a lifetime. I wished never to see such a one again. But I was surprised to see Alicia dressed all in white. White dress, white stockings, white shoes, white hair ribbon. Had it not been for her dark glossy hair, the faint flush tinging her milky white cheeks, she could have been a ghost. The thought brought a prickle to my scalp.

She had walked straight up to her brother. How had she known he was there? But of course he had spoken to her, and she had moved in the direction of his voice. He kissed her cheek and placed his arm about her waist. She was not going into mourning, he explained to me, nor was she going to the funeral. It would be too taxing for her. "Besides," he concluded, "a few days without any distracting influences will give you both the chance to become better acquainted."

Miss Selina must have guessed, as I did, that this last remark was directed against herself, but she chose to ignore it, sensibly, I thought. I let my gaze travel to Alicia. There was no smile on her face, no evidence of pleasure at the prospect of a few days alone with me. I remembered the limpness of her hand in mine at our first meeting. She had evinced no sign of pleasure then, no glimpse of friendship. On the face of it she had no desire for my companionship. And I, I must admit, at that time was not overeager to provide it.

Conversation at the dinner table was not easy. Miss Selina and Lord Denton, while not exactly arguing, rubbed angry sparks off each other, and the atmosphere was far from relaxed.

I withdrew into myself, wishing yet again that I had never come to Rosemont, a house thick with tensions, where the occupants seemed not to like each other very much. Where the girl I had come to be companion to was blind and dumb, and with whom it would be difficult if not impossible to strike up any sort of relationship.

And yet I must try to be friendly. Make her like me. I had to get along with her somehow. Lord Denton expected it.

Miss Selina wanted to be my friend. If I had come to be her companion, my job would have been easy. Yet — she was a lady of quick-changing moods and might very well change toward me. She had already shown her impatience toward me. But perhaps I was being unfair to her. She had not treated me unkindly, and though I felt I should have to watch my step with her, she was someone I could communicate with. Which was more than could be said of either of the others.

But Lord Denton had made it perfectly clear that I was to be Alicia's companion, not Selina's, and that he expected to be obeyed.

I glanced at him sitting at the head of the table: arrogant, superior, cold, impervious to the needs and wants of others. Only when his glance fell on his sister did his features soften. Only she held the key to the case of ice which

46

surely entombed his heart. There was a caustic lift to his mouth as he conversed with his aunt. I was staring at him again, and let my glance fall just as he switched his gaze to me.

I picked up the thread of conversation.

"So you knew him?" Miss Selina was saying.

"Only slightly. I did not cultivate his friendship. Our tastes took us in different directions."

"The papers said he died in debt."

"Yes, I'm afraid he did. He had a penchant for dangerous pursuits and ran up debts of enormous proportions in order to indulge his craving. And when he wasn't gambling with his life, he gambled at cards. He gambled away his entire fortune one way and another and left his only daughter destitute."

"A thoroughly selfish man."

"Yes."

They were talking about my father.

"But he wasn't like that." I rushed breathlessly to his defence. "He wasn't selfish. He was kind and thoughtful." I glared angrily at Baron Denton and the Honorable Miss Selina Denton, imperious descendants of Normans, and slave or not, my voice grew stronger. "How dare you describe him so?"

"Is it not a true description? One to which you have yourself subscribed?" the baron asked with a sarcastic lift of his eyebrows.

"No, it is not. And I never said a word against him in my life. He was a dear man. A kind man. The best father a girl could have."

"Yet he left you without two ha'pennies to rub together," he rasped.

"What did that matter?" I was almost weeping. "I loved him. He was very dear to me. I won't have you blacken his name."

"I'm very glad to hear it," he said quietly, and quite took

the wind out of my sails.

Was he applauding my loyalty, my quick defence of my father? Or was it simply sarcasm again? How could I know. I couldn't read his expression, nor see if his eyes were warm or cold as he lowered them to raise his wineglass to his lips. But why was I even questioning it when I knew the only warmth in him was for his sister, Alicia? And why should I care? What did it matter what he thought of me?

The meal over, we rose and adjourned to a small parlor nearby. A fire blazed in the hearth. Modern couches and chairs of soft leather piled with cushions invited us to sit down and relax. There was a bookcase, its shelves full of works by popular novelists. Dickens and Austen rubbed shoulders with present-day novelists like Mr. Arthur Conan Doyle and Mr. Wells. On a side table rested piles of magazines and newspapers. Photographs of members of the Denton family were placed here and there—I noticed a very good study of Lord Denton standing tall and proud beside a horse whose reins he held with the light touch of an expert horseman.

It was a warm room, a welcoming room. It became my favorite room. I called it the Little Parlor in my mind. But for now Miss Selina occupied a chair placed near the fire and poured coffee out of a silver pot into small, blue and white fine china cups. She signalled me to hand one to Lord Denton who had taken up a position at the other end of the fireplace and was leaning nonchalantly with one elbow atop the marble mantelpiece.

He took it from me with a muttered thank you. I did not raise my eyes to his face and turned back quickly to take a second cup from Miss Selina, this time for Alicia, only half full, I noticed. Then I received my own and sat back against the cushions on the couch where Alicia sat and listened to Lord Denton discussing funeral arrangements with his aunt.

I sipped my coffee and looked at him propping up the

mantelpiece — and hated him. He was so sure of himself. So sure he had everything just as he wanted it. So sure his aunt would meekly do his bidding and go with him to Witchet Towers, though it was the last thing she wanted to do. So sure he had put me in my place. But I would show him. I was not one to meekly follow his dictates. Yet that was just what I must do for the present, till I had scraped enough money together to enable me to quit Rosemont for good and tell him exactly what I thought of him.

Until then — I had to make the best of things.

I turned to Alicia. "Do you like music?" I asked. She might not be able to see or talk, but she could hear perfectly well, so I thought this a good opening gambit.

She turned towards me, astonishing me with her clear gaze — it was difficult to believe she was blind — and for the first time, I detected the vaguest semblance of a smile lift the corners of her mouth.

"My sister is very fond of music, Miss Conway," Lord Denton said from the fireplace. "She derives great pleasure from it. Do you play an instrument at all?"

"I play the piano and the violin."

"The violin? How fortunate. Alicia plays the piano."

"If you can call it playing." Miss Selina's voice zoomed like a wasp into the conversation.

He ignored the interruption and continued, "Perhaps you could play duets together."

"Personally, I think it would be better if she left the pianoforte entirely alone."

"Aunt Selina!" Lord Denton swung round on her with an angry hiss.

She was unabashed. "I can see no point in pretending she is anything she is not."

"No one's pretending anything. Alicia . . ."

"Might be many things, but a pianist she most certainly is not. She's had tutors," she remarked to me, "but you can't make a silk purse out of a sow's ear."

49

"Aunt Selina!" Lord Denton thundered, an expression on his face I thought I should never like to see directed at me. It was ugly, brutal. He looked as if he would like to strike her, even made a little lunge towards her—but he managed to hold himself in check. It was more than enough to silence her.

He addressed me once more. "My sister is a very good pianist. She has an ear for it. Play or sing something to her and she will reproduce it accurately on the keyboard."

"I shall be most happy to p—"

I held my breath as I turned to Alicia again. Her behavior was taking on a frightening mold. Her hands had fisted into tight balls and she began beating a feverish tattoo with them on her knees. She threw her head back and opened her mouth in a terrifying silent scream. With a moan her brother dropped down beside her and caught her hands in his.

"Alicia! Alicia!" he mumured, his face contorted with agony.

"Oh, lord, she's at it again." Miss Selina threw up her arms in mock alarm. "Ring for Murkett. Ring for Murkett."

I hardly heard her. In any case I was frozen to my seat beside Alicia, rigid now in her brother's grasp.

"Yes, ring for Murkett." He turned to me, his eyes, those hard pebble eyes, filled with pain and deep compassion. I saw how vulnerable he was where his sister was concerned, how he might easily be hurt through her. Just like anyone else, he had his weak spot. A weakness that could be exploited if one was inclined to be so ruthless.

A tremor of sympathy ran through me and I wanted to help him, relieve him of the pain that filled his heart. "I'll take her to her room," I said gently. "I'll look after her."

But as I touched her arm she reared away from me and began threshing about, trying to dislodge herself from her brother's grasp. If he had not been holding her so tightly, I felt certain she would have attacked me.

"No." He shook his head. "It's no good. Ring for Murkett. She's the only one who can help her now. All I can do is try to keep her still. Keep her from hurting herself."

And others too. I could not prevent the thought from entering my mind. And I trembled with fear.

Murkett came, neatly garbed and frizzed, and immediately took charge of the situation. She gathered Alicia into her arms. Alicia nestled against her, quiet as a dove now.

"There, there, my pet," Murkett began soothingly, rocking Alicia to and fro. "Has someone been upsetting my little darling then? Well, don't you worry any more. Murkett's here now. She'll see nothing happens to you." And a baleful glance winged its way towards me. "Come along, my pretty. Just you let his lordship carry you up to your room, and I'll put you to bed. That's right. That's my girl."

I watched and listened and felt slightly sick. It was all so very strange and frightening. Murkett talking to Alicia as if she were a baby; Alicia responding to it; the others accepting it; as if it were all quite normal.

But it was not normal. Far from it. Alicia was not a baby. She was not a child. She was a grown woman and in spite of everything I sensed a keen intelligence behind her dark expressionless eyes.

Yet she chose to respond to their babying ways. Why? Was it her way of escaping from reality? Was it by choice she behaved the way she did, aided and abetted by Murkett, and not because she could not help it?

Puzzling over it I saw her coil her arms around her brother's neck. He picked her up as easily as if she were a doll, and with a nod at Murkett preceded her through the doorway to Alicia's room.

"Tut-tut! Such tantrums!" Selina spoke calmly from her chair. "She certainly knows how to play upon her brother for sympathy, that one."

"You mean it was all an act?" I searched her face. She had not been taken in by all that baby talk, either.

"Oh, no," she said quickly, then shrugged. "Well, who knows? Thank God for Murkett, that's all I can say."

"Who *is* Murkett?" I had still not got over the venom in the woman's baleful glance. "Her nurse?"

"You could call her that. Since Alicia's illness she's had complete control of her."

"Illness? What sort of illness?"

"Oh, some sort of nervous breakdown. The doctors never really understood the nature of her illness. It was quite a few years ago now. She hasn't improved much. In fact, in some ways, she's worse."

"But isn't there some sort of treatment she could have?"

"We've tried everything. No, I'm afraid there's no help for it. She's as she is and we must accept it. We're just lucky to have someone like Murkett to look after her. She was undernursemaid in Nanny Perrot's time and took over when Nanny found it impossible to deal with the child. She was the only one Alicia seemed to be at ease with. She could quieten her where everyone else failed. Now she's the only one who can do anything with her when she gets into these moods."

"Does she have them often?"

"Often enough. And when they are on her, she can become quite violent. Well, you saw for yourself."

"So they are not just tantrums."

"Well, maybe they are, maybe they aren't. I have my own views on the matter. Charles may not agree with them but . . ." She shook her head speakingly. "One has to be so careful with her. One word out of place and . . ."

Still shaking her head she left the rest of her sentence unfinished, and I asked myself, that knowing all this why did she not watch her words more in front of Alicia. I could not help feeling she must take a lot of the blame for Alicia's sudden outburst just now. Ridiculing her — in front of me, a stranger. It would have angered anyone.

But to such an extent?

Lord Denton returned, reproval on his lips. "I do wish you'd be more careful about what you say in front of Alicia, Aunt Selina," he said, echoing my thoughts. "You know how she reacts."

"She doesn't understand," his aunt retorted. "She only has the mind of a child."

"Children can be as easily hurt as adults. I've begged you to guard your tongue in her presence. Why did you not try? Why do you continue to torment her?"

"I, torment her?" Miss Selina looked at him in outrage. "What are you talking about? I treat her with every consideration. Is it my fault she can't behave like any other normal human being? I've said it before and I'll say it again. She should be in an asylum."

"And I've said I shall never countenance such a thing. Please get that into your mind once and for all. It's out of the question. If I have to keep her locked up here at Rosemont all her life, I will do so. But I will not have her locked away in an asylum. She is not mad, Aunt Selina, just — disturbed in her mind."

"Isn't that madness?" she threw at him.

"Things have been going so well lately." He swung away from her to pace the room. "Each time I have seen her recently, I have thought her much improved."

"You should not set too much store by that. You do not see as much of her as I."

"But she has improved, Aunt. You must admit that. That was why I engaged a companion for her. I thought . . ."

His voice trailed away into a hopeless whisper.

"You will have to have her put away sooner or later," said his aunt with light assurance.

"Never! I have told you I will never . . ."

"You will have to in the end," she asserted as his voice broke again.

Was she mad, that lovely young girl? I tried to view her dispassionately as the argument continued. After my initial revulsion at finding her so afflicted I had pitied her, and as I saw how calm, how obedient, how normal she was in other ways, my compassion had grown. I had sensed intelligence behind those lovely dark eyes. But her outburst during coffee, her behavior at the luncheon table, had these been the actions of a normal intelligent woman?

Blind. Dumb. Mad? It was all too much. I excused myself and went to my room. I don't think they even noticed I had gone.

I sat on the chest at the foot of my bed and gazed into the flames licking up the chimney making distorted visions to fit my mood. How *could* I stay at Rosemont? How *could* I be expected to make friends with a madwoman?

Was she mad? Miss Selina thought she was, and even Lord Denton, though he denied it, hinted by his very vehemence that he thought so too. *"If I have to keep her locked up here at Rosemont all her life . . ."*

Locked up! There was already one locked door at Rosemont that I knew of—the big solid door on the landing at the stair head guarded by two monstrous pilasters. Why was it kept locked? Because someone had already been locked up at Rosemont? Shut away because of insanity? Or worse?

I was letting my thoughts run away with me. Just because of my strange experience outside the door earlier on, I mustn't place weird and mysterious reasons for it. It had happened in my imagination . . . because I was tired and hungry . . . Why, the door was probably not even locked. I had only imagined it so.

Or had I?

I had to know.

The only way to find out was to go and try the door now.

Now that I was no longer tired and hungry, no longer liable to hallucinate. In control of my imagination.

I ran swiftly, candle in hand, trying not to notice the flickering shadows, and arrived at the door with a thumping heart and the beginnings of a stitch in my side. It was quiet, very quiet in the richly furnished corridor overlooking the stone-flagged hall which still retained its original hammerbeam roof and great fourteenth century cartwheel-like chandelier.

I stood outside the door and felt nothing. No icy coldness seeping out to chill my bones. I looked at the carvings on the pilasters. That's just what they were, carvings, mad-made, man-hewn. They had no life of their own. They could not jump from their positions to claw at me.

I suddenly felt extremely foolish. I did not even wish to try the door now. If I did, and it opened, and I found it occupied, how would I explain my temerity?

I turned to go back to my room and all but bumped into Lord Denton. His face was livid. He stood over me like a giant, and I backed away fearfully, my heart beating painfully.

"What are you doing, Miss Conway?" he hissed angrily. "Why are you at that door? What do you want?"

I opened my mouth, but no sound escaped my lips.

"There's nothing for you there. Kindly return to your own quarters and stop snooping about the corridors."

I fled from him as from a demon, the rush of air caused by my flight blowing out my candle, so that I had to feel my way along the stone passageways and up the winding staircase to my room. Once inside I banged the door shut and stood with my back to it heaving noisily. He had been so angry at finding me outside that door that all my fears regarding it had returned to plague me. But as my breathing eased, I grew angry with myself for running from him like a craven coward.

But I was afraid. Afraid of everything that was around

55

me. Rosemont that had so enraptured my heart on sight had become a place of fear for me. Fears imagined, fears real, what did it matter? I had not known a moment's peace since entering its portals.

I had to get away.

I sat down and penned a letter to Mr. Morrison. He had to take me away from here, not matter how his wife reacted. I poured out my troubles and fears to him and felt better after it. He would not let me down and Mrs. Morrison, when she knew of my fears, would surely relent and agree to have me back. But I must wait till morning before I could post the letter, so I started to undress. Bed was the place for me now, where hopefully I would fall asleep quickly and forget my worries till dawn.

A knock came at the door. "Come in," I called, expecting it to be Doreen come to help me prepare for bed, then, "Oh! Oh!" in a lather of agitation as Lord Denton entered.

He halted momentarily when he saw me in my shift, then calmly handed me my dressing gown.

"Forgive this intrusion, Miss Conway," he said, "when you are getting ready for bed, but I feel I owe you an apology for the way I spoke to you earlier. It's just that I was so surprised to see you there. That doesn't seem much of an excuse, I know, but it's the only one I can offer."

Feverishly wrapping my dressing gown around my near-naked body, I mumbled something about it being all right and that it would have done in the morning.

"I did not wish to delay it," he said.

Hot-cheeked and trembling I waited for him to go. But he stood his ground.

"There's something else," he said. "About my sister. I should have informed you of her condition . . ."

"I should not have come if I'd known about it," I burst out, unconsciously echoing Miss Selina's words, though in truth I should have had no say in the matter. I think he knew so, too, for something flickered across his eyes, but he merely agreed.

"Of course you would not. What young woman would?"

He regarded me silently for a few moments while the frown etched itself more deeply into his forehead. Then he continued.

"My aunt believes you will not wish to stay now you have met Alicia." His eye fell upon the letter I had placed upright on the mantelpiece as he moved to take up his favorite stance, and he turned back to me with an urgent cry. "I beseech you not to go. My sister needs you. She's so very lonely. Lacking in companionship. Oh, I know she has Murkett and she is invaluable, of course, but she's more than twice Alicia's age. Alicia should have young people about her. A friend of her own age. Someone like you."

He left his place by the fireside and came towards me. Stood close to me. My heart hammered painfully as he caught hold of my hands and peered searchingly into my eyes.

"I love my sister very deeply. There's nothing I would not do for her. I don't find it easy to beg, Miss Conway, but I'm begging you now. Stay. I'll go down on bended knee if that is what it will take . . ."

"That will not be necessary," I said hoarsely.

His face brightened. "You will stay?"

"I did not say that. Your aunt says . . ."

"I know what my aunt says," he scowled, flinging himself away from me. "She thinks Alicia is mad and should be shut away in an asylum. But she's *wrong*! Alicia is *not* mad! She's blind, yes. She was born so. But she has not always been dumb. That came as a result of — an illness she had. Since then she has gone steadily downhill. Her mind has deteriorated and she's given to outbreaks of . . ."

"Violence." I finished the sentence that became too difficult for him.

"As you saw this evening," he conceded dejectedly. "Yet if only you could have known her as a child. She was the

57

sweetest liveliest little thing . . . I'll never forget the day I found her hiding in the old oak."

"Hiding in the old oak?" I echoed, puzzled.

"It's an old oak tree with a partly hollowed-out trunk where my brother and I played as children," he explained. "I showed it to Alicia once. When she disappeared, just before her illness, we searched everywhere for her without success. Then I remembered the old tree and went to see if she was there. She was. Cowering inside. Trembling like a leaf—and unable to utter a word. She has not spoken since."

"But . . . I don't understand how such a thing could happen."

"Nor do I. Nor did anyone else. She's seen doctors galore. None was able to explain it. She recovered her health, but . . ."

He threw up his arms and let them fall in a defeated gesture.

"I'm sorry," I said.

"I hoped you'd become her friend," he cried accusingly. "Perhaps I hoped for too much."

"Perhaps you did."

"There's not much I can do to make my sister's life easier, but anything money can buy I will give her. Anything, Miss Conway. State your sum."

"You can't buy friendship, Lord Denton," I exclaimed. aghast, appreciating the lengths he would go to for his sister's sake. "Money can buy governesses, companions, but not friendship."

A silence ensued between us. A log spluttered in the hearth. A bright golden flame went shooting up the chimney. He searched my face with eyes that glittered blackly in its dancing light. What was he looking for? Whatever it was, he did not appear to find it.

"You're right," he said at last. "Forgive me for suggesting it could—yours, anyway. I will bid you good night. Tomorrow I will arrange for your return to the Morrisons."

He turned to go. His shoulders drooped. His sister's happiness was of great importance to him, and he had failed to provide her with the thing he thought she needed most. The company and friendship of a young woman her own age.

So would things go on in the same old way, with Murkett babying and Miss Selina belittling her? Would the intelligence I felt sure she possessed be finally crushed beneath the two-pronged onslaught? Would her violent outbreaks grow more frequent? Would Miss Selina's wish to have her shut away in an asylum become too hard to resist? I shuddered at the thought of the lovely girl immured for the rest of her life. Inwardly I did not believe she was insane. And I knew I must save her if I could from such a terrible fate.

"Wait!" I stopped Lord Denton in his tracks. "I will stay. Friendship can't be bought, but it can be given. I'll offer Alicia my friendship. I think she'll reject it, but at least I can try."

The chill seemed to leave his eyes and for a brief moment a little of the warmth he lavished on his sister was shed on me.

Chapter Four

They had gone, Miss Selina and the baron. I was left standing on the doorstep with Alicia. It was early and we both shivered in the cold morning air as we watched the carriage quickly swallowed up into a thick mist.

"Let us go in," I said, touching her arm only to drop my hand quickly as she reacted as she would have done to a scald.

"Don't be afraid of me," I begged. "I want to be your friend."

For a moment I sensed an unsurety in her, but then she left my side and re-entered the house, moving without hesitation in the direction of the staircase while I gaped after her in astonishment. Seeing Selina's solicitude, Lord Denton's careful guidance, Murkett's constant attendance, I had taken it for granted she needed assistance in finding her way around. I could see now she did not. She was ascending the stairs with all the confidence of one who could see.

My heart jumped again. Could she see? Was her blindness all pretence? But of course it was not. She had been blind from birth, Lord Denton had said. So she had probably been given a sixth sense to make up for it. But if so, why did she hide it from the others and not from me? Was I of so little account that she cared nought for what I thought?

I started to follow her up the stairs faithful to my pledge to try to be a friend, then with a little quiver of fear I saw the black-garbed Murkett come into view at the top of the stairs. Alicia moved quickly towards her. They hurried away together. They entered a room and closed the door. As I approached it, I heard the key turn in the lock.

What was I to do? I was clearly not wanted. Yet Lord Denton had gone saying, "Spend all the time you can with her. She needs to be with someone her own age. Murkett is too old. Too old." I had felt he wanted to add something more, but he had set his lips together in a thin straight line and walked away.

So what should I do? Knock on the door and ask, beg, demand that she come out or let me in?

I did not know what to do.

In the end I went downstairs again and tried to settle down with a book. If Alicia did not wish for my company, I would not force it on her. But I could not concentrate. Alicia's beautiful face kept coming between me and the printed page.

I tossed the book away and went out for a walk. The mist still lingered, but the sun was trying to get through. It would be a fine day later on. Perhaps I would do a little more sketching.

Only I should be with Alicia.

I could not stop thinking about her. Her afflictions. To be blind was bad enough, but to be dumb as well! Her years of loneliness, without friends. Only Murkett for company. Murkett who babied her and kept her from enjoying life as she should. Was it Murkett who encouraged her to play her game of dependence? Encouraged her to pretend a stupidity she did not possess? In which case she must take the blame for Miss Selina's harsh way with Alicia. She was a lady who could not abide stupidity. Did Lord Denton believe this? Was this what he might have told me, if he had not restrained himself?

I believed I had hit upon the truth of the matter. Murkett was to blame for everything. She was jealous of her role of protector and saw me as a threat to her influence over Alicia. She had already shown open animosity towards me. She wanted me out of the way quickly before Alicia could form any sort of attachment to me. Who knew what poison she poured into the girl's ears?

I went back indoors determined to wean Alicia away from such an objectionable woman. Ordering hot chocolate for two to be brought to the Little Parlor I went to knock on her door. For a while I thought she was going to ignore the summons, but then I heard the key turn in the lock and the next moment Murkett's black bombazine confronted me.

My heart reacted turbulently. I felt the woman's hate as she waited, unspeaking, for me to make the first move. Looking past her I saw Alicia sitting by the fire, her head slightly to one side, listening.

I called out to her, ignoring Murkett. "Alicia, it's me, Deborah. I have ordered hot chocolate to be sent to the Little Parlor. Will you come and share it with me?"

She gave no indication that she had even heard me.

I continued. "We could get to know each other. I could tell you about myself. Then we could play together, if you like. I love music and I know you do, too."

My heart leapt as she half-rose and I thought she was going to come with me, but then she fell back on her chair and shook her head.

Murkett sniffed and her bosom swelled with satisfaction. Smugly she attempted to close the door in my face, but I was not going to be put off so easily. I brushed past her and went to lay a hand on Alicia's arm. She reacted as violently as she had done earlier.

"Alicia," I pleaded, "please don't reject me. I'm so lonely down there all by myself." Instinctively I felt this was the right approach, an appeal to her sympathies. "I didn't want to come here any more than you wanted me here, but I was forced into it. I had nowhere else to go. I would like us to be friends. We're both about the same age. There's lots we could do together. As you know, I'm all alone in the world. I need someone . . ."

I could see I had reached her at last. She seemed racked by indecision. She wanted to come with me and yet . . . I waited eagerly, but she shook her head. Bitterly disappointed I turned to leave her, deliberately refusing to look at Murkett whose triumph I felt.

The door closed on my back. The key grated in the lock.

I went to drink a solitary cup of chocolate. Sipping it in front of the fire in the chair Miss Selina had occupied the night before, I looked at the place where Lord Denton had leant his impressive height. His personality was so strong it seemed as if he still stood there and I felt my face go fiery red. I did not like him, but I could not ignore him. Behind my concern for Alicia had been a deep awareness of him, of all he had said to me. I found I could remember every word he had addressed to me, almost all of them about his sister. I experienced a sudden irritation with his overwhelming concern for his sister.

I steered my thoughts back to her. What was her attitude towards me really like? Was it shaped by Murkett, her maid, her nurse, her—jailor? On the face of it she had no need of any companion other than Murkett. She seemed to have complete faith in her, was obviously very fond of her, relied on her completely.

Her brother, Lord Denton—Charles—however, believed she needed the companionship of someone her own age, and I found myself in complete agreement with him on that point. To me Murkett was like an octopus, all-embracing, smothering.

"Hello. Who are you?"

The voice startled me. I looked up to see a tall young man observing me from the doorway. Dark-haired, dark-eyed, he had the most engaging smile. I recognized him at once as the man in the silver-framed photograph.

"I'm Deborah Conway," I replied, returning his smile. "Alicia's new companion."

"Are you indeed?" He came forward to take my hand. "I'm Jonathan Denton."

"I know," I said, deeply conscious of the warmth of his hand, the firmness of his grip. He raised his eyebrows. "I recognize you from your photograph," I added.

"And do you think you will stay long enough for us to become better acquainted? So many young ladies have come and gone during the past few years, I've lost count."

His smile was humorous, teasing. "I hope so," I said.

And I did hope so. There was something so likeable about this young man. Enough to make up for the lack in others.

"Where is Alicia?" he asked.

"In her room. Resting. Would you like me to call her?"

"No, no. I'll surprise her."

He raced up the stairs, banged on her door. When he found it locked, "Alicia," he called, "it's me, Jonathan. Your loving brother home from foreign parts."

I stood at the bottom of the stairs and waited. Would they come down together or would he stay with her and talk to her in her room? Suddenly they appeared at the top of the stairs. His arm was round her waist. She was smiling happily, transformed in his presence. And why not? He was a man of tremendous charm and gaiety. Eager and friendly. Not a bit like his dour brother.

"I've just met your new companion, Alicia," he was saying. "She's lovely. Has anyone described her to you? She's dark and small and neat, with fascinating green-gray eyes, a shy smile, and dimples. There. Can you see her now?"

Alicia nodded and smiled as he hugged her to him.

But I thought, How can she know what anyone looks like from a description, when she has been blind from birth?

She had nothing to go on.

Then as they reached me, "Here she is," he said and Alicia put out her hands, and I felt her sensitive fingers caress my face—my lips, my cheeks, my nose. She nodded again and smiled, this time at me. Then she took hold of my hand.

I could not believe it. She had accepted me. Through nothing I had done, but because her brother had introduced us in the only way she could relate to. I felt a little light-headed as I was drawn with them back into the Little Parlor. I felt Rosemont held something for me after all, that I might begin to feel at home there. And it was Jonathan who had brought this about. I smiled at him with all the warmth and gratitude in my heart.

He deposited Alicia on the sofa facing the fire. "Now just you sit there, my darling one, while I bring you something."

He dashed from the room, he seemed to do nothing at a quiet gentle pace, and returned almost at once with a large flat box which he placed on her lap.

"There. All the way from Venezia," he said.

He stood back and allowed her to remove the lid herself. I gasped as she drew from between folds of tissue paper a shimmering white satin shawl fringed with long silken tassels.

"It's a shawl for evening wear," Jonathan explained to his sister and began describing it for her. "It's white satin embroidered with seed pearls and in one corner there is a large rose woven in richly colored strands. Let me place it round your shoulders. There." He stood back admiring his lovely sister. "It suits you. I knew it would. As soon as I saw it I thought of your dark tresses, the creaminess of your skin, and I knew I had to buy it for you."

"It's truly lovely," I breathed. "You look like a princess."

"I'll take a photograph of you in it later," Jonathan promised and smiled at me. "I'm a keen photographer.

Always have been. My brother says I was born with a camera in my hand. It is my dream to turn professional one day. Own my own studio. Charles doesn't like the idea, but as I say, it's my life. I can do what I like with it."

"Your aunt told me you were interested in photography. She said most of the photographs in the house were taken by you. They're very good."

His smile broadened with pleasure. "Thank you. They're family photographs, of course, but I like to take outdoor scenes, too. I have a vast collection in my photographic room. Perhaps you'll let me show you some of them?"

"I should be delighted."

"Good. Where is Aunt Selina, by the way? She's not usually so tardy with her greetings."

"She's not here. She and Lord Denton have gone to Devon. To Witchet Towers."

"Witchet Towers? But she can't abide the place."

"I'm afraid your Uncle James died suddenly and they have gone to the funeral."

The levity left his face and he frowned. "Poor old Nunc. What a shame. Charles must have been devastated. Still," his voice lightened a little, "he'd had good innings. He must have been well on the way to seventy. When is the funeral to take place?"

"I don't know. They only left this morning. But Miss Selina did say she hoped they would not be away too long."

"Yes, she won't want to be there longer than is absolutely necessary. Can't think why she doesn't like the old place. I love it. So does Charles. In fact I think he prefers it to Rosemont. At least he did until . . ."

A shadow crossed his face and he gulped down the remains of his chocolate without finishing what he had been going to say. Then he sprang up with a decisive air.

"Well, I had better be on my way there. There's a train back to London in a couple of hours, just time for me to wash and change and have a bite to eat. Wonder what time there'll be a train for Devon? I'd better ring and find out. There might not be another today, but I can spend the night in London. I must get to Witchet as quickly as I can. I might not be in time for the funeral, but with luck I should not miss the reading of the will."

He grinned and was gone, bounding up the stairs with an urgency that had me thinking, He's not really concerned about his uncle's demise, he's only interested in what he had left him in his will. Then I cast such an unworthy thought from me in disgust.

Alicia was removing her shawl and feeling for the box which lay on the sofa beside her. I had to restrain myself from going to her aid, feeling she would much rather manage by herself, and as I watched her carefully fold the shawl back into its box and replace the lid I knew I was right. She was perfectly capable of managing for herself. There was no need for Murkett's babying ways.

She set the box carefully beside her and I waited, frowning, expecting her to rise and leave me now, go back to her room and Murkett. Now that her brother had left us she would not wish to stay on her own with me. But to my surprise she remained seated, her face set in soft relaxed lines. She *had* accepted me.

Tentatively, almost voicelessly, I asked her if she would like another cup of chocolate. She shook her head and settled back against the cushions. I stared at her, swallowing anxiously, striving to find the right thing to say for this tenuous start to our friendship.

"Your brother is very charming, isn't he?" I voiced at last.

She nodded, smiling.

"You are very fond of him, aren't you?"

Another smile, another nod.

"If I had a brother, I'd like him to be just like Jonathan."

A broader smile.

"It's a beautiful shawl he has brought you."

She nodded happily.

"Such a pity he has to leave again so soon after arriving."

Her smile disappeared and I hastened to add, "But it won't be for long. He'll be back soon."

Her smile returned.

"They'll all be back soon."

But that was the wrong thing to say. Her smile faded, her head fell, her shoulders drooped, her whole attitude one of dejection. I stared gloomily at her glossy dark head and wondered what I could say to restore her earlier contentment. But it was difficult to know what to say. There was not much help to be had from one whose only replies were smiles and nods and droops.

With a strange mixture of sadness and relief I saw her rise and cross the floor, open the door, and let herself out. She was going back to Murkett after all. Murkett, with whom she felt at ease.

Jonathan left on the afternoon train after an hilarious luncheon during which he regaled Alicia and myself with witty stories of his adventures abroad, mimicking some of the people he had met—he had a great talent for mimicry. He drove himself down to the station in his brother's white motor car. Flat-capped, voluminous-caped, and goggled against the inclement weather, he looked like a creature from another world waving good-bye to us from the scarlet leather seats. I laughed to see him and wished Alicia could see him, too. But as I looked at her with her mouth open laughing soundlessly, I almost felt she could.

It seemed so quiet when he had gone. For a while none of us seemed able to settle. His quicksilver presence had affected us all—Alicia, me, Croft, the servants, even Murkett. However, we eventually adjusted and life progressed in the way it had before he arrived to disrupt it.

Murkett took control of Alicia again and I found it as difficult as ever to get near her. Then one day I came across her in the Music Room playing quietly to herself at the pianoforte. I listened in amazement. It was a Chopin piece she played and she played it brilliantly, putting the lie to Miss Selina's statement about her being no musician.

I started to clap as she came to the end and she reacted wildly, but when I spoke she calmed down and a smile spread across her face. I told her how much I had enjoyed listening to her. She rose and showed she wished me to take her place, then she stood back waiting for me to play.

I played a piece by Franz Liszt that I was particularly fond of, at the end of which she was as unstinting in her applause as I had been.

After that we were often in each other's company — in the Music Room where we spent many pleasurable hours playing duets together, she on the violin, I on the piano; in the Little Parlor where I read to her from the books of Miss Jane Austen, her favorite author and mine; in the gardens and grounds of Rosemont where we walked and talked — at least I talked, she listened — whenever the weather permitted.

There was nothing wrong with Alicia's hearing. She could detect sounds long before I did. She loved to hear the tales I had to tell of my childhood at Conway Place, and though I had not meant to dwell on the deaths of my father and Aunt Susie, such was the quality of her silent sympathy that I found myself telling her how much I had suffered afterwards, how I had sunk low in the world and been rescued by Mr. and Mrs. Morrison.

Tears had begun rolling down my cheeks, and she halted our walk, turning to me and cupping my face in her hands, tracing its contours, discovering its wetness. Tears sprang to her eyes, rolled down her cheeks, and we hugged and kissed each other in mutual sympathy and affection.

Our friendship grew in spite of Murkett's opposition. Alicia still spent the greater part of her time in her nurse's company, but I noticed no babying, no babyish response during those few days, and there were no outbreaks of violence.

I felt the seal was set on our friendship when she allowed me into her room. We had both decided to change into lighter garments as the day had grown steadily warmer, and as I was ready first I went to knock on her door. She opened it herself and beckoned me in. Murkett was nowhere around. She had not undressed, being unable to reach the buttons that fastened her gown at the back. I offered to help her. She readily turned her back to me and my fingers were soon busy with the tiny buttons that spread from neck to waist.

She opened her large wardrobe—it almost filled the whole wall—and I blinked in surprise at the array of color that met my eyes. Blue, green, purple, apricot, yellow, red—every color imaginable. It seemed obscene somehow, all that color for a girl who could not see.

I wondered who chose her clothes. Miss Selina? Murkett?

Alicia was searching through the clothing holding each garment up to her face. It was her way of seeing, her sense of touch equal to that of sight in another. She found the dress she was seeking, a light flowery silk, and with my help put it on. She looked like a flower herself in it, a marguerite, a tall foxglove. I thought, Why shouldn't she have beautiful colorful clothes? She's a beautiful girl, her beauty ought to be complemented by beautiful clothes. If she could not see the effect herself, others could.

Then a strange scene was enacted. She drew me back with her to the wardrobe and commenced searching through the clothes once more. Almost immediately she brought forth a gown of creamy satin overlaid with flounces of lace, decorated with tiny bows at the heart of which lay a seed pearl. Just to look at it was a joy, the feel of it was enchantment.

Alicia guided my fingers over the material, caused them

70

to fondle the little lace-covered buttons and all the while she was looking up into my face—Looking? It seemed like that—to see what my reaction was—Only she could not see it. I had to keep reminding myself of that fact.

She was nodding and smiling, her lips moving as if she were trying to tell me something. What? How I wished she could speak.

"What a beautiful gown," I said, and she jumped a little distance away from me.

She began miming putting on a dress with extreme care, smoothing the skirt lovingly with her hands. Then she bent to pick up an invisible something and placed it carefully on her head, drew something down to cover her face, then looked behind her to see if something trailed there.

It seemed a cold hand clutched at my heart as I breathed, "It's a wedding gown."

She smiled and nodded, came back to me, and took the dress into her own hands.

"Yours?" I squeaked.

She nodded and smiled.

"You are to be married?" My voice rose in disbelief. I thought she was playing some sort of game with me.

But she nodded again, though a little less certainly.

"To whom? When?"

She bit into her lip.

"There's no one, is there?" I said quietly.

She shook her head and turned with a dejected air to return the gown to the wardrobe. It suddenly struck me that the style was rather old-fashioned.

"Was it your mother's wedding gown?" I asked gently.

She nodded and pushed it right at the back of the wardrobe, her earlier gaiety quite gone, and I was angry with myself for not playing her game with her. But mostly I was angry with the cruel fate that could deny the fulfilling of a desire natural in every girl for a husband, children, a family of her own.

71

Alicia had that desire and tried to fulfil it in the only way open to her — by dreaming. By pretence.

Then my anger moved on. How had the gown come to be in her possession? Who had given it to her? Whoever it was must have known it would lead to dreams of marriage, must have known it would be well nigh impossible for those dreams to come true. For what man would be willing to take on a wife so sadly afflicted as she? Yet as she turned to me again, so lovely, so touchingly vulnerable, I thought it was just possible she might find someone romantic enough to want to marry her and care for her.

I hoped so. Oh, I hoped so.

Miss Selina and her nephews returned. Alicia was at once subdued with the withdrawn expression on her face I had not seen since their departure. Her two brothers were not the cause, I knew that, for they had greeted her with hugs and kisses, and she had returned them affectionately. No, it was Miss Selina who had this dampening effect on her, despite the fact that solicitous as always, she had taken Alicia by the hand and led her indoors where she settled her in a chair with the injunction to remain there till Murkett came.

She indicated that I should go with her to her boudoir, which I did, but not without a worried backward glance at the pale young girl who only minutes ago had been happy, smiling, and carefree.

"I suppose you have been unutterably bored while I've been away," were Miss Selina's first words on entering her boudoir.

"No," I said brightly. "I've thoroughly enjoyed myself."

Her glance was one of astonishment. "Indeed. You had no trouble with Alicia?"

"None at all. I found her charming and we have become great friends."

"I'm glad to hear it," she said, pulling off her soft kid gloves. "I must admit to having been worried about you. My niece is such a strange creature. One never knows where one is with her. But if you say you have had no trouble with her . . ." She sat down at the dressing table. "Remove my hat for me, dear, will you?" she begged.

She watched me silently through the mirror as I searched through black feathers and veiling for the long jet-headed pins anchoring the hat to her hair. Then, "Thank you," she said as I lifted it from her head and set it down on a chair. "Now you may go. Just ring for Lister first."

But Lister, Miss Selina's personal maid, was already entering the room, aware as everyone at Rosemont of Miss Selina's impatience with tardiness.

"Tell Murkett I wish to see her," Miss Selina called after me as I went, and I felt a curious coldness down my spine at her words, innocuous as they were.

I found Murkett and gave her the message then went back to Alicia still sitting patiently as we had left her. A lump came to my throat at the sight of her drooping frame. I placed an arm about her shoulders. "Let's go for a walk," I said.

But her aunt had told her to remain where she was and she shook her head.

Murkett came up in her black bombazine, trailing the ribbons of her black lace cap behind her like the forked tongue of a snake.

"Miss Selina says I'm to take Miss Alicia's hair down," she said curtly.

"What?"

A tingle of shock ran through me and I stared at her in angry bewilderment. I had lately persuaded Alicia to wear her hair in a style more becoming to her age, piled on top with a single ringlet drawing attention to her long slender neck and delicately shaped ears. After all, she was nearly eighteen, the Alice-in-Wonderland style was for children.

Murkett had reluctantly agreed the new hairstyle was an improvement, and I had counted it a little victory when she continued to dress Alicia's hair in this way, thinking it heralded the start to the cessation of hostilities between us.

"Miss Selina's orders," she said with a slightly shame-faced air.

"Don't do anything," I exclaimed. "I'll go to her and persuade her to change her mind." I turned to Alicia. "Jonathan admired it. He said so. Charles — Lord Denton — also approved. I could see he did."

I started to go, but Alicia restrained me with her hand.

"It's all right," I said. "I won't be long."

But she began shaking her head violently, and I realized she did not want me to go to her aunt. Was she afraid of what her aunt would do if I did?

She rose to leave with Murkett in obedience to her aunt, and I stood back to let her pass, defeated. But as she went I saw from the set of her mouth, as clearly as if it had been put into words for me, that fear played a subordinate part in her attitude towards her aunt. It was not fear alone that made her pinch her lips together in such a fashion, it was hatred.

Alicia hated her Aunt Selina.

I wandered out of the drawing room through the long windows that opened out onto the terrace overlooking the gardens and vistas created by Capability Brown over a century ago. The sun shone down warmly and the air was filled with the scents and sounds of spring. Laburnum trees dripped gold from their branches. Lilacs raised fat candles, purple and pristine white, heavenwards. Wistaria draped the terrace walls below me with lavender-colored fragrance.

I descended the wide stone steps and walked towards a fountain where a huge green fish spouted water from its mouth. Drops of water cascaded like crystals upon the sailing lily pads beneath. I sat down on my favorite seat nearby and listened to the water falling, splashing, dancing and felt my worried heart ease.

It was all so peaceful after the tensions and unhappiness within the house. I closed my eyes and let the peace steal over me.

I must have dozed momentarily, for when I opened my eyes again a pied wagtail was hopping about on the grass a few paces away and Lord Denton was sitting next to me on the bench.

"He doesn't seem concerned at his misfortune," he said nodding towards the bird.

The wagtail had only one leg.

"No," I whispered hoarsely, wondering how long he had been sitting there.

"I wonder how he lost it," he mused.

"A cat, maybe," I offered, my voice no less hoarse than before.

"Maybe." A look of pain crossed his face. "Or maybe he was born like that."

I knew he was thinking of his beloved sister, how she had been born blind, and I wanted to dispel the dark sadness from his eyes.

"He seems quite happy," I said, "quite competent. Nature has a way of compensating those who . . ."

"Don't give me that," he interrupted me harshly. "I've heard it all before and it's not true."

"It is." I felt an almost obsessive desire to ease his pain which at the time I did not question. "Alicia is blind. She can't see with her eyes, but she can see all the same. By touch. She can find her way about as well, or almost as well, as you or I."

He snorted disbelief and looked at me with loathing. "How can you say that when you know she has to be guided everywhere?"

"But she hasn't. That's what I'm trying to tell you."

"Please, Miss Conway, that's enough."

"I'm sorry." I rose abruptly and the wagtail flew away.

75

He rose, too, detaining me with his hand.

"Don't go," he ordered roughly, standing close to me. Too close. His nearness was not objectionable, but it was disturbing, and my heart started hammering painfully. "How have you got on while I've been away?"

"With Alicia, you mean?"

"Precisely."

"Very well. We have become friends."

He sighed as if greatly relieved and said, "I'm glad. I delayed our return for as long as I could to allow you time to get to know one another without—distraction. I knew once you got to know her, you would love her."

Love her! I had not reached such a positive conclusion. He saw my hesitancy and put his hand on my arm. "You do love her?" he said anxiously.

I looked up into his pebble gray eyes. They were no longer stony and repressive, but soft as they always were when he spoke of his sister. I thought madly, if only they could be soft for me, and shook the thought away as soon as it was made, as being inconsequential and silly.

"I'm very fond of her," I said.

It seemed to satisfy him.

"And you do not regret your decision to stay."

It was a statement not a question. Our eyes held for a moment, and I was aware of the heat of his hand through the thin material of my sleeve.

"No," I whispered and the voice sounded a long way off to my ears, as if it belonged to somebody else.

His hand fell from my arm. "Shall we go indoors?" he urged. "My aunt sent me to tell you we are taking tea in the parlor."

I fell into step beside him.

"By the way," he said, "I like the way Alicia has done her hair. Was that your idea?"

"Yes. But Miss Selina was not impressed. She ordered it to be taken down again."

I looked up to see how he would take it. He frowned slightly, but all he said was, "Pity. I thought it suited her."

"Then why don't you do something about it? Countermand your aunt's orders."

His glance was cold when it fell on me.

"My aunt usually has good reasons for her actions," he snapped.

"What good reason can there be for this? It wasn't harming anybody."

His eyes narrowed. I had gone too far. But then he smiled, and his cares seemed to fall away from him as his features softened, and I could almost think I was looking at a different man.

"It wouldn't do for me to interfere in such womanly things, but you might try persuading my aunt yourself."

Chapter Five

Baron Denton returned to London sole owner of the Lockhart shipping empire. The bulk of his uncle's fortune had passed to him, including Witchet Towers and the house in Grosvenor Square which had been his home for so many years in preference to Rosemont. Sizeable legacies had been left to Miss Selina, Alicia, Jonathan, and Jenny and Fanny Lockhart, James's elderly spinster sisters. The sisters had received an assurance from their nephew that Witchet Towers was their home for as long as they lived.

"What will happen when they die?" I heard Miss Selina ask Lord Denton shortly before he left for London. "Will you sell the place? After all it has unfortunate memories for you. I take it you will not wish to live there yourself."

"I'll worry about that when it happens," he had replied and gone off with a scowl on his face.

I wasn't sorry to see him go. After our conversation in the garden he had paid scant attention to me, only noticing my presence when Alicia and I appeared together. His was an abrasive presence. He and Miss Selina never seemed to be at ease with each other, and she complained about him to me all the time. An abrasive presence, a gloomy presence, it provoked tension in the atmosphere. Even Jonathan was less lighthearted when his brother was near.

Only Alicia seemed to fully enjoy his company, and only

in her company did his features soften and he became almost human. There was no doubting Alicia's affection for him. She loved both her brothers, but it was plain she held the elder in greater esteem. I wondered what it was she saw in him that others did not, what qualities she perceived in him with her sixth sense.

If there were any, they were too deeply hidden for me to appreciate. I preferred Jonathan's company. He was friendly, full of fun, always ready with a merry quip — and yet, out of his presence I hardly thought about him, whereas the baron was rarely out of my mind. But the baron was that kind of man. You might dislike him, hate him, loathe him, or love him, you could not ignore him.

The days settled into a peaceful routine. Alicia and I walked in the grounds and played duets in the Music Room. Sometimes, when it was warm enough, we sat on a bench in the garden and I explained what was going on around us — which flowers were blooming, which birds were flying about, if the gardeners were at work, what they were doing. And sometimes I would tell her about my childhood and Conway Place, my father and Aunt Susie. I found it easy to talk about these things to her and found balm in it.

When I was not with Alicia I was with Miss Selina. We spent many hours sketching together as she had promised we would, always indoors, never out. She seemed to have an aversion to going outside.

Jonathan took up the reins of management again, though I often wondered when he got any work done, for he always left the house with his tripod slung over his shoulder and his camera in his hand. Alicia and I often came across him on our walks, photographing something or other, then he would insist we pose for him. These were delightful occasions, he made us laugh so much, though it was heartbreaking to see Alicia's lovely face alive with enjoyment, yet no sound of laughter issued from between her parted lips.

Then Lord Denton came back to Rosemont.

In a flash everything was changed. Peace went out of the window and strife came in. Jonathan was taken to task for his "mismanagement" of the estate. Voices were raised and there was much ill-feeling in the air.

But I was the first to receive the rough edge of his tongue.

I had gone to the drawing room to meet Alicia as previously arranged. She was not there, but Miss Selina was.

"Ah, Deborah," she exclaimed, her face lighting up. "Just the girl I want to see. I'm bored, Deborah. Come and talk to me."

"I'd arranged to go for a walk with Alicia," I said. "I thought she was with you."

"So she was. I sent her away. What use is she to me, or anybody? One might as well talk to oneself as to her."

As always her slighting of Alicia made my hackles rise and I retorted pertly, "I find her most responsive."

"Oh, you!" Miss Selina shrugged peevishly. "You have a way with her."

"I think I'd better go and find her," I said. "I promised to take her down to the village . . ."

"You can't take her there. I forbid it. She's not to go outside the grounds."

I swallowed anxiously at Miss Selina's sudden ferocity. "Well of course I won't, if you object, but . . ."

"Do not argue with me. Just do as you are told. Alicia is never to set foot outside these grounds."

"Very well," I said and turned to go. "If you'll excuse me . . ."

"Yes, go. Go and find Alicia and keep her company. Don't worry about me. I'm used to being on my own."

I sighed to myself and halted on hearing the pitiful whine enter her voice. Her complaints of loneliness, I had discovered, were not completely true. She had Jonathan's company, she had mine, she had Alicia's. And she had Lister's, her personal maid with whom she played cards, often well into the night. I did not play cards, and when Miss Selina had tried to teach me, had made such a hash of it she had thrown the cards down crossly and banished me from her sight. And another thing, I did not believe she really minded being on her own. She often sent me away within minutes after begging for my company.

However, I turned with a placatory smile. "I will come and sit with you later, if you wish."

"That will be nice . . ."

Miss Selina broke off as footsteps were heard outside the door which I had left open and a moment later Lord Denton stepped into the room. His face darkened when he saw us together, and after respectfully kissing his aunt demanded of me, "Where is Alicia?"

I never seemed to be with Alicia whenever he came home. Each time he expected to see me with her and found me with his aunt. Have I not made it clear you are my sister's companion, not my aunt's? his eyes sparked angrily. He believed me neglectful in my duties and I longed to put myself right with him, tell him that I was much more often in Alicia's company than Miss Selina's. But why should I humble myself before him? He had begged me to stay on at Rosemont. I had agreed, set my own plans aside, what right had he to treat me so discourteously?

"I don't know," I said coolly. "I can't find her. I thought she was in here."

"Can't find her?" His voice rose sharply. Fear came to his eyes and he turned in distress to Miss Selina.

"She's with Murkett, Charles," she said irritably. "Don't get so worked up. Deborah is not often out of Alicia's company, I might tell you."

"That's what she's here for," he grated.

But he had sighed with relief and I wondered why he was so fearful for his sister. What harm could befall her at Rosemont? I knew, I had told him, she was not incapable of finding her own way about. And even if she were not, there was always someone to watch out for her—myself, Miss Selina, Murkett, any number of servants, and now there was Jonathan.

Yet I could understand his concern, just as I could understand Miss Selina not liking the idea of Alicia leaving the confines of Rosemont and going down to the village. Alicia would be an object of wonder, of pity, amongst the village folk. I could see that now I had had time to think about it. On the other hand I felt it would be no more than a nine days' wonder if she got into the habit of mixing with them. In time they would begin to accept her as she was. In my heart I was sure it would be good for her to meet and mix with other people, enlarge her sphere of life. I hoped to persuade Miss Selina to this way of thinking.

Lord Denton went to see Jonathan and I went in search of Alicia. I could not find her anywhere, but as Murkett also seemed to be missing, I presumed they were together and did not worry. I went back to Miss Selina in the drawing room and we settled down to a chat.

Then came the explosion. Lord Denton had found Jonathan taking photographs of some of the servants while Benson struggled with figures in the office ledgers.

Accusations and excuses came thick and fast. Jonathan was told firmly to pull his socks up or take the consequences. "The books are all to pot," Lord Denton said, "and I can't blame Benson for it. He can't be expected to do his own job and yours as well, and keep them both up to scratch. *Jonathan!* It's getting so that I can't *trust* you. Doesn't Rosemont *mean* anything to you any more?"

"Of course it does," Jonathan declared. "I'm sorry, Charles. You're right. I have been neglecting things here of late. But don't worry. Not any more. Leave things to me. I'll soon set everything straight."

"See you do," his brother scowled.

Unfortunately Jonathan's good intentions did not last

long. He was soon back to his old ways of leaving Benson to do all the work while he indulged his love of photography.

Two weeks later Lord Denton was back again.

"You're honoring us a lot with your presence lately," Miss Selina remarked sarcastically as soon as he had greeted her. "I should have thought you'd be off on another voyage long before now."

"I may be . . . sometime in the future . . . but at present I have nothing planned. Running the company is taking all my time at present."

"Are you sure it's not because you wish to spy on Jonathan?"

He did not deign to reply, but I could see by the sudden tightening of his lips and the throbbing of a pulse at his temple that the jibe had hit home—or hurt him by its unjust utterance. I could not decide which, though I still believed I would put nothing past such an ill-tempered man as he. However, I did think Miss Selina's words a little uncalled-for, particularly when they were said in front of me, no more than an employee whichever way you liked to look at it.

He turned to me. There was no need to ask, "Where's Alicia?" for she was sitting on the sofa beside me.

"I've a letter for you," he said, handing me a blue perfumed envelope. "It's from your friend."

"Elizabeth?" I cried excitedly. This was the first letter I had received from her, though I had written to her almost as soon as I had arrived—after tearing up the letter to her father when Lord Denton persuaded me to stay.

"You will wish to read it straight away," he said, his voice low with understanding. "I'm sure we will all excuse you if you wish to retire and peruse it at your leisure."

"Thank you," I whispered, hugging the letter to me and dipping a swift curtsey. I left the room on winged heels.

I couldn't wait to reach my room before opening the

letter, and made my way instead to the Little Parlor which I knew would be empty at this time of the day. My fingers trembled as I opened it. I had longed so much to hear from Elizabeth, it was almost painful to see her dear familiar handwriting.

It was a long letter full of things she knew I would wish to hear and I read and re-read each paragraph as I went along, till a paragraph towards the end stopped me in confusion and bitter disappointment. I read it over again and was still bemused at the end of it.

"Mama is looking forward to a summer wedding and is constantly arranging trips to London to search the shops for suitable material for a wedding gown. She has already decided on my bridesmaids for me and the color of their gowns. And each day brings the question, 'Do you suppose we should invite Lord and Lady So and So, or Sir Somebody or other?' I declare I am quite at my wits' end by it all."

The words danced before my eyes. Married! Elizabeth was going to be married! And I was not to be her bridesmaid! She had always vowed I should be her chief bridesmaid, as she would be mine if I married first. Yet the bridesmaids had already been chosen. Their gowns were being decided upon. Had I missed something? Had she mentioned my name?

I read back quickly. No, there was no mention of me. Deeply hurt, I read on. Suddenly . . . *Baron Denton* . . . The name leapt like a flame from the page.

"Mama says Baron Denton's aim is clear. He wishes to make me his wife and will declare himself any day now. She is certain of it, she says. So we must be as ready as we can be for that moment, so that the wedding can take place with as little delay as possible.

*She says we cannot afford to let such a prize slip
through our fingers. And he is a prize. I am fully
aware of how great a catch he is. But it is all happening so quickly. I'm not sure of myself, not sure I am
not letting Mama's enthusiasm run away with me. . ."*

I let the pages flutter from my hand. Elizabeth and Lord
Denton? Bride and groom? I could not believe it. It was too
awful to contemplate. My bright good-natured friend and
that dark saturnine man downstairs. The thought filled me
with abhorrence.

With a curious little twist of my heart, I realized he must
have become a regular visitor to Hunt Park. If I had
thought about it, I might have known Mrs. Morrison
would not let so unique an opportunity pass her by. She
was ambitious for her children and had marked Baron
Denton down as a future son-in-law from the start. When
the invitations had come, he had accepted them. The lure
of Elizabeth was too great to ignore.

But what about Elizabeth? Did she find his lordship
irresistible? It did not appear so from her letter. ". . . *It's all
happening so quickly . . . I'm not sure . . ."* Such phrases
could have resulted from too much harrying by her mother.
Then again, it was quite usual for a young bride-to-be to
express a certain reluctance as her wedding day drew near.
Indeed it was considered desirable. Too much anticipation
was to be eschewed by any well-brought-up young lady.

I picked up the pages and scanned them again. No wedding date had been fixed. In fact no declaration had yet
been made.

But Mrs. Morrison expected it to be made any day now.

I do not know how long I sat alone in the Little Parlor,
pondering the letter and its contents. It became very clear
to me that Mrs. Morrison had deliberately left me out of
any coming celebrations. My present situation did not
qualify me to be included among Elizabeth's friends. Did

85

she know Elizabeth had written to me, I wondered. It was doubtful. She would most probably have confiscated the letter if she had seen it.

I could have wept. I had always thought Mrs. Morrison a kindly soul. I knew better now. She was a fair-weather friend. I had thought her motherly. But her motherliness had not included accepting me as a daughter-in-law. Not that she need have worried. I could never care for William in any other way than as a brother. She had not believed my protestations. William was paying more than brotherly attentions to me and that was sufficient for her to want to cast me out. I could understand that in a way, but that she should cut me off completely, banish me from Elizabeth's circle of friends! That hurt and was very hard to stomach. Very hard.

"There you are." It was Jonathan who found me. "What are you doing sitting here all alone? I've been looking everywhere for you. Had you forgotten you were to sit for me this afternoon?"

I stuffed the letter into my pocket. "Yes. No. I mean . . . Your brother is here. Lord Denton. Perhaps we'd better put off . . ."

"Oh, that's all right. I've just seen him riding over the bridge on Templer. He'll be gone for ages."

He took me up to the room at the top of the house he used as a studio. Studies of his sister, his aunt, and others I did not know lined the walls. There was even one of Lord Denton, I noticed with a slight stumble of heart. The portrait was so lifelike, the eyes so mocking. They seemed to follow me about the room.

"Sit down here," Jonathan said and arranged my skirts for me. "Cross your ankles," he said. "That's right. And put one arm along the chair arm. Yes. Rest your other hand on your lap. Good. Perfect."

He started moving lights about, focusing them on me. Then he decided on another backdrop. "That one's too stark for you," he explained. "You need something more romantic, something to project your femininity."

At last he was ready.

"Now sit still. Very still. And smile. No, not too much. Yes, that's right. That's what I want to capture. The Mona Lisa look."

"How long will it be before it's ready?" I asked as he took the plate out of the camera.

"Not long, once it's in the dark room."

"May I see your dark room? I've never been inside one."

"Yes, of course."

I was very impressed.

"It's all right," he said, "but I've got bigger ambitions than this. I haven't told anyone else, but I want to open a studio in London. I want to be a professional photographer."

"Professional! How marvelous. I'm sure you'll be a great success. You have an artist's eye. All your portraits are excellently composed."

"Thank you," he cried, taking my hands in his hand holding them to his lips. "You don't know how much your praise means to me. I know you're an artist yourself. I'll tell you another secret. I want to do more than just take still photographs. I want to take moving pictures."

"But . . . You can't . . . It's impossible."

"No, my dear Deborah, it's not impossible. There are men in the United States of America experimenting on it now. And there are men here who . . ."

There was a brisk tap on the door and in walked Lord Denton. His brows met in the middle of his forehead when he saw us standing close together with my hands in Jonathan's. My first instinct had been to draw away, but Jonathan refused to let my hands go.

"Forgive me." Lord Denton turned to go. "I did not mean to intrude."

"You're not intruding, Charles. Come in," cried Jonathan gaily, and now his arm slipped round my waist. "I've just been taking photographs of Deborah." At Jonathan's use of my Christian name Lord Denton's frown increased. "She's most photogenic."

"I'm sure she is." The comment was clipped, sarcastic. He was angry at finding me here. I should have been with Alicia.

My cheeks burned and I withdrew myself from Jonathan's restraining hold. "I was just going," I muttered, plunging for the door.

"Please don't let me drive you away . . ."

But I was already out of the door.

"If you would like to reply to your friend's letter," he called out after me halting me in my flight, "I shall be glad to deliver it for you when I leave tomorrow."

"Thank you, my lord," I whispered and hurried to my room.

I never felt at ease with Lord Denton, arrogant descendant of arrogant Norman barons, invaders of England, slayers of Hereward the Wake, and it would be worse now that he was courting my best friend.

I did not want to see him married to Elizabeth. He was too cold and forbidding a man for so sweet and bright a personality as she. He would crush her with his pebble eyes and repressive manner.

Or was he different with her? Was he more like the man who softened at the sight of his sister? Did Elizabeth share the warmth he showered on Alicia? I wondered and wondered and then I started to write.

The following morning I handed my letter for Elizabeth to the man intent on marrying her. He accepted it with a smile, and a tinge of guilt stirred in me as he said, "I'll see she gets it as soon as possible. I know she is dying to hear from you."

If he could have known what was in it, he would have been greatly surprised and would have declined to deliver it.

But he could not know that I had cautioned Elizabeth against marrying him. Consider carefully, I had written, the sort of man he is. You are obviously uneasy about him and your instincts do not play you false. Don't be misled by your mother's ambitions for you into making a mistake you will rue for the rest of your life. A good match he may be, but a kind man he is not.

I had hesitated over those words. Should I scratch them out, or leave them in? I left them in, but not without a qualm of conscience, for I had seen some kindness in him — but it was only for his sister, and I was concerned about my friend.

I had continued, I don't believe he'll make a loving husband. You deserve better than he. Hesitating again I had wondered if I was going too far, taking too much upon myself, then Miss Selina's words sounded in my head, *"He is not a man to entertain tender feelings for. Many a foolish young chit has been taken in by him, to her cost."* My pen flowed again. I should be failing in my duty as a friend if I did not put Elizabeth on her guard.

Or so I had told myself, feeling very superior and moral, not facing the real truth of the matter. Not realizing there was any other truth to face.

"By the way," he said, "did I see you coming from the west wing this morning?"

I nodded silently.

"You mean you're still there, in that Elizabethan monstrosity of a room?"

I nodded again, a little surprised at the vehemence he exhibited, and felt a further twinge of guilt as he continued, "But I gave orders for you to be moved into more attractive quarters weeks ago."

Not a kind man, I had told Elizabeth. Here was evidence to the contrary.

"Why hasn't Miss Conway been moved as I instructed?"

he turned an inquiring eye upon his aunt.

"I just haven't got around to it, Charles, but don't worry, I shall see she is moved today."

"See that you do, Aunt. She should be nearer to hand if Alicia wants her."

All my guilty feelings departed. It was Alicia he was concerned for, as always, not my comfort. My telling of his character was the correct one. I had done well to set Elizabeth on her guard. He might have a charming smile when he chose to exercise it; he might appear to have a gentle heart when his features softened; but behind such outward appearance was the chilling, harsh reality of a cold, stony-hearted man without a scrap of affection for anyone other than his sister. I was not even sure he had any brotherly feeling towards Jonathan, and I was convinced he cared little or nothing for his aunt.

It came as something of a shock, then, when I had to revise my too certain conclusions about him.

But that time had not yet come.

"Deborah. You're daydreaming. Penny for your dreams."

I looked up startled to see Jonathan's merry brown eyes looking down at me.

"Oh, they're not worth anything like that," I laughed self-consciously.

"A halfpenny, then."

"They're not worth so much as a farthing, I assure you."

"From the expression on your face, I should have said they were worth a lot more than that. However, if you wish to keep them to yourself . . ."

"Stop quizzing her, Jonathan. Can't you see you're embarrassing her?" his aunt said with an indulgent smile.

"I wouldn't embarrass Deborah for the world," Jonathan said.

"Patience Jonathan. We know what you're after, but give her time. Slow and easy is the key to success, is it not,

Deborah?"

"I don't know what you mean," I protested.

But I did. I could read her meaning plainly in her eyes, just as I could read the message in Jonathan's, and my heart started beating faster. I liked Jonathan. A lot. But I had never thought of him in that way. Now, as I looked into his eyes, conscious of his extremely potent charm, I did begin to think of him in that way, and thought how very handsome he was. How nice. How pleasant it was to be with him. Life with him would be one long laugh. Any girl would count herself lucky to be able to attract him.

And I attracted him. And he attracted me. But . . .

His growing interest in me became apparent to everyone and was fostered by Miss Selina. Doreen remarked the servants were placing bets on the day of the wedding. I told her to discourage them at once, but she smiled as she got on with her work, and I knew she believed with everyone else that one day I would become Jonathan Denton's wife.

Chapter Six

Jonathan was a soul who could not stay put. His was a nature that craved excitement, variety. "He leads such a busy life," Miss Selina had said on one of the many occasions when she spoke about Jonathan to me. "I wish he could be here with me more often, but he has so many friends, so many outside interests . . . He's miserable if he stays too long in one place. He's always looking for something new, something different." So it came as no surprise to me when he announced his intention of going up to Scotland to visit friends — and take a few photographs.

But what he said to me before he went, did.

"Come with me," he said. "My friends will love to meet you. We pass through Gretna on the way up north. We can be married over the anvil. What do you say, Deb?"

It was not the most romantic of proposals. Not the sort I had always dreamed of. He had not even said he loved me, though that omission he rectified moments later after I replied, "I can't. What would people say?"

"That I must love you to distraction, as I do, to take such a step."

To have taken him at his word, to have married him and become his wife would have solved all my worries for the future. He was handsome, full of fun. I liked him. Was very fond of him. Why, then, did I prevaricate?"

"I can't leave Alicia."

"Why not?" he demanded with astonishment. "She doesn't really need you. She's got Aunt Selina — and Murkett. I need you more."

"Need? How?" Why could I not say yes at once? I wanted to, but something held me back.

He looked surprised, then shrugged and laughed, "I don't know. I just do. Oh, Debbie, sweet adorable Debbie, say yes. Come away with me. Now I'm not penniless. Uncle James left me a tidy sum. Properly invested it will bring in a reasonable income. And there's my salary. We shall not be poor. And we get on well together. We like the same things. Don't we?"

"Well . . . yes," I said, but was I really sure? His was a wandering spirit. He offered me a life full of interest and adventure. But what about a home? I needed the security of a stable home. Would I be happy wandering around the world with him? And if there were children? Should I be able to leave them behind to be with him wherever he might wish to be? And would I be asking myself all these questions if I loved him? *Really* loved him?

With these thoughts racing through my mind, gazing up into his eager, smiling face, wanting to say yes, yet hesitating still, he suddenly swept me up in his arms.

"Come, I won't take no for an answer."

And he kissed me.

I had always dreamed of being kissed by the man I loved. Jonathan's kiss told me he was not that man. Beneath the pressure of his lips my world stayed rock steady, and I knew it should not have been like that. If I had been in love with him, his kiss should have sent me rocketing skywards.

"I'm sorry, Jonathan. I'm not in love with you."

The light died in his eyes. "Debbie," he whispered, "you can't mean that."

"I'm fond of you, Jonathan, very fond." I hated to see bright eagerness leave his face. "I appreciate the honor you

93

do me. But you deserve more than I could give you."

"I said I would not take no for an answer. I shall ask you again," he said, and left me to prepare for his journey to Scotland.

"I'll miss him," Miss Selina sighed sadly as we watched the carriage pull away. Then her blue eyes looked into mine. "We both will, won't we?"

"Yes," I murmured truthfully, wondering if Jonathan had intimated to her his intentions towards me. There was indeed a knowing air about her which suggested he had, but she made no mention of it and I remained silent on the matter.

She walked away, obviously wishing to be left alone. Alicia and I took a turn about the garden, coming to rest on my favorite seat by the fountain. I had been unusually quiet during our walk, occupied by thoughts of Jonathan. Of his proposal. Of my refusal. Had I done the right thing? I believed I had, and yet I still kept questioning myself. Had I been a fool to turn him down? There was no certainty I should ever receive another proposal of marriage. And I *could* have been happy with him. He showed a certain irresponsibility, ready to drop everything to gratify a whim of the moment, but he was affectionate and kind and gentle.

Had I blighted my chances of a happy marriage?

"I won't take no for an answer. I'll ask you again."

He had said that before we parted. Did I want him to ask me again? I wished I knew. And what I would answer if he did.

As we sat beside the fountain, caressed by the sound of dropping water, Alicia's hand crept into mine, as if understanding the reason for my unwonted silence and sympathizing. Yet there was no way she could have known what had ensued between her brother and myself. Unless he had told her. Whether he had or not, I was grateful for her sympathy and squeezed her hand in return.

Just as everybody had found it hard to adjust to Jonathan's departure the last time he had vacated the house, so they found it now. It was suddenly so quiet, with the laughter he evoked missing. However, we soon got used to his absence. All of us except Miss Selina. She continued to be unsettled, idling her time away, often sitting just staring into space, snapping if anyone spoke to her.

I endeavored to keep Alicia out of her way as much as possible. She was all too easy a target for Miss Selina's wayward tongue, and scenes of distress began to happen more often than they had done of late. I found it better to leave Alicia with Murkett while I sat with Miss Selina, listening to her whine about her lonely existence. Strangely enough she did not seem to object to my presence.

As the days passed she improved, till at length she was able to laugh and talk about other things than her loneliness and sadness at Jonathan's departure. Jonathan was her favorite nephew and she took no pains to hide the fact. And no one was made more aware of it than her other nephew, the baron.

The baron went out of his way to try to please her. I noticed how he never came to Rosemont empty-handed. There was always a gift for her of flowers or her favorite chocolates, as well as any gift he brought for Alicia, yet she never had a good word to say for him. And though he tried to hold on to his temper, she goaded him to such an extent with her sly remarks that he was rarely successful. No wonder he did not come to Rosemont as often as he might.

It was three weeks since his last visit and I sat with Miss Selina in the drawing room sketching the firescreen with the golden cockerel emblazoned thereon, trying hard not to include the remembered figure I had seen so often stationed beside it. I was thinking about him now because Miss Selina had briefly referred to him in a derogatory way in the midst of compiling a list of Jonathan's many good qualities for my ears — for my benefit. She had fallen silent

95

now, however, and was staring into space, her pencil idle in her lap.

Shading in the proud young cock's comb, I wondered if Lord Denton had seen Elizabeth again. But of course he had. He was her swain, hoping to become her husband. He would wish to see her, be with her, as often as possible.

He would have delivered my letter to her by now. What had she made of it? Had I been wrong to write so slightingly of the man who might one day be married to her? Had I done him a disservice, robbing him of a charming, delightful wife? For all I knew he might be deeply in love with Elizabeth. Had I done her a disservice in that case, robbing her of a loving husband and the title her mother so dearly coveted for her? There was no denying she would make a magnificent Lady Denton, gracing Rosemont with her beauty and charm as no other could.

I had thought myself into a dark depression, and as I tried to shake myself out of it, noticed with alarm the tall masculine figure my unrestrained fingers had outlined leaning nonchalantly against the mantelpiece.

With a swift movement I tore the page from my pad and, crumpling it in my hand, thrust it into my pocket.

Selina, caught by the sudden movement, asked, "What's the matter? Aren't you pleased with it?"

"No," I said without explanation.

I bent to retrieve the pencil she had let fall to the floor and held it out to her.

She ignored it. "Oh, I don't want to do anymore. Let's go out for a walk."

It was a fine sunny day and I agreed gladly, eager to be out of the room that seemed to be haunted by the presence of the absent lord of Rosemont.

"I'll go and get Alicia. I'm sure she will wish to come."

There was an imperceptible pause before she agreed. "Oh, very well. But hurry. I don't wish to be kept waiting."

But Alicia was not in her room. Nor was Murkett. I

looked in other rooms for her, the Little Parlor, the Music Room, the library. I could not find her anywhere.

"She's probably out already. Walking in the grounds with Murkett," Miss Selina said when I ran back to her in some anxiety.

"Maybe, but . . . I wonder. There have been quite a few times lately when I have not been able to find her. It's beginning to worry me a little."

"Don't fuss so, Deborah. She'll be perfectly all right. Murkett will not let her come to any harm. She was looking after her long before you arrived on the scene."

There was a tartness in her voice and I had no option but to accept her reasoning and follow her out into the warmth of a June afternoon.

We wandered past herbaceous borders starting into brightly colored life, through the extensive rose gardens where the buds were beginning to burst, and out onto the sloping greensward. All the time I kept an eye open for Alicia and Murkett, but had no sight of either of them.

Was Alicia deliberately avoiding me? I sensed that she was, and yet when we were together there was no constraint between us. But there was something: something I could not put a finger on. It seemed to stem from the day I mentioned that Elizabeth might be going to marry Lord Denton.

"You will have a sister-in-law," I said. "One who is as good as she is beautiful. You will not fail to love her."

She had reacted strangely, grabbing at my arm and shaking her head violently from side to side.

"It's true," I sad, thinking she did not believe me.

She continued to shake her head.

"Don't you want him to marry?" I asked.

She shook her head more slowly, then stopped and let her hand fall from my arm. For a moment she looked angry, then sad, extremely sad.

"Well, perhaps it will not come to pass," I said with a

frown of concern. The bond between brother and sister seemed almost abnormal in its intensity, and I felt momentarily afraid.

I had kept away from the subject after that.

Selina's breath was becoming a little labored. She had been keeping up an endless stream of chatter to which I had been lending only half an ear. Now I noticed the catch in her breathing and felt guilty at having allowed her to walk so far, knowing her heart condition.

"Shall we sit down for a while?" I suggested, nodding towards the trunk of a fallen oak tree.

"I used to sit here a lot in the past," she murmured, spreading her skirts and tapping the gnarled wood with her long slim hands. "This has been here since . . . I can't remember when."

"It must evoke a lot of memories for you."

"Yes. A lot." She was silent for a moment, looking inwards, or backwards to the past. Then she said, "I wasn't born here. It wasn't until my grandfather died and my father inherited that I came to Rosemont. Till then we had lived in Essex. I don't remember anything of that time. I was only two years old when we left to come to Rosemont. Rosemont has always been my home as far as I am concerned. Father died when I was twenty. My brother, Samuel, was two years younger. But he inherited Rosemont. The eldest son always inherits."

A resentful look came over her face.

"It should have come to me. I was older than Samuel. Rosemont should have been mine. Now it belongs to Charles — for all he cares about it. And if he weds Elizabeth Morrison, as he will for he must produce an heir, I shall be of less account than ever. At least now the running of Rosemont is in my hands, but even that will be taken away from me."

She fell silent. Her expression did not welcome further conversation.

I fell to wondering why she had never married. She would have had a home of her own to run and maintain and have no cause to be resentful of others. She must have been very beautiful when young. Why, then, had she remained unwed, a spinster, an old maid aunt?

Would I become like her, old and unwanted? Not if I married Jonathan. If I married Jonathan the whole course of my life would change direction. If Elizabeth married Charles and I was as convinced as Miss Selina that she would—he was too great a prize to let slip—she would become my sister-in-law. Lord Denton would become my brother-in-law.

My heart skipped a beat at the prospect and I tried not to dwell on it. If only I was in love with Jonathan . . . But deep down inside me I knew I was not.

My thoughts ran away with me and I found myself wondering what Charles had been like as a little boy. *Charles,* not Jonathan, not even Lord Denton, but *Charles.* I imagined him running wild through the grounds of Rosemont, climbing trees, swinging conkers, getting into all the kinds of mischief boys usually got into. And later as a tall youth, dark, slim, yet with the powerful physique of his maturity evident even then, playing cricket, tennis, fishing, maybe in this very stretch of river rippling past our feet. Then I saw him on board his ship. Captain Lord Denton. Strict disciplinarian . . .

I gave a startled yelp as Miss Selina's long fingers poked me in the ribs.

"You were a long way off, Deborah. Daydreaming again?"

"I'm sorry," I murmured, lowering my head quickly to hide the sudden rush of color to my cheeks, half-afraid she would question me as to what my faraway thoughts had been. And how would I answer her? With the truth? Impossible. How would I explain it? I could not explain it to myself.

However, "Let's go in," she said tapping my knee gently. "It's not as warm as it was."

I did not think the sun had cooled. It seemed to me to be hotter than ever. But I turned obediently towards the house with her, my breath catching in my throat, as it always did whenever I looked upon the rose-red walls and glinting sun-lit windows from this vantage point. Then I gave an involuntary cry as I caught movement at one of the upstairs windows and thought I saw a woman in white looking out.

"Who is that?" I exclaimed, pointing urgently.

"I can't see anybody," Miss Selina frowned, shading her eyes and looking up at the window I pointed out.

And neither could I now.

Feeling suddenly cold in the sun, I declared, "I could have sworn I saw somebody . . . moving the curtains."

"It must have been the wind."

"But there is no wind. In any case the windows are closed."

"Then it was a maid you saw, cleaning in there. It could have been no one else. No one uses it. The door to that room is always kept locked."

But the woman had not looked like a maid. And why should a maid bother to clean a room that was never used by anybody?

I guessed it was the room with the locked door and thought it must be a very large room. Most likely a suite of rooms. I knew it was kept locked because I had tried it after learning Lord Denton did not inhabit it, his room being at the end of the corridor on the left next to his brother, Jonathan's. It was not Alicia's, nor yet Miss Selina's, and there was no one else living at Rosemont who could occupy so important a room. So I had felt at liberty to turn the knob.

I had tried the door and found it locked.

But I did not know why it was kept locked.

And I was curious.

"Why is it kept locked, Miss Selina?"

Blue eyes swept over me coldly. "I hardly think that is any of your business," she snapped.

Snubbed, I said no more, and we walked in silence side by side till Miss Selina exclaimed with a furious click of her tongue. "There's Charles in his smelly motor car! And Jonathan away, too! Oh, how provoking!"

We could not see him, but we heard the chug chug of his automobile and my heart joined in its loud rhythmic beat. Because he would see me yet again in company with his aunt instead of his sister and I feared the hard displeasure of his pebble gray glance, I told myself.

Turning through the archway leading into the courtyard, we reached the massive iron-studded front door as the motor rumbled over the wooden bridge astride the dry moat.

"Hello," he called, waving cheerily at us. Soon he was drawing to a halt beside us.

He leapt down from his high leather seat smiling broadly. Thank goodness he's in a good humor, I thought, and immediately afterwards, How nice he looks when he smiles.

His good humor did not last long.

"If you've come looking for Jonathan," Miss Selina said starchily after receiving his kiss on her cheek, "you'll be unlucky."

"That wasn't my prime purpose . . ." Wary puzzlement chased the smile from his face. "Why will I be unlucky?"

"Because he's not here," she replied smugly. "He's in Scotland. Staying with friends."

Puzzlement gave way to anger. "Scotland! I don't believe I'm hearing this. *Scotland!* After all I said to him the last time. After I made it plain what the consequences would be if he didn't . . ."

"He has every right to visit his friends."

"Not if it interferes with his work. Not to indulge a whim

of the moment. He's supposed to be my estate manager. Yet he's hardly ever here. Does he expect the place to run itself?"

"There's Benson. He . . ."

"Benson! Yes, that's his favorite cry, isn't it? 'There's Benson. Let him take over. He's a good man. He can manage.' Well, so he can and so he will. I warned Jonathan what would happen if he didn't keep his word. If Benson can manage the estate when he's not here, he can manage it when he is."

Miss Selina's face whitened. She had been enjoying herself at Lord Denton's expense, going out of her way to antagonize him, knowing his temper would flare, but she had not expected this result.

"You can't mean to make Benson estate manager—over your own brother?" she rasped.

"I mean just that," said his lordship grimly.

Jonathan would not be pleased that Miss Selina had lost him his job, but she tried to make light of it. "As to that," she said, "I doubt it will cause him any distress. Thanks to James's beneficence, he has ample means of his own now. I fancy he will be glad of the opportunity to start up the photographic studio he has been talking about so much lately."

But a note of self-pity entered her voice. The last thing she would want would be for Jonathan to set up in business on his own—a business that would take him away from Rosemont. She adored Jonathan, and if she had her way he would never leave her side—not even to visit friends.

"But that's all it is. Talk." Lord Denton allowed a sneer to enter his voice. "He flirts with the idea of becoming a professional photographer, but he'll never do it. It's all very well as a hobby, but no way for a gentleman to earn his living."

"I don't know why you don't come and run Rosemont yourself if you're not satisfied, instead of frittering your

102

time away in London."

"I assure you, Aunt Selina, I do not spend my time in London frittering it away, though Jonathan seems disposed that way. It was decided years ago he would run Rosemont so that I could go to sea. You know my heart had always been inclined to the sea and ships."

"Yes, and the devil take Rosemont. Eh? Eh? But you've stopped going to sea now, haven't you? What's to stop you from coming back and taking your share of the responsibility? Why should Jonathan. . .?"

"Lockhart's needs me."

"Rosemont needs you."

They battled on and I edged away from them, slipping through the open doorway into the cool weapon-hung hall where I saw Alicia standing at the top of the stairs palefaced and frightened, obviously having heard every word of the heated argument below.

She heard my footsteps cross the stone floor and moved away quickly.

"It's only me," I called out softly.

But she ignored my call, and when I reached the top of the stairs she had vanished.

I hurried along to her room and knocked on the door. There was no reply. Yet she must be in there. I had run up the stairs quickly as she fled, expecting her to be waiting for me further along the corridor and surprised when she was not.

I knocked again. Still no answer.

Where was she? Where was Murkett? Were neither of them in there? Cautiously, I turned the knob and pushed open the door calling Alicia's name.

The room was empty.

I crossed the pale blue carpet and knocked on the door leading to Murkett's private chamber.

No answer. I opened the door. That room was also empty.

I retraced my path across the pale blue carpet and let myself out. Where would Alicia be? What other room could she have gone into? She must have gone into one of them. She could not simply vanish into thin air.

My eyes was drawn towards the door guarded by the two pilasters. Was she in there?

No, she could not be. I would have seen her, heard her go in as I ran up the stairs. Then my hair started prickling at my scalp as I remembered the woman I had seen—thought I had seen—at the upstairs window had been wearing white.

Alicia had been dressed in white.

Had it been Alicia I had seen?

I believed now it had. It was the logical conclusion taken together with her present odd behavior and disappearance.

Did Miss Selina know Alicia went in there? Did Murkett know? Did Murkett go in there with her? She was missing, just as Alicia was missing. But why was Alicia behaving so secretively? Why was she avoiding me? Miss Selina had pointed out to me that Murkett had been taking care of Alicia long before I set foot in Rosemont. Was this her way of showing me she preferred Murkett's company to mine? Had I outlived my novelty value?

With these questions tumbling over themselves in my mind, I heard the front door bang shut. The argument was over and the protagonists were coming up the stairs. I drew back behind a suit of armor in an attempt to escape detection, but only Miss Selina mounted the stairs and her quick eye sought me out.

"Deborah! What are you doing propped up against the wall like that? Are you waiting for Alicia? Where is she? What's she doing?"

But she was not really interested in my stumbling response, continuing onwards and entering her boudoir while I was still in mid-sentence.

Three and a half hours were still to pass before dinner-ime. Plenty of time for a bit of sketching. Sketching always soothed me, eased the worries out of my mind. And so it did now. I made a few lightning sketches of the fountain with its great green fish—something I had been meaning to do for ages and never got around to—before wandering down towards the river bank where I was lucky enough to find a dragonfly lazy enough to keep still on a stone till I had captured its elegant form on paper. Then, as always, I finished up facing the house.

I decided to concentrate on sketching the West Tower. My room was in the West Tower. Miss Selina had not had me moved as she had promised Lord Denton she would, and I was, in a strange sort of way, becoming attached to it. I still felt a little afraid making my way along the cold stone passageways and up the narrow staircase, but now that Doreen occupied a room nearby, not so alone, so cut off from the world.

The window at the top belonged to my room. Absorbed in committing it to paper I did not hear the man come up and it was with a shock that I heard him rasp, "Ere! Wat d'you think you're doing?"

I looked up in alarm to see a man with a face as brown and wrinkled as a walnut waving a gnarled old stick at me. After the initial shock I realized he must be one of the gamekeepers. He was not a gardener, for I knew every one of them by now.

I smiled and said pleasantly, "I'm making a sketch of the house."

"I can see that. And I can tell you now, you can pack up and be on your way."

"But . . ."

"Now. This ere's private property. We don't allow no drawin' 'ere."

"But I have permission," I explained patiently. After all the man was only doing his duty. "I am . . ."

He shook his gnarled old stick at me again. "Get movin'

young woman. I've seen the likes o' you before. And I'll 'ave that what you've done." He made a grab at my drawings. "Don't think I don't know what you're up to. Got accomplices, 'aven't you? Think you're going to get into the 'ouse with the help o' these."

"Oh, please," I cried out anxiously, seeing all my work about to be crumpled in his huge hands. "If you'll let me explain . . ."

"Out!"

"But I'm Miss A—"

"Out!"

"You're very rude," I admonished him angrily. "I tell you I'm . . ."

"You can tell me all you like, it won't make no difference. You're trespassing on private property."

"What's going on here?" A new voice joined the fray. "What's all the shouting about Newman?"

"It's this young lady, m'lord." Newman doffed his cap. "I've told her to leave and she won't."

"Of course not. She lives here. This is Miss Conway, Miss Alicia's new companion. don't you recognize her?"

Newman scowled. "No, I don't. I didn't know Miss Alicia had a new companion. What's happened to Murkett?"

"Murkett's still here."

"What do we want 'er for then?"

Lord Denton's relaxed manner left him. Suddenly he was all nobleman and master.

"This is Miss Conway, Newman, and you will treat her with respect, or I will know the reason why. You may go about your business now, Newman."

"Yes, m'lord." Newman touched his forehead and went away grumbling to himself. "Nobody told me about a new companion. Nobody tells me anything anymore. I'm only the watchman. Not important enough to be told what's going on."

Lord Denton smiled ruefully. "Poor old Newman. I'm

afraid his age is catching up with him. I told him about you myself weeks ago. But he'll never admit he's forgotten. It's funny, he can remember things that happened way in the past, but recent events often evade his memory."

"He need not have been so rude," I exclaimed hotly. "He's ruined some of my sketches."

"You must forgive him, Miss Conway. He's well over seventy, you know."

"Age is no excuse for rudeness," I countered.

He flopped down beside me chuckling. It was a deep, rich indulgent sound and somehow very satisfying to hear. The two chocolate-colored pointers that had been at his heels came up to investigate me, and he shooed them away with a quick and easy command, immediately obeyed by the dogs who went lolloping away, perfect specimens of their breed.

With their departure I became very much aware of who it was sitting beside me on the grass. Till then I had been too full of annoyance with Newman. Now my cheeks began to burn. He was very close. If either of us moved an inch we would be touching. At the thought my heart started racing and if I could have moved I would have done—but my limbs seemed petrified.

He sat back resting on his hands and stretched his long legs out in front of him. "He should be in his cottage with his feet up," he said. "He's an old gamekeeper of ours, retired years ago. But he was always an active man and after a few months of enforced idleness he cornered me and asked if he could have his old job back. 'You know that's out of the question,' I said. 'But growin' a few veg'tables and lazin' about aint for me,' he said. 'I've always led a active life. Always on me legs, out wi' me gun. Can't you find nothin' for me to do in me old age, m'lord? I'll die, else.' "

He was giving a very passable imitation of the old man's voice and manner and I listened to him in growing astonishment, hardly able to believe this smiling, humorous man was the stern, cold-hearted Baron Denton of Rosemont.

He chuckled again. "The old devil. He knew that would get me. I told him he could patrol the grounds if he liked. Be the eyes and ears of Rosemont. Keep trespassers at bay." His lips spread into a grin. "I never expected you to fall foul of him." He subjected me then to a questioning scrutiny and said kindly, "You mustn't mind him. He's tetchy with everybody. And never having met you . . ."

"Well, I hope he remembers me when he sees me again," I responded chirpily, suddenly very much at ease with him.

"I shouldn't think there's much doubt about that," he said, and there was a caress in his voice I could hardly mistake.

"Once seen, never forgotten,' he quipped. "And I mean that in the nicest possible way."

I blushed to my hair roots and I felt dizzy beneath the glance he bestowed on me. The world toppled sideways and we swayed towards each other. In another moment our lips would meet. But his face passed mine and he bent to pick up the papers scattered around my feet and I spiralled downwards into a yawning abyss that suddenly opened up in front of me.

"Are these your drawings?" he murmured from the other side of the abyss. "They are good. My aunt said you had a gift. She's right. They're excellent."

His glance rested on me again, but I saw nothing in it other than admiration for my work. And what did I expect to see? What had I thought I had seen? I could not understand myself—or him.

"I'm glad you feel able to give my aunt a little of your spare time. But don't let her monopolize you completely."

"I don't," I said with some asperity detecting a rebuke in his words. "Alicia is always my first priority. But if I am free, and Miss Selina requests my company, why then, I am happy to give it. She's so much on her own, particularly

108

now that Jonathan has gone away."

His eyes narrowed at his brother's name. "Yes. He's the only one she cares about. The rest of us might not exist . . ."

He broke off, drawing in his breath quickly as if fearing his tongue was running away with him, and I thought, He resents Jonathan, resents the place he holds in his aunt's heart. And yet, I thought, it's not only that. There's something more. He looks as if he actively dislikes Jonathan.

They were complete opposites in every way. Jonathan was charming, happy-go-lucky, somewhat selfish, and something of a rogue. Lord Denton was a man of the sea, strongly disciplined, with his emotions very much under control. They were, in their aunt's words, as different as chalk from cheese. It was not so difficult then to see how Lord Denton might hold someone like Jonathan in aversion.

But what about brotherly feeling? Did he have any? Or were all his tender feelings reserved solely for Alicia?

"She's become something of a recluse over the years," he was continuing. "Abhors meeting new people. She's taken to you though. She says you're different. She can talk to you. You know how to listen."

I met his gray puzzled stare, heard the surprise in his voice. "And you have difficulty in believing this," I said.

"No," he returned. "I agree with her."

The look I did not know how to interpret, but which caused my heart to stumble in its beat, sprang to his eye again and I withdrew my glance quickly. For a few moments there was silence between us. Then he broke it. In a voice that held a kind of wonder he said:

"Rosemont *is* a beautiful house, isn't it?"

"Oh, yes." I agreed at once. "Warm and mellow with the sun on it like this, the windows sparkling like jewels — I should love to paint it. A charcoal sketch is all very well, but cold. It can't convey the warmth of the place."

109

"You find it warm?" He sounded surprised.

"Yes, I do. I didn't at first. At first I . . . well, perhaps I wasn't in the right mood to appreciate it. But now, I've grown to love it."

We were silent again, then he said, "Why don't you?"

"What?" I turned to him innocently to find my eye caught and held by his.

"Paint Rosemont."

I answered him breathlessly. "I—haven't any paints; I left my easel behind me at Hunt Park. I—I'm not sure water colors would do it justice anyway, and I've never painted in oils."

"There must be an easel or two about the place. In an attic somewhere. And paints can always be bought."

It was a perfectly normal conversation, and yet I had the feeling there was something momentous about it—as if it would affect the rest of my life.

"Alicia likes you," he declared abruptly, changing the subject completely.

"We've become great friends," I said, finally managing to disengage my eyes and set them to look upon the grass, each verdant blade of which seemed to stand out in such stark relief that if I had wished, I could have counted each one separately.

"I know. I've seen you both together. Watched you. There's been a great change in her since you came. I'm grateful to you."

"We get on extremely well together. She is really very intelligent."

"I've always known it."

He was looking at me earnestly, listening closely.

"I think it would be a good idea to allow her more freedom."

A scowl crossed his face, but now that I had started on this course, I continued.

"I think she ought to get out and about. Mix with other

110

people. Even get away from Rosemont altogether. For a holiday. Go to stay at Witchet Towers in Devon, perhaps."

I was unprepared for the look that settled on his face. It held a mixture of bitterness, sadness, hate.

"Out of the question," he snarled.

"But why? She's not mental, whatever Miss Selina might think. She intelligent and perfectly capable of . . ."

"I know you mean well," he interrupted me, "and I'm not quite as unobservant as you might think. I've seen how she can relate to you, but you are the exception. With others she would not be forthcoming. They would not be so kind to her as you. They would recoil from her, mock her."

"At first, maybe," I admitted, "but when they got used to seeing her around . . . She's so lovely and sweet, they would soon learn to accept her as she is."

"You don't know the world as I do, Miss Conway. People are cruel. I should have thought your own experience would have told you that."

I was reminded of how my friends had shunned me after Conway Place was sold; remembered how tradesmen, previously obsequiously survile, refused to extend my credit; remembered how my servants laughed at me, saying I was no better than they now, and it did their hearts good to see me down on my knees scrubbing floors.

"But surely this is a different case," I said, banishing unpleasant remembrance.

His lips curled into a sneer. "Oh, yes. Different indeed. They would be faced with something they couldn't understand and be all the more vicious because of it."

"I think you are being too pessimistic," I responded, remembering now that although I had met with cruelty in my despair, I had also met with kindness in the shape of old Mrs. Wood who had brought freshly baked bread to my door and vegetables from her garden; and Mrs. Hinkley who had concocted herbal drinks for my aunt — and very helpful they were too; and the greatest kindness of all, my deliverance by my father's old friend Mr. Morrison.

"Do you, indeed!" His tone was clipped, his temper rising. I should have noted it and kept quiet, but I soldiered on regardless.

"*I* think it's cruel to keep her so closely confined. It can't be right to keep her shut up away from the world."

"I see. After so short an acquaintance, you think you have the answer to all Alicia's problems."

Blithely I replied, "I have come to know her; understand her."

"Better than those who have known her all her life?" Steel was in his voice, flint in his eye. "I suggest you stick to your duties, Miss Conway, and leave those more fitted to decide what is best for Alicia."

Hot under the collar at the rebuff I hit back. "Miss Selina would have her shut away in an asylum if she could. You say you will never countenance such a thing, yet you keep her as closely confined as any inmate of Bedlam."

He stiffened and for a moment anguish flecked his stony glance. He appeared about to retaliate, but thinking better of it, rose instead, called the dogs to heel, and left me sitting on the grass looking after his tall athletic figure, impatient with myself. We had been getting on so well together and now I had spoiled it all.

I should have kept quiet, kept my views to myself, but as usual my wayward tongue had run away with me. *"You should not be so impulsive. You should think before you speak."* How often had Aunt Susie said that to me? If only she were here now to caution my unbridled tongue.

But she was not. She was gone. Just as my father was gone.

My throat tightened as I thought of my father, his tortured body moldering away beneath the mighty ocean's waves. I could see it now as I saw it often in my dreams, with the flesh falling away, empty sockets where his eyes had been, his bones glistening white with fish swimming

112

round about and in and out . . .

I threw myself down on the grass, burying my face in it, battling to keep back the tears it would be useless to shed.

A sudden cry brought me bolt upright, my heart hammering against my ribs. What was it? Who had made so agonizing a cry? I stared all about me. There was no one in sight.

Yet the cry had been close, very close to my ear.

A bird hovered high above my head, its wings whirring, its body motionless. A kestrel. Had it been the kestrel's cry I heard, or its victim's, snatched unaware.

I knew it was neither.

It was not a bird's cry I had heard, nor an animal's. It was a human cry. The cry of a soul in torment.

A living soul?

Or a dead one?

Chapter Seven

I gathered my things together, dropping them in my haste, trying not to panic, but all my old fears and forebodings had been resurrected, and I was very much aware that the "thing" that had threatened me from the start still lurked within the environs of Rosemont. It had lain dormant for weeks, lulling me into a false contentment it was now preparing to shatter, and as I hurried towards the house I knew I should not be safe from it even there. Wherever I went it would seek me out and . . .

I pulled myself up sharply and allowed common sense to counsel me. These black thoughts had been brought about because I thought I had heard the cry of a tormented human being. But it was not so. It could not have been a human cry, but that of a bird or some animal in distress. It was the only sensible explanation.

Gradually my sense of doom departed, and by the time I reached the house I had fully accepted the only sensible explanation, sad only that I had not been able to help the suffering creature.

Miss Selina waylaid me on the stairs. "What were you doing with my nephew down by the river?" Her eyes showered me with particles of blue ice.

"We — were talking," I replied, taken aback by her angry confrontation.

"About what?" she demanded.

"Oh—this and that."

"Don't be flippant with me, my girl. I demand to know what he has said to you."

"Well . . . we just . . ."

"You know he's to marry Miss Morrison?"

"Y-yes."

Her words acted on me like a blow to the head. Everything started spinning round and I felt sick. For a moment it seemed a black blanket fell to cover me, blotting out all light, suffocating me so that I could hardly breathe.

"And yet you encourage him . . ." Miss Selina was continuing as I fought my way out of the smothering blanket, gasping for air, ". . . I told you, I warned you, not to be taken in by him. He's not the man for you."

"I—I don't know what you're talking about," I managed a breathless response, frightened by the livid expression on her face, the reaction her words had evoked in me.

"I think you do," she snarled, baring her teeth like a tigress. "I told you to keep him at a distance."

"This conversation is quite unnecessary, Miss Selina," I said stiffly, angry with her and myself now that her meaning was plain. "Keeping Lord Denton at a distance is no task at all. He keeps the distance between us quite wide enough."

"So! You have thought about him in *that way*." Her eyes no longer showered me with ice. Sparks of fire fell upon me now.

"What way?" I swallowed anxiously. "I don't understand you."

"Don't be mealymouthed. You know full well what I'm talking about. You're falling in love with him, aren't you?"

I had read in novels of maidens' hearts standing still when confronted with unpalatable truths and dismissed it as fantasy. Now I knew it was true, for mine stopped then. Was it true? Had Miss Selina hit upon the truth? Was I falling in love with Baron Denton?

"No!" I cried defensively. "Of course I'm not!"

"Why didn't you take my words to heart, Deborah? I warned you to beware of him. Now there's no knowing what will happen."

"Nothing will happen. I'm not falling in love with him. He's the last man on earth I would fall in love with."

Miss Selina stared at me intently, her eyes holding mine, probing deep into my soul, searching for the truth, till at last they softened and she said, "Well, I hope that's the truth, for I should hate to see you hurt. Take Jonathan. You'll be happy with him. Leave Charles for Elizabeth to contend with."

Lord Denton had brought me another letter from Elizabeth. In it she had thanked me for mine, been delighted to hear from me at long last, and appreciated my concern for her in her predicament, but could not really believe Lord Denton to be as black as I had painted him. In fact, she had owned, she was finding him quite charming.

My heart had sunk as I read it. She had been taken in by him; no doubt been encouraged by her mother to see him in a good light. It was obvious from the tone of her letter that she had made up her mind that marriage to him would not be a bad thing after all. So when I wrote back I made no more mention of Lord Denton's character. I had done all I could to enlighten her in that respect. I could go no further without antagonizing her. I contented myself with other matters. Told her how I was now enjoying life at Rosemont, and on impulse, little realizing where it would lead, told her about Jonathan's interest in me and how the future might possible see us as sisters-in-law.

Now as I held the letter in my hand I wanted to throw it away—tear it up into a thousand tiny pieces. We would never become sisters-in-law. I would never marry Jonathan. I would never marry anyone.

Why then, did I take the letter and go in search of Lord

116

Denton and ask him to deliver it for me on his next visit to Hunt Park? What demon stopped me from tearing it up as instinct prompted me to?

Leaving the winding staircase and stone passages behind, I traversed quickly the silent corridors of the west wing, emerging into the main part of the house just as the man I was seeking was ascending the magnificent Elizabethan staircase. He scowled when he saw me. He had not forgiven my criticism of his treatment of Alicia and my heart, already knocking and tumbling about in a frenzy of activity, lurched agonizingly as he came towards me — a tall, powerful figure — and I thought my bones would melt with fear when he halted before me. There was irritation on his face.

"Miss Conway!" he said, but before he could treat me to the length of his tongue, as I felt he was about to do, I held out my letter and made a breathless request.

"Will you be so kind as to deliver this to Hunt Park, my lord? It is for Elizabeth."

"I should be most happy to do so," he said as the letter passed between us, "were I going to Hunt Park, but I intend to remain at Rosemont for the foreseeable future. However, I shall instruct Croft to see it is posted at once."

"Thank you," I whispered throatily. *He was staying at Rosemont.* I felt myself tremble.

"If you should wish any further mail posted, just leave it on the silver salver in the hall. Croft will see it is promptly dealt with."

"Thank you." *Was I glad or sorry? Why question myself?* I swung away to seek the sanctuary of my room.

Sanctuary? Yes, that was how I thought of it. Sanctuary from him. From life. From despair. A place where I could be alone to work out my salvation — whatever it might be.

"Miss Conway!"

I was halted by his bark of a command. "Yes, my lord?"

"Where are you going?"

"To my room—in the West Tower."

His black brows met, cleaving a deep inversion in his forehead. "You are not still resident in that Elizabethan relic of past grandeur?"

"Yes, I am, my lord."

"But I gave orders for you to be moved out of there weeks ago. Why have they not been carried out?"

"It's of no consequence, my lord," I declared, seeing his volatile temper about to explode and wishing to terminate the interview. "I don't mind. I—I quite like it there."

"Nonsense! No one could like it there! Come with me!"

I had no option but to follow his purposeful tread to Miss Selina's boudoir door which he opened, after an exasperated knock, and entered without waiting for permission.

"Why is Miss Conway still in the West Tower, Aunt?" he demanded without preliminary. "Why has she not been moved as I ordered, nearer to Alicia?"

So it was for his sister's sake he wished me moved, not mine. How could I have been so foolish as to believe for a moment it was because he cared about my comfort? Would I never learn he cared not one whit for my comfort?

Miss Selina was sitting in her favorite chair by the window, looking a little startled at our abrupt entrance and her nephew's sharp attack. But she responded easily, "I'm sorry, Charles, I just haven't had the time to see to it. She shall be moved tomorrow. I promise."

"Today, Aunt Selina," he barked. "Now."

Within the hour I was rehoused in a comfortable airy suite next door to Alicia's. There was a room for Doreen to inhabit adjoining mine and she bubbled over with excitement as she unpacked for the two of us, never in her life expecting to occupy such a room—and all to herself!

I could not enthuse. It mattered little to me now where I was housed. It was only a temporary resting place. Before Elizabeth was installed as mistress of Rosemont, I must be elsewhere. Never mind about becoming an independent career woman, I would take anything, any servile post, just to get away from an ostensibly humiliating situation. Miss Selina, I felt, would help me in this. She would understand why I could not remain an employee in the house of one with whom I had known the intimacy of friendship on an equal status.

Oh, coward that I was, refusing to face up to the truth — the unpalatable truth!

Whether Alicia had been deliberately avoiding me or not I had no way of telling, but quite suddenly she was seeking my company again, and after an initial restraint on my part, we were back on our old friendly footing.

However, I noticed Murkett much more in evidence than usual. Wherever Alicia and I went, there she was hovering about within calling distance. It worried me, and wondering about it, came to the conclusion that either Miss Selina or the baron himself had instructed her to keep us under observation, fearing I might somehow persuade Alicia to go down to the village with me.

I felt angry and sad that they did not trust me and in my hurt tackled Murkett upon it. "Is it by instruction that you follow Miss Alicia and me about?"

She met my eye boldly. "Miss Selina says you want to take Miss Alicia down to the village and I'm to see you don't."

"Miss Selina?" I asked sharply. "Not Lord Denton?"

"Lord Denton has said nothing to me on the matter."

I felt a surprising and inordinate relief at these words. It was not the baron who mistrusted me, it was Miss Selina.

"But how could she think I would do something she expressly forbade me to do? Surely she must know I wouldn't dream of disobeying her."

Murkett said, "It's just that she's very fearful for Miss

Alicia."

"Yes, I know," I murmured, then, as I had tried to do on occasion before, sought to make an ally of her. "But, Murkett, don't you agree with me it would be good for Alicia to go out and about . . . meet other people?"

"Miss Selina thinks it wouldn't be wise."

"But what do *you* think, Murkett? You must know as well as I, Alicia is no simpleton. You, who are so close to her."

Something flickered behind her eyes before she lowered her head. "It's not my place to say what I think, Miss Conway. If I spoke out of place, I should be dismissed. And I wouldn't be able to bear that. Miss Alicia needs me, whatever you might think."

"Of course she does. I know that. But it's not fair to her to keep her from doing things. Things she is perfectly capable of doing."

"Like what, Miss Conway?" Murkett raised sad brown eyes to me. "What can she do in her condition? She does all that can be expected of her."

"But there's so much more she could do. Life could be made much more interesting for her. She could be taken for carriage rides, for instance, outside of Rosemont. She could take a holiday. Mix with people. Make new friends. Oh, there's so much . . ."

"She doesn't need new friends." Murkett interrupted my flow of ideas. "She doesn't like meeting new people. She's better off staying with the people she knows and loves."

"You just want to keep her to yourself," I snapped. "You're not concerned with what is best for Alicia."

I could have bitten off my tongue at the hurt look that came over her face. Whatever else I had discovered during my stay at Rosemont, Alicia meant the world to her. Her one purpose in life was to ease Alicia's path.

"Oh, Murkett," I cried as she turned from me. "I'm sorry. I didn't mean . . ."

But her departure was swift and she disappeared before I could finish my apology. Yet another friendly overture had been aborted by my too impulsive tongue. Well, why should I care? Why should I bother myself about Alicia's future? She and everyone else in this household would soon cease to be any concern of mine whatsoever.

A sudden upspring of tears had me darting for the front door. I gulped them back — had I not shed the last of them long ago? Exercise was what I needed. A good long walk in the fresh air would do me a world of good. A good long walk and a good long think. There was such a lot to think about.

"Miss Conway." Croft stopped me opening the door. "The mistress invites you to take tea with her in the boudoir."

An invitation from Miss Selina was a command, so I toyed only briefly with the idea of turning it down and climbed the stairs. I hesitated at the top, breathing fast, as Lord Denton came out of his room and reached my side in seconds with his long stride. I had not known of his return from a trip to Norfolk with Benson.

"Good afternoon, Miss Conway." He greeted me without the semblance of a smile.

"Good afternoon, Lord Denton," I responded huskily, my mouth having dried at his sudden appearance.

"Anything happened while I've been away?"

"Such as what, my lord?"

He frowned down at me. "Such as anything," he rasped.

Wondering why he seemed so angry I murmured, "I can't think of anything. Everything's as usual."

"Is it? Are you sure?"

His eyes burned into mine. He was hinting at something. But what? I tore my eyes away. We had reached Miss Selina's door. He knocked and I was glad to hear Miss Selina reply at once.

"Come in."

I could still feel the burning power of his eyes scorching my head as he stood aside for me to enter the room ahead of him. His hand retained its hold on the door knob so that in passing I brushed against his outstretched arm. My dress seemed to flare up and spread fire through my veins. I almost fell into the chair Miss Selina offered me as my legs were robbed of their power to sustain me.

"I have something to tell you, my dear," she smiled at me, "that will please you greatly — when Alicia gets here."

"I hope we're doing the right thing," Lord Denton said, crossing the room quickly to take up his favorite stance at the mantelpiece, "and not making some frightful mistake. I've been wondering if we ought . . ."

"Don't say you wish to change your mind now," his aunt interrupted him sharply, "just when I've managed to come to terms with it. We've discussed the whole thing thoroughly. There's no going back. We've made our decision."

"I know, but . . ."

"It was you who insisted upon it in the first place."

"Yes, but . . ."

"No more buts, Charles. We'll abide by our decision come what may. It will settle matters once and for all."

Their exchange made no sense to me, but it seemed to have a bearing on what Miss Selina wished to tell me and I contained myself in impatience for Alicia to arrive.

She came, shepherded by the faithful Murkett, stunningly dressed in lime green silk, a color admirably suited to her dramatic good looks, and I thought, not for the first time, that if her beauty could be enhanced by animation, she would be absolutely ravishing. Her brother bestowed a tender kiss on her cheek and brought her to sit beside me on the sofa.

Murkett departed and Croft entered with a footman and maidservant in tow. Clearing Miss Selina's table he threw a lacy white cloth over it and transferred the silver Georgian tea service and delicate china cups, saucers, and plates from the tray the footman was holding onto it. Then at a snap of his fingers, the maid brought the three-tiered cake stand she had been minding to set beside her mistress, then stood back waiting with the footman to serve the freshly poured tea and cake and sandwiches to the assembled company.

It was quite a performance and one which I had seen enacted many times before, so rather than observe it again I focused my eyes on the man propping up the mantelpiece. This had not been my intention, I vow. Why should I wish to look at him? I did not even like the man. Yet I could not help admiring the strong uncompromisingly masculine line of him, the firm set of his jaw, the dark sheen of his hair.

Suddenly his gaze was upon me, starting my blood churning through my veins, my pulses throbbing, my heart hammering, and he was saying with an air of mockery, "Your tea, Miss Conway."

In confusion I took the proffered cup from the footman and a dainty sandwich from the maid, and nibbling, thought, What on earth is the matter with me? Dry mouth, a burning in my blood, pulses throbbing, heart hammering. I was exhibiting all the signs of a high fever.

"Daydreaming again," Miss Selina observed drily. "She has a propensity for doing that, Charles. A pity she refuses to share her dreams. I'm sure they must be most interesting."

"Dreams are very precious things," he said, "to be safeguarded at all costs. Is that not so, Miss Conway?"

His glance rested on me, pebble hard. I could see he was angry with me, and I could not think why. I was aware he was trying to tell me something—or ask me something—but what? Oh, I could not understand him. I did not like him. He was cold and cruel, stern, unkind . . . I began listing all the reasons why I did not like him against a barely heard background of conversation till, "Deborah!" Miss Selina's sharp call brought me out of my reverie.

"My dear girl, where *do* you get to in your daydreams?" she remonstrated. "Well?"

"I . . . I . . ." How could I tell her what I had been thinking about?

But she did not want to know about that.

"I said will you not be delighted to see your friends again?"

"Friends? What friends?"

"The Morrisons, child."

"The Morrisons! Oh! Are they coming here? Or am I to go there—to Hunt Park?"

Miss Selina's tongue gave a click of annoyance and her nephew's mocking voice came sailing across the room.

"I'm very much afraid Miss Conway hasn't heard a word you've been saying, Aunt Selina."

"Well, really!" Miss Selina's tongue clicked again and she looked away from me in disgust.

"We are to give a ball," Lord Denton explained, "on the first of August in honor of Alicia's eighteenth birthday. We feel—my aunt and I—that we can't let it pass without some sort of celebration."

"A ball! But that is wonderful!" I beamed at him, forgetting my dislike of him, for I knew it must be he who was the instigator of this. "It is exactly the sort of thing . . ."

I remembered Alicia was sitting beside me, listening if not seeing. I must not let her know we had been discussing her. It might embarrass and upset her. But he knew what I had been going to say. He had thought over my ideas and the suggestions I had made. He was not unfeeling where his sister was concerned. He wanted her to be happy. He had noticed the change in her. The marked improvement in her behavior. He intended this to be the first step in a new life for Alicia.

For a while I was elated, but then I wondered anxiously if it might not be too big a step. A ball was necessarily a large and lavish affair. A great many people attended such events. Would it be too much for Alicia to cope with all at once?

Miss Selina was saying, "It will not be possible for her to be presented at Court . . . Well, look at her, how could it be? . . . So a ball is the next best thing. Charles thinks I am being overambitious wanting to hold a ball — he would have preferred a smaller affair — but I say . . ."

So it was Miss Selina who wanted the ball, not Lord Denton as I had supposed. I was surprised, for Miss Selina herself did not like mixing in company. She shunned society of any kind. Yet for Alicia's sake she was prepared to invite a large number of people to a ball in her honor.

"I must invite the Prince of Wales," she was continuing, "and the Princess, of course."

"No!" Lord Denton's response was swift and firm.

"But we can't give a ball and not invite him. He'll take it as a snub."

"Then we won't give a ball. We'll have a small party of friends and neighbors, as I originally intended. I will not have that man within a hundred yards of my sister."

I understood his reasons. His Royal Highness had a bad reputation where women were concerned, and Alicia's beauty would be bound to commend her to his notice. Lord Denton was fearful for her, afraid she might be compromised. Miss Selina, however, did not appear to appreciate his concern.

"But I've set my heart on a ball," she pouted.

"Then you must unset it, for I've made up my mind."

Her eyes sparked anger at him then she smiled thinly, "If you insist, then of course, it shall be as you say. Perhaps it is just as well, anyway. She will probably spoil it all by having one of her tantrums. I'm afraid I can't feel as sanguine as you as to how she will behave in public. I . . ."

"Another cup of tea, if you please, Aunt Selina."

Lord Denton's interruption, accompanied as it was by an angry frown, made it perfectly plain he did not wish her to continue along this road.

She ignored him.

"Of course, she can always go to her room if she proves tedious. You must keep her under close observation, Deborah. At the merest sign of trouble you must whisk her away. My nephew seems to have set his mind on marriage and we don't want Miss Morrison frightened off, do we?"

I had expected it to happen. Ever since Elizabeth first broached the matter to me in her first letter, I had been preparing myself for it, her marriage to Lord Denton. But I had not been prepared for this cataclysmic effect on my body, this awful deprivation of breath, the freezing of my blood. Numbed, paralyzed, I could not even react to Alicia's sudden rise which sent her cup flying and her swift dash from the room.

"Now look what you've done!" Lord Denton yelled at his aunt. "Will you never learn? Come, Miss Conway, we must catch her before . . . MISS CONWAY! This is no time to go off into one of your dreams. My sister needs you."

Unceremoniously he grabbed hold of my arm and dragged me from the room with him.

Alicia was nowhere in sight.

"She'll be with Murkett," I gasped. "It's Murkett she needs, not me."

He dragged me to Alicia's door and burst in. Alicia was in Murkett's arms sobbing silently. Murkett mouthed above the girl's head, "It's all right. Leave her to me, my lord."

I knew he wanted to spring forward and gather his sister into his own arms and comfort her, but he nodded and drew me from the room, confident that Murkett's ability to soothe and calm her young mistress was greater than his — or anyone's.

"I thought it was a good idea," he grated once the door was closed. "I thought over your advice and followed it — and look what's happened. I should have listened to my aunt. She was against it from the start."

126

I was stung to retort, "It was your aunt who caused this with her unkind words."

"I know." He turned on me angrily. "But can't you see, if Alicia can't cope with a few unthinking words from one who has loved and cherished her all her life, how will she manage if strangers . . ."

"Unthinking! They were downright cruel."

He was silent and I continued impetuously, "Why won't you admit it?"

"Because it's not true. My aunt's tongue might run away with her, but she's not deliberately cruel."

"Maybe not, but you can't deny she is always slighting Alicia and making her unhappy."

"That will do, Miss Conway. You forget yourself. Kindly remember you are an employee in this house and mind your own business."

It was a whiplash and I reacted sharply to it.

"I shall remember. You need not fear I shall step out of place again. In fact, I shall not be here much longer. Very soon I shall be out of your way, out of your house, out of your life."

"Oh?" he said very quietly. "How's that?"

I was silenced. How could I answer?

"You are thinking of getting married, perhaps?"

Taken by surprise I stammered, "N-no . . ."

"Then where will you go? What will you do?"

"I . . . I . . ."

"You're not going anywhere. There's nowhere for you to go. Unless . . ." his voice was tipped with anger again, "you think to join Jonathan."

"Jonathan?"

"He has asked for your hand, has he not?"

How could he know? Who could have told him? Jonathan, himself? But Jonathan was still in Scotland. Miss Selina? But Miss Selina didn't know. Or did she? Had Jonathan told her he had proposed to me before he left?

What did it matter who told him? He knew. And he was not at all pleased about it. His next words made it clear why and explained his simmering anger.

"And he's quite a catch, isn't he? With Uncle James's money in his pocket and his twenty-fifth birthday coming up and my management of his trust funds at an end, you think he can afford to disregard my wishes—but I shall put every obstacle I can in the way of your marriage. Depend upon it."

I held my breath as his face took on the brutal expression I had hoped never to see directed at me. I would have run away—if I could have moved—but I was gripped by a strange paralysis again. Nor could I disclaim his accusation, for my tongue was incapable of utterance.

"Why didn't you try for me? I'm a much better bet with a title, lands, an income of over £50,000 a year . . . But no doubt you considered him easier meat. He's young and gullible, easily taken in by a pretty face . . ."

My hand came up then to smite him across the face with every ounce of my outraged strength. With a muttered oath he caught hold of my wrist on its way down and fear curdled my blood as his eyes blazed down into mine. Then with a sudden wrench he crashed my body against his and took my lips with brutal savagery. Then as suddenly he let me go and I went reeling with humiliation against the wall as he stalked away and I slid helplessly to the floor.

Chapter Eight

My future looked bleak. If I had thought about accepting Jonathan's proposal, it was out of the question now. Lord Denton had made it impossible. I went about with downcast head and heavy heart, afraid to look up lest I see his black, accusing, censuring gaze.

Alicia, sensing something was wrong, hardly left my side. I was grateful for her silent sympathy. Miss Selina, however, demanded to know why I was so quiet.

"Don't you feel well?" she inquired. "You are looking a bit peaky."

I seized the opportunity of telling her of my desire to leave Rosemont and seeking her help in acquiring a new situation.

"But why? What has happened. Has Charles been upsetting you?"

"No," I cried quickly at the sudden perspicacity of her glance. "It's just that . . . well, you must see that when Lord Denton and Elizabeth are wed, it will be impossible for me to stay here—as an employee."

"I see nothing of the sort," she countered, "and I shall certainly not help you acquire a new situation. I can't do without you here. As for being an employee—you must know you're more than that. You're a friend."

"But . . ."

"Not another word."

It was all settled as far as she was concerned.

Jonathan came home. Happy, carefree, smiling Jonathan. Everyone fussed around him as usual, none more so than his aunt. The sight of him raised my spirits, but when he planted a smacking kiss on my lips and demanded to know if I had missed him, I drew away in embarrassment, more conscious of Lord Denton's derisive gaze than anything else. But then, as if my courage had returned with Jonathan, I returned the baron's glance, refusing to be cowed any longer. After all, I had done nothing wrong. The wrong was all at his door. He had accused and abused me intolerably.

Not a great deal of time was allowed to elapse before he informed his brother that he had been relieved of his job as Rosemont's manager and that Benson had superceded him.

Jonathan accepted the news joyfully. "That's grand. Now I can do what I've always wanted to do and set up a photographic studio in London. I would have done it sooner only I didn't want to let you down. Can I have a room in your house in Grosvenor Square to set up in?"

"No, you can't," his brother snapped, trying to hide his surprise behind a scowl.

"But there's loads of space. You could let me have a whole floor to myself and not notice it . . . You know, that's a damn good idea. Why didn't I think of it before? I can live and work all under one roof."

"Lockhart House isn't a commercial enterprise," was the grating reply. "You can live there with pleasure for as long as you like, but you must set up your studio elsewhere."

"But Charles . . ."

He got no further. Miss Selina was clutching at his coat sleeve, "Jonathan! You can't go to live in London. What about Rosemont? What about me?"

"Rosemont's not my responsibility any more," he said. "And I must do this, Auntie. It's something I've always wanted."

"But you've a studio upstairs. You could use that. You don't need to go to London."

"I do, Aunt Selina. London's where I want to be. There's so much happening there. It's so exciting. I don't know how I've managed to exist all these years buried here in the wilds."

"But you love Rosemont!" she declared wildly.

"Of course I do. It's my home. And I shall come to see you often. But I must live in London. Do you know I met men in London — I stayed there for a few days before coming home — who are experimenting with moving pictures, and not only moving pictures, but with color. Think of it. Color! Real color, actually in the pictures as it's being taken."

"But Jonathan . . ."

But Jonathan was chasing a dream.

"I intend to go to the United States eventually. There's a man there I must meet. George Eastman, the man who invented the first machine for making rolls of transparent film. You must have heard of him, Charles. He's Kodak Films. If anyone makes a breakthrough with color, it will be him. I've got to be there when it happens."

All through the rest of the evening and through dinner talk was of films and cameras. Jonathan even insisted there would be talking pictures before very long. I found this hard to believe and Miss Selina pooh-poohed the idea roundly, but I noticed Lord Denton took it quite seriously.

After coffee in the Little Parlor Jonathan leapt up, caught hold of my hands, and drew me up from Alicia's side.

"Come and help me pack up my studio," he cried gaily. "I shall need to transport everything to Grosvenor Square. Oh, don't worry, big brother," he added with a quick grin as Charles reared, "I shan't set it up there, but it'll have to be housed there till I find a suitable place."

131

"Do you have to do it now?" Miss Selina frowned. "Can't it wait till morning? You've only just got back."

"Sorry, Aunt Selina," he returned gaily. "Must be away at sunrise tomorrow."

He drew me out of the room with him. I kept my eyes averted from Charles Denton's face. I knew I should only see disapproval written there. I didn't care, anyway. Let him think what he liked. I was resolved not to let it worry me. And why shouldn't I help Jonathan pack? Why shouldn't I marry him, if I chose? I wouldn't be marrying him for his money. I would be marrying him because he was nice and charming and fun to be with . . . because . . . because . . .

A sudden constriction in my throat brought my thoughts to a stumbling halt.

"Right. You start emptying that cupboard while I find some boxes," Jonathan cried, and I was glad to shelve my thoughts in a frenzy of activity.

In no time at all it seemed, we were finished. Jonathan placed one last box of film in the last packing box and slammed the lid shut. "There's a lot of film there I've never developed," he said. "Can't think why. Must see to it when I get the chance. There might be some good stuff among it."

We left the studio and began to make our way back to join the others downstairs, but at the head of the stairs I halted.

"What's the matter?" Jonathan asked.

"Nothing," I replied, but my voice was a croak, and fear stampeded my soul as the same icy coldness I had experienced seeping into my bones at that very spot once before seeped into my bones again, and I stared in terror at the grotesque carvings on the guardian pilasters expecting them to come to life again, expecting this time to be torn to pieces by the angry lion and leopard.

"But you've gone quite pale," he said, putting his arms round me. "And you're trembling. I hope you're not sickening for something."

In the warmth of his arms, my fear receded. "I'm all right. I felt cold suddenly, that's all."

"On a warm night like this?" He tilted my chin to look into my eyes. "Are you sure that's all it was?"

"Yes. What else could it be?" I tried to laugh away my fear and his concern.

"I don't know," he responded thoughtfully, "but, somehow, you seem different from when I last saw you."

"Different? In what way?"

"You don't seem — happy."

"Nonsense. I'm perfectly happy. I'm just tired. I — I think I'll go to bed. If you'll excuse me . . ."

His arms tightened around me. "You remember I asked you to marry me before I left for Scotland?"

"Yes," I whispered.

"And have you thought it over?"

"Yes."

He drew in his breath swiftly. "I said I'd ask you again," he said huskily, his face very close to mine.

"Please, Jonathan . . ." I tried to push him away.

"I'm asking you again now, Deb. Will you marry me?"

"Oh, Jonathan, I . . ." Say yes, said a voice inside me. Say no, said another. "I don't know," I prevaricated.

"Well, that's an improvement on your last answer," he beamed and kissed me joyfully. "It means I stand a chance."

As he released me I saw Charles Denton at the bottom of the stairs looking up. When he caught my glance he answered it with withering scorn, then turned his back, and let himself out of the house.

Next morning after kissing his sister and aunt good-bye, Jonathan pulled me into his arms. "When I'm settled I'll send for you," he said, not caring that he could be heard by all.

"No, Jonathan," I began a little wildly.

But kissing me he laughed away my protestations and

133

clambered confidently up beside his brother, sitting straight as a ramrod at the wheel of his white automobile waiting to drive him to the station.

Miss Selina tucked her arm in mine and smiled as we watched the tail end of the motor car pass under the ancient portcullis and cross the wooden bridge. "Jonathan's proposed to you, hasn't he?" she said.

I admitted with a gulp that he had.

"And you've accepted him?"

"No."

She withdrew her arm abruptly. "Why not?"

"I don't love him."

"You can learn to love him." She eyed me stonily. "I advise you to marry him."

"I know it would solve all my problems," I said, thinking this was what she had in mind, "but I can't."

"It's Charles, isn't it?" She almost spat the words in my face.

"No."

"You're in love with him."

"No."

"I'm not a fool, Deborah. See that you're not one, either."

She left my side quickly and I watched her ascend the stairs. She had spoken harshly to me, but it was only because she was concerned about me, about my future happiness. She thought I was in love with Charles and, knowing nothing could come of it, warned me against it. *I'm not a fool, Deborah. See that you're not one, either.* But I wasn't a fool. I knew nothing could come of it. And I wasn't in love with him, anyway. I wasn't. I wasn't.

I swung round at a light touch on my arm. It was Alicia's cool hand. I had forgotten she was there. But she had been listening and had heard every word.

I said quickly, "Miss Selina has got hold of the wrong end of the stick. Because I am not in love with Jonathan,

134

she thinks I must be in love with Lord Denton, which is absurd."

For a few moments we stood perfectly still looking at each other. Looking? A chill ran down my spine as I reminded myself that though her dark eyes were on me, she could not see me. Then she caught hold of my hand and began drawing me with her up the stairs, along the corridor, and into her room.

Murkett was nowhere about and I watched in surprise when Alicia locked the door. She took my hand again and drew me with her towards her dressing table where she began feeling about for something. Her hands found a small Chinese lacquered cabinet with two doors and five drawers. She opened the doors and revealed more drawers. She removed three and pressed a hidden spring. To my astonished gaze a cavity appeared and from this secret place she withdrew a small velvet box. She opened the box and held it out to me, and for the first time I gazed upon the periwinkle brooch.

I never coveted anything before or since as I coveted that sapphire brooch so daintily made in the shape of a periwinkle flower—and not only did I covet it, but it coveted me. Ridiculous, I know, but that is how it was. Its tiny diamonds and larger sapphires winked a message at me.

"Take me, take me," it seemed to say. "Take me and hold me. I'm yours."

And my hand was drawn towards it.

I lifted it from the box and pinned it to my bosom. Immediately something seemed to leap from it and clutch at my throat. Terrified, I unpinned it and returned it to its box, then felt foolish. As if anything could leap up from a brooch, an inanimate object. Nothing could. Any more than a carved leopard could leap down from its frame.

Alicia was standing opposite me and as I looked into her face, I had the uneasy feeling she knew how I had been tempted to take up the brooch and keep it. Did she know why I had put it back?

Don't be stupid, I admonished myself severely, how could she know? But I sensed something hidden behind her dark shining eyes—something she wished me to know, something she wished to tell me, if only she could.

Lord Denton invited George Benson and his fianceé, Nancy, to dinner. Benson had popped the question as soon as he had officially been made Estate Manager. The dinner was to celebrate both his promotion and his betrothal.

I liked Benson. He was always friendly and polite with me, treating me as a member of the household and not an employee. I liked Nancy, too. She helped in the dairy and sometimes in the house if any of the servants happened to be sick. So I looked forward to a pleasant evening.

And so it proved to be—and so much more.

Alicia wished to retire early so I escorted her to her room and handed her over to Murkett. When I returned to the drawing room where coffee was being served the other four were deep in conversation. Not wishing to intrude I went out onto the terrace and breathed in the balmy evening air. A few moments later Lord Denton was at my side.

"It's a lovely evening," he said.

"Lovely," I agreed.

"Do you mind if I ask you a question?"

"No. What is it?"

"It's advice I'm looking for. Could you give me a few ideas on what to get for my sister's birthday? I usually buy her clothes. She can't see them, but she likes the feel of different materials. Hats, shoes and gloves—I tend to fall back on those, too. But she has more than enough of them. More than she'll ever wear."

I stared up into his face. All those lovely clothes in Alicia's wardrobe. *He* was responsible for them.

He gave a deprecating little laugh. "Not very imaginaive, you'll agree. Can you suggest something a little more — adventurous?"

"What about jewelry?" I said, and held my breath as the beautiful periwinkle brooch popped into my mind.

"She has plenty. That is something else I fall back on — and she can't see that, either."

I was still holding my breath. The brooch had escaped from my mind and was floating about in the air in front of me. I put out my hand to grasp it. It faded away at my touch.

"Miss Conway!" Lord Denton caught hold of my hand. "What's the matter? Aren't you feeling well? Shall I call my aunt?"

"No, no. I'm all right." *Was I going mad?*

The brooch had vanished now. But I had seen it, floating in the air in front of me, and it had frightened me more than I cared to admit. *Was* I going mad, seeing things that weren't there?

"Are you sure," Lord Denton sounded worried. "You look — peculiar."

I gave myself a shake and tugged my hand away. "I was thinking that will always be a problem with Alicia — getting her something she will appreciate even though she can't see it." He was standing far too close to me, his eyes too intent upon my face. I moved away from him. "I've been giving a lot of thought to it myself."

"What to give her?"

"Yes."

"And have you come up with anything?"

"Yes."

"But you don't want to tell me what it is, in case I steal your idea."

I turned quickly. "Oh, no, I . . ."

I broke off. Turning I had encountered Miss Selina's cold blue gaze. It sped across the room and onto the terrace where I stood to flay me like a whip, scouring away at the

137

outer layers of my being leaving my nerves exposed and raw. Had she seen Charles take hold of my hand and misconstrued what she saw? It was plain she was displeased at seeing us so close together. More—she was enraged.

"You're quite right," I heard Lord Denton chuckle "That's probably exactly what I should do."

"There's one thing you could give her that I could not," I said swiftly—the sooner this conversation was ended, the better. I could not think why he had opened it, unless it was to atone for his reprehensible behavior to me, his way of apologizing. "A boat trip."

"A boat trip?" He looked and sounded incredulous.

"Alicia and I were walking by the river one day recently," I went on to explain, "and I noticed a small boat half-hidden among the reeds. It was old and rotten and tied by a length of rope to an iron peg on the bank. I mentioned it to Alicia and was surprised at her swift reaction. She became excited and intimated to me that I should pull it in. I did so—it was easier than I expected—and she knelt down and touched it, lovingly. I asked her if she had ever sailed in a boat. She nodded eagerly tapping at the boat's rotting side. 'This one?' I asked her, and she nodded again. It was a long time before I could get her to leave the old boat's side."

"That must have been the boat my father gave me when I was a boy," he mused wonderingly. "Fancy it still being there! And fancy her recognizing it!"

"If you arrange a boat trip for her, I'm sure it will please her more than all the gowns and jewelry you could give her."

"I wonder." Suddenly his face clouded over. "She used to love going out on the river with me . . . when she was little . . . before Mother died . . . All those years ago! But one day she begged me to let her take an oar—she wasn't dumb then—and promptly lost it in the water. I was angry with her. Said I'd never take her out in the boat again. She burst into tears . . . sobbed uncontrollably. I was a fool. A crass

138

nsensitive fool. I should have been horsewhipped."

He was staring through and beyond me, blaming himelf, angry with himself, and I thought, This is the reason vhy he pampers Alicia now, why he goes out of his way to grant her anything that might make her life of darkness nore bearable. It was his way of trying to make up for the iurt he had caused her on that long ago day.

"If only I'd known . . . If only we could see into the uture . . . I'd give anything . . ."

His face was bleak and my heart went out to him. "I lon't think she remembers that particular day," I said gently. "Her face bore only signs of pleasurable rememrance as she stroked the old boat."

"Really?" His eyes came alive to my presence again. "Do ou honestly think that?"

"I do."

"And you think she would like a boat trip?"

"I'm sure she would."

His face cleared at last. "Then a boat trip it shall be. Maybe a picnic, too. What do you think."

"Marvelous. I think she'd enjoy it enormously."

"Miss Conway, you're a treasure," he beamed. "What should I do without you and your clear-headed advice?"

My heart fluttered at his praise. I curtailed its momenum with peremptory severity. I was a treasure only in so far as I was useful to him, to Alicia's happiness.

"Now tell me," he continued, "what you have decided upon. You have no excuse for holding out on me now that you know I shall not steal your idea."

"Perfume," I said, and was annoyed it came out as no more than a breathless whisper.

"Perfume!" he repeated. "Now why didn't I think of hat?"

I felt sure he must have done, many times.

"And bonbons," I added, glad it came out more strongly.

"And bonbons. Perfect. You were wise to keep your own

counsel on the matter. I should not have been able to resist copying it."

I was conscious of laughter behind his words. "I'm sure the idea's not new to you," I said with a rush of asperity. "You must have given her perfume before — and bonbons."

"Well, maybe . . . but I assure you I had not thought of them on this occasion."

There was a twinkle in his eye and a lift to the corners of his mouth. In spite of myself I began to smile. Suddenly we were both laughing.

"That's better," he said. "I had begun to think you would never smile at me again."

"Is it any wonder?" I said, sobering.

"No wonder at all." He sobered, too. "I had no right to speak to you the way I did. Will you accept my apology?"

"Gladly," I said, and was surprised at myself.

A moment later he asked, "And how do you intend to go about purchasing your gifts?"

"I don't know. I don't think the village shop will stock the sort of thing I want. I was wondering . . . Do you think . . . Could I have the use of the carriage to take me to King's Lynn?"

"With pleasure, Miss Conway, and I shall escort you there myself."

"Oh, but there's no need . . ."

"I think there's every need."

"But I shall be perfectly all right on my own. Doreen can come with me."

"Don't argue." He put his finger to my lips. "I shall escort you. Doreen will not be needed. We'll go tomorrow. Can you be ready by eight o'clock?"

I nodded. My lips were burning from his touch and longed to put a cooling hand over them, but dare not make such a move. My hands weren't cool, anyway. No part of me was cool. A fire had been kindled in my blood again and there was no way of putting it out.

Benson and Nancy were waiting to take their leave.

Lord Denton went into the hall with them. Miss Selina turned furiously on me.

"What was all that about?"

I did not pretend to misunderstand her. "Lord Denton and I were discussing Alicia's forthcoming birthday."

"And?"

"He asked my advice on what sort of present she might like."

"And?"

"That was about it."

"I don't believe you."

"I'm sorry, Miss Selina, but it's true."

I was growing out of patience with her. What right had she to probe into my private conversations? Besides, I wanted to get away to be by myself. I wanted to think over the conversation in the privacy of my own room, sort out my feelings which were confused and at the same time amazingly clear.

"There must have been more," Miss Selina refused to let the matter drop. "You were out there such a long time and I saw . . ."

"Lord Denton kindly offered to drive me into King's Lynn," I cut in quickly, "on a shopping expedition."

"Did he, indeed?" she said drawing in her breath. "Then we'll all go," she added promptly.

"All go where?" Lord Denton inquired entering the room.

"Up to Lynn. It will be a nice outing for all of us. When are you leaving?"

"Miss Conway and I are leaving first thing in the morning," he said equably. "And we're going alone. We're going to buy Alicia's birthday presents and we can't do that if she is with us. And you will not wish to come and leave her with nobody but the servants for company, will you?"

"She'll have Murkett."

141

"Yes, but I still think it best you do not come. Alicia is bound to suspect something is afoot if you come with us, and more than likely hit upon the truth. No, it's better you stay here with her. After all, you have already bought a present for her. Did you not send Lister to purchase it for you?"

She scowled at him. "And if I did — I should still enjoy a trip into Lynn."

"You wouldn't," he said sharply. "I've offered to take you there many times and you've always refused, saying you didn't enjoy long carriage trips."

"I can change my mind," she snapped. "Anyway, there's no need for you to put yourself out. I shall accompany Deborah. You can stay behind with Alicia."

She was determined I should not be alone with her nephew again. I enjoyed the battle, happily guessing at the outcome.

"No, Aunt Selina," he said, his determination more than equalling hers. "You shall stay behind with Alicia. I shall accompany Deborah."

Miss Selina rose, lacing and unlacing her fingers in front of her. Tall and defiant, she faced him angrily. I waited for the explosion, but it never came. He outstared her till at length, pale and tight-lipped, she withdrew without another word or glance in my direction.

The morning brought me face to face with her again. Standing just inside the open doorway of her boudoir I did not see her till she stepped out in front of me. I knew it was not a chance encounter. She had been waiting for me.

"So you're going then," she spat contemptuously. "You're a bigger fool than I took you for. You've been taken in by him. I warned you. I warned you to be wary of him. How many times is it now? But you didn't listen. And now . . ."

I heard the carriage wheels rattle over the cobbles in the courtyard, the front door open, and Lord Denton's voice.

"Excuse me, Miss Selina," I said, glad of the excuse to get away from her, "Lord Denton's waiting . . ."

"Yes," she whispered, hissing low, "he's waiting. Waiting for you to fall into his arms like a ripe plum. Don't think I haven't seen you holding hands, seen your sheep's eyes."

She was about eight inches taller than I, but her face had come close to mine and for a moment I was afraid of her. Then she said gently, "Oh, Deborah, don't be a little fool. There's no future for you with him. He doesn't care for you. He's a philanderer. He plays with women and their affections, but his heart is cold."

"Miss Selina, please . . ." She was hitting below the belt and I was beginning to tremble.

She laid a sympathetic hand on my arm. "Forgive me, my dear, but I must speak out. You have no one else to guide you. I know you think you are in love with him . . ."

"I do not. I am not," I cried wildly, shaking off her arm.

She gave a little sound of aggravation and continued, "You are so young, my dear, unused to the ways of the world, of men. They are wicked. All of them. Charles is no exception." She caught hold of my arm again. "My dear, I must tell you something about him — something you should know — "

But I did not want to hear. I pulled my arm away. "I must go, Miss Selina. I must go."

"Go then, but remember what I've said. Don't trust him."

Her fingers made a final bite into my arm and I was free.

Hastening down the stairs I was aware that she followed me. Charles was standing by the open door so tall and good-looking that my heart leapt at the sight of him.

"There you are at last," he grumbled, but with a smile.

Then I saw his smile went beyond me and when I looked round Alicia was descending the staircase, unaided. I expected Miss Selina to rush to her side, and when she did not, evincing no surprise, concluded I was right in my assumption that she was well aware of Alicia's capabilities and always had been, though she would not acknowledge it.

She called out from where she stood, "Good morning, Alicia. Come and see Charles and Deborah off on an outing. They are going to Lynn."

Alicia's step faltered on the stairs. She soon recovered — and the others had not seemed to notice — but I wondered what her thoughts were on the matter, if she thought it strange that I should be going on an outing with her brother. Such a thing had never happened before. The smooth skin of her forehead was marred by a frown. She certainly did not appear to like the idea. Perhaps she was annoyed that I hadn't mentioned the outing to her, not realizing I had not had the opportunity.

My thoughts were interrupted by Charles who, having saluted his sister with a kiss, was now anxious to be off. "Come along, Deborah. The morning will be over before we get there."

Deborah. He had called me Deborah again. I could not get used to it. Would he expect me to call him Charles? But though I found it easy enough now to think of him as Charles, I knew I wouldn't dare.

I poked my head out of the carriage window to wave good-bye and with a shock saw Alicia smile and wave back for all the world as though she could see. But of course, it was at her aunt's instigation. Smile, she would have said. Wave, she would have said, and Alicia would have obeyed.

Nevertheless, the incident disturbed me and set me wondering about Miss Selina and why, if she knew Alicia's capabilities, she pretended ignorance of them. I was certain now she did know of them. She was an astute woman. Very much aware of all that was going on around her. She had fathomed my secret before I had fathomed it myself — I was falling in love with Charles Denton.

My eyes slid to his face. He was looking out of the

window and his profile was towards me. It was a strong profile with a high-bridged nose, firm lips, square jaw. What could I read there? Nothing but that he looked stern, that he appeared to be very self-contained. My eyes fell to his hands, strong and brown with little tufts of black hair at the base of each finger. One hand was resting on his knee, the other held the window strap, loosely but firmly, and I wondered what it would be like to be held in his arms, to feel those strong hands caressing, stroking . . .

I looked away quickly, stifling a moan as my body reacted with shameless desire. But he heard the sound and turned.

"What's wrong?"

"Nothing."

"You seem worried. Are you wishing you hadn't come?"

"Why should I do that?"

"Well, sometimes, I think . . . Are you afraid of me?"

"Of course not. Whatever makes you think such a thing?"

"I don't know. The way you recoil from me sometimes. My aunt hasn't said anything to make you fear me?"

"Good heavens, no," I managed to laugh. "What could she say?" But I suddenly felt desperately afraid and was beginning to tremble. Why should he ask that, if there was nothing to fear?

"What, indeed?" he said turning to look out of the window again.

What a strange conversation, I thought, trying to still my trembling limbs and wishing I had taken notice of Miss Selina and not placed myself in this position. We were alone together in a confined space, in close contact. I would be alone with him for the rest of the day and try to deny it as I might, I feared it. I feared him. Or was it myself I feared and the effect his nearness had on me?

I was still trembling. I wondered if I would ever be able to stop. I had never experienced anything like this before.

Never longed to be with someone so much, and at the same time longed desperately to be somewhere else. But I knew, somehow, I had to remain calm, not let him see the effect he had on me, not give him the chance to—to what? I hardly knew. My thoughts were like chaff blown hither and thither by feelings I could not control. One moment I wanted nothing so much as to feel his arms around me, to give myself up to whatever might be the result—the next to put an ocean between us.

"Tell me about yourself."

The suddenness of his question made me jump, but it also eased things for me by setting my provocative thoughts to flight.

"There's not much to tell," I said. "You know my background. That I'm the only child of Sir Raymond Conway, that he was killed while ballooning over the English Channel, that the house I lived in from babyhood was sold over my head to pay his debts, and that after my Aunt Susie, my only living relative, died, Mr. Morrison took me in for the sake of his friendship with my father, and that I now bide at Rosemont as companion to your sister, Alicia."

"Yes, yes, I know all that," he said, clicking his tongue rather in the way his Aunt Selina did when annoyed, "but what about *you*, yourself? What goes on behind that cool, calm exterior? What dreams lie behind those lovely eyes?"

Cool, calm, was that how he saw me? If he only knew how his glance set my pulses throbbing! I turned away from him quickly, lest he should see the dreams that lay behind my eyes.

"You're right," I heard him say. "It's none of my business."

He had lost interest. I knew without turning round he was looking out at the passing countryside, as I was, though I saw none of it. The silence that developed between us lasted all the way to King's Lynn.

"Would you care for some tea or coffee before we go in

146

search of Alicia's birthday presents?" were his next words to me as he helped me down from the carriage.

"I'd love a cup of coffee," I said.

"I know just the place."

He piloted me to a little restaurant where he seemed to be very well known. We were served with coffee and cream and little sticky biscuits, all puffy and sweet. Then he took me to a shop that sold all manner of exotic things including a range of French perfumes, soaps, colored bath crystals, as well as sweet-smelling English lavender.

I chose a tiny bottle of French perfume because of its elegant shape and then found I had not enough money left for the bonbons I had intended to buy. As soon as he realized this, Lord Denton insisted on advancing me sufficient funds for my purchase.

Then he took me to lunch at The Duke's Head in the bustling marketplace and afterwards we joined the throng among the stallholders, many of whom he knew and chatted away with as if they stood on equal terms. As he talked the years seemed to fall away from him, the careworn lines on his face were eased away, and he was almost a boy again.

Before long I found myself entering the Custom House, an interesting old building dating from the seventeenth century—built by Henry Bell for Sir John Turner, a local vintner, my erudite companion informed me. He was very well known there also and welcomed as an old friend. I was looked at with great interest. Did they see me as his lordship's future wife? They treated me with as much respect as if I were. Then I was asked by one of the officers, "Do you like the sea, Miss Conway?" obviously expecting me to say yes.

I said, "No. I hate it."

He looked taken aback. "May I ask why?"

"Because it took my father's life."

"But the sea was not to blame for your father's accident," Lord Denton pointed out reasonably. "He could as easily have come down over land. Would you then hate every blade of grass, every flower, every tree?"

"Yes," I cried unreasonably. "But he didn't, he came down over the sea and it gave him no chance. It's vicious, cruel."

And suddenly I was weeping, pouring out my heart, telling him how much I missed my father.

"But from what I hear," he said and it was at this point the officer responsible for opening up the wound moved discreetly away, "he was hardly ever at home."

"But when he was, we were always together. And he's with me still, ever-present in my thoughts, my dreams. I see him in my dreams with the waves billowing over his head, drowning his cries . . ."

"I'll have to take you out on the sea one day, so that you may face it and overcome your hatred of it," he said softly.

"Never," I croaked through tears streaming down my face. Tears I thought I had done with. Tears I should have shed sooner. Tears that would have healed the wound left raw within me, if I had not been determined to keep them at bay.

He gathered me to him and held me close. "It's the only way you'll ever lay your father's ghost to rest," he said.

Chapter Nine

"So you're back at last." Miss Selina was looking distinctly put out. "Where have you been all day long? Do you know what time it is? What have you been doing? It couldn't take you this long to buy a birthday present for Alicia. I've been worried sick."

It was two thirty in the morning.

"I'm sorry you were worried, Aunt. We would have been home sooner only I decided at the last minute to take Deborah out on a fishing trip," Lord Denton explained.

"A fishing trip!"

"It was marvelous," I enthused. "I thoroughly enjoyed myself."

Miss Selina glared at me malevolently. She was annoyed with me anyway for disobeying her wishes and going out with Charles, but that I had enjoyed myself in the bargain was fuel to her annoyance.

"Well, I'm glad somebody did," she snapped. "I've had a very trying time. Alicia has been at her most awkward. She went off on her own somewhere and stayed away for hours. I didn't know where she was. Neither did Murkett. We had the servants searching all over the place for her. Then just when I'd decided to contact the police, she turns up unconcerned as you please. Where she'd been, what she'd been doing, how could we tell? But the time will come, Charles, when we shall no longer be able to excuse her escapades."

I felt Charles stiffen beside me, worried as always about Alicia and fearful of his aunt's prognostications. I wanted to tell him not be afraid. I had long suspected Alicia had secret hiding places to which she repaired when she felt the need to be alone. She even hid from me on occasion—and Murkett. And Miss Selina was aware of this also. She did not usually show concern over her niece's disappearances.

Miss Selina was continuing in a plaintive tone. "You could have taken me with you. Alicia would never have missed me. And I should have enjoyed a fishing trip."

"No you would not," Charles said abruptly. "You would not have liked it at all. You don't like the sea and you don't like going out. When was the last time you accepted an invitation from me, or anyone, to go out? Even Jonathan hasn't been able to winkle you out of your groove for years."

"Things are different now," she retorted sullenly.

"How—different?"

She pouted and did not explain, but turning to me asked in the same tone, "What did you get for Alicia, anyway?"

Lord Denton's swift intake of breath led me to think he would insist on an answer to his question, but he left us without another word and climbing the stairs two at a time entered his room closing the door behind him with an ear-splitting bang.

Miss Selina winced and sighed extravagantly. "Tut, tut, such temper. Now you are seeing him as he really is."

I got away from her as soon as I could. She had soured the whole day for me. I undressed and got into bed, lay on my back, and looked up at the ceiling, picking out the shapes of plaster roses and rampant vine leaves encrusted thereon as my eyes adjusted to the dim light of the room. Then suddenly they weren't there any more.

My ceiling had become a kaleidoscope with the events of the day crowding in one upon the other to arrest my attention. The tense morning during which I tried desperately to resist the strong magnetic pull I felt towards Lord Denton. The shopping expedition and luncheon at the hotel which saw the tension relaxing between us. The visit to the Old Custom House where I had broken down and been comforted by him. The sea trip.

The sea trip!

It was late afternoon. A chill wind was blowing in off the sea. I did not at all want to go on a sea trip. But having thought of the idea, nothing would satisfy Lord Denton but the putting of it into immediate action. My vehement protestations brushed aside, Rogers was instructed to take us with all possible speed along the coast to a little fishing port where, after a little persuasion, the skipper of a boat just about to put out to sea, agreed to take us on board.

I stood at the rail beside Lord Denton and stared down at the chilly brown waters, and as I looked it seemed I saw my father's bones, all washed white, gleaming in the murky depths. I began trembling violently.

"Cold?" Lord Denton slid his arm round my waist and drew me close to his side.

Inside that warm enclosure I listened to him talking about the sea. He told me of his great love for it, of the great ships he had sailed in, of the many voyages he had been on, and gradually I began to see the sea as he saw it and enjoy the sting of the salt spray on my face. My trembling ceased. The terrifying vision of my father's bones departed.

From that day onwards I was never troubled by such visions again. My father's ghost had indeed been laid to rest.

I began taking an interest in what was going on around me, amazed and delighted to see the quantities of silvery fish flooding the deck as they were released from their prison of strong black net; but there was sadness, too, in my heart for the poor creatures leaping and gasping in their

151

death throes.

It was past midnight when we returned to shore. Rogers was fast asleep.

"It seems a shame to disturb him," I said, seeing him stretched out inside the carriage snoring gently.

"Let's leave him a while longer," Lord Denton said, "and go for a walk."

The moon was bright, the sands soft where the tide had not reached them. The wind had dropped and the air was warm, redolent, now that we had left the smell of fish far behind, of the scent of flowers escaping from unseen village gardens. It was a night for love and I was walking by the side of the man I loved. I felt exhilarated and could no more conquer the feeling than I could fly to the moon. Though he was indifferent to me, yet could I dream.

"Deborah," he said softly and I turned to him. "We must go back."

"Oh, not yet," I cried, not wishing to relinquish my dream. "This is so wonderful. I've never walked like this before . . . so late . . . at night."

My words limped to a halt as a look came into his eye that seemed to sap the breath from my body, and then his lips came down on mine, hard, urgent, demanding, awakening a blaze of desire in me and I answered him kiss for kiss like an abandoned woman and could not help myself.

"Deborah, Deborah," he breathed, his hands straying to mold my thighs, my breasts, sending shivers of terror and delight through me, his lips travelling over my eyes, my cheeks, my lips, my throat. I wanted it to go on and on, but in a tiny ever-watchful portion of my mind I knew I must put a stop to it — or pay the price of folly.

He felt the change in my response. His arms slackened and fell. We started walking back towards the carriage, a wall of silence descended between us.

I began to wish I had not drawn away from him in the way I had, though I failed to see what else I could have done and retained my innocence and his respect. Innocent as I was of men and the ways of the world, I was nevertheless aware that the onus fell upon a woman to preserve her honor. A man's passions were less easily subdued.

Seeking to set myself on an easy footing with him again, I asked, "Do—do you think you'll ever go to sea again?" I was not fool enough to think his kisses had meant anything, but I needed him to like me. I needed him to be my friend, if nothing else.

"Because of Lockhart's, you mean?" he answered me, and I detected no rancor in his voice. It meant he had not been unduly disturbed by my withdrawal—and it hurt.

"Yes," I whispered chokily.

"I doubt I shall ever go back to being a full-time sailor."

The wall of silence divided us again. Then a few paces further on he stopped, and looking out to sea said, "I have a yacht moored down in Devon. I sail in her whenever I can. One day I hope to go round the world in her."

"Round the world?" A rising tide of pain threatened to engulf me. "That will take you away for a very long time."

"A very long time," he agreed and turned to me. "Supposing I were to ask you to sail round the world with me?"

My heart stumbled, stopped, then raced madly. Was he proposing?

"But—how—could—I?" I gasped.

His eyes were searching my face. For what? For the answer I would give if he asked me to marry him? He must know the answer would be yes.

"You've proved yourself a good sailor. The sea was very choppy today and you didn't turn a hair."

My heart sank. "Oh. Is that—all?"

"It's a very necessary requisite."

The tide of pain gushed forth again flooding my eyes. It was a proposal, but very different from the one I had hoped for. It was the kind of proposal put to a woman whose behavior proclaimed her to be of easy virtue. And I could not blame him for it. I had given such an impression with my earlier response. Even though I had drawn away, it had been a belated withdrawal, easy to construe as guileful coquetry.

I turned away from him with a groan that would not be held back.

"Is the idea so very repulsive to you?" he demanded harshly.

"As it would be to any virtuous female," I whispered, my voice tight with misery.

He swung me round to face him. "Did you think," he grated, "I was asking you to be my mistress?"

I could not deny it.

"Oh, Deborah," he reproached me gently, tilting my chin upwards, and as he caught sight of my tears, "Ah, don't cry, my love . . . my sweet . . . my darling . . ."

His voice was losing its steadiness, thickening, causing him difficulty in his speech, then suddenly he was crushing me to him once again, claiming my lips with the same demanding urgency as before. And this time it was not I who drew away, but he who thrust me from him with a sudden angry movement. Then with a swift impatient gesture he took me by the arm and hurried me back to the waiting carriage.

Inside the carriage we sat apart from each other, hardly speaking, afraid to touch. But gradually, as if we could not help ourselves we drew closer and closer together till I was nestling in his arms and he was kissing me hungrily, longingly, and with a sweet intensity that spoke of love and desire and filled me with ineffable joy. His kisses evoked a passionate response in me and for a while we were oblivious of everything but ourselves and the sensations we aroused in each other. Then, as if afraid of where those sensations would lead us, he withdrew his lips from mine and did not seek them again.

But I was happy. I knew he loved me. His kisses had told

me so. He loved and wanted me as much as I loved and wanted him. He knew I would never be his mistress. He did not want me as his mistress. So he must want me for his wife. He would ask me to marry him. When? It was only a matter of time.

And I never even thought of Elizabeth.

A sudden sound outside my door dispersed the pictures from my ceiling. Had it been a knock? Did someone wish to speak to me? But who, at this hour of the night? I sat up listening intently, but moments passed and there was no recurrence of the sound that had disturbed my dreams. Yet I had heard something . . . someone. I got up to investigate.

I threw open the door. There was no one there. I must have been mistaken. But as I was about to shut the door, a sound, faint but distinct, reached my ears and I put my head out into the dark and shadowy corridor — and held my breath. In slanting moonlight I caught a glimpse of someone in a flowing garment entering the room at the head of the stairs. *The room that was always kept locked.*

Alicia! It must be Alicia! I believed she had a key to that room and often shut herself away in there when she wanted to be alone. But in the middle of the night? What possible reason could she have for shutting herself away there in the middle of the night? Should I find out?

None of your business, I told myself. Don't get involved. She won't thank you for it. But I found myself running along the corridor and tapping on the door.

"Alicia. Alicia. Are you in there?"

There was no reply. Did I expect one? I turned the big brass knob and pushed at the door. It did not budge. She had locked the door behind her. I stood looking at the door, nervously clasping my hands together. For some reason I was worried, wondering if something was wrong, if she was ill — though it hardly seemed likely she would shut herself away if such were the case.

I tapped on the door again. "Alicia. It's me, Deborah. Let me in."

No answer came.

All about me was a gravelike stillness. Giant shadows on the walls seemed to move with quiet stealth as I glanced around, dry-mouthed. And I began to wonder if I had been mistaken and not seen Alicia at all, not seen anyone, but been misled by the silent dancing shadows.

Silent dancing shadows. But I had heard a sound.

On a swift decision I sped to Alicia's room. Outside her door I hesitated. What excuse would I give for disturbing her should I waken her from sleep? But in my heart I knew her bed would be empty, that I had seen her go into the locked room.

I pushed open the door. Moonlight illumined the bed. My heart began a painful tattoo. Alicia was lying there, fast asleep, with her dark hair spread like a mantle about her shoulders.

I retreated and closed the door. My heart beating ever more agonizingly, I hurried through the shadowy corridor back to my own room and fell into bed drawing the sheets high to cover my face, huddling into a ball beneath them in an effort to combat the shivering that had taken possession of my limbs. If it had not been Alicia I had seen entering that room, then it must have been a ghost, for no one else ever went in there. A maid might go in to clean occasionally—but not in the middle of the night. Many old houses were reputed to be haunted by shades from the past, why not Rosemont? There was something at Rosemont, something frightening and unseen, that I had been aware of from the beginning. Was this it, then, the shade of a long-dead woman roaming the corridors at night?

My thoughts ran on keeping sleep at bay till the morning sun fingered its way into my room through the chinks in the curtains. Then at last I slept.

Startled into wakefulness by Doreen sweeping aside the

the curtains, the thoughts I had fallen sleep on rushed back to plague me. But with the bright sun lighting up every familiar object in my room, and Doreen's cheerful chatter as she poured water into a bowl for my ablutions, they were quickly dispersed. Ghosts had no place in daytime.

Other, different, thoughts came to occupy my mind which led to a buoyancy of spirits that had me walking on air and I hastened downstairs to breakfast hardly able to contain my excitement at the thought of seeing Charles again.

But Charles was not sitting at his usual place at the table. Only Miss Selina looked up to greet me.

"Good morning, Deborah. Didn't you sleep well? There are huge rings under your eyes."

"Not very," I murmured. Were there really rings under my eyes? I hadn't noticed them.

"Too much excitement yesterday, I expect," she commented shrewdly.

I went to help myself to scrambled egg and bacon. Where was Charles? Imagining him as eager to see me as I to see him, I had not dreamed he would not be here to greet me. Was he sleeping in? Breakfasting in bed? Had he breakfasted early? Had he gone out riding, as he often did before breakfast?

Pondering all these possibilities I sat down.

"Coffee?" Miss Selina pushed the coffee pot towards me — then dealt me a blow from which I thought I would never recover.

"Charles has gone to London. He left on the early morning train. There's some business he must attend to in the City. Afterwards, he intends calling at Hunt Park."

Hunt Park! Elizabeth! Too late I thought about Elizabeth.

"Did he leave a message for me?" I cried.

"Why, no. Were you expecting him to?"

A cry rose within me from some deep dark well of misery. Had what had happened between us meant so little to him that the leaving of a message for me was unimportant? And from that same deep dark well of misery came the answer. It had been a night of dalliance for him. He was a philanderer, just as Miss Selina had said. I should have listened to her.

He was away for almost a week — unable to tear himself away from Elizabeth's side. I made a conscious effort to think of the two of them together, trying to school myself into an appearance of indifference so that he would never see how much he had hurt me. I had been misled into thinking he cared for me and he, realizing from my response I was taking his lovemaking seriously, had chosen to show me my mistake by ignoring me, leaving his aunt to remind me that Elizabeth was his intended bride.

It was a bitter pill to swallow.

I knew he would be wary of me on his return, wondering how I had taken it, if I would make a fuss. He need not worry. I had my pride. I would be circumspect. So I greeted him coolly with the due deference of a paid employee. After a few awkward moments he followed my lead and seemed grateful for it.

But my composure was a fragile thing, easily fractured if I allowed my guard to slip, which it did, at night, alone in my room — but by day my emotions were admirably controlled and cold politeness became habitual between the two of us.

The following Sunday morning after church, Charles announced his intention of going down to the river to fish. "Don't wait luncheon for me," he said to his aunt, "I'll cook my own meal over an open fire."

Miss Selina took herself off to her boudoir and Alicia and I, evading Murkett — who admittedly did not keep so close a tail on us now — set off for a stroll round the gardens. Finishing up on our favorite seat by the fountain and listening to the gentle sound of water dropping on water,

158

we suddenly found ourselves being accosted by a cheerful personality.

"So this is where you've got to. Come on, both of you, we're going on a picnic."

"Jonathan!" I cried as Alicia, springing up with a joyous smile, steered herself unerringly into his brotherly embrace.

But his eyes were on me and there was nothing brotherly in his glance nor in the embrace he gave me when Alicia was released. I drew away from him as quickly as I could, embarrassed by Alicia's presence. Though I knew she could not see, I felt she knew I had been kissed. What her feelings were on the matter, I could not gauge.

"We're going to join Charles and share his alfresco meal," Jonathan announced and my heartbeat quickened.

"I got the impression he wanted to be on his own," I murmured.

"No man roasting fish over an open fire can expect to be left on his own," was his response, and slipping an arm round both our waists hurried us along to join Miss Selina who was waiting with a retinue of servants bearing picnic baskets, chairs, and other such accoutrements she had deemed necessary for the occasion.

Charles was bending over the glimmerings of a fire, puffing and blowing it into flame when we reached him. He looked up at our approach and scowled at the procession bearing down on him.

"Hope you've made a good catch, brother," Jonathan called out in his usual cheerful manner. "We've come to help you eat it."

Charles rose. "So I see," he grunted disagreeably. "And what's brought you back to Rosemont? When I saw you in London recently you said nothing would drag you away from there."

"Well, yes, I know I did, but . . . well . . . er, I mean to say . . . it's Alicia's birthday soon and I couldn't miss that."

"It's not for another ten days yet. Are you intending to

159

stay that long?"

"Well, yes, of course I am. Why not?"

He did not sound at all like his usual confident self. Alicia's birthday had the trappings of an excuse. I wondered why, then thought I found the answer. His brother's antagonism was to blame.

"How do you expect to fill in your time—in this backwater?" Charles was being deliberately rude and sarcastic. "I doubt you'll find sufficient to hold your interest for ten whole days."

"Oh, I shall find plenty to occupy my time," Jonathan smiled, with a glance at me which was not lost on Charles. "I might even take up the reins of management again."

"That you won't." It came out like the crack of a whip. "Benson's in charge now."

Jonathan flushed. "You didn't waste much time, did you?"

"Did you expect me to after you'd cleared off?"

"I didn't expect you to act so swiftly. You might have waited a bit, given me a chance to change my mind. After all, this is my home."

"But not your inheritance. Not yet. And while I live, the running of it will never fall into your hands again."

Charles's voice was razor sharp—cutting, lacerating— and Jonathan recoiled visibly. A fleeting spasm crossed his brother's face as though he regretted the words and wished them unsaid.

But they could never be unsaid, and I felt deeply for Jonathan as the blood drained from his face.

"No," he said hoarsely, "Rosemont is not mine and probably never will be, for I don't doubt you will marry Elizabeth and beget an heir, but I've always loved the old place, always given of my best to it, always . . ."

"Loved going off and leaving it without a second's thought to indulge whatever might be your whim of the moment."

ACCEPT YOUR FREE GIFT
AND EXPERIENCE MORE OF
THE PASSION AND ADVENTURE
YOU LIKE IN A
HISTORICAL ROMANCE

Zebra Romances are the finest novels of their kind and are written with the adult woman in mind. All of our books are written by authors who really know how to weave tales of romantic adventure in the historical settings you love.

Because our readers tell us these books sell out very fast in the stores, Zebra has made arrangements for you to receive at home the four newest titles published each month. You'll never miss a title and home delivery is so convenient. With your first shipment we'll even send you a FREE Zebra Historical Romance as our gift just for trying our home subscription service. No obligation.

BIG SAVINGS
AND FREE HOME DELIVERY

Each month, the Zebra Home Subscription Service will send you the four newest titles as soon as they are published. (We ship these books to our subscribers even before we send them to the stores.) You may preview them *Free* for 10 days. If you like them as much as we think you will, you'll pay just $3.50 each and save $1.80 each month off the cover price. *AND you'll also get FREE HOME DELIVERY.* There is never a charge for shipping, handling, or postage and there is no minimum you must buy. If you decide not to keep any shipment, simply return it within 10 days, no questions asked, and owe nothing.

Zebra Historical Romances
Make This Special Offer...

*IF YOU ENJOYED
READING THIS BOOK,
WE'LL SEND YOU
ANOTHER ONE*

FREE

(a $3.95 Value)

No Obligation!

—Zebra Historical Romances
Burn With The Fire Of History—

ACCEPT YOUR FREE GIFT
AND EXPERIENCE MORE OF
THE PASSION AND ADVENTURE
YOU LIKE IN A
HISTORICAL ROMANCE

Zebra Romances are the finest novels of their kind and are written with the adult woman in mind. All of our books are written by authors who really know how to weave tales of romantic adventure in the historical settings you love.

Because our readers tell us these books sell out very fast in the stores, Zebra has made arrangements for you to receive at home the four newest titles published each month. You'll never miss a title and home delivery is so convenient. With your first shipment we'll even send you a FREE Zebra Historical Romance as our gift just for trying our home subscription service. No obligation.

BIG SAVINGS
AND FREE HOME DELIVERY

Each month, the Zebra Home Subscription Service will send you the four newest titles as soon as they are published. (We ship these books to our subscribers even before we send them to the stores.) You may preview them *Free* for 10 days. If you like them as much as we think you will, you'll pay just $3.50 each and save $1.80 each month off the cover price. *AND you'll also get FREE HOME DELIVERY.* There is never a charge for shipping, handling or postage and there is no minimum you must buy. If you decide not to keep any shipment, simply return it within 10 days, no questions asked, and owe nothing.

Zebra Historical Romances
Make This Special Offer...

IF YOU ENJOYED
READING THIS BOOK,
WE'LL SEND YOU
ANOTHER ONE

FREE

(a $3.95 value)

No Obligation!

—Zebra Historical Romances
Burn With The Fire Of History—

"That's unfair. Benson was always willing to take over a and . . ."

"Now he's taken over for good."

"You forget — you put me in charge of Rosemont because you wished to *indulge* your passion for the sea."

"But no longer. I've turned a blind eye to your mismanagement for the last time."

The two brothers faced each other eye to eye, one truculent, self-justifying, the other condemning.

Jonathan gasped. "You can say that to me after . . ."

"I thought we'd come out here for a picnic, not a dog-fight." Miss Selina's coldly angry voice splintered the air, and I marked the ice in her eye single out her nephew, Charles, for its target.

The two men responded at once, apologizing to us and, thankfully, to each other.

"Forgive me, Jon," Lord Denton said. "I didn't mean any of that." He held out his hand to his brother who looked at it resentfully. "Come on, Jon, let there be no bitterness between us."

After another moment's hesitation Jonathan relaxed and his pleasant smile broke out again as he shook the hand held out to him. "Nothing to forgive," he said. "If brothers can't sound off at one another occasionally, who can?"

All tension removed as suddenly as it had started, they both began skewering plump little trout on to long-handled forks and handed them round. We were each to cook our own. The servants had laid the contents of the picnic baskets onto a cloth draped over the grassy bank and had gone to stand a little way off trying to pretend they had not heard a word of the previous heated exchange. Croft, stationed beside his portable trolley, cast his expert eye over the bottles thereon and gave the glasses an occasional extra polish. A perfect, peaceful English country scene.

"By the way, Benson's getting married," Charles said to Jonathan as if he had never been a bone of contention between them.

"Is he, by Jove?"

"To Henry Day's girl, Nancy."

"Well, would you believe it? The old slyboots. He never gave me an inkling of the way the wind blew. Little Nancy Day, eh? A peach, if there ever was one. I've often re- marked to him how unfair it was that she should have all that long ash blond hair, those big baby blue eyes, that trim figure," and here he made a shape in the air with his hands, "and not offer it around . . . And he never said a word."

"You forget yourself, Jonathan," his aunt scolded him with mock severity.

He laughed. "I only meant she would make a good model, but I could never get her to pose for me. Shy, I think."

"Stick to your society ladies, Jon," Charles instructed him caustically. "They're more used to that sort of thing."

"What sort of thing?" Jonathan was his old self again, full of banter which on this occasion bordered on ribaldry.

"You know," Charles said and changing the subject, "These are about ready, I think."

The appetizing aroma of roasting fish was filling the air around us and we commenced our meal. Croft served us with champagne and Charles ordered him to leave the bot- tle and join his fellows in a meal of their own. Jonathan was sitting beside me and I took the opportunity to ask him about his new studio and how it was faring.

"Not bad," he said. "Got a fair number of clients. All my friends are rallying round."

But he did not raise his eyes from his plate and I won- dered if all was going as well with him as he tried to make out. My suspicion that something was worrying him had already been aroused. Might this be the reason? Or was it just that he was homesick for Rosemont? Or had it to do with the bitter exchange between him and his brother in which Charles had all but accused him of falsifying the

162

accounts in order to line his own pockets? Had he been defrauding his brother?

I found this last totally unbelievable. Lord Denton himself had admitted he had not meant it. So it must be something to do with his new venture. Perhaps photography was not proving to be the fulfilling occupation he had been expecting.

Having reached this conclusion I set the matter aside.

As usual with Jonathan around, there was fun and laughter at Rosemont. He paid a great deal of attention to me encouraged, I suspected, by Miss Selina. I knew she looked upon our friendship with favor and would not be averse to see it grow into something deeper and more lasting. If Lord Denton noticed the closeness of our relationship, he did not comment on it, but I had not forgotten his threat to put every obstacle in the way of marriage between us, nor, I could tell by his black looks, had he.

There was a tremendous build-up during this time towards Alicia's ball. Miss Selina had defied her nephew's instructions and it was to be a great event after all, with people coming from all parts of the country to attend. With most of them having to be accommodated for at least a night or two, the west wing was opened up and rooms long neglected made ready for use.

Alicia was tremendously excited, almost beyond herself, her face flushed, her beauty burgeoning. She was constantly squeezing my hand in delight. I was surprised she was looking forward to it so much. Although I believed it was exactly the sort of thing needed to bring her out of herself and launch her into Society, I had not expected her to welcome something that would see her as the center of attraction with so much ease.

I was also surprised at Miss Selina's anticipation. Charles had told me, and I had seen for myself, that she did not go out of her way to seek company, preferring to live an almost hermitlike existence. She saw no one outside her immediate family and the servants at Rosemont. Even the weekly excursion to St. Martin's Church where we all sat in an enclosed pew, saw us the last to arrive and the first to leave so that she need speak to no one. Yet here she was looking forward to entertaining a vast crowd of people.

Surprised, too, that Lord Denton made no remonstrance. Perhaps as the Prince had not been invited, he saw no reason to be concerned.

Alicia's birthday dawned in a haze of heat. There was a great deal of activity with an army of servants scurrying back and forth attending to the wants of the guests who had arrived the night before. Others were carrying armfuls of flowers and arranging them in bowls and vases all over the house. Eggs and milk and freshly churned butter were brought in from the dairy and taken to the kitchens where Cook and her assistants were turning out concoctions of superlative quality. Croft was in his element, supervising and organizing the wines for the occasion. If tempers became a little frayed as the heat of the day increased, it was hardly to be wondered at.

After breakfast Alicia was pressed to open the vast array of presents she had already received, and I sat beside her making a note of each and its giver so that I might write and thank them on Alicia's behalf at a later date. My little bottle of French perfume was quite overshadowed by the many expensive gifts she unwrapped, but I noticed with joy it was my small offering she kept clasped in her hand and took with her to her room, while the rest were left for the servants to transport.

I went with her to her room and saw lying on a chair the white kid gloves Charles had bought her as an extra while we were in King's Lynn — a mute reminder of my brief trip into a fool's paradise. Beside them was Jonathan's gift: white satin shoes with jewelled buckles and a satin purse to match.

Both gifts, brought to her room by her loving brothers

before she had risen, were in impeccable taste. Even though their sister would never see what they gave her, it was always the most beautiful and best.

She surprised me by throwing her arms around me and embracing me with a show of affection more intense than any she had shown before. Then she took me by the hand and drew me towards the dressing table and my heart started thumping violently as her fingers reached for the little Chinese cabinet which I knew housed the periwinkle brooch that still haunted my mind. She opened it, the secret drawer sprang open, the blue velvet box was withdrawn. The next moment sapphires and diamonds were winking up at me.

She took out the brooch and held it out to me. My hand closed over it greedily. Immediately I opened it again. What was it about this brooch that compelled such base instincts to rise up in me?

"Do you wish me to pin it on your dress for you?" I asked.

She shook her head and pointed to my own dress.

"You . . . can't wish me to wear it?" I gasped.

With a quick impatient gesture she pointed to the bottle of perfume I had given her, then to herself, then to the brooch, then to me. The inference was clear.

"You want to give it to me?"

She nodded vigorously.

I remained silent contemplating the enormity of her gift, longing to thank her and keep it — but such a course was impossible.

"It's very sweet of you," I said, "but I can't accept it. It's . . . too valuable. But I thank you from the bottom of my heart for thinking of it."

She sighed deeply, then her mouth started working as if she were trying to persuade me to keep the brooch, her face so full of hurt and sadness that I began to think I should not have refused, particularly as her distress showed signs of becoming hysterical.

I touched her arm and said quickly, "If you really want me to have it, of course I will accept — gladly."

She drew in her breath again and closed her mouth, but her face lost none of its sadness and pain. However, I was unable to concern myself about it any more. I looked down at the periwinkle brooch shining in my hand. It was mine. Mine! That was all that mattered to me. All I cared about.

"I'll wear it at the ball tonight," I breathed.

Chapter Ten

Strains of music pervaded Rosemont. Guests were arriving in a continuous stream and already the ballroom was crowded. Alicia greeting her guests alongside her aunt looked breathtakingly lovely in a white satin gown strewn with silk rosebuds. Murkett and I had conspired to do her hair in the style I had created during the days when the rest of the family were in Devon attending James Lockhart's funeral, and though Miss Selina had frowned when she saw it, she had to accept it for the houseguests were loud in their praise of it. The white satin gloves Charles had given her encased her long slender hands and the jewelled purse which had been Jonathan's gift to her swung from her wrist. The matching shoes peeped from under her gown. Gleaming pearls encircled her throat.

I was wearing my black silk, the best gown I possessed, though it was hardly a ballgown. As I watched the female guests arriving in their rainbow colors and jewel-bedecked bosoms, I felt dull and dowdy.

I slipped away to my room. Earlier, I had pinned the periwinkle brooch to my dress. It had brightened it at once, but for some reason I could not explain, I had unpinned it and put it back in its box. Now I took it out again and went downstairs wearing it. I knew it would be outshone by the blaze of jewels below, but I felt better for the lift it gave my plain appearance.

Most of the guests were unknown to me, but there were a few I recognized as friends. However, after a brief exchange of words I found them edging away from me. Fairweather friends, not wishing to be seen talking to a mere lady's companion.

Then Miss Selina came towards me with Alicia on her arm, raising her light, clear voice, "Deborah, my dear, where have you been hiding yourself? Jonathan has been quite demented not knowing where you were. Here she is, Jonathan. I've found her for you," and my fair-weather friends looked on and listened in unfeigned amazement to her warm familiar greeting.

Then her eye fell on the periwinkle brooch pinned to my gown and something in her bright blue stare sent a cold chill to my heart and I knew I should not have accepted so valuable a gift from her niece.

Then Jonathan came into focus, dark, handsome, superb in evening dress, with his love for me shining from his face and in his smile, but his smile faded when he, too, noticed the brooch and a strange expression chased the love from his face.

It was only momentary, he was soon smiling again and so was Miss Selina, and I was left wondering if I had seen a change of expression on their faces at all.

"The Morrisons have arrived," Jonathan said to his aunt. "Charles is just seeing them out of their carriage."

My heart started thumping. My cheeks flamed. I wished I could remain cool and unperturbed whenever Charles appeared, but I could not, and this would be my first meeting with him since this morning. Not only that, I would be seeing him with Elizabeth.

"Well, I suppose we'd better go and meet them," she said, whisking her niece away with her.

Jonathan took my arm and we followed on behind.

Charles brought Elizabeth, magnificent in emerald

green silk and lace, and wearing what I knew to be her mother's diamond and emerald necklace, forward to meet his aunt. I was vaguely aware of her parents smiling proudly beside her and of William just behind. But it was Charles and Elizabeth together who held my attention and set me adrift on a fresh tide of misery. They made such a good-looking couple — so right for each other.

". . . and you know Deborah, of course . . ." They were standing in front of me and Elizabeth was reaching out to embrace me when in a change of tone he rasped, "Where did you get that brooch? Take it off at once," and he thrust an arm towards it with snakelike speed.

"No!" I cried with involuntary force, backing away and covering it with a protective hand. "Don't touch it! It's mine!"

He glared down at me, eyes burning with a wild light, and I feared him at that moment more than I had ever done hitherto. I fully expected him to rip the brooch from my dress without more ado, but suddenly he swung away from me and cut a pathway through the converging throng of interested guests, like one of his great ships cleaving through the ocean.

Agape with curiosity, everyone crowded round and above the growing murmur of comment and question I heard Elizabeth's cry. "Charles . . . Charles . . ." Then she turned to me and asked, "What was all that about?"

"I don't know," I said, but I was trembling from head to foot. What was it about the brooch that it aroused uncharacteristic acquisitiveness in me and such ferocious anger in him?

Miss Selina took Elizabeth and her family to meet other guests and I turned to Jonathan.

"What *was* all that about?" I asked.

He took my arm and swept me out to a quiet corner of the terrace. "That brooch," he said, "I should do as Charles says and take it off."

"Why should I," I demanded belligerently, "just because he demands it?"

"It reminds him of someone."

"Who?"

"Miranda."

"And who is she?"

"I do honestly believe," he insisted, not answering my question, "it would be better all round if you removed it. My brother wasn't being as high-handed as he appeared. It really is offensive to him."

"But . . . Oh, very well."

I unpinned the brooch and placed it inside my purse.

"How does it come to be in your possession, anyway?"

"Alicia gave it to me."

"Alicia!" He looked stunned. "Where did she . . . ?"

But there was no time to say any more. William Morrison interrupted us, requesting a place on my dance card.

"Whichever you like," I said. "My card's empty."

"Then put my name down for the next one and the one after that and as many as you care to allow me, only . . . I must save a couple of dances for . . . someone else."

"Someone else?" I teased as I saw the color creep into his cheeks, and could not make out whether I was glad or sorry that he seemed to have got over me so quickly.

"You may have the next dance, Mr. Morrison, but that is all. The rest are reserved for me," Jonathan informed him smartly.

William glanced from one to the other of us, eyebrows shooting upwards. "Is that the way of it?" his glance seemed to say, and the color flooded to my cheeks even more strongly than his had done.

"He's enamored of you," he said as we walked back to the ballroom together.

"Oh, no," I returned swiftly.

"Oh, yes. It's as plain as a pikestaff from the way he looks at you and his proprietorial air. Do you feel the same way about him?"

"I . . . I . . ."

"Well, you're not averse to him, I can see that."

"No, but . . ."

The set of his face as he looked down at me was so serious that I wondered if I had been wrong in assuming earlier that he had forgotten his previous attachment to me. I tried to make light of the situation by asking teasingly, "Are you jealous, William?"

"Good heavens, no!" he exclaimed with more exuberance than I might have wished for. "You know as well as I there was never anything really serious between us. Mother made more out of it than was there. I was furious when I found out she'd sent you away. Were you terribly unhappy to leave Hunt Park? Elizabeth said you were."

"At first—but I soon got over it."

"I'm glad. I want you to be happy, Debsie." His pet name for me struck a chord in my heart that sent a wave of nostalgia through me, making me both glad and sad at the same time. "You deserve it," he was continuing, "after all you've been through."

William was a good dancer, very light on his feet, and as he whirled me away to the strains of a Viennese waltz I lost my griefs and worries in the sheer enjoyment of it. When it was over and he walked me off the floor through my haze of euphoria I heard him say quietly, "Alicia Denton is a very beautiful young woman, isn't she?"

"Indeed, yes," I responded. "It's such a pity she is so sadly afflicted."

"Being blind, you mean."

"And dumb."

"Some men might consider that an advantage."

"How do you mean?"

"A woman who can't speak, can't nag."

"William!"

"Oh, not I! Don't class me among them. It was a taste-

171

less joke. I can't think why I made it, unless it was because if I hadn't I would have made a fool of myself ranting and raging at the evils of fate . . . I think it's the saddest thing I've ever come across. Do . . . Do you think she would dance with me, if I asked her?"

"No, William," I said. Was this the "someone else" he had referred to? "She can't dance."

"I can't believe that. Every woman can dance."

"Not Alicia. She's blind, remember. She's never learned."

We both looked at her sitting with the dowagers like a diamond among dross. "Then its about time she did," he murmured angrily.

Elizabeth came hurrying towards us pursued, as was usually the case, by a throng of adoring males. During the course of conversation I noticed Elizabeth's attention seemed to be straying and after a while she drew me away from the men, laughing aside their protests at being deserted, "I wish to speak to my friend alone," she said. "It's an age since I last saw her."

We went to sit in an alcove.

"Are you happier at Rosemont now than you were?" she asked me.

"Well . . ."

Without waiting to hear either affirmation or denial, she hurried on, "You seem quite happy."

"I . . ."

"Miss Selina treats you kindly?"

"Yes, she . . ."

"She's a very handsome woman, isn't she?"

"Very." I gave up trying to make conversation and just answered her questions.

"And Alicia is astonishingly lovely, is she not?"

"Yes."

"Would you call Lord Denton handsome?"

"Why, yes, I suppose so."

172

"Yes. They're a very handsome lot the Dentons, aren't they? Particularly Lord Denton's brother."

"Jonathan?"

"I think he's the handsomest man I've ever seen. Oh! There he is . . . and he's coming over. Thank goodness I make it a habit never to fill in my dance card. I need not refuse him."

But after a courteous bow to Elizabeth, it was to me he turned. "Our dance, I think, my sweet," he said.

I had never seen Elizabeth at a loss, but I did now. She could not hide her amazement at being passed over in favor of another. It must be the first time it had ever happened to her. She could not know, of course, that Jonathan was in love with me.

The more I got to know Jonathan, the more I liked him. He was easy to get on with, amusing, and, for all his boyish exuberance, a man of taste and artistry. He had spun me a rapturous tale of the holiday he had spent in Venice in the spring and shown me the pictures he had taken. I had been greatly impressed and enthused over them.

"I knew you'd appreciate them," he said. "I may not be an artist like some I could mention—but I'm a dab hand with a camera."

"I'd love to go to Venice," I had said. "It must be a very beautiful place."

"Oh, it is. Absolutely fantastic. It almost defies description. It's a fairy tale land. Magical. Luminous. A Canaletto come to life. I tried to capture with my camera the scenes he painted. Look! I've tinted them to try to achieve the same effect. But it's a poor substitute."

He was talking now, as we danced, about Scotland, the views he had taken there, with the same degree of enthusiasm and use of picturesque language that had made Venice seem so real to me, almost as if I'd been there myself.

"Would you like to see them?"

"The photographs? Oh, yes, I'd love to."

"I'll get them and show them to you in the library."

"Now?"

"It's as good a time as any."

"But . . . should we? I mean, should we leave the floor in the middle of a dance? People might . . ."

"Notice and jump to conclusions? Let them. Why should we care?"

He was already guiding me through the throng of dancers and I glanced around self-consciously as he whispered in my ear with his arm about my waist, quite certain everybody was taking note of our exit. My eye fell on Charles looming in the doorway ahead of us, and I stumbled at the unexpected sight of him.

Jonathan's arm tightened around my waist. "What's the matter? Ankle give way?"

I nodded mutely.

"Would you like to sit down?"

I shook my head.

Charles was glancing round the room in his usual disdainful manner. How handsome he looked. How proud. How cold. His glance rested briefly on us, his lips curled thinly, then his eyes moved on to find what they were seeking. Elizabeth.

She was dancing a few couples away from us, her beauty outshining the diamonds sparkling round her throat. He threaded his way towards her, passing so close I could have touched him, and tapped her partner on the shoulder. She turned to him with a radiant smile and melted into his arms.

It all happened within the space of a few moments, but each separate moment seemed to last an eternity to me.

Inside the library with the door closed, shutting out completely the sounds of gaiety, it was like being in another world, and with the picture of Elizabeth going into Charles's arms engraved on my heart, I wished I need

174

never leave it.

Jonathan stood very close to me. "Quiet, isn't it?" he murmured as his arms went round me.

I experienced a moment's panic. "The photographs," I whispered urgently.

"There's no hurry," he said and planted a warm firm kiss upon my parted lips.

"Now, Jonathan, please," I begged, pushing him away. "We mustn't stay here too long."

"I don't see why not," he grumbled a trifle truculently, then, seeing I was serious, gave a resigned shrug. "Oh, all right, then. But don't go away. I won't be long."

Another peck at my cheek and he was gone and I stood like a statue staring at the door, my mind racing. Should I wait as he bade me and risk his amorous advances, or go out and rejoin that other world where all that lay before me was pain, the pain of seeing Charles and Elizabeth together, the fountainhead of all my future unhappiness.

The door opened. Jonathan was back. I had tarried too long.

He drew me to sit beside him on a low couch, closer than was proper for two people of the opposite sex, and knowing he would try to kiss me again, I quickly made some distance between us. His eyebrows rose a little but he made no move to close the gap and opened the album he had brought.

"Here we are," he said, "Scotland, wild and spectacular." Scene after scene of Highland grandeur were displayed for my approbation. Lochs, mountains, castles, all brilliantly executed. "If only you could see them in color," he added wistfully.

"It will come in time, like you said," I encouraged him, "and when it does you can go back and take them all again. Meanwhile, why don't you try tinting them?"

I had seen him tint some portraits once and thought how much it improved them. If it worked with people, why not with views?

"I had thought about it," he said. "Maybe I will . . . one day . . . when I get the time. Just now, all I want to do is kiss you."

"No, Jonathan," I cried, trying to avoid his advances. His arms closed round me. "Why do you insist on keeping me at arm's length, Deborah? You know I love you and want to marry you." He kissed me deeply, then with a strange sort of urgency whispered against my lips, "I want to take you away from here. Come with me to America."

Here was the answer to my problem. Marry Jonathan and leave Rosemont forever. In the faraway land of America I would forget Charles. In setting up a new home with Jonathan and bearing his children, the thought of Elizabeth in Charles's arms would cease to bother me.

Yet still my heart would not consent.

The sound of music and laughter drew us apart and we looked up to see Miss Selina standing in the doorway smiling. She did not chastise her nephew, nor me, but looked thoroughly pleased to see us in so compromising a situation.

"Forgive this interruption," she said, "but you are wanted on the telephone, Jonathan. Croft said he couldn't find you, but I had seen you come in here with Deborah and undertook to deliver his message for him. I believe it's important or I wouldn't have disturbed you."

When I rose to follow him out Miss Selina barred my way.

"No," she said, "you stay here and wait for him to come back."

When Miss Selina used that particular tone of voice, I knew there was no room for argument. It was an order. I sat down signifying my acquiescence and with a satisfied smile she departed.

To while away the time till Jonathan's return I picked up

the album to look through it again, and as I did so a loose photograph slipped from between the pages onto my lap. I realized at once it must have got in there by mistake for it had nothing to do with the scenic content but was a studio portrait of an incredibly lovely young woman.

Wondering who she was I studied the lovely face. She could not be a relative. There was nothing remotely Denton-like about her. Nothing of that proud reserve, that aristocratic arrogance so characteristic of all the Dentons, even Jonathan, for all his easygoing charm. Was she an old flame of Jonathan's and had he clung on to this photograph because he couldn't bear to part with it? She was certainly lovely in an angelic sort of way—there was an aura of innocence about her.

I guessed Jonathan had taken it and had tinted it—her hair was golden, her eyes sky-blue—and was about to replace it in the album when the eyes took on a sad, brooding expression. "Help me," they seemed to say.

I shook myself irritably. It was the atmosphere of this old house affecting me again, making me imagine that a girl in a photograph could communicate with me. I laughed at myself, but my throat was dry with sudden nervousness.

"I saw Jonathan leave and knew you were still in here." The harsh rasping voice of Lord Denton proclaimed his entrance into the room. "You're waiting for him, I suppose."

"Yes." Why let him think differently?

"It's all to no consequence."

"What?"

"This fantasy you have for marriage with him. I won't allow it, you know."

"You can't stop it."

"You'll find I can."

"I don't see that it has anything to do with you," I cried out, goaded by his sarcastic mien.

"It has everything to do with me," he returned coolly.

"Because you are the head of the house? Do you expect Jonathan to ask your permission before he marries? Times are changing, my lord, had you not noticed? He's in charge of his own life, his own fortunes. As you said yourself, he is no longer dependent upon you for support."

He was staring down at me hard-eyed and furious, looking now as if he would like to throttle me. I returned his stare steadily despite my quivering knees and his steeple height. Then he said abruptly, "What's gone wrong between us, Deborah? I thought we had reached an understanding?"

"An understanding!" I whispered. "I don't understand you at all."

"What has turned you against me?" he demanded. "What did I do that made you reject me so completely? I think I'm entitled to an explanation."

I gaped at him. "I reject you? You rejected me. It was you who went away without so much as a word . . . without even seeing me . . . You who went to Hunt Park . . . What was I to think? I thought you had been playing with me."

"Playing with you? My dear girl, I don't play with people's emotions. What do you take me for? I was called away suddenly. I had no chance to speak with you."

"You could have left me a message."

"I did. With Aunt Selina. I asked her to tell you what had happened and that I would ring you from London as soon as I could."

"She didn't tell me."

But he was too angry to listen.

"I telephoned you on three separate occasions and each time I was told you were out or not available. It should have dawned on me then, I suppose, but it didn't. It should have prepared me for the treatment I received from you when I saw you again, but it didn't. Funny, isn't it?" He laughed harshly. "It doesn't usually take a ton of bricks to fall on my head before . . ."

"I didn't know . . . No one told me . . ."

He gave an angry snort. I could see he did not believe me. My head was in a whirl. Did he blame me for our estrangement? Would he have liked to continue what had been started that day in King's Lynn?

But how could it have continued? If there had been no Elizabeth, then maybe . . . maybe . . . there might have been a future for us together. But there was Elizabeth and he was going to marry her.

I said, carefully careless, "What difference does it make? It doesn't matter now, does it?"

"Doesn't matter! Of course it matters! What do you mean, it doesn't matter? Because of Jonathan?"

His vehemence surprised me. He was angry, very angry.

"Because of Elizabeth," I gulped.

"Elizabeth? What has Elizabeth to do with this?"

I stared at him in astonishment. "You're going to marry her, my lord."

He scowled dangerously. "Who told you that? Jonathan?"

"It's common knowledge."

"Is it, indeed?" He drew in his breath and his anger seemed to subside a little. "Listen to me, Deborah . . ."

But I did not want to listen to him. What could he tell me that I did not already know? He was going to marry Elizabeth. Yet he wished to conduct an illicit relationship with me, her best friend—in spite of all his previous protestations to the contrary. He was, as his aunt had said, an unprincipled man. He flirted with women, led them on to believe he cared, used them for his pleasure, and tossed them aside when he tired of them. I would not allow that to happen to me.

He was going to marry Elizabeth. But was he in love

with her? I failed to see how he could not be completely captivated by her. Knowing him as I did I feared for her future happiness.

"I like Elizabeth," he continued earnestly. "Certainly I do. She's lovely to look at, good company, as kind as she is merry, but . . . Oh, do put that thing down."

He stretched out his arm to relieve me of the album still clutched in my hands and the photograph fluttered to the floor.

He picked it up. His expression changed alarmingly. He looked as if he had seen a ghost.

"Where did you get this?" he asked hoarsely.

"Do you know who she is?" I countered.

"She's my wife," he said. "Or she was. She's dead."

There was a rushing sound in my ears as a train began thundering its way round my head. My wife, my wife, my wife, my wife. She's dead, she's dead, she's dead, she's dead. The wheels hammered the words into my brain and above them I heard my conventional comment, "I'm sorry."

"Don't be," he grated, tearing the photograph into tiny pieces and letting them fall like snow upon the carpet, "I'm not."

I stared at the torn fragments in something of a daze. Why had he torn up the photograph of his wife? Why wasn't he sorry she was dead? Was it because she had been desperately ill, so wracked with pain that death had come as a merciful release to her? Had he been glad of that? And had seeing the photograph showing her as she used to be, so young and lovely, been more than he could bear? Was that why he had torn it up?

I raised my puzzled gaze seeking explanation and found it in his stricken face, the naked misery in his eyes. "Charles," I whispered, pitying him, myself, any woman who might have the misfortune to fall in love with him, for though he might flirt with them, use them, take all they had to give, he could offer nothing in return. His heart was buried in the grave with his dead wife.

It explained the coldness, his unresponsive attitude, careless indifference to anyone other than his sister, and why he shook off my sympathetic hand with a cry like a wounded animal and went blindly from the room bumping into Jonathan in the doorway.

"Hey!" Jonathan laughed. "What's the rush? Where's the fire?"

Charles did not even see him.

"What's got into him?" Jonathan asked, then, seeing the torn pieces of the photograph on the floor, "what's all this?"

Haltingly, I told him what had happened.

"Oh, no!" he groaned. "How did it get into the album? I thought I'd got rid of them all. There'll be no living with Charles now. Ah, well," concern was quickly despatched, "no use crying over spilt milk. Come and dance."

It was the supper dance and as soon as it was over everyone made a beeline for the supper room where long tables were spread with every kind of fish, meat, and fowl. Boars' heads. Game pies. Flans, savoury and sweet. Fruit pies and fools. Lemon creams. Chocolate creams. Pavlovas. Melbas. Dishes piled high with fresh fruit of every description. Punches and wines. An army of servants stood behind waiting to carve and serve and pour.

Elizabeth came to join us closely followed by Charles. I was surprised to see him there. I had imagined him going off alone somewhere, nursing his grief. Instead he had been dancing with my friend.

"Deborah, my love," she cried out affectionately, "Charles tells me he knew nothing about your birthday tomorrow."

I gulped and swallowed.

"Birthday? Tomorrow?" Jonathan exclaimed. "Why didn't you tell us, Deborah?"

"She wouldn't have wanted to steal Alicia's thunder." Elizabeth smiled up at Jonathan. "But we remembered. We've all brought gifts, so it won't go unmarked."

We were joined by Mr. and Mrs. Morrison.

"Isn't it like Deborah not to mention her birthday to anyone, Mama?" Elizabeth said gaily.

Her Mama smiled thinly at me. "Yes, indeed, just like her." Then directing a warmer smile at Charles, "Quite a coincidence her birthday being so close to your sister's, my lord."

"Quite," he answered her with a supercilious glance from his towering height, and moved forward to join Elizabeth and Jonathan who were considering the delights laid out upon the table nearest them.

"They make a lovely couple, don't they?" Mrs. Morrison said to me with a satisfied smile. "I fully expect *an announcement* before we leave Rosemont. She'll make a splendid baroness, don't you agree?"

Our eyes were on Elizabeth standing majestically beautiful between Charles and Jonathan, almost of a height with them. Yes, she would make a splendid baroness.

I could not stop a shuddering sigh escaping me.

"Is anything wrong, my dear?" Mr. Morrison looked down at me tenderly. "You seem a little sad. Aren't you happy here?"

"Of course she's happy." Mrs. Morrison had a great fondness for answering questions directed at me. "If she's not she ought to be. She should be thanking her lucky stars to have achieved such a felicitous position. And once Elizabeth is installed as mistress here, she should be even more thankful."

"Don't you think you are being a little precipitate, Millicent, my dear? After all, Denton has not yet spoken to us of his intentions."

"Oh, tush! You can see it's only a question of time—and I don't believe that time is very far off."

She smiled at her daughter's back again, and Mr. Morrison resumed his questioning of me.

"Do they treat you well, child?"

"Of course they treat her well," Mrs. Morrison answered for me complacently. "They treat her like one of the family, do they not? Just like Lord Denton said they would. What more proof could you want than to see her here now, present at Alicia's ball, enjoying herself like everyone else?"

"They're all very kind to me," I murmured and forced myself to add, "I'm very happy here."

"So I should hope. You'd be a most ungrateful girl if you were not. Now, what shall I have?" It was our turn to be served at the supper table. "I'll have some of that game pie, if you please."

With our plates full we looked round for the others, Charles, Jonathan, and Elizabeth, but they were seated at a table already fully occupied, and though Jonathan sent me a rueful glance, I had perforce to join the Morrisons somewhere else.

"Look, there's William and Alicia just being served." Mrs. Morrison directed my attention towards them. "Don't they look attractive together. Wouldn't it be wonderful if . . . ? She's a great heiress in her own right, I believe?" She looked at me for corroboration. "Yes, a very attractive couple."

And so they were. I thought how supremely confident and happy William looked with Alicia, flushed and smiling, holding on to his arm. I had seen them dancing together earlier and been astonished to see Alicia twirling round so surefootedly. Can she really not see? I had wondered. It seemed incredible that a girl, blind from birth, should be able to dance so well, so unconcernedly. Then I had noticed how firmly William's arm encircled her slender waist. She could afford to be carefree in that strong protective hold.

He led her now to sit beside her Aunt Selina while he went to collect her a plateful of food and my heart skipped a beat at the ardent devotion on his face, the way he treated her as if she were the most precious thing in life to him.

Mrs. Morrison had been babbling on, but I had been listening to her with only half an ear. Now her words came through to me.

". . . I'm sure it won't be long before we are celebrating more than one betrothal at Rosemont."

"You think William and Alicia will marry then?"

"Why . . . yes . . . It's possible, I suppose . . . But I was talking about you and Jonathan in this instance. Oh, you might well blush, but I've seen the way he looks at you." She dug me in the ribs. "You haven't wasted much time, have you?"

I opened and closed my mouth like a fish, completely flabbergasted at her remarks.

"Well, I always said you were a dark horse. But you've got your head screwed on the right way, I'll allow. He's a wealthy man now, by all accounts. Not as wealthy as his brother, Lord Denton, of course, nor will he inherit property, but he's a fair catch for all that, and far above anything you could have hoped for after your father died leaving you penniless."

"There's nothing between Jonathan and me," I said, angry and hurt by her words.

"Nonsense. I've got eyes in my head, haven't I? Play your cards right, my girl, and it will be your turn next. Don't let him slip through your fingers, you'll never get another chance as good as this."

She continued in this tone and every time Mr. Morrison or myself tried to steer her away from it, returned to it in the next breath. But at last the ordeal was at an end. The musicians started up again and Jonathan came swiftly to beg me for a dance.

"I say," he said almost as soon as we moved away together, "Elizabeth's a dashed attractive girl, isn't she? And what a sense of humor! She's had us all in fits over there."

It hadn't escaped me.

"If I weren't so hopelessly enamored of you, dearest Deborah, and if she weren't so enamored of Charles, I swear I could fall for her."

It was only to be expected, of course. Her magic had been bound to work on him sooner or later, as it did on everybody. Why should I expect him to be impervious to her charms?

But then he danced me out onto the terrace. It was shadowy and deserted. We stopped dancing, but his arms stayed around me—tightened. "Debbie," he whispered urgently, "when are you going to marry me?"

I was aware of his strength, of his love, and I relaxed against him, needing his warmth, the knowledge of being wanted, and I let him kiss me.

It was a mistake. His kiss went deeper and deeper and I wept in my soul as he kissed me. He loved me. He wanted me. But he was the wrong man.

Chapter Eleven

I woke to the sound of my curtains being drawn back
and a churning in my stomach and in my mind. I had
slept only fitfully and with each awakening had been as-
saulted afresh by the question demanding an answer I
could not give.

Jonathan loved me and wanted to marry me. He cared
for me deeply. He had declared himself more than once
and at last had requested an immediate answer to his
proposal of marriage, but I, tasting the misery of being
held in the wrong arms, had been unable to give him the
answer he sought. I had given him no positive answer at
all. The question was still open.

Yet still my heart rebelled against acceptance.

"Good morning, Miss Deborah," Doreen called cheerfully.

"Good morning, Doreen." I raised my aching head to
look at her. She was smiling gleefully. "Why are you smiling like that?" I added somewhat testily. What right had
she to be so cheerful when I was so miserable?

"Look, Miss." She pointed towards something that
made me sit up and take notice.

"An easel!" I exclaimed. "But . . . who . . .
what . . . ?"

"And paints, Miss. Look. Lots of them."

186

"But . . . where did they come from? . . . Miss Selina, of course! Oh, how kind of her. How thoughtful."

I slipped out of bed to caress the easel and turn the paints over in my hands. There were paint brushes and tablets of drawing paper, too, for me to drool over.

"No, they're not from Miss Selina, they're from . . ."

"Jonathan! I should have known! He showed great interest when Elizabeth told him . . ."

"No," Miss Deborah," Doreen broke in with mock annoyance, "they're not from Master Jonathan, either. They're from his lordship. He asked me to place them there before you woke, so they would be the first things you saw on your birthday. Is it your birthday, Miss?"

I nodded, bemused by what she had said.

She smiled hugely. "May I wish you many happy returns, Miss?"

"Thank you. But are you sure it was his lordship who . . . ?"

"Of course I'm sure. I know his lordship when I see him, and he stood at that very door giving me clear instructions while everyone was at the ball."

I could not believe it. Charles had had them placed there? It did not seem possible. He might have done something like this for his sister, possibly even his aunt, but for me . . . ? No! And yet — I looked at Doreen going about her duties. She had been adamant. ". . . *his lordship asked me to place them there* . . ."

Doreen caught my eye. "I expect you'll want to go out straight away with them. I know how you've longed to paint Rosemont," she chirruped merrily. "I've poured your water. I'll go and prepare your breakfast while you wash and bring it up to you, then . . ."

My thoughts, still pounding through my brain, buried the rest of her words. I was remembering telling him of my desire to paint Rosemont and his response that there must be an old easel stored somewhere inside the house.

But that was a long time ago. He had not mentioned it since, and I had not liked to broach the subject again, thinking it was not of sufficient importance to him. And now, here was an easel, paints, and paper. New. From him. For my birthday. But he had not known it was my birthday until Elizabeth mentioned it at the ball.

I found it all very puzzling.

I lingered over my breakfast before going in search of him to thank him for his gift. I found him in the middle of a crowd of departing guests and hovered on the fringe, glad of the reprieve no matter how short from the execution of the duty beholden upon me. I noticed Miss Selina standing beside him, but there was no sign of Jonathan, nor of Alicia, then arms slid round my waist and Jonathan was smiling down at me.

"Good morning, my beloved," he greeted me.

"Don't call me that!" I muttered, glancing round anxiously to see if anyone had overheard.

"Why not?" he replied unabashed. "It's what you are, repulse me as you may." And he kissed the back of my neck, tightened his hold, and pressed his body against mine.

"Jonathan, stop it!" I hissed.

He nuzzled my ear. "Many happy returns of the day, my sweet. What would you like for your birthday? Just say the word and I'll make it a diamond ring."

Just then, much to my relief, someone in the crowd called out to him, "Jonathan, may I have a word with you?" and reluctantly he left my side.

I saw Lord Denton's eye was upon us. How much had he seen of what had passed between us and what interpretation had he put on it? The worst, of course. His cold, calculating stare proclaimed it. I turned away and caught sight of Elizabeth entering the drawing room. I hastened after her.

"Good morning, Elizabeth."

"Good morning," she returned without a smile.

"Is something wrong?" It wasn't like Elizabeth not to smile.

"Should there be?" she frowned.

"Well, I—I don't know."

She walked across to the window. I joined her. Guests were issuing out from the hall and piling into carriages.

"It was a good ball last night, wasn't it?" I murmured, more for the sake of something to say than anything else, to break the silence between us, a silence unlike any we had shared before.

She shrugged.

I could not understand her. I had never seen her in this mood before. She was being very short with me, giving me the distinct impression she did not wish for my company. But that could not be. I was her best friend.

"I'm looking forward to the picnic, aren't you?" I persisted.

"I suppose so."

No, this was not Elizabeth at all—quiet and withdrawn—when she was usually so enthusiastic about everything, bubbling over with fun and laughter. I placed a hand on her arm and drew her round to face me.

"Something is wrong, Elizabeth. What is it? Can't you tell me?" Her eyes fell before mine. "Is it me? Have I done or said something to upset you? Please tell me. If I have, I'm sorry. You must know I wouldn't deliberately hurt you for the world."

She looked at me then and I recoiled at the animosity in her glance. "Why didn't you tell me?" she asked.

"Tell you what?"

"That you're going to marry Jonathan."

"But I'm not. At least . . ."

"Don't lie to me. Mama says your betrothal will probably be announced before we leave tomorrow."

"No. She meant yours. Yours to Charles."

"You might have told me." Hadn't she heard what I said? "Given me a hint. You never used to be so secretive, Deborah. We used to share everything."

"Well, for what it's worth," I said huffily, needled by the fact that she seemed not to want to believe me, "I did tell you in my letters that he was paying attention to me."

"You made brief mention of it, I believe. I didn't take much notice of it."

"Then perhaps you should have done," I snapped, then overtaken by remorse, "Oh, Elizabeth, forgive me. Why are we getting at each other like this? It's all your mother's fault. She had no right to say what she did."

"Why not? It's true, isn't it? I knew it was last night when I saw you both on the terrace — kissing!"

"You saw us?"

"Yes. Charles, too."

"Charles?" So that was the reason behind his cold calculating stare.

"And he wasn't best pleased, I can tell you. I don't think he views an alliance between you and his brother with much favour."

She sounded spiteful. This was not the Elizabeth I knew and loved. What had changed her? It could not be any attachment Jonathan and I might have for one another. It must be something else, and suddenly I knew what it was.

"You're not in love with Charles, are you, Elizabeth?" I said.

She reddened. "What makes you say that?"

"Well, you don't behave as though you are, and you've never once said you were in your letters."

"What does that matter? It doesn't mean I'm not in love with him."

"Are you, Elizabeth?"

"Yes. Yes, of course I am. I'm going to be a baroness. That's something you'll never aspire to."

I gasped. Her hand flew to her mouth. "Oh, Deborah,"

190

she breathed then turned and fled.

I gazed after her, wondering if I should follow her. She was unhappy, that was why she had said the things she had. But would she thank me for going after her? Wouldn't it be best to leave her alone?

While I was wondering thus the Denton brothers entered the drawing room. Jonathan came straight to my side. "Well, thank goodness they've gone at last. Now we can concentrate on enjoying ourselves. What time are we starting out, Charles?"

Charles did not answer him, but addressed himself to me.

"Where is my sister, Miss Conway?"

"Miss Conway!" Jonathan exclaimed sliding his arm easily about my waist. "Why so formal all of a sudden?"

Charles continued to ignore him.

"She should have been here to bid her guests good-bye. It was up to you to see that she was."

"I'm sorry, I . . ."

"Go and find her, Miss Conway, and be good enough not to leave her side again till the Morrisons have gone."

"I don't understand," I said, perplexed.

"It's not necessary for you to understand. Just do as you are told."

"Charles!" Jonathan rebuked his brother as my cheeks turned scarlet with humiliation and indignation. "There's no need to be so abrupt."

"I'm sorry," Charles said, "but you must have seen the way young Morrison behaved last night, ogling Alicia, monopolizing her. I had to take him to task more than once."

"He wasn't ogling her," I cried. "He was admiring her. He finds her attractive. In fact, I think he has fallen in love with her."

He looked at me as if I were something that had crept out from under a stone. "You know very well he was only paying attention to her in order to make you jealous," he said.

"What?" Jonathan stared at him and me in amazement.

"Didn't you know?" Charles said smugly. "He's in love with her and she's in love with him."

"That's not true!" I gasped.

"Mrs. Morrison hoped that by placing you out of his reach he would forget his attachment to you, but fears now that it was a mistake to bring him here where you can weave your spell over him again."

"Weave my spell! But this is ridiculous. I'm no more in love with William than he with me. He might have thought at one time . . . but it never amounted to anything. His mother made too much of it."

"God, what an actress you would have made! I could almost believe you. As I believed you shy and demure when I first saw you. An innocent little thing, I thought, under the thumb of a dominant woman. I was never more fooled. Neither, it seems, was Jonathan."

"I think you should know before you say anything further," Jonathan said with quiet remonstrance, "that Deborah and I are going to be married."

"Over my dead body," was his brother's prompt and decisive reply.

"If that is what it comes to—so be it."

"You can't be serious."

"Never more serious in my life. I love Deborah and she loves me."

"You and William, both."

I could not stand any more. I tore myself out of Jonathan's encircling arm and ran from the room and out of the house, down to the river bank where I buried my face in the grass and wept as if my heart would break.

I did not know my tormentor had followed me till I heard him say, "Tears, Miss Conway?"

"Oh, go away," I moaned. "Leave me alone."

"You do well to weep with your schemes in tatters around you. Mrs. Morrison will not allow you to wed William and I shall not allow you to wed Jonathan."

I stumbled to my feet. "I hate you," I sobbed. "I hate you."

"That hardly surprises me now that I've shown you up for what you are in front of Jonathan—a scheming little gold digger."

Instinctively my hand rose to wipe the mockery off his face, but before it could achieve its purpose he had seized my wrist and held it in a viselike grip.

"That hit the mark, didn't it?" he sneered. "And I thought you were different. But you're just the same as all your sex; cold, scheming, calculating."

I struggled in his grasp. "Let me go. You're hurting me."

I was stunned beyond belief by his contempt, and it was this that pained me more, much more, than the hand trapping my wrist.

"I mean to," he ground out. "By God, I mean to! You're not overconcerned about whom you hurt. Women! You're all the same. Nothing matters but that you gain your own ends. It's all a game with you, isn't it, manipulating the emotions of others?"

"Oh, please . . ." Tears were streaming down my face. I did not know how much more of this I should be able to take. But he was not concerned with my feelings. My misery meant nothing to him.

"You came to Rosemont in the hope that 'absence makes the heart grow fonder' would be proved true in William's case, and if it wasn't, well, there was Jonathan as a second string to your bow. But I don't care about them. They're grown men and should be able to take care of themselves. It's your willingness to use Alicia as an innocent pawn to further your scheme I can't stomach."

"But I . . . Oh, I never used Alicia . . . You must

believe that, if nothing else."

The cry came from my soul and it seemed to give him pause. An odd look came to his eyes and he peered at me as though he longed with all his heart to believe me—and couldn't. Then releasing his hold in my arm he said hoarsely, "Oh, get away from me. I can't be bothered with you anymore."

I watched him stride away from me, hating him, loving him, hating myself for caring. Why should I care about a man who treated me the way he did? Why should I let it concern me if he thought such terrible things about me? Did he really believe all he had said? Yes, he did. I had seen he did. I should have hated him for it, but I could not hate him—I could not.

I do not know how long I remained there, but the tears I shed were bountiful as I watched him out of sight. When at last they dried and Rosemont came into focus again, I stared up at its beautiful brickwork and oriel windows, standing strong and firm as it had done through the centuries buffeted by the elements and fate alike, and I thought: If only I could emerge from my slough of despond calm and blessedly at peace like that, all vicissitudes at an end. Ah, if only I could.

Heartsore and as weary as if I had trekked for miles, I made my way back to the house I had grown to love as my own. I had been afraid of it at first, felt it boded me ill, but gradually as I settled in, I came to regard it as my home. Yes, I loved it now and should be heartbroken to leave it. Yet leave it I must and without delay. I must seek out Mr. and Mrs. Morrison and beg them to take me back to Hunt Park. Somehow I must make them believe I had no designs of their son, William. They would have to take me back anyway. Charles—Lord Denton—would not wish me to continue my employment at Rosemont believing I was only using Alicia to further my own selfish ends.

Go and find Alicia. Was I still expected to? Did it

matter now? She was probably with Murkett, anyway. A curtain twitched and suddenly I was running angrily across the grass. Alicia had hidden herself in the locked room again, and because she had done that and not been present to bid her guests good-bye, I had had to take the brunt of her brother's displeasure. If it had not been for her, he would not have been so harsh, so unreasonable.

I was running up the wide oaken staircase, my breath coming in loud painful gasps, unreasonable myself, blaming her for all the hurt and pain I suffered.

My hand reached for the big brass knob. It began to turn.

"Deborah! What are you doing?"

I jumped and let the knob go at the sound of Miss Selina's sharp accusing voice. She was dressed for going out in a lightweight suit of a becoming shade of mauve and a large straw hat with a chiffon scarf of a deeper shade tied over it and under her chin. She was approaching me swiftly.

"Alicia's in there!" I exclaimed.

She looked startled for a moment, but recovering quickly said, "Nonsense. I've told you, that room is never used."

"Alicia uses it. I know she does. I saw her at the window just now."

"You couldn't have. You imagined it."

"Well, if it wasn't her, it was someone else," I argued belligerently. "Perhaps it's haunted."

"Haunted? Yes, you could say that."

I gulped. "You're joking."

"Yes, of course I'm joking. Come along now, it's time for the picnic, so go and get your hat . . ."

"Well, we can't go without Alicia." I turned to the door and turned the knob again—only this time it did not turn.

I began to rap on the door.

"Alicia! Alicia! It's me, Deborah! I know you're in

195

there. Open the door and stop pretending . . ."

"Deborah, this is foolish." Miss Selina eyed me with something akin to hostility. "But if nothing else will satisfy you, I will go and get the key and prove to you there is no one in there."

But before she could move, William's voice attracted our attention, "Alicia, please wait. Listen to me. You've got it all wrong," and Alicia came running up the stairs.

I called out to her weakly as she passed by and went into her own room.

Miss Selina's eye met mine in triumphant satisfaction.

I tried to get out of going on the picnic, but Miss Selina would not hear of it, so it was with reluctance that with Alicia's hand in mine I followed the others down to the river bank where a hired boat awaited us. Charles was leading the way with Miss Selina on his arm. Mr. Morrison and his wife were a step or two behind. William and Elizabeth were some distance away from them and appeared to be arguing quietly but ferociously. I could not see Jonathan.

Then suddenly he was beside me, linking his arm through mine.

"Hello, my love," he said softly, but with an odd tone to his voice.

"Hello, Jonathan," I whispered, conscious of Alicia listening beside me.

"Only you're not, are you?"

"What?" Alicia's fingers bit deep into my hand.

"My love," he grated. "You're William's."

I realized Charles was to blame for this. He had given Jonathan his version of how William and I felt about each other. He had been too arrogant, too sure of himself, to listen to the truth—but Jonathan would understand when I explained it to him.

"I'm not William's love, nor he mine," I declared, and felt Alicia's hand relax in mine and knew my answer meant as much to her as anyone. "We have never been anything more than brother and sister to each other," I added firmly.

"Is this the truth?" Jonathan demanded hoarsely.

"I'm not in the habit of telling lies."

It was pleasant gliding along the river, the wide East Anglian countryside stretching away at either side of the boat in interminable miles to merge with the hot summer sky, and everyone appeared to be enjoying it. Yet there was an atmosphere of unease that disturbed me so that I was not sorry to step ashore at a previously determined spot and help set out the picnic fare on gaily colored cloths spread out on the grassy bank.

I was not hungry. After making a feeble attempt at eating something, I excused myself saying I wished to stretch my legs. Elizabeth rose immediately to join me.

We walked in silence for a while. In truth I hardly knew what to say to her after our last parting. But at last she spoke.

"Do you remember the long walks we used to take together at Hunt Park?"

I smiled. "They were happy days."

Elizabeth sighed plaintively. "If only you hadn't left."

"I wouldn't have, if your mother hadn't turned me out. If she had believed me when I told her I wasn't in love with William, I would still be there. But she didn't. She still doesn't and she's spreading the most awful lies about me. Do you know she told Lord Denton she had to get rid of me because I had designs on William, that I still had? And now he believes I'm a scheming hussy using Alicia to trap William into marriage . . . And it's not true! You know it's not true, Elizabeth."

"Yes," she whispered almost inaudibly. "I know."

"And now he's told Alicia and Jonathan, and goodness

knows how many others. I shall have to leave Rosemont. I've been thinking of doing so for some time . . . so many things have happened to . . . and now this . . . I don't know what I'll do or where I'll go, but . . ."

It was a blessed relief for me to talk like this and I was on the verge of pouring out all my troubles to the only one I could unburden my soul to, Elizabeth, confidante of my childhood, my adolescence, when she rounded on me, flaring angrily.

"Oh, stop it! Stop it! You know you won't leave Rosemont. You know you're going to marry Jonathan and . . . Oh, why didn't you stay at Hunt Park and marry William? Why did Mama have to turn you out?"

"It wouldn't have made any difference, Elizabeth," I said anxiously, startled by the vehement outburst. "I couldn't have married him. I wasn't, *I'm not,* in love with him."

"You could have learned to love him. We could have been sisters, instead of . . . of . . ." She caught my arm eagerly. "There's still a chance. He's still in love with you."

"He's not," I said sternly. "He never was. Not really. Not the way he is with Alicia."

"Alicia!" Her voice rose hysterically. "He's not in love with Alicia!"

"Have you seen the way he looks at her?" I said slyly.

"Yes, but it doesn't mean anything. He won't marry her. He can't."

"Why not? Your mother can't have any objection to her on grounds of money and background. In fact she said to me . . ."

"She's blind!" Elizabeth cried out.

"Yes, but that's no drawback. Believe me, she's highly intelligent and perfectly capable of doing most things unaided and she's . . ."

"Dumb! What sort of wife would she make for him. He deserves better."

"I can't understand you, Elizabeth," I said unbelievingly. What *had* happened to change my dear, sweet, adorable friend? I hardly knew her. "You're not usually so . . ."

"You. It should have been you," she cried. "And if you had thought for anyone other than yourself . . ."

"Elizabeth!"

Checked, she gulped, then continued. "Anyway, you were wrong about Mama. It wasn't she who told Lord Denton about you and William, it was I. *I* told him. *And* Alicia. *And* Jonathan!"

"Elizabeth!"

"Oh . . ." She choked on the word as tears began pouring down her face. "Forgive me, Deb. Forgive me. I shouldn't have done it. I didn't mean to. It was wrong of me, but I couldn't help myself. Oh, Deborah . . . I'm so unhappy."

She collapsed in my arms. I had never seen her cry before, even as children, but now her sobs choked her and I grew fearful for her.

"Hush. Hush," I whispered, clutching her tightly as I staggered back against the trunk of an elm the better to take her weight, patting her back in the time-honored way of a mother soothing a fretful baby, and when her sobs eased, "Tell me what has happened. Tell me all about it. I might be able to help."

"You can't help," she moaned. "You, least of all." She pulled away from me. "Oh, Debbie, if only . . . Oh, someone's coming! I must go. They mustn't see me like this."

"Elizabeth . . ." But she was gone like a startled fawn.

I would have followed her, startled likewise, as Charles came into view, but he reached my side before I could move.

"Why did Elizabeth hurry away like that?" he demanded.

199

"I . . . She . . ."

"Never mind. It's not her I wish to speak to, it's you. You might remember if you cast your mind back that I asked you not to leave my sister's side till the Morrisons had gone."

"I remember," I said more coolly than I felt, "but what harm can she come to surrounded by her family?"

"She is not surrounded by her family now," he snapped, and I followed his gaze to where she was walking with William while the others went off in differing directions, exploring their surroundings.

She looked as lovely and delicate as the wild rose blossoms that bloomed in the hedgerows and William was guiding her gently and tenderly through the wooded area we were in. His face was earnest as he talked to her. Was he trying to persuade her that there was nothing of a romantic nature between him and me? If so, I wished him better luck than I had had with her brother, Charles. In any event I did not feel inclined to interrupt them.

"She'll come to no harm with William," I said briskly. "I never did."

His lordship's eyes surveyed me with a narrowed thoughtful expression. "No?" he murmured.

"No," I said. "I've known him all my life and never known him do anything dishonorable or mean." Then because I should be leaving Rosemont soon and have no cause to fear him any more, I started to walk away from him — without permission.

He started to walk with me.

"Do you think he is sincere in his regard for Alicia?" he asked.

Surprised that he should ask me, I stopped and turned to him again. "I believe he's in love with her," I said boldly.

"So do I," he said.

"Will you . . . allow them . . . to marry?" I ventured.

200

"I doubt it," he replied.

We started walking again, I fuming inwardly against him.

"Why didn't you tell us it was your birthday today?"

"I—I didn't think it was important."

"You little goose," he chaffed, and I glanced up at him to see a gentle smile playing about his mouth.

"Thank you for the easel and paints," I gulped, glad he was not angry with me anymore, yet in some odd kind of way not trusting his new pleasant mood. "I would have thanked you sooner," I continued, averting my eyes again, "only . . ."

"Only I was in no mood to receive your thanks."

I looked straight ahead of me.

"Was it what you wanted?"

"Oh, yes." My eyes flew back to him. "But how . . . I mean, you didn't know it was my birthday . . . and they're all brand new. How did you manage to get them at such short notice? I mean . . ."

"I know what you mean," he laughed as I got myself all tangled up. Then he grew serious. "I've had them ever since my last visit to London. That was my main reason for going there—to get them for you. I remembered the look in your eyes as you told me how much you loved painting and wished you could paint Rosemont. I looked forward to seeing your face when I presented them to you on my return, but your attitude towards me was so cool . . . you treated me with such disdain . . . I hadn't the heart. And then the opportunity to give them to you did not seem to present itself, until I heard it was your birthday, then I got them out and instructed Wicks—Doreen, I believe you call her—to place them where you could see them when you woke in the morning."

"Yes. She told me. It was very kind of you. I'm overcome with gratitude."

I waffled on trying to sort out the meaning of his

201

words. They suggested . . . suggested . . . My heartbeat quickened, thundered inside my breast, as he said:

"It was nothing compared with what I would give you if you . . . Deborah . . ." His voice dropped, thickened. He was standing very close to me. His hands reached out to grasp my arms. "Deborah . . ." there was a desperate kind of urgency about him, "tell me I didn't imagine what happened in Lynn. Tell me . . . Damn! We'll talk later."

He let me go as Mrs. Morrison's voice sailed towards us, steely and full of suspicion. "Hello, you two. Miss Selina says we ought to be getting back." She took up a stance between us and her glance fell coldly upon me. "There's a long way to go and . . ."

"Yes. Yes," Charles said testily. Mrs. Morrison put her arm through mine, and despite his angry scowl, kept herself between us all the way back to the boat.

Once there and sure she could not be overheard, she hissed in my ear, "What do you think you are up to, young lady? Is no man safe from your grasping hands?"

William made sure he sat beside Alicia on the trip back. Charles sat at the other side of his sister, Elizabeth next to him, and Mrs. Morrison firmly wedged herself between us, plainly opposed to any chance there might be of Charles and me engaging in conversation again. Miss Selina and Mr. Morrison chatted amiably together at the other end of the boat and Jonathan, with his arm about my waist, seemed quite content to sit beside me.

"We haven't had much chance of being alone together," he complained softly. "We'll make up for it tomorrow. We'll go off on our own somewhere."

I tried to withdraw myself from his arm, but every time I made the slightest move Mrs. Morrison cast a baleful eye on me and pressed herself closer against me. So unless I wished to make a fuss I must remain where I was, hot and sticky, enduring her hostility, Charles's black accusative stare, Elizabeth's returned resentment. At least Miss Selina looked on me with favor—and that did not last.

Detaching herself from Mrs. Morrison's side as we crossed the greensward on the way back to the house, Selina joined the little group Jonathan, Alicia, William, and I made, and catching my arm held me back from the others.

"What's this I hear from Mrs. Morrison?" she demanded furiously.

"What do you mean?" I asked, a tumultuous volcano starting up inside me.

Her nails bit viciously into my arm. "She says that you and Charles are . . . more than friendly. That you are egging him on to marry you. Is it true?"

"No. No. Of course not. I . . . I . . ."

Her grip relaxed. "I knew it wasn't. I told her she didn't know what she was talking about. I told her it was Jonathan you were interested in. She laughed and said, 'You'll see. All our plans for an alliance between our two families will come to nought if she's not stopped.' But if you tell me it isn't true, I am relieved." Her nails started to bite again. "It had better be true. Miranda thought she could . . . Well, never mind about that now. But it's not wise to harbor thoughts of marriage with Charles. It can only lead to unhappiness all round. Leave it to Elizabeth to find out the cost."

I stared at her, the volcano inside me in no way eased by her words.

"But there's nothing for you to worry about, my dear— if you are sensible," she continued. "Elizabeth will have to look out for herself, and if she gets hurt, well, that's her problem, but I'll not have you hurt, if I can help it. I'm too fond of you for that."

She left me to join Mrs. Morrison again, no doubt to tell her there was no need for worry. Was there need? No. My heart was a well of misery and pain as I followed on. Even if Charles wished to marry me, a wedding between us would never take place. The opposition was too strong.

I had been pondering Charles's words to me under the elm. Did they contain the promise of a proposal? Or was he still hoping to make me his mistress? And now I wondered, if he did propose, would I accept after Miss Selina's warnings?

"... *It's not wise to harbor thoughts of marriage with Charles* ..." Why not? "*Leave it to Elizabeth to find out the cost* ..." What cost? "*Miranda thought she could* ..." What? And who was Miranda? His dead wife? Had he harmed her in some way? Was that what Miss Selina had been hinting at? But he had loved his wife. Loved her still? "*Elizabeth will have to look out for herself* ... *but I'll not have you hurt* ..."

What *did* it all mean? If only I could make some sense out of it all. If only I was clear in my mind about Charles, about his feelings towards me. I wanted to believe he was in love with me, but was he? I wanted to believe there were no flaws in his nature, but I had seen there were. And Miss Selina was forever hinting at other, deeper, hidden flaws that it would be wise not to evoke.

But within the space of the next half hour all my questions, all my doubts, had been routed, utterly and completely.

I felt a hand at my elbow. It was Charles. "Deborah," he said, "don't go in yet. I want to talk to you. I *must* talk to you."

I went with him like a sleepwalker being led in a dream to something, somewhere, beyond knowledge, only dimly aware of the rhododendron bushes we walked between and the little rustic summerhouse ahead. But once inside the wooden structure, as he gripped my arms and turned me round to face him, my dreamlike trance fell away and my breath became painful to me.

With the nearness of him, his breath feathering my cheek, all Miss Selina's warnings flashed into my mind and I trembled with apprehension. What was I doing here alone with him in this quiet secluded place? *Don't trust him . . . Give him a wide berth . . .*

"Why have you brought me here?" I murmured, annoyed that I sounded plaintive when I wished to sound stern. "What do you want?"

"I want to know about you. About us," he said harshly. "I want to get things clear. Are you in love with Jonathan?"

"No," I whispered in some surprise.

"With William Morrison?"

"No."

"Are you in love with me?"

I could not answer that, even in a whisper. I dared not answer.

"You are silent," he said coldly, then with a force that seemed to stem from his innermost being, "Did Lynn mean nothing to you? Do I mean nothing to you?"

His hands fell from my arms and he turned away from me, facing outwards along the rhododendron walk. If I had allowed my heart to speak I would have told him then he meant everything to me, but cautioned by my brain, no words came from my mouth.

He started speaking again, as if to himself.

"I shouldn't be surprised. I'm a lot older than you. Many years older. Not old enough to be your father, perhaps, but . . ." He indulged in a bitter laugh. "I love you, Deborah. God help me, I love you."

I was dreaming. I must be dreaming. He would not be saying these things to me if I were awake.

"I've loved you from the very first moment when you faced me so crossly . . . You were so small . . . frowning at me like a veritable demon . . . and like a demon you fastened yourself onto my heart and made it your own . . . for good or ill."

It *was* a dream and I never wanted to wake from it.

"I fought against it. You were so young. No older than my sister, and like her, I thought, you had a lot of growing up to do. Besides, you plainly didn't like me. I knew I wanted you for my wife, but that I should have to wait, hoping you would change towards me, begin to care for me . . . it didn't matter how much, the smallest amount would suffice . . . But then you and Jonathan . . . I could see you didn't care for him. I believed you were leading him on, coaxing him into a marriage that would lift you out of your present demeaning position and place you back in your rightful niche. I determined to thwart your plans. And so I persuaded you to go with me to King's Lynn."

I gasped in my dream. It was taking an ominous turn. Becoming a nightmare.

"I am not unversed in the arts of love and I intended to bring them all into play to make you fall in love with me so that I could confront Jonathan with . . ."

"You said you would put every obstacle in the way of our marriage," I whispered, "but that you should go as far as to marry me yourself . . ."

He swung round to face me. "Marry you! I didn't intend to marry you, only to let you believe I would, so that my brother might see you for the scheming woman you were. At least, that is what I told myself. The truth is I was head over heels in love with you myself and could not bear the thought of you as another man's wife.

"I didn't bargain for your sweetness, your softness, your ardent response. It made me feel ashamed. I saw I was wrong about you and tried to draw back, but you made it clear your feelings were the same as mine, and I vowed I should never give you a moment's unhappiness again. I would make you my wife and give you everything your heart desired. I would be your slave.

"But there was a message waiting for me when we got back, and I had to leave early the next morning without seeing you, and when I returned it was to find you cold and distant, obviously regretting what had happened between us. Then Jonathan came home and as I watched you together I had to face the fact that I might be wrong about you, that you might be in love with him after all. In any case he was obviously besotted with you, and so I swore I would interfere no more."

My dream was changing yet again, making it clear where things had gone wrong, and that it required only explanation on my part to put things right.

But then he continued. The voice that had softened grew hard and brutal. "That was until Elizabeth put me in the picture regarding your relationship with her brother. How you were dismissed from Hunt Park because you tried to seduce him and that you still pursued him, even though by now you had a second string to your bow. And then I saw you in Jonathan's arms. You were, after all, everything I despised in a woman. A cheat, a liar, using your sex to ensnare any man foolish enough to be taken in by your air of sweet innocence."

I put my hands over my ears.

"Stop. Stop. It's not true," I cried. "Any of it. I don't want to marry Jonathan or William. There's only one man I want to marry. Only one man I love. And it's you. *You*. And you hate me."

I darted out of the summerhouse and ran blindly down the avenue of crowded rhododendron bushes with great sobs tearing at my throat. He had made me say things I had not meant to say . . . I hardly knew what I had said . . . but it had been too much, and all I wanted to do now was hide from him and his power to hurt.

Suddenly I was hauled to a halt and swung around.

Through a blur of tears I saw a strange grotesque being, an escaped creature from the carved pilasters, and I screamed. "Let me go! Let me go!"

"Deborah! Deborah!" Charles's voice rang through my

nightmare as he shook me into silent submission and held me close.

I crumpled against him. "Let me go," I moaned.

He held me away from him but kept a grip on my arms. "Is it true?" he demanded. "Do you love me?"

I nodded wordlessly. There was no point in doing anything else. He knew I loved him. I had told him I loved him.

But it did not seem to be enough for him. "Say it. Let me hear you say it," he commanded.

"I love you," I whispered and saw wonder spread across his face.

Against all odds hope surged within my breast.

"Will you marry me, Deborah?" he asked.

And I replied, "Oh, yes. Yes. Yes. Yes. Yes."

Every fiber of my being leapt to life and love as his lips pressed down on mine. All heaven and earth fused into one resounding sea with wild waves crashing and roaring. I was carried on a turbulent tide to a destination I had neither the will nor the wish to avoid.

That should have been my happy ending.

I did not know the half of it.

Chapter Twelve

Mrs. Morrison was very angry with me. "You ungrateful wretch!" she raged, cornering me in my room later that night, "After all I've done for you!"

And so began a tirade of accusation and abuse. I was the lowest, cunningest creature under the sun. Base. Disloyal to my friends, but most of all to Elizabeth.

"The friend who loves you as a sister! Who has always treated you kindly and spoken up for you! You know she is enamored of Lord Denton! From my own lips you heard they were to become engaged! And yet you . . . you . . . How could you descend to such depths of duplicity? Pretending a penchant for Jonathan when all the time . . . How could you be so serpentlike? Really, Miss, words fail me! There aren't sufficient to describe your underhanded dealings!"

Deeply wounded, I tried to explain, to beg her forgiveness for something that had happened in spite of myself, but her ranting and raving did not cease till she left my side.

She was right of course, I had been disloyal to Elizabeth. However unintentionally I had deceived and hurt her and I regretted it. She might not be in love with Charles, nor he with her, but they would have married and been happy enough if I had not declared my love.

When Charles had announced our engagement she had stared in disbelief before congratulating us almost voicelessly. She had paled, become subdued, kept throwing me strange, furtive glances. I had longed to be able to speak to her, tell her how sorry I was that she should have heard this way, that I would much have preferred to tell her myself when we were alone and plead forgiveness and understanding, but no private moment presented itself.

I left my room in search of her. Somehow I must make her see I had not deliberately come between her and Charles, that I had given him no encouragement till he had revealed his feelings for me. I could not bear her to think ill of me. She might not be able to forgive me, but she would understand and not think the awful things her mother did. But as I ran along the corridor Miss Selina stepped out from her boudoir to confront me with a frosty blue gaze that sent icicles stabbing into my heart.

A veil had dropped over her face after the first few moments following the announcement Charles made, when she had cast a look of utter stupefaction at Jonathan standing nearby like a man stunned. He had turned and stalked from the room while she kissed me dutifully and wished me every happiness. But her kiss had been cold and I sensed her angry disapproval. And now the veil had been removed.

"So," she hissed, detaining me with a long-fingered hand, "you are going to marry Charles. After all I said to you—after all you said to me."

"You have every right to criticize me, Miss Selina," I said faintly, trembling at the confrontation, "I must appear very two-faced, but . . . circumstances change and . . ."

Her fingers dug deep into my flesh. "Yes, circumstances change. Or do they? It seems to me this was meant from the start. Oh, you fool, Deborah! You fool!

You should have taken notice of me. I told you not to trust him. But it's too late now. He'll never let you go. You're here . . . for the rest of your life . . . whatever it may bring."

"It will bring me happiness," I cried with an attempt at bravado as her words dredged buried fears to taunt my joyous heart.

"I'm not saying you won't be happy . . . for a month or two . . . maybe longer . . . but once there's a child on the way . . ."

"He loves me," I cried.

"Don't you listen to anything I say?" she asked witheringly. "I've told you, there's only one person he loves other than himself, and that's Alicia. Hasn't it entered your silly little head that she's the main reason behind his proposal of marriage? An heir is important to him, yes, but he could have got that with Elizabeth Morrison. But Alicia's happiness is of great importance to him, too, and she doesn't care for Elizabeth, whereas she does care for you. He'll do anything to keep you here to dance attendance on her. When he saw you and Jonathan together, saw how Jonathan worshipped you, he grew afraid you would marry him and leave Rosemont—and Alicia. And he saw he had to act quickly if he was to chain you here forever."

I had been listening to her in stunned silence. Now I began spluttering defensively, "No. No. It's not . . . true. I d-don't b-believe you."

She shrugged, and shaking her head sadly, went back into her boudoir.

"Ah, well," she said as she closed the door, "You've made your bed. You must lie on it."

I ran back to my own room in no fit state now to face Elizabeth—or anyone else—and spent a restless night in ceaseless questioning. Even my brief bouts of sleep were riddled by doubts and fears, so it was hardly surprising I rose in the morning pale and haggard so that Doreen exclaimed at the sight of me.

"I couldn't sleep," I excused myself.

"That's hardly surprising, Miss, with all the excitement. Oh, you'll make a lovely bride. And his lordship will make you so happy. We all knew it would happen sooner or later. It was only a question of when—if you'll pardon my saying so, Miss."

"You knew? Who?"

"In the servants' hall. Everybody knew. It was obvious his lordship adored you. The way he looked at you! None of us could understand how you could prefer Master Jonathan to him." As if afraid she had said too much, she left me quickly, murmuring that she would bring me some breakfast to eat in bed.

I lay back against my pillows thinking over what she had said, all so different from Miss Selina's interpretation of the situation. Were the servants right, or was she, who knew her nephew so well?

But servants in great houses were notoriously clearsighted where their masters were concerned, and though they might keep silence where there was contempt, they would not hesitate to proclaim their favor for one who was honorable, just, and kind.

The servants at Rosemont believed their master was honorable, just, and kind. They believed he loved me—adored me, had been Doreen's word. I believed it, too, and so, I believed, did Miss Selina in her heart. It had been her displeasure speaking out last night. Her displeasure at the fact that I should prefer her nephew Charles to her beloved Jonathan.

By the time Doreen returned with my breakfast tray I had improved immeasurably, ready to talk and laugh and discuss my forthcoming wedding.

After I had eaten and Doreen helped me dress, doing up the buttons at the side of my black cotton skirt while

I dealt with the dozen or so tiny ones down the front of my pale cream blouse, she said, "I can hardly wait to dress you as a bride. That is," her voice dropped, "if you still want me to be your maid."

"But of course I do," I cried.

"Only I thought you might want somebody more experienced now you're going to be a baroness."

I turned and gathered her to me. "How can you think such a thing, Doreen? No one will ever take your place. You are my friend."

She beamed at me like a ray of sunshine and I left her happily tidying my room as I went to seek another friend, one I feared I might have lost. It was essential I heal the rift between Elizabeth and myself. We, who had been more sisters than friends, could not become enemies. I did not think she was very deeply in love with Charles — if at all. But she had been expecting to marry him, and she would have been hurt by my seemingly apparent deceit, therefore I must beseech her understanding by explaining . . .

"Deborah."

Jonathan brought me to a halt placing himself squarely in my path. He looked angry. Hurt and angry. Another friend lost? Another friend to explain my actions to? Another friend from whom to seek forgiveness and understanding?

"Jonathan," I began unhappily, but he was in no mood to listen to explanations.

"How could you do it? Why keep it such a secret? Why didn't you tell me instead of leading me on? I made a real fool of myself, didn't I, believing you cared for me, when all the time it was my brother you were setting your cap at?"

"No, it wasn't like that. You've got it all wrong . . ."

"Have I? I don't think so. I think you're the one who's got it all wrong. If you expect Charles to settle down with a baby like you after Miranda, you're more of an innocent than I took you for."

"Please, Jon, I . . ."

"You're not like her, you know. Not one little bit. In looks or anything else. Miranda was a golden girl. Cool and remote, yet full of fire. Like an ice queen with a flame in her heart to set alight all who came near her."

He was describing the girl in the photograph that Charles had torn up with such cold deliberation, and I shivered as I recalled the pain and anguish I had seen on his face which had led me to believe he was still in love with her. A golden girl. Full of fire. Not a bit like me. Why was he telling me all this? To set me on my guard against Charles in the hope that I would turn back to him?

Or was there another reason?

Had Jonathan kept the photograph of Miranda because he had been in love with her himself? And had Charles been aware of the fact and been resentful? Did it account for the antagonism that existed between the two of them? It simmered so gently beneath the surface most of the time that it was barely noticeable, but it was there. Had Charles observing Jonathan's growing attachment to me seized his opportunity for revenge?

Revenge? What had put such a word into my mind? It suggested Charles had something to be vengeful about. *Had Jonathan been Miranda's lover?* Did Charles want to marry me, not because he was in love with me, but because he wished to be revenged upon his brother?

As always at Rosemont, just when I began to feel at ease something rose to check my progress—the ever-present "something" that still lurked in the background eager to torment me.

How swiftly these thoughts passed through my mind. They were here and gone in the bare moment Jonathan paused for breath before continuing, "Still, I wish you

214

well."

I was left undecided as to whether he sneered or commiserated.

"Deborah."

I heard my name called again and looked to see Charles in the hall below with his aunt. Abandoning her side he raced up to me and I was shaken by the lovelight that shone from his eyes.

"I've been in a fever of impatience to hold you in my arms again," he murmured as he bent to kiss me. And I thought, If he can look at me like that and hold me like this, what have I to fear?

Keeping an arm about my waist he said, "Come on down, my darling. The last of the guests will be leaving shortly and they will want to say good-bye to you."

"I must go and see Elizabeth first," I said. "I must speak to her."

Miss Selina heard me and called up, "She's in the conservatory with her brother."

"I'll come with you," Charles said. "I want a word with that young man."

"Don't be too hard on him," I begged, knowing William found no favor in his eyes.

"No harder than I need be," was his response.

"If you're going to chastise him," Miss Selina said, "it might be better if you spoke to him alone. Why don't you go and speak to him in the conservatory and send Elizabeth out here to Deborah?"

He bowed to the wisdom of her words.

Miss Selina said to me, "There goes your future husband. I dare say it thrills you to think on it. I only hope you don't live to regret it."

"I won't," I said confidently.

She scowled. "He's so much older than you are."

"That's nothing to worry about. Lots of girls marry older men."

"Yes, but . . ."

She broke off abruptly and went quickly from my side as Elizabeth approached.

"You wished to speak to me, Deb?" Elizabeth asked.

"Yes," I said hesitantly, searching her face for the unhappiness I expected to see there and being surprised by the carefree expression that met my gaze. "About Charles and me, I . . ."

"I know what you're going to say," she interrupted, "but don't. It doesn't matter." And she beamed and clasped me to her bosom, hugging and kissing me and telling me I was her best, her dearest friend as she had always known me to be. "Why didn't you tell me it was Charles you loved? It would have saved us both so much heartache."

I drew away from her and gazed up into her face.

"But you were going to marry him."

"Only because Mama wanted me to. She wanted me to be a great lady, mistress of a great house. I wasn't in love with him, but I would have married him if he'd asked me . . . how many girls marry for love, anyway? . . . only then I met Jonathan."

"Jonathan?" Light began to dawn. *Jonathan!* Elizabeth, are you . . . ?"

"Yes." She blushed crimson. "I'm in love with Jonathan. And now that I know you are not, I shall do my best to make him fall in love with me."

"Oh, Elizabeth . . ."

"There's been a lot of misunderstanding . . . I've been hateful to you . . . to everyone . . . but now at last things are clear and . . . Oh, I do wish you every happiness, sweetest Deb."

"And I you, dear, dear Elizabeth."

We hugged and kissed again.

"And you forgive me?" she whispered.

"Need you ask?" I said. "I only wish I had opened my

heart to you and . . ."

"Well, we're off. Are you ready, Elizabeth?"

I was stopped from finishing my sentence by the arrival of Mr. Morrison and his wife. Not that it mattered. All that needed saying had been said.

Miss Selina re-appeared as if from nowhere and the genial gentleman who had given me his blessing unstintingly on hearing of my engagement addressed her affably.

"Thank you, Miss Selina, for a most enjoyable visit. We've never been so agreeably entertained, have we, Millicent? And we think Rosemont is a beautiful, splendid old house, don't we, Millicent?" Then he kissed me fondly. "I know you'll be very happy here, my dear. Your father would be proud of you. The Baroness Denton of Rosemont. What a splendid title. Splendid."

Poor man, he was being so tactless and did not even know it. Seeing his wife's lips purse more thinly, I knew he would be in for a fine old harangue on the way home and when I curtsied before her, it was as much as she could do to be civil to me, in spite of my new status.

Charles and William joined us and we all went out to the carriage waiting to convey the Morrisons home. When William embraced me as he said good-bye, I whispered, "Have you seen Alicia? Have you said good-bye to her?"

I really wanted to ask him what Charles had said, but that was impossible.

He answered me sadly. "I haven't been allowed to see her."

"Not allowed . . ."

A touch of censure entered my heart against Charles. Why must he be so ruthless? So unbending? Could he not see William and Alicia were made for each other? I sent him a scalding look which seemed to surprise him. I did not care. He was denying them both a future of happiness together, refusing them even a last meeting for farewell.

The carriage pulled away and Charles touched my arm to lead me back indoors.

"You might have let William say good-bye to Alicia," I muttered crossly.

"I couldn't," he replied.

"Why not?"

"She's being kept to her room. She had a bad night last night."

"Oh. I'd better go to her."

"No. Leave her to Murkett. Murkett knows how to deal with her best when . . . under such circumstances."

"You mean . . . she's had another attack?"

He did not reply. There was no need. His face said it all.

A footman brought a message from Benson. He urgently required his lordship's assistance on some matter.

I wandered out into the garden thinking about Alicia. Not expecting any adverse reaction from her to the news of my engagement, thinking she would be overjoyed to receive me as her sister, I had been surprised to see her face turn ashen and her mouth open in that silent scream that terrified me. She had started shaking from head to foot and all the signs of a bout of violent hysteria were in evidence.

Markett had been summoned to take her to her room, but as she was led away, she had turned and looked at me—it had seemed as if she looked at me—and pleaded with me not to marry Charles.

I told myself I had misinterpreted her glance. Why should she not want me to marry Charles? She liked me. We got on wonderfully together. Perhaps it was a sudden shock to hear it like that. We should have prepared her.

I sat down on my favorite seat and closed my eyes. Suddenly Alicia appeared at my side. She pressed something into my hand, something hard and cold that seared my skin like a flame, then slipped away leaving me to stare down at the periwinkle brooch lying in the palm of my hand.

The sight of it froze my blood. It emanated evil and I closed my hand over it to banish it from view. It ground into my flesh till I screamed in agony.

"Deborah. My darling. Wake up. Wake up."

Charles was beside me. There was no brooch in my hand. I had been dreaming.

"Are you all right?" he asked. "You were having some sort of nightmare."

"Yes, I—think so."

"You gave me a fright."

The warm concern in his voice tempted me to pour out all my fears and anxieties. But I resisted the temptation. It would sound ridiculous to him, the ravings of an hysterical female. Strange dreams about a brooch that seemed to have a life of its own—a watcher at the window of a room that was always kept locked—a ghost flitting through the corridors at night—a fear that some unknown thing lurked within the confines of Rosemont waiting . . . waiting . . . for the moment when it would show itself and deliver my death blow.

No. No. "Nonsense," he would say and look at me warily, doubting my sanity, as I doubted it on occasion, as I began to doubt it now.

"It was a dream," I said—and to myself, "It *was* a dream. *All* of it."

Accepting my assertion he said, "Shall we take a walk? I shall be leaving shortly to escort my aunts Lockhart back to Witchet Towers. I shall stay there a day or two, then go on to settle some business in London. But before I go I need to talk to you."

We ambled down towards the river. His arm about my waist gave me a warm, safe, protected feeling.

"It's about Alicia and William Morrison."

"If you are going to enlist my help in quashing the romance between them, I'm afraid I shan't be able to oblige," I said quickly. "To me the alliance seems ideal."

"No, I'm not going to do that. If there is any quashing to be done, I shall do it myself. I shall not require help from anyone."

I grimaced to myself. Of course he would not, adept as he was in the art. I had been his victim more than once.

We walked on in silence. The sights and sounds and smells of summer wrapped us round. In the distance the haymakers were at work. I felt blissfully at peace walking by the side of the man I loved. Newman, self-appointed watchman, came into view, touched his forelock, and moved on.

"I tackled him before he left," Charles said, and it took me a moment or two to realize he was talking about William again. "Asked him man to man what his intentions were. I must admit I thought he spoke up honestly and sincerely. Do you think he is sincere, Deborah?"

"I'm sure he is."

"You sound so certain. Yet only a short time ago it was you he was after."

"I've explained all that."

"Yes, but . . ."

"You don't believe me?"

"I — find it difficult to accept that he's not in love with you."

"Oh, Charles," I said with exasperation, "he *isn't*. He never was. But he *is* in love with Alicia — and I believe she is in love with him."

"I wonder if you're right."

"I am."

"He says he wants to marry her."

"There you are, then," I crowed triumphantly.

"But she's such a vulnerable little thing. I'm so afraid she'll get hurt."

"She won't. Not with William."

"Marriage is such a big step. And Alicia's not like an ordinary girl. She needs a deal of looking after. A deal of understanding. You know what she's like . . . can be like . . . why only this morning . . . she wasn't fit to come down to say good-bye to her guests."

"But such attacks are becoming less and less frequent. You've said so yourself."

"Yes, but what young man would willingly take on the responsibility for such an unstable woman?"

"William would."

"She's an heiress and he's not a wealthy man."

"Neither is he a fortune hunter," I returned sharply. He seemed determined to look with disfavor on any union between the two young people. "And he's not poor. He's heir to a great estate and I know he has a fortune, left him by his grandmother in trust which he will be entitled to receive intact when he's twenty-one, less than a year hence. He does not wish to marry Alicia for her money."

"She's never been away from Rosemont."

"Then it's about time she was."

"Oh, Deb, if only it were that simple."

"It is."

He threw back his head and laughed—that deep rich sound I loved to hear and which was so rare. "Oh, my sweet girl, how wonderful you are," he said and drew me into his arms.

Chapter Thirteen

Charles had gone, leaving me with only the memory of his kiss to sustain me through the long days ahead without him. Seven whole days! An eternity.

Alicia had been well enough to leave her room and see her brother off. We had been tentative with each other at first, but soon became inseparable again, and when I asked her if she would be my bridesmaid in company with Elizabeth, she hugged me happily and accepted with tears in her eyes.

Miss Selina continued to argue against my forthcoming marriage. Every now and then she would make some derogatory remark about him, and say it was not too late for me to admit I had made a mistake and change my mind.

I closed my ears against her. Nothing she could say now would shake my faith in him.

With Jonathan it was different.

"I'm going back to London tomorrow," he said after he had sought me out and begged my forgiveness for the things he had said to me. "There's nothing to keep me here now. But I want you to promise me one thing before I go. If you should need me, don't hesitate to send for me."

"Why should I need to send for you?" I asked, suddenly apprehensive.

"Perhaps you won't need to, but promise me anyway."

"Why should I promise? Is there something I don't know? Something to do with Charles? Miss Selina keeps hinting . . ."

He looked away from me quickly and something about his manner disturbed me so, my legs almost gave way.

"What is it?" I cried. "Tell me!"

"I just want you to know you have a friend you can turn to, if the need should arise."

I did not press him further. I was afraid to.

I did not want to think ill of Charles, but, with Miss Selina's detrimental tales about him filling my ears, and the impression that he knew more than he was willing to say left behind by Jonathan, by his return I was doubting him again.

Because of my uncertainties my greeting was reticent and I endeavored by all possible means not to be left alone with him. Towards the end of the day he took me by the arm and piloted me out of the house down to the riverside.

"Now," he said, turning me to face him at the water's edge. "What's wrong?"

"Nothing," I mumbled.

"Then why have you been avoiding me like the plague ever since my return?"

"I haven't."

"Oh, yes you have. Something's troubling you and I want to know what it is." Tucking his hand under my chin he forced me to look up at him. "Come on. Tell me. There should be no secrets between us."

"Are you sure you have no secrets from me?"

"What? What do you mean?" He was suddenly on his guard.

"N-nothing."

"Nothing? Nothing prompted such a question from

223

you? Don't try to pull the wool over my eyes. Someone's been filing your head with tales. I demand to know whom?"

His eyes were hard, his voice rasping. I wished I had kept quiet. My words had roused him to such anger, I was afraid it signified he *had* something to hide which I would not like to hear.

"It doesn't matter," I whispered.

"It matters," he snapped. "Tell me who it was."

He started to shake me.

"Please Charles . . ."

"It was Aunt Selina, wasn't it?"

"Yes, but . . ."

"Don't believe her." His grip tightened urgently on my arm. "Don't believe anything she says about me."

"I don't but . . ."

"But?"

"Well Jonathan said . . ."

He drew in his breath with a hiss. "What did Jonathan say?"

"Just . . . just that your . . . that I . . . He said that I . . . I'm very different from . . . from your . . . from Miranda."

"Is that all? Is that it?"

He was glowering blackly and I knew I had gone too far. I had trespassed on a part of his life he was not prepared to share with me. I expected him to break away from me, leave me standing at the water's edge, our romance at an end.

But he did not. Instead he enfolded me in his arms and kissed me fiercely.

"Oh, my darling girl," he said. "Of course you're different. Completely different. And I thank God for it."

I should have left it at that, but I could not help asking, "Was she very beautiful?"

"You saw for yourself how beautiful she was."

"Did . . . did you love her very much?"

"Very much — at first. But let's not talk about her . . ."

"Do you still?"

His hands dropped to his sides. "What is this, Deborah? Why all the questions? First it was Elizabeth. Now it's Miranda. Are you to be forever wondering about my past, about my love for you? Isn't it enough that I've said I love you?"

It should have been, but it wasn't. Miss Selina's warnings had borne much fruit.

"Very well." His voice fell flatly into the silence. "I should have preferred never to speak of her to you. Stupid, of course — it's only natural you should be curious."

He turned away from me and looked out across the water. Everything went quiet momentarily. Even the birds stopped singing. I remember it all so clearly — the evening sun warming my shoulders through the thin silk of my blouse; the cloud obscuring it briefly causing a shiver to run through me; the sudden splash in the water. A water vole diving in? A woodpecker starting an urgent knocking on the bark of a tree. A blackbird etching his golden notes upon the bars of encroaching night.

"Five years ago — I'd just returned from a voyage to the West Indies — a friend introduced me to the most gorgeous female I had ever set eyes on. Blue eyes, golden hair, the face of an angel. I fell in love with her on sight. Within the year we were married. I gave up going to sea. It was what she wanted — I thought. It was a mistake. If I hadn't, maybe . . ."

He broke off, seemed to wrestle with something inside himself, and continued.

"It didn't last. I strove to make the marriage work for the sake of . . . even after . . ."

Bitterness ravaged his face as he broke off again, and I hated myself for reviving what were obviously very painful memories for him. Immediately my love asserted itself casting out my doubts and fears. What did it matter what his feelings for a dead woman were? It made no difference to the way he felt about me now. And he loved me. He had told me so.

"Don't say anymore," I pleaded, raising my arms to bring his head down to meet mine.

It needed nothing else for him to draw me close. "My love," he whispered. "My dearest love." Then he set me gently away from him. "But I must tell you . . . I have to tell you . . . there are things you have a right to know, then nothing will stand between us."

My lips sought his again. "I don't want to know," I asserted.

And believed what I said.

Whatever had gone wrong with the marriage, it could not have been Charles's fault. Of that I was certain. The cold contemptuous face he showed the world was a facade. It hid a kind, gentle, thoughtful soul, a man of wit and humour. These qualities must have always been there, though I had failed to see them—or acknowledge them. I could hardly believe he was the same man I had met at Hunt Park and been afraid of.

I made a remark to this effect to Miss Selina and she responded darkly. "A leopard can't change his spots."

But I believed he had not changed. It was simply that there was more depth to his character than anyone realized. He did not suffer fools gladly. He had a sharp tongue which he did not scruple to use should the occasion demand it, and admittedly he had a strength and firmness of purpose that led to ruthlessness in his dealings with other people. I had seen evidence of this in his treatment of Jonathan. Though he loved his brother dearly, he was not blind to his shortcomings, and showed

226

no mercy when reprimanding him on his careless attitude towards his work at Rosemont, nor compunction about depriving him of his post as estate manager.

Yet with his sister he was gentle, caring, infinitely patient. With me warm, loving, tender, passionate. With his Aunt Selina respectful, allowing her to run the household as she wished, never interfering, accepting her wounding comments calmly, only losing his temper when her barbs were hurled at Alicia.

Yes, I was discovering many and varied facets of Charles Denton's character.

Jonathan returned to London. I wondered if he would seek out Elizabeth—she was, I knew, paying her annual visit to her Aunt Fanny in Curzon Street. To ensure a meeting I handed him a letter for her with the request that he deliver it at his earliest convenience, and watched him go thinking how wonderful it would be if they could make a match of it. It would be ideal. They had so much in common. Both were sociable and fun-loving.

I began to dream of a double wedding.

A couple of days later Charles followed him on one of his periodic visits to his shipping offices. While he was away, William called to see Alicia. Miss Selina was far from pleased and made her disapproval obvious, but as William had come with Charles's permission, she could not very well turn him away.

Alicia bloomed like a summer rose.

I began to dream of a triple wedding.

I missed Charles desperately and took to going out with only my easel and paints for company, sitting on my little stool at the spot where I had first sat with him, and endeavored to capture Rosemont's beauty in color as I had long wished to do.

Now, it was almost done and I was putting the finishing touches to it ready for his return on the morrow. I drifted away into daydreams about the future. A threatening rumble of distant thunder brought me back with a frown of dismay. Could I finish my painting before the storm came nearer? Was there much left to do? I scanned the painting quickly—and held my breath. A small, white face was staring out at me from the big oriel window.

I shook my head and blinked. I must be seeing things. But there it was—still staring at me.

I could not understand it. There had been no face at the window when I had painted in the leaded panes reflecting the sun—and I could not paint what I did not see. Or had I done it unconsciously? My mind had wandered, after all. There might have been someone looking out whose likeness I had captured without realizing it. That must be the explanation.

But what a face! Small, white, pointed—disembodied.

Thunder rumbled nearer. Great dark clouds were massing overhead. Soon it would rain. Glad of the excuse to pack up my things, I headed back for the house, a strange feeling of unreality upon me. Thunder followed me as I ran and lightning slashed the sky. Great drops of water exploded round my feet and I flew the last few yards.

I tore through the door and slammed it shut behind me just as the rain came down in a sheet. Stopping to regain my breath in the dim and silent hall, my eyes were drawn to an object standing against a wall, an object not usually there, and as it was cast into sudden relief by a flash of lightning, my ragged nerves screeched with terror and I all but turned and ran out again into the storm. The object was a full-length portrait of a young woman standing with one hand on a marble table, the other at her breast.

I recognized the smiling face surrounded by a halo of golden curls at once. It was the face of Miranda, Charles's dead wife.

My heart thumping madly, questions hammered at my brain. What was it doing here? Why had I not seen it before? Had Charles had it placed there? And if so, why?

A sound reached my ears and I looked up the stairs. A wraithlike figure was floating down them. I stood perfectly still, unable to move, unable to cry out.

"You've seen the portrait? Beautiful, isn't it? It's a Sitcairn."

It was Miss Selina, and relief flooded through me as she came to stand at my side.

"He's a genius, is he not?"

A footman appeared with a taper to light the candles in the sconces and my eyes became rivited on the painting. The girl was dressed in a gown of palest blue with a chiffon scarf caught round her neck and floating away behind her like wings—and the gown seemed molded onto living flesh. But it was not that which trapped my breath and stilled my heart, it was the shape of the earrings and brooch she was wearing. They were all made in the shape of a periwinkle flower.

The brooch was identical to the one given me by Alicia; the brooch I had coveted against all my natural instincts; the brooch that I felt held a message for me.

Was this the message then—that it had belonged to Miranda?

As I gazed at her, the girl's blue eyes also seemed to hold a message. Was it that Charles still belonged to her? Was that why he had reacted so strongly when he caught me wearing the brooch? Was he still in love with her?

My heart flinched.

The bright blue eyes seemed to mock me.

It always came down to this. In spite of everything, of all that had happened between us, I was still unsure of Charles.

"It's Miranda, isn't it?" I whispered.

Miss Selina's eyes widened. "You know?"

"I saw a photograph of her once."

"Ah, I see." She smiled up at the lovely face in the portrait as if she smiled at a living person. "That was painted in the first year of her marriage. She was just nineteen. The same age as you."

Ignoring the warning in her voice I murmured. "How beautiful she was. What a pity she had to die so young."

"If she is dead."

Thunder hit the roof of Rosemont as if it would force an entry.

Lightning silvered the hall.

Rain lashed the window panes.

My tongue glued itself to the roof of my mouth.

"I've never been fully convinced the body Charles identified was Miranda's. After all it was months after she went missing . . . and the body had been in the water for a very long time, constantly battered against those vicious rocks along the Devonshire coast . . . They said the face was virtually unrecognizable. Still, he managed to convince the authorities . . . and she did have yellow hair . . . and she had left Rosemont with her bags packed, intending to go to Witchet Towers . . ."

Selina, the portrait, the hall itself, whirled into a spin, sucking me up with them into the spiral of darkness where Miss Selina's voice echoed sepulchrelike, "Only she never reached there."

Only she never reached there.

"My dear, are you all right?" The darkness lifted. I was back in the hall and Miss Selina was searching my face with grave concern. "You look dreadful. It's all my fault. I shouldn't have blurted it out like that, only . . . I didn't realize you didn't know the whole story. I took it for granted when you said you'd seen the photograph that Charles had told you everything."

"He told me she was dead."

"Well, yes, so she is . . . must be."

"Miss Selina!" I grabbed her arm in sudden dread.

Gently she disengaged herself. "Come and sit down, my dear. It must have been quite a shock hearing how she died . . ."

The great front door suddenly burst open and Charles, wet through, hair plastered to his head, entered, smiling ruefully at us, and shook himself like a dog.

"Car broke down half a mile up the road. Couldn't fix it. Had to walk the rest of the way. Can't wait to get into a warm bath, eh, Finch?"

"Not 'alf, m'lord," grinned his valet from behind, equally soaked and carrying a valise. "See to it at once," and bowing to us was away up the stairs.

Then Charles saw the portrait and his face became suffused with rage.

"What's that doing there?" he bellowed. "I told you to get rid of it."

"I couldn't," said Miss Selina. "It's a Sitcairn. A work of art."

"I told you I never wanted to see it again. Destroy it."

Astonishing me by the malevolence of his expression, he lunged at the portrait as if to destroy it there and then with his own hands. Selina screamed to him to leave it alone, and of their own volition my arms reached out to restrain him. Even in my present state, I knew its worth as a work of art and that it should not be destroyed.

His eyes as he turned to face me were the eyes of a madman.

Miss Selina sighed audibly. "If you hadn't come back before you were expected, you wouldn't have seen it. I only had it put there for Deborah's benefit. I knew she would appreciate it being an artist herself. But I'll have it taken back to the cellars immediately if it offends you so."

"And see that it goes in the boiler," he barked, joining

Finch who stood gaping halfway up the stairs.

I accompanied Miss Selina into the drawing room where she rang for Croft, gave him his orders, including that tea be brought within the next half hour. "Now sit down," she said to me when he had departed, "and tell me what you have been doing with yourself this afternoon."

My mind was in a turmoil over what I had just witnessed and I turned to her reprovingly. "Miss Selina, how can you turn aside so easily from what has just occurred? I cannot."

She raised her finely arched eyebrows. "My dear, my nephew is given to outbreaks of temper over the most trivial things. I should have thought you would have found that out by now. I find it pays not to take any notice. You would do well to follow my example if you do not want your nerves in a frazzle."

I was wondering what it was that spilled out of the grave to cause such rage in Charles. Was it hatred, or the fact that he knew the girl he had identified as Miranda was in fact someone else?

It was a frightening possibility, but Miss Selina believed it. Did I?

"Why did the portrait affect him so?" I demanded, wanting to know, yet afraid of the answer.

"Because . . ." Miss Selina paused. "Because he doesn't like to be reminded of her."

Why had she paused? my nerves screamed. There must be something else.

I said, "Was she so hateful?"

"Hateful? No, she wasn't hateful." My heart sank. I had wanted her to be hateful. "Just stupid."

The spite overlaying those final two words stunned me for a moment, so that more questions eluded me.

I listened to the thunder still trying to hammer its way into the house, to the rain battering against the window

232

panes. It seemed they hammered and battered at my heart which only wanted to rest and be at peace—but I had to know more.

"In what way was she stupid?"

"If she'd listened to me," Miss Selina spat, "she wouldn't be where she is now—dead and buried in Devon."

I felt in some way she was unleashing her venom at me for not listening to her. She had cautioned me often enough, heaven knows.

"Let's not talk about it anymore. I find the subject distasteful, and Charles won't thank me for talking to you about her. I saw you leave the house earlier armed with your easel. What have you been painting?"

"The house."

"The house? I should like to see it."

I had not wanted to show it to her, not with the face at the window, but now I thought, why not? It was time for questions and answers. Someone used that room. I thought it was Alicia. She did not, insisting that only the servants ever went in there. But the face I had painted was not the face of Alicia, nor any one of the servants. It was not the face of anyone I knew. I wanted her to see it and admit it.

I handed her my painting.

"Excellent!" she exclaimed. "Excellent! Hello, what's this?"

I had been holding my breath while she looked at it. Perhaps she would not notice the face at the window. Perhaps it was not there. Perhaps it appeared only for me. Now I breathed again.

"So you see it, the face at the window. Who can it be? It's not the face of a servant, she wears no cap. And it's certainly not Alicia, so . . ."

"Oh, Deborah," she chuckled, "you and your imagination. You even paint what you think you see. I believe you really do think we have a ghost in the house."

"It's the only explanation if . . ."

"Rosemont has never had a ghost in its entire history. Why should one appear just for you?"

"I don't know, but . . ."

She sighed wearily and handed the painting back to me. "Put it away and let's talk about something else. Have you named the day yet?"

"What day?"

"Your wedding day. When is it to be?"

"Oh . . . the first week in October."

"That's a bit soon, isn't it?"

"We see no point in waiting."

"Where?"

"Where? In the village church, of course."

She pursed her lips and drew in her breath, shook her head sadly.

"What's the matter? Is there anything against it?"

"Well . . . I'd be only too happy to see you married in St. Martin's, but . . . Have you discussed it with Charles?"

"Not yet."

"Then I should not set my heart on it if I were you. You see, he married Miranda there. I doubt he'll wish to be married there again."

"I don't see why not."

"Oh, my dear, you don't know Charles very well, do you?"

"I know him . . . quite well. I admit I have a lot more to learn about him, just as he has a lot to learn about me. That is something every newly married couple has to face."

"But Charles is such a hard man . . . difficult to understand. He can be extremely cruel." Her eyes looked challengingly into mine as I made to protest. "It's true, however you might like to think it isn't. I think you ought to know that he turned Miranda out of the house when she displeased him — without a qualm of conscience."

"No," I whispered. "I can't believe he'd do that."

"Why do you think she left Rosemont for Witchet Towers? I told her to go there. She had nowhere else to go. But as I have already told you, she never reached there. I'm still not convinced that the girl we buried in Devon was actually Miranda. You see . . . Oh, my dear, you've turned quite pale. I'm upsetting you again. I don't mean to, but I would be failing in my duty if I did not apprise you of all the facts. Take no notice of this foolish fancy of mine. Of course it was Miranda — it must have been."

The arrival of tea coincided with the arrival of Charles and Alicia. His loving smile caressed me as he led his sister to sit beside me. I watched him take up his favorite stance by the fireplace, trying to see in his face the cruelty his aunt insisted was in him. I failed to see it. I saw only a firm strong jaw, the farseeing eyes of a sailor, a tightly held, but not insensitive mouth, and when Miss Selina said, "Deborah tells me you've set your wedding date for the first week in October," and he answered, "Yes, we see no point in waiting," I saw nothing but love and admiration in his glance as he looked at me.

"So she's been telling me," Miss Selina responded sulkily.

We sipped tea and ate dainty cucumber sandwiches followed by rich fruit cake.

"That boy, William Morrison, came while you were away," Miss Selina said suddenly, and I felt Alicia stiffen beside me. "He came to see Alicia. He said he had your permission to do so."

"Yes," said Charles. "I gave him permission to come any time he chose."

"You might have had the courtesy to let me know and

not leave me to find it out from him."

"I thought I had told you."

"Well, if you did, I can't remember. In any case I did not expect him to turn up out of the blue like that — as if he were an old friend. He wanted to take Alicia for a drive with him in the gig. I soon scotched that little plan."

"Why, for heaven's sake?"

"You can ask me that? Would you expect me then to allow my niece — your sister — a girl who has led a completely sheltered life, to go off alone with a hot-headed youth, just because he wishes it?"

"She would have come to no harm with William," I protested on his behalf.

"Mind your own business, Miss," she rounded on me. "He would have upset her, if nothing else. He behaved badly enough when he was staying here."

"He behaved perfectly honorably."

"He could do untold damage. I think, Charles, you should reconsider . . ."

"I shall not withdraw my permission, if that is what you are after, Aunt."

"Well, I must tell you I am not at all pleased about it," she said frostily.

"I'm sorry, but this is my house and Alicia is my ward. In future I intend she shall go where she wants, do what she wants, see whom she wants. I agree with Deborah, she has been kept close for far too long."

The animosity between nephew and aunt — she trying to impose her views on him, he refusing to accept them — had never been more overt. Her eyes sparkled angrily and she rose with all her Norman dignity.

"I can see my counsel counts for nothing with you now, so if you will excuse me, I will retire to my room. I have a great deal of thinking to do and adjustment to make. I am only just beginning to realize that I shall have to take second place to Deborah from now on."

I jumped up to follow her as she went through the door. "I must go to her, Charles. I can't let her think I wish to oust her from her position here."

"But that is what will happen, my darling. As soon as we are married you will be mistress here. Aunt Selina knows this must be. It will be hard for her to accept, but she will do so. Now sit down again and have another cup of tea. I should like one, too."

It was true, of course. As Baroness Denton I would be mistress of Rosemont — but I wished he had not sounded so careless, callous, about the change it would bring to Miss Selina's life.

I poured him his tea and asked Alicia if she would like another cup. She shook her head and rose, signifying her desire to leave. I rose to accompany her, but when we reached the bottom of the stairs she made it clear she wished me to return to Charles in the drawing room. Nothing loathe to do this I watched her mount the stairs and disappear from my sight, then went to join him with fast-beating heart.

We went straight into each other's arms.

Chapter Fourteen

Rain ceased hammering on the window panes. Thunder rumbled only distantly. I stirred in my lover's arms and murmured, "It's passing, the storm."

Mumbling assent his lips traced a pathway over my forehead, my temples, my cheeks.

"It must be nearly time to go and change for dinner," I continued breathlessly.

His lips strayed down the bridge of my nose to my lips, where with gentle persuasion they blinded me once more to the passage of time and stoked up the fire in my blood.

"Five weeks," he murmured. "Five weeks to our wedding day. How shall I be able to wait that long? I should have applied for a Special Licence so that we could be married straight away."

My earlier conversation with Miss Selina thrust its way to the forefront of my mind and I asked with a little shiver of apprehension, "Have you approached the vicar of St. Martin's yet about the reading of the banns?"

Did I sense a stiffening in him as he replied, "You want to be married in St. Martin's?"

"It is the parish church."

"Yes it is. But I was thinking St. Margaret's, Westminster, would be better, then we could spend our wedding night at Lockhart House which would be handy for catching the train to Paris the next morning. However, if you . . ."

"Paris!" I clutched at him excitedly. "Paris! I've always wanted to go to Paris."

He smiled and said, "I got the tickets this morning. We'll spend a fortnight there, then go to Switzerland, and on to Venice. I know how enthralled you were by Jonathan's tales of Venice . . ." he broke off with a smothered oath and gathered me to him. "How can I go on talking to you," he muttered, "when you keep looking at me like that?"

"Isn't it time you two were changing for dinner?"

Miss Selina's sour tones parted us and we rose at once to vacate the room I, at least, rose-hued with embarrassment.

The painting of Miranda was still in the hall facing us.

Charles roared with rage. "Croft!" and when that hapless man arrived flayed him with a glance. "Why hasn't that thing been removed? I ordered you to get rid of it."

"Yes, my lord, but Miss Selina said the morning would do."

"It will not do in the morning. I want it disposed of now. In fact I'll do it myself. Get me an axe."

"An axe, my lord?"

"An axe, Croft. A chopper. The thing that chops wood."

"But . . . my lord . . . You're never going to . . . You can't . . . Miss Selina says it's worth a fortune."

"It's worth a fortune to me to see it in pieces at my feet," said his lordship grimly.

"But you can't mean to destroy it?"

"I shan't rest till I see it go up in flames."

As scandalized as Croft at Charles's intention I laid a hand on his arm. Dearly as I would have loved to see Miranda's lovely face disintegrate beneath his hands, the artist in me could not allow it. It was a Sitcairn. A masterpiece.

"Croft's right," I said. "It's much too valuable. You can't destroy it."

"Can't I?" he snarled. "I'll show you I can. Did you hear me, Croft? Get me an axe. At once."

As Croft scuttled away I pleaded again with Charles. "Don't destroy it. You mustn't. It's a Sitcairn. A work of art."

"If a thing displeases you, you get rid of it, no matter what it is."

"But why . . . like this?"

"Because I hate the sight of it. I hate her. With every breath in my body. I won't have anything connected with her remaining at Rosemont to remind me of . . ."

"The fact you are still in love with her?"

Oh! Why had I said that? I had not meant to. My tongue seemed to pluck the words from the air and utter them without any regard to my wishes.

His look was blank and incredulous, his voice like the hiss of waves breaking on the shore. "Is that what you believe, after all I've said . . . after all we've . . . ?"

"I don't know!" I cried. "I don't know what I believe. I don't even know if I believe she is dead."

Again I had no control over the words that came out of my mouth. I heard myself speak them in utter dismay.

"Take my word for it—she's dead," he grated.

"Miss Selina said the woman you identified was unrecognizable."

"There was no mistaking that golden hair . . ." He turned away from me. "But what does it matter?" His shoulders sagged; there was hopelessness in his voice. "What does anything matter if you can't believe me when I tell you it's you and only you I love? Let it stay then. I can't be bothered with it any more."

"Oh, Charles," I whimpered, reaching out to touch

240

him, to make amends.

He recoiled from me.

"I thought . . ." he said in a voice low and husky, "I really believed . . . you loved me."

"I do! I do!"

"No." He shook his head. "Love that is riddled with doubts is no love at all. If you truly loved me, there would be no room for doubt in your heart."

The tables had been turned. He doubted me now and I could not bear it.

"I do love you. I do. Please believe me. It's just that I'm so mixed up . . . I've heard so many different things . . ."

"And if I told you I was still in love with Miranda? What then?"

A shiver ran down my back.

"I should still love you," I whispered.

"And be willing to marry me?"

"Yes."

He turned to face me again, his expression cold, hostile.

"And you think I would marry you under those circumstances?"

"I don't know," I cried wildly. "I only know I love you, will always love you. My greatest happiness would come from being your wife—if only you would want me."

"Want you!" His hostile expression fled. "Oh, my beloved, if you knew how much . . ."

I was in his arms. Our lips met. I listened to the words he breathed between kisses—"I love you, only you. I couldn't bear to lose you now,"—and my joy knew no bounds.

"I didn't want to destroy the portrait for any reason you could surmise. What can you know of a hate that can sour your soul, your whole life? I hated Miranda like that. I hated her so much it became an obsession, and when I saw her portrait standing there, looking so life-like, it was as if she stood there in person, taunting me in my happiness, I wanted to kill her—*kill* her. But now . . ." he looked back at the portrait and smiled as he went on lightheartedly, "that's all gone . . . because of you. I can look upon her likeness and feel nothing. So let it remain, but in the cellar—in the dark. Let it never see the light of day again. I will have nothing of her anywhere near you, my own sweet, innocent darling."

As I savored these words Croft reappeared bearing the axe he had been sent to find. He held it out to his master with a resentful air, and I smiled to see his astonishment when Charles told him to take it away again.

With our arms about each other, my love and I climbed the stairs.

"What did she do to make you hate her so?" I asked. It was easy to talk to him about her now.

"She poisoned everything she touched," he said. "She was evil. There was something in her that made her want to hurt people, and this she did with assiduous application. She had the looks of an angel, but no heart, no pity. She was greedy, selfish, vain, incorrigibly immoral. She had a constant stream of lovers and cared not who they were or whence they came. Many of my friends were caught in her net. Their marriages wrecked. Remonstrance had no effect on her. She was immune from it.

"I should have divorced her, scandal or no, but there was the family name to consider. She said she was expecting a child. It wasn't mine. With all the lovers she had, it could have been anybody's. So . . . I let her stay. But then something happened that . . . It was the last straw.

"I was walking with Alicia along the river bank . . . I came across Miranda, naked on the grass, making love with one of my tenant farmers. A black rage swept over me like nothing I had ever known. What I would have

242

done if Alicia had not been with me . . . I'd have killed them both. As it was I thanked God for her blindness and hurried her away from the scene and later evicted the man and turned Miranda out of the house. I ordered everything belonging to her to be packed and stacked ready for removal, then I left Rosemont and did not return till I knew she had gone."

"Miss Selina said she went to Witchet Towers."

"Yes."

"But she never reached there."

"No."

"She was drowned. I wonder how it happened?"

"We'll never know."

We had halted at the head of the stairs, but with things still to be said we could not part from each other.

"What I can't understand is why Aunt Selina ignored my specific instructions to have the painting destroyed and had it stored in the cellars instead."

"Perhaps because she recognized its value. It's a Sitcairn after all."

"Yes. But why bring it out for you to see — now? Why fill your head with her nonsensical theories about her death? Why rake up the past like this?"

"Why bother your head about it? Let's not think about it. Let's put Miranda out of our minds, our lives. She's dead. There's no place for her at Rosemont. We have the future to look forward to."

The future meant our marriage to each other.

Arrangements were made for the wedding to take place in London, and from London came dressmakers laden with patterns and materials. An array of colors and textures were set before me that turned me quite dizzy after being accustomed to wearing blacks, browns, and grays for so long. I tried on shoes and gloves and hats. Alicia helped me choose. Her sensitive fingers traced the shapes, caressed the satins and silks; her smiles told me which she liked and advised me to take. I could not fault her choice. All I needed to do was decide on color.

It was a blissfully happy time for me. I felt like Cinderella.

Alicia was happy for me, too, I knew that, yet I still sensed a certain sadness within her. I said to her one day, "You are happy about the wedding, aren't you, Alicia? You know I love Charles with all my heart and that all my life will be dedicated to making him happy?"

She nodded vigorously, but then her teeth came down over her lower lip and a frown creased her lovely brow.

"But something's worrying you, isn't it? What is it? Can't you find a way of letting me know? I might be able to help."

After a moment's pause she went to my dressing table and felt about till she found the little drawer in which I kept my treasures. She knew where it was because I had shown them to her once, letting her fondle them as I described them to her; my father's gold watch, a silver thimble of my aunt's, a crucifix that had belonged to my mother—things I could not bear to part with. To these I had added the periwinkle brooch.

She drew it out and handed it to me.

"Do you want me to wear it?" I asked in some surprise.

I had not worn it since the night Charles had attempted to snatch it from my bodice, and since learning it had belonged to Miranda I had vowed I never would. I wondered now how it had come to be in Alicia's possession. Had she borrowed it from Miranda and forgotten to give it back?

She was flailing her arms about in frustration as she strove to communicate with me. Her lips opened to form a word and I froze into immobility as a small sound issued forth. I could hardly believe I had heard it, and when her mouth snapped shut as a knock came at the door, I was sure I had not.

"Ah, there you are Alicia. I told you she'd be here, Murkett."

Alicia dropped the brooch back into the drawer and closed it at her aunt's entrance into the room. Her face became a blank as she turned round.

"We've been looking everywhere for you. You should not go wandering off without first letting Murkett know where you are going. Really, Alicia, you grow more tiresome with every passing day. This is not the first time you have had the house in an uproar with everybody searching for you."

Miss Selina was exaggerating, as was often the case where Alicia was concerned, and it was having its usual effect on the girl. Her cheeks were drained of color and she was breathing rapidly.

"Alicia's been with me all morning, Miss Selina. It would have been better if Murkett had come and checked before setting the house in an uproar."

I sent the black clad figure hovering behind Miss Selina a frowning glance. She gazed back at me miserably and I knew this was not her doing. It was all Miss Selina's work.

Miss Selina caught hold of Alicia's shoulders and propelled her through the door. "Go with Murkett, my dear. The new gown you are to wear for the wedding has just arrived and you are to try it on before the dressmaker departs."

Alicia half-turned to me. I took her hand. Our plans for her to be my bridesmaid had been thwarted by her aunt. "It would be unwise," she had said—and that had been that. "I'll come with you," I said.

"No." Miss Selina stopped me forcibly with her hand. "You can see it later."

"But why not now?" I demanded. "I'd like to see how Alicia looks in it."

"And I want to show you over the house," she snapped. "You said you wanted to see over every part of it, and I promised I would take you round when I had the time. I have the time now. If you don't take advantage of it, I don't know when I'll find the time again. Besides, you must be made cognizant of the state of the linen and plate. If you are to be mistress here . . ."

Murkett led Alicia away.

"I'll show you the schoolroom first." Miss Selina guided me along the corridor and down the oaken staircase. "I dare say you will be opening it up again soon."

"I — suppose so," I said coloring slightly at the inference. She eyed me obliquely. "I only hope . . . You should have accepted Jonathan, you know. I hoped so much you would. He was in love with you and you let him down."

"I didn't. He knew I felt nothing more for him than friendship. He knew I didn't love him."

Her expression was disbelieving.

"Oh, well, what's done is done. Mind the stairs. They're steep."

She had opened the door I knew led to the cellars.

"This can't be the way to the schoolroom," I cried.

"It's a shortcut to the nursery wing in the North Tower."

"But that's part of the old castle."

"Exactly, and reaching it entails a long trek round the outside of the house or the traversing of innumerable corridors. My heart is not very strong, as you know, I have to take care not to overtire myself." The old familiar whine crept into her voice. "This way is much easier. Just a few steps and . . ."

"But it's a ruin. You warned me against going near it when I explored the grounds."

"Oh, no, no, no. You misunderstood. I told you to be careful. It is crumbling away in parts, but far from

246

ruined. In fact it's remarkably well preserved. Various ancestors of mine, those who saw the need to preserve our heritage, restored it from time to time. My own father was one of that farseeing band. Maybe now that the nursery will come into use again, Charles will bestir himself to action and see that it is fully restored to its former glory."

Refusing to be drawn into argument about Charles again, I thought how strange it was that the nursery wing should have been located so far from the family's main living quarters.

I remarked on this and she replied, "Until children are of an age to mix agreeably in society, it's best they are kept at a distance."

This might be true. But so *far* away? I gave thanks for being brought up in a household where children were not kept so strictly apart from the family and felt sorry for all those past Dentons who had had to spend their childhoods so far removed from their parents and vowed mine should not suffer a similar fate. I would insist on a nursery being set up in the main part of the house that I could visit regularly and with ease.

"Come."

Miss Selina proceeded down the cellar steps and though I could not see much point in looking at a nursery wing I had no intention of using, I could do little but follow her. In any case, it would prove an interesting excursion and one which I would not willingly miss.

She led me past shelves stocked with dried footstuffs of every description. Sacks of flour and potatoes stood on the floor. I was faintly surprised to see the gas lamps lit, then realized Miss Selina had ordered them to be when she decided she had time to show me round.

"As you can see," she said, "it's a veritable storehouse down here. There's a variety of rooms where we keep old furniture, bric-a-brac and suchlike. Most of them are not in use—but this one is. I'll show you."

She tried to open a heavy door which groaned loudly as it moved slightly.

"Let me do it," I cried. It's much too heavy for you."

"Oh, thank you, my dear. I'm afraid I tend to forget I have to take care not to overexert myself. I've lived with this heart murmur of mine for so long now that . . . Oh, Deborah, be careful. There are steps leading down."

I clutched at the hand stretched out to me gratefully as I stumbled, but it was not the steps that had caused my stumble, it was Miranda's portrait standing by the far wall. Caught in the sudden light of the lamps she seemed removed from the frame and her blue gown seemed to swirl as she moved towards us. It was a momentary illusion that set my heart pounding.

I was more than happy to close the door on the lifelike vision in answer to Miss Selina's instruction and follow her lead to the wine cellar. She seemed not to have noticed the portrait, or if she had, deemed it unnecessary to comment upon it.

Sherries, clarets, wines of every description stretched endlessly, row upon row, tier upon tier. Racks full of dusty green and brown bottles stacked over the centuries by the masters of Rosemont.

"These shelves were already full when my father inherited. Some of these brandies go back to Napoleonic days," Miss Selina informed me proudly.

But I was not so concerned with them or the men who had bought them as I was with the whole underground network of passages and rooms beneath this house I lived in and of which I was soon to become mistress. It excited me. Were there any secret passages? I wondered.

"We'll need to take this for the rest of the way."

Miss Selina took a lantern down from a shelf. Its wick was already burning. Then she picked up a large iron key and with this opened a door made out of thick iron bars through which nothing was observable—only thick impenetrable darkness lay beyond.

I followed her in her wake. More steps. More passages. I tried to keep close to her. The swaying lantern cast weird shadows. They mounted the walls and swirled around our feet like fearsome demons.

"Are we still on our way to the nursery wing?" I asked in hushed tones, lest the demons were disturbed and rose to slay us.

"Of course."

Her voice was reassuring.

"It can't be much further, surely?" I said.

"No. We'll soon be there."

The passages grew colder and narrower. Our breath sailed out on the dank air like steam from a kettle. I wished I had picked up a cardigan before embarking on this journey, but I had not realized it would take so long, nor be so cold—and Miss Selina had not suggested I might need one, though I realized now she was wearing one herself.

I caught fleeting glimpses of iron rings attached to the walls linked by rusty chains, large shapes lurking in the shadows—they might be pieces of furniture stored away long ago and forgotten, or old farm implements that outlived their use—or they could be instruments of torture.

We were going through the dungeons.

"Let's not go any further," I urged, my enthusiasm for the excursion waning completely. "I'm so cold."

She did not appear to hear me and continued on her way swinging the lantern so that our own shadows loomed large upon the walls threatening our progress. Then suddenly she stopped and turned to me with a smile.

"Here we are, my dear," she said and my knees almost gave way as I looked into the pale blur of her face.

Where eyes should have been were two bottomless black holes; catching the gleam of lantern light her teeth appeared like fangs.

I told myself not to be so silly and tried to pull myself together as she pushed at the door which I was certain would lead us into brightness again as we entered the nursery wing in the North Tower.

"Help me, will you, my dear," she panted. "It's a bit stiff."

I leant my weight against the door and glimpsed a bare vaultlike place before being projected headlong into turgid gloom. "Miss Selina," I screamed as I fell — and heard the door slam shut behind me.

It was pitch dark.

Terrorstruck, I scrambled to my feet and felt for the door, searching frantically for the handle when I found it. There did not seem to be one. I hammered at the door with my fists and called out.

"Miss Selina! Miss Selina! Help me! The door's jammed. I can't get out."

I received no response.

"MISS SELINA!"

Why didn't she answer? Why didn't she open the door? Did she find it too difficult to open by herself? Had she gone to find someone who could? Had she left me here alone in the darkness where I had fallen without leaving word . . . Fallen? Had I fallen? I remembered feeling a thud in the small of my back. I had been pushed. By whom? Miss Selina? Nonsense!

I started hammering on the door again. Splinters ran into my hands. I hardly noticed the pain.

"Miss Selina, are you there? Miss Selina, answer me."

But could she hear me? The door was thick. Perhaps it muffled all sound. I moaned and started to wail.

Then I heard her voice, faint yet clear.

"Hush, Deborah. Don't take on so. I'm still here."

"Oh, thank goodness. Can't you open the door. Try. Please try. I can do nothing. There's no handle."

"I must go . . ."

"NO!"

"Try to get some sleep. It will be better if you go to sleep. I'm sorry there's no blanket, but you won't be needing one after . . ."

Her voice trailed away.

"Miss Selina. Miss Selina-a-a-a!"

I waited for her response. I heard nothing. Was she still there? Was she playing some ghastly macabre game with me?

I pounded on the door again. My hair lost some of its pins and fell down over my face. I pushed it away impatiently. I felt a warm wetness ooze from my hands to my face. It was blood. I could feel pain now from the splinters which had worked their way into my flesh. I cradled my bleeding hands one inside the other. Oh, why didn't Miss Selina free me?

I started pounding the door again, but found it agonizing for my cut and bleeding hands. I desisted and tried to calm my thudding heart, to consider the situation calmly. There was no point in pounding on the door. Miss Selina knew I was in here. She had not answered my last call, therefore, she must have gone for help. She had said she was going . . . She had told me to be patient — more or less — so patient I must be. It would be a little while before she could bring someone back to rescue me.

Rescue! As the word entered my mind, my heart pumped madly again. Rescue suggested danger. Was I in danger — here? But where was I? How big was this room I was in? Room? I knew it was a dungeon.

Be calm. Be still. Sit down. Don't let anxiety get the better of you. Be patient and sit down. Someone will come — soon.

But I was already sitting down. No, not sitting, huddled in a heap at the door. How had I got into that position? How long had I been here?

Be calm. Be still. Someone will come soon.

I was cold. My fingers were numb. I ached in every limb. Had I been asleep? I had not been aware of falling asleep, yet realized I must have done, when as I tried to rise, I cried out in agony. I felt as if I had been tied up in one position for centuries. Gradually, I forced myself to my knees, then to my feet. With my head swimming, I put my hands out to steady myself against the wall.

The wall! I had been by the door! How had I got by the wall? I panicked and started tracing my way round the wall searching for the door. At last my hands came into contact with wood and I sighed in relief. It was as if I had found a friend.

I leaned wearily against the rough wood and began to whimper like a child. When would somebody come and let me out of this dark and awful place? This cell? This dungeon? I collapsed in a heap on the cold stone floor again.

I slept again. I must have done, because I dreamed. Nightmarish dreams. I was dreaming now. Miranda was with me, smiling across the dungeon floor at me, dressed in her sky-blue gown and . . . Oh! Her face was disintegrating before my eyes. Soon only a skull remained, and as her flesh continued to fall away, a skeleton.

I turned away retching with terror. Then suddenly she was whole again and bending over a trunk. She turned and beckoned to me. Unwilling, but curious, I went to her side. The trunk was full of periwinkle brooches, blue and shining, and as I gazed at them they melted away and Miranda was lying at the bottom of the trunk with her golden hair spread all around her—dead.

But then her eyes opened and they were not eyes at all but flowers, periwinkle flowers, sapphire blue and hard as stones.

I screamed — and awoke. There was no trunk, no Miranda, and I was still huddled beside the door. But had I woken from a dream? It had all seemed so real and I expected to see Miranda again any minute. I knew she was here somewhere in the cell with me.

I fought down a rising panic. Of course she was not here. Of course it had been a dream. I tried to coax some sense into my thinking. I began to work out how long I had been here, how long it would be before someone came to let me out. But how could I tell how much time had passed while I was incarcerated in this dark place? How could I tell if it was day or night?

Panic threatened to engulf me again. Would I ever get out of here?

My eyes were growing used to the dark and I saw now that the cell was not all that big and that it was bare, completely bare. There was nothing to be afraid of here — if I did not fall asleep again.

But how to keep awake? By reciting poetry to myself — and it would help pass the time till my rescue came. I knew Lord Tennyson's "Lady of the Lake" by heart and embarked upon it at once, but before long found I was repeating the same lines over and over again. I started on something else and the same thing happened — so I gave up. Quietly and without fuss I gave up. I knew I would never be released. I would die here.

A blissful sense of relief swept over me as I accepted my fate. Quite calmly I wondered what Charles would do when he couldn't find me. He would be heartbroken, of course, never knowing what had happened to me. His aunt would not tell him. She would tell no one. She would keep it secret to herself. I saw everything plainly now. She had never wanted me to marry Charles, she had wanted me to marry Jonathan, and when I wouldn't, condemned me to die.

Would it be painful to die? I had read somewhere once that it was easy to die of starvation, if you just closed your eyes and went to sleep. Death crept stealthily then to take you away. So I would go to sleep. That was what Miss Selina had told me to do out of some kind of pity.

I closed my eyes and composed myself for sleep—but how could I sleep with all that noise going on?

Noise?

I sat bolt upright. Was I dreaming again? I pinched myself. No, I was not dreaming. There was a noise . . . people talking . . . someone was coming. At last. At last.

"Help!" I called.

Silence.

"Help! I'm in here."

Why didn't they come. I couldn't hear them now. Had they gone?

I called again. "Help! Help! Help!"

It was no use. They had gone. Or it had been a dream after all. Fate playing one of her cruel jokes on me again. I burrowed down into myself in my misery, folded myself up into a ball, in a desperate effort to ease my unhappy soul.

Into my despair came Miss Selina. She came through the black stone wall in garments of shining white.

"Marry Jonathan," she said, "and I will set you free."

"Yes, yes, I'll marry Jonathan," I responded cravenly, holding out my arms in supplication.

But she only laughed and vanished.

Then Jonathan himself stepped out of the shadows, eyes shining with wrathful indignation.

"You should have taken me," he said. "Charles is not for you."

"Let me out, Jonathan. Please let me out. I'm cold . . . so cold."

But he too vanished.

"Deborah. Deborah."

That was Charles calling my name. Was he to be my next visitor and would he vanish as the others had done, impervious to my pleas? Take no notice. Take no notice. Haven't I misery enough?

I felt something pushing at me. It was the door opening. I scrambled out of the way not knowing whether I dreamed or not. There was a blaze of light and I shut my eyes against the sudden glare.

"Deborah. My love. Thank God! Thank God I've found you!"

He caught me to him and I buried my face in the soft wool of his jacket. I clutched at him wildly. If this was an illusion I did not want to lose it.

"My darling. My darling." He was kissing my hair, my closed eyelids, my cheeks and murmuring endearments over and over again. I could hear his heart beating. Was it real? Was it true?

I opened my eyes and looked up into his dear face.

"Oh, Charles, is it really you?"

"Yes, my dearest. I'm here. I have you safe."

I sobbed against his chest. My ordeal was over.

Chapter Fifteen

I was safe. I was warm. I was in bed. The doctor had been and dosed me with laudanum. I was drowsy and holding on to Charles's hand. "No more than a minute or two," the doctor had said, allowing him access to the room on his way out. But I was having none of that.

"Don't leave me," I begged.

"Don't worry. I won't," he promised.

I sighed and relaxed. "You were such a long time coming for me, I began to think you never would."

"I didn't know where you were, my love. I nearly went mad with worry."

"But didn't Miss Selina tell you where I was?"

"No. How could she?"

"Because she knew. She was with me when . . ."

"Oh, Deborah, how can you say such a thing?"

Miss Selina's face came into focus. I had not seen her enter the room with Charles, but she was there standing just behind him looking every bit as concerned as he.

Yet she had not told him where I was.

I started accusingly, "You took me down to the cellars . . ."

"Yes. To see the wines and stores, but we didn't stay there long—with so much else you hadn't seen. You'd always wanted to see the room where Mary, Queen of

Scots, was kept prisoner for a short while so we made our way there. Unfortunately this wretched heart of mine started playing me up and I had to go and lie down. I left you looking at the tapestries . . ."

"I never saw any tapestries . . . We never went to Queen Mary's room . . . We went down to the cellars. You were taking me to see the nursery wing in the North Tower."

"Nursery wing in the North Tower!" she echoed. "Poor girl! The experience has been too much for her. She's raving."

"There's no nursery wing in the North Tower," Charles said gently.

"She said it was a shortcut."

"You must have imagined it. The North Tower has not been used in decades."

They eyed me pityingly. Had I imagined it? Everything? No, not everything. Even with my head growing fuzzy, I knew I had not imagined the happenings of the last few hours. They knew it, too. Why did Miss Selina insist . . . ? What? What did she insist on? Oh, why couldn't I think clearly? A lantern. Yes, there had been a lantern . . . I had followed its wavering light . . . and a key . . .

"There was a key . . . lantern . . . dark passages . . ."

"What's she mumbling about? I can't hear her very well."

That was Miss Selina.

"I think the laudanum's beginning to take effect. She'll be away soon."

That was Charles answering her.

I tried to fight my way through a thickening fog. I had to tell him she had unlocked the door before I forgot.

"The key . . . door . . . she . . ."

But the fog was relentless. It smothered me beneath its gray blanket.

* * *

"How are you feeling, Miss Deborah? Are you better? You did give us all a fright yesterday."

Bright sunshine flooded the room. What was I doing here? What a foolish question. Why shouldn't I be here in my own bed? But how had I come to be here? I had been in a deep dark dungeon. Charles had rescued me. Charles. "Charles!" I called out.

"His lordship's downstairs, Miss. Shall I tell him you're awake? He's been very anxious about you."

"Yes. No. I'll get up and go down to him."

"Do you think you should, Miss?"

"There's nothing wrong with me, Doreen. I'm not ill. I was just exhausted after . . . after . . ."

Doreen bit her lip. "It must have been a dreadful experience for you, Miss Deborah," she said as I stumbled into silence.

A light tap came at the door. Miss Selina in wine moire silk, pearls at her throat and wrists, skimmed the carpet's surface. "My dear, how are you? I've been so worried about you."

She bent to kiss me. I recoiled from her kiss. She had been responsible for my plight and had no right to look at me with such sweet concern.

"I hardly slept all night for thinking about you and considering the awful consequences that might have ensued if Alicia had not discovered you."

I squeaked in surprise. "Alicia discovered me?"

"Well, it was she who led us to you. We'd searched the house, the grounds—even the village. Charles was just about going out of his mind when Alicia came tugging at his sleeve. She was extremely agitated and made it plain she wanted us to follow her. She led us back down to the cellars. We'd already searched them, but she insisted on leading us right through the wine cellars again—and opened the door to the dungeons. We were astonished and mystified to find that it opened. We had not even bothered to try it earlier, knowing Father had had it locked and barred years ago when the boys were little and into every kind of mischief. So afraid was he of them coming to harm in there that he had had the key thrown away. At least that is what everybody believed."

I had seen her take a huge key from the shelf. I had seen her unlock the door.

Or had I? I could not be sure now. She seemed so concerned about me. Could it be possible I had imagined her with me when in fact I had been alone?

"You must have been terrified down there all alone in the dark."

"Yes. Terrified. I thought I was going to die."

Miss Selina shuddered. "Don't think about it anymore, my dear. It's too terrible to contemplate. It's all over now. Nothing like that will ever happen again. I'll see the greatest care is taken of you from now on. But how pale you look. Go and bring your mistress something to eat, Wicks. Something good and nourishing to build up her strength. We can't have her looking pale and drawn on her wedding day, can we?"

Doreen sped away and must have informed Charles that I was awake, for within the space of a minute or two he was at my bedside.

Kissing me and embracing me tightly he said with mock severity, "Never do that to me again, young lady. I could never live through another day like yesterday."

"I was just telling Deborah that if it had not been for Alicia we should never have known where she was."

"You knew, Miss Selina."

Miss Selina gasped, and I gasped as I made my accusation. Nevertheless, I continued. "You were in the cellars with me. You took a lantern down from a shelf . . . and a key . . . you unlocked the door . . . and shut me up in the dungeon."

"Deborah!" Charles expostulated. "You mustn't keep repeating such a wild accusation. It's preposterous! Aunt Selina was in bed all afternoon—Lister can vouch for it. She was mortified when she heard you were nowhere to be found. I'm sorry, Aunt Selina, you can see she is still very much distrait."

"No, don't apologize for her, Charles." Miss Selina eyed me coldly. "I've gone out of my way to make allowances for you, even to supposing you must have banged your head against something that caused you to think such uncharitable thoughts, but this is too much. I know you have a vivid imagination and enjoy exploring, but that you should involve me in your wild escapades, and blame me for them when they go wrong, is more than I can tolerate. I suppose you went looking for ghosts," she added sneeringly. "Did you find any?"

"Yes, I . . ."

"Oh, Deborah!" She turned away from me in disgust. "I think her incarceration has unhinged her mind, Charles."

"If so, you caused it," I cried.

"Darling, stop it," Charles said hastily. "Can't you see how much you've hurt Aunt Selina?"

"But she shut me up in a dungeon!"

"No. She didn't." He was trying to hold on to his patience with me. I could see it was difficult. "For heavens' sake, see the truth of it. You went exploring, found the key, and shut yourself up in the dungeon."

"I didn't . . . I never . . . at least . . . perhaps I did . . . Oh, I'm so confused. I was so sure . . . now . . . I'm not." Looking back I saw myself taking the key down from the shelf, taking the lantern in my hand, and holding it high to light my way along the dark dank passages. I *had* been exploring and locked myself in the dungeon for my pains. *And I had blamed Miss Selina for it*. "Oh,

260

Charles," I whispered fearfully, "I think I must be going mad."

"No, my love," he fell to his knees and enclosed me in his arms again. "You've had a bad experience . . . shut up alone . . . in the dark. It's bound to have had a disturbing effect on your mind. But it won't last. You'll soon forget all about it."

"Oh, I hope so. It was terrible . . . so dark . . . I was so afraid."

"Of course you were, my dear." Miss Selina turned back to me in quick sympathy. "Please forgive me for being so tetchy. I should have shown more understanding."

"It is for me to beg your forgiveness, Miss Selina," I said humbly. "How I could ever think you capable of . . . You and Charles are right, I have become so disoriented in my mind through my incarceration, I hardly know what is real and what is not."

"This is real, my sweet—you in my arms and surrounded by those who love you," said Charles.

"Yes," smiled Miss Selina, "remember we all love you and wish only for your happiness."

Doreen came in with a tray of food. There was the appetizing aroma of freshly made coffee and at sight of the pile of fluffy scrambled eggs on a plate with snippets of mushroom and bacon attendant upon it, I knew how hungry I was and fell to with will. Miss Selina departed, but Charles stayed and joined me in a cup of coffee.

"Feel better?" he asked as finishing my repast I fell back luxuriating in satisfaction against my pillows.

"Yes. Much."

"Foolish notions all gone?"

"Yes."

"Good."

We laughed together then I sprang forward.

"I think I'll get up now," I cried.

261

"No you won't," he said lightly. "Aunt Selina thinks you ought to stay in bed for the rest of the day and I am in total agreement with her."

"Pooh. I feel fine. Now go away and let me get dressed."

"Am I to understand that I am contracted to marry a woman who will be disobedient to her husband's wishes?"

"Only in some things, small things, I promise you," I laughed at his show of mock dismay. "Now go away and let . . ."

Doreen interrupted us.

"Master Jonathan to see you, Miss Deborah."

"Jonathan! How lovely to see you! I didn't know you were here!"

"I've only just arrived. Hello, Charles." The brothers shook hands. "What's all this I hear about you being locked in a dungeon?" He turned to kiss me. "Aunt Selina was full of it."

"Oh, it's nothing," I laughed, surprised at myself for being so lighthearted about it. "I stupidly went exploring by myself and got lost, that's all."

"You call being locked in a dungeon for hours nothing? You're taking it all very calmly, I must say."

"It's taken time," Charles said. "She was in a dreadful state earlier on."

"I bet!"

She had us all scared out of our wits. We didn't know where she was. It took us the best part of nine hours before we found her."

"And then it was Alicia who led them to me. She must have had a sixth sense or something."

"Yes," Jonathan said, "she can often sense things others can't. I think it's a kind of compensation. But how did you get through to the dungeons? They were sealed off years ago, weren't they Charles?"

262

"I always thought so. Father had the entrance locked and the key hidden or thrown away when we were nippers. We were always playing hide and seek down there and he thought it dangerous. Is it possible Father's orders were disobeyed? I've never bothered to check."

"Who would have dared disobey Father's orders?"

Charles shrugged. "Who, indeed?"

"Charles." Jonathan laid his hand on his brother's arm with a quick sudden urgency. "I must talk to you."

"Certainly old chap. What about?"

A swish of skirts heralded Miss Selina's entry into the room.

"I thought I'd find you here," she said, looking at Jonathan.

Jonathan's hand fell from his brother's arm. "Never mind," he said softly. "It doesn't matter."

As he turned to his aunt his eyes were bleak.

Something was troubling Jonathan. I did not know if he discussed it with Charles. I did not concern myself about it once I was up. I became too wrapped up in preparing for my wedding day.

The wedding went off without a hitch. In fact, it all went too smoothly, according to Miss Selina, as if it boded ill.

The day was bright and golden as only an October day can be. I wore a creamy gown trimmed with gold lace and a veil kept in place by a coronet of orange blossom. That was the something new in the old saw: Something old, something new, something borrowed, something blue—which all brides paid tribute to and I was no exception. The old was my prayer book given me by my father when I was a little girl. The borrowed was a

handkerchief loaned by Alicia. The blue was the periwin
kle brooch which I wore concealed under a flounce o
lace at my breast. I do not know what evil genius sat o
my shoulder when I pinned it there; I only know tha
when my eyes fell upon it as I looked for somethin
blue, the impulse to wear it had been too great to resist

Charles and I stepped out of the church with th
strains of Mendelssohn's Wedding March in our ears
wreathed in smiles. Congratulations were poured upo
us. We were photographed by one of Jonathan'
friends—Jonathan was, of course, Charles's best man—
who would take other, more formal ones later, the
under an onslaught of rice and confetti, Charles tucke
his arm through mine and piloted me to the carriag
waiting to drive us back to Denton House where th
wedding reception was being held.

It had been by Miss Selina's request that Dento
House, closed for a number of years, had been opene
up and refurbished. "You and Jon may stay at Lockhar
House," she had said. "Alicia, Deborah, and I will sta
at Denton House. It is not fitting that a bride an
groom-to-be should live under the same roof, days befor
the wedding." Charles and I had smiled in amusement a
each other—we had been living under the same roof fo
a very long time now—but he had bowed to his aunt'
wishes without demur.

My heart had fluttered unbearably as I entered th
church and saw Charles waiting for me to join him a
the altar; now, as I stood beside him greeting our guest
in the high-ceilinged, white-pillared ballroom hung wit
mirrors and crystal chandeliers, it soared till I thought i
would burst from my breast with happiness.

I could not forbear looking at him with love an
pride. He was so tall and handsome. How could I eve
have thought him less than handsome? Why, he was th
handsomest man in the room. And he was my husband

264

I was his wife. Now and for always.

Why did I feel a sudden chill of foreboding?

Was I too happy? Was Fate, jealous of my happiness, seeking to blunt it?

It was only a temporary chill. Nothing could blight my happiness for long on this day of all days; not even Miss Selina's ill-concealed resentment as she wished me every happiness; not even Mrs. Morrison's muttered, "So you are Baroness Denton at last. I hope you won't be disappointed, as his lordship's first wife was." I knew it was said out of spite. She had not forgiven me for usurping, as she termed it, Elizabeth in his affections. Even now, when it was obvious Elizabeth had no regrets and that her heart was set elsewhere — her adoring eyes followed Jonathan about wherever he went — she could not withold hurtful comment.

But all this passed me by. With Charles at my side, his smiles falling upon me every now and again, his eyes alight with love, I was aware only of him and our love for each other.

However, when Jonathan took me aside and urged me to "Be happy. Don't let anyone come between you and your happiness," I confess to a feeling of slight alarm.

Then it was time for the guests to depart. Miss Selina and Alicia, who were to be escorted back to Rosemont by Jonathan, were the last to leave.

Then everyone was gone.

Charles and I were left alone.

Just Charles and me standing amidst the chaos of food and wine.

Charles turned to me, desire in his eyes, the intensity of which brought color flooding to my cheeks. He drew me to him and kissed me sweetly, gently, then picked me up in his arms and carried me up the wide winding staircase to the room we were to share together.

Once inside he locked the door. I smiled shyly at him,

then looked quickly down at my feet as his eyes sent hot irons to scorch my skin. Then his arms were round me and he was kissing me again, not as he had done earlier, but crushingly with a passion that frightened me. I already knew him for a man with strong passions, but they had always been tightly controlled, now as they were unleashed, I suddenly realized what marriage to such a man would mean. Such a man would make passionate demands. Was I woman enough for him?

His fingers ranged through my hair undoing the pins that kept it in place till it fell down to my waist, then they slid down to unbotton my dress and I submitted, frightened, but deliciously so. I knew this was not at all as it should be—it was only half past four in the afternoon. What would the servants think? Their master and mistress closeted together in their bedroom in the daytime hours! But there was an urgency about him and I was powerless to resist. My own passions blazed and I kissed him with as much ardor as he kissed me, eagerly awaiting that which was to come.

Then his hand fell upon the periwinkle brooch.

Oh, fool that I was! Why had I not removed it sooner? Why had I worn it at all?

Too late I questioned myself. I tried to speak. To explain. But how could it be explained—even to myself?

He raised his eyes to mine. I quailed beneath the scorn in them. His lips bared his teeth in a terrible sneer and with an angry cry he thrust me from him—and was gone.

He was gone and I stared at the door left wide open as he went, longing to call him back, but uttering no sound, longing to run after him, but remaining where I was. I had done the unforgivable in wearing the brooch that had belonged to Miranda—and on our wedding day. I knew I would never be able to repair the damage I had done.

I heard the front door bang. It brought me to with a jerk. I rushed to peer over the banister. "Charles! Charles!" But he had gone. He had left me on my wedding day. And I could blame no one but myself.

No *one,* but some *thing.* The periwinkle brooch. The periwinkle brooch was to blame.

I tore it from my gown and dashed it to the floor. It was evil, inhabited by an evil spirit that wanted my unhappiness. What had Jonathan said to me? *Don't let anything come between you and your happiness.* I had laughed and said, *I won't.* But I had. I had allowed this evil thing to come between me and the man I loved. There it sat on the carpet winking at me, unheedful of the tears scorching down my face. I stared at it with hate—that foul thing that seemed to be alive, that seemed to possess a life of its own, that propelled me to do things against my will. And with groans dredged from my innermost being tearing me apart, I slid to the floor grasping at the stair rails for support and thought my heart would break.

"Miss Deborah . . . my lady . . . whatever is the matter?"

Doreen, the little frightened serving girl who had become my friend, slid to the ground beside me and enclosed me in her arms.

"Oh, don't take on so. You'll make yourself ill."

"He's gone, Doreen. He's gone," I moaned. "Charles has gone."

"Well, he can't have gone far. He'll be back soon. There's no cause for you to . . ."

"No, you don't understand. He's gone and he's never coming back."

"Nonsense!" she said taking on the role of a Nanny with a recalcitrant child. "You're overwrought, my lady. You've had a tiring day. You were up before dawn. I said you should have had another hour or two in bed." Her glance caught the periwinkle brooch lying on the carpet. Without questioning me about it she picked it up and put it in her pocket. "Come along, I'll help you change. His lordship will be back, never fear."

I believed her because I wanted to believe her, and allowed her to lead me back to the bedroom where she picked up my veil from the spot where it had fallen and divested me of my wedding gown. She garbed me in soft blue velvet and pinned my hair back into position, fastened a strand of pearls—a gift from Miss Selina—round my neck and pronounced me ready.

I went to the drawing room to await my husband's return. I sat with a book in my hands, but turned not a single page. I listened to the servants dismantling the evidence of earlier feasting.

The hours went by.

I stood by the tall windows looking out at the traffic in the street below, but searching, searching all the while for the tall handsome figure of the man I had married— how long ago? It seemed an age.

Dinner was served to me. It was removed uneaten despite Doreen's adjurements.

And still he did not come.

I knew he would not come.

The hour was late. The servants had all gone to bed, all except Doreen, dear faithful Doreen, who was as tired as any of them. I told her to go to bed.

"I don't like to leave you, Miss D—my lady," she said.

So in order that she should get some sleep, I said I would go to bed, too.

She had laid out my nightgown—my beautiful new white silk nightgown with the forget-me-nots and rosebuds embroidered on the bodice and round the hem. A lump came to my throat as I saw it and I could not control the tears that rolled down my cheeks as I put it on. It was my wedding night and my husband had left me to spend it alone. He would never come back to me. Through my own stupidity I had lost him. I would never smile again.

I wept long into my pillows and found no relief from the awful, aching emptiness inside. This was how it would be now—a continuing void stretching to my life's end. I heard a distant clock strike the hour, every hour, right through the night and not once did I sink into the blessed oblivion of sleep, but lay staring into the darkness bitterly, despairingly, self-condemningly unhappy. I became aware of the servants starting about their business, of cabs trundling through the streets, of vendors crying their wares. Another day had dawned.

"Good morning, my lady."

Doreen swept back the curtains onto a gray and gloomy aspect. Rain was trickling silently down the window panes. A fitting start to my life as an unloved wife.

"Lucy's bringing your breakfast up. His lordship's already had his."

"What?" I sat up suddenly as if released by a spring.

She smiled with a slightly self-conscious air, as if she did not wish to appear too knowing. "He asked me to let you lie in for as long as possible—but the train leaves at half past ten, so . . ."

I hardly heard her. He was back! He was back! I wanted to rush downstairs and throw myself into his arms, beg his forgiveness—but common sense restrained me. He had come back not for love of me, but for appearance' sake. He had made it appear to Doreen as if we had spent the night together. But we had not. I did not know what time he had come back, but whatever time it was, it had not been to claim me as my beloved bride.

I bathed and dressed, gulped down a cup of coffee, and sent the food away untasted. There was no joy in me at Charles's return. He had come back, but not to me.

He had come back for duty's sake, not for love's. We would go away together—on our honeymoon—but it would mean nothing to him. Nothing.

The periwinkle brooch was sitting on my dressing table where Doreen had placed it—strange she had not returned it to its box—and it was winking up at me as if it were amused by the events it had been responsible for. In sudden anger I raised an arm and swept it to the floor. It dropped at the foot of the bed. I kicked it savagely underneath and left it there.

Charles came forward to greet me. He was spruce and smart, but unsmiling. I thought I detected a certain wariness about him. Was he afraid I would make a scene?

I responded calmly and with dignity. "Good morning, Charles."

He seemed to breathe with relief.

"You look very nice," he said, eyeing my dark blue suit with its sable collar and matching hat appreciatively.

His lips brushed my cheek. I stiffened and stepped quickly back from him. A frown of annoyance crossed his face. What did he expect of me? I knew it was done for the benefit of the watching servants, but it was a game I found difficult to play. He placed his hand firmly under my elbow and led me to the waiting carriage.

"Are you warm enough?" he asked after tucking a fur rug round my knees. "It's very cold this morning."

"Yes, thank you," I said stiffening again and drawing further into the corner as he sat beside me.

He frowned, drew back into his corner, and lapsed into silence.

I remembered being with him in another carriage driving back from King's Lynn. We had sat apart then, but been drawn together by a compulsive bond of love. That bond no longer existed. The clip-clop of the horses hooves on the cobblestones and the cries of the flower sellers and other such faded as I withdrew into a private world of grief.

"We're here."

Charles brought me back to the bustle of London life and helped me down from the carriage. Finch and Doreen were waiting for us. They had left early to see to the luggage and locate our reserved compartment. As we commenced to follow them along the crowded platform, Charles put his arm through mine, guiding me with all the care of a seemingly loving and solicitous husband. All show. All for appearance' sake.

Once we were settled in our compartment, the servants left to take up their own seats further down the train. They had provided a pile of newspapers and magazines for us to read. I picked one up and pretended to read it.

Charles sat opposite me in silence for a few minutes, then he rose and excused himself. A moment later I saw him striding off along the platform and panicked. Was he leaving me again? But then he was striding back again and presenting me with a large box of chocolates.

"Your favorites," he said.

He was playing the solicitous husband remarkably well.

I thanked him and set them down on the seat beside me.

"I could change them if you would prefer something else," he said.

"No, thank you. There is no need."

He was observing me closely. I picked up the box and opened it, held it out to him.

"Perhaps you'd like one," I said.

He shook his head, frowning irritably. Was he annoyed that I showed so little interest in his gift?

Perhaps I should eat one. I looked down at the confectionery attractively set out. Some had sugared violet petals decorating them, some rose-colored geraniums. Others were wrapped around in gold and silver paper, and one or two in little ridged paper cups. But I was gorged on misery and set them aside.

He buried himself in a newspaper. I tried to concentrate on my magazine. The words blurred and ran together. I looked out of the window at the passing countryside. I saw little of it. The windows were smeared with raindrops — or was it the tears in my eyes making them appear so?

We pulled into Dover and boarded the cross-channel steamer. It was a rough crossing, but, as Charles had once told me, I was a good sailor and I adapted to the pitch and toss of the ship with ease. Doreen, however, suffered badly, and though I felt sorry for her, I was glad of the opportunity it gave me to remain by her side in her cabin and so obtain respite from trying to keep up appearances with Charles.

The train journey from Calais to Paris put a further strain on me. I had deliberately thrust away thoughts of what would happen at the end of our journey, but now they came crowding in on me, making me edgy and less than polite with Charles, who was correct in every way. He made many attempts at conversation in spite of my lack of response and bowed to my request for silence when I complained of a headache.

It was no lie. I did have a headache. And the nearer we got to Paris the more it developed.

Questions ran round my brain over and over again. Would we share the same room? Would we share the same bed? Would he consummate our marriage? Would I be able to bear it, knowing he did so only because convention demanded it, because he needed to produce an heir, even one born of a loveless marriage — at least on his part? Or would he demand a separate room for himself? Perhaps he had no intention of consummating our marriage. If he could walk away from me on our wedding night with so little concern, he would find it no problem to stay away from me altogether. But if he did share my bed—with my pride so much less than my love for him—what would I do? What would I do?

We reached Paris later that same night.

Charles had booked a suite of rooms and made no demur when the manager of the hotel bowed and scraped his way before us as he escorted us to them himself.

The manager departed after assuring us a great many times that he was at our disposal, and that nothing we might require would prove too great a task for him or his staff to provide, and as he left, Finch and Doreen, whose rooms were nearby, presented themselves for service.

Charles shut the door on them saying, "We'll ring when we want you."

We were on our own and I was afraid. "I wish you hadn't turned them away," I said starchily. "I need Doreen to help me . . ."

"Deborah, how much longer do you intend to keep this up?"

"I don't know what you mean."

I turned my back on him to hide my trembling. He caught me savagely by the arm and swung me round to face him.

"You know damn well what I mean," he cried. "Oh, Deborah, I can't stand any more of this. I've never known you so cold. I know I've hurt you and I'm sorry. I've been trying to tell you I'm sorry all day—trying to make amends—"

"You can never make amends for what you did," I said hoarsely, trying to hold on to my pride, yet all the time knowing my defences were crumbling.

"No. It was a terrible thing I did. You have every right to hate me. I can only hope one day you'll find it in your heart to forgive me. I swear I never meant to hurt you."

"Yet you left me alone on our wedding night. Why?"

273

"It was that damned brooch. I thought I'd got over such feelings, but when I came across it . . . nestling against your breast . . . on our wedding day . . . I saw red. I thought . . . I thought . . . I don't know what I thought. I only knew I had to get away from it, from you, from Miranda."

"I knew I shouldn't have worn it," I moaned, "but I thought I'd have removed it before . . . and it was only a brooch."

"Only a brooch! It was my wedding gift to her—Miranda. That and a pair of matching earrings . . . They had belonged to my mother and I wanted my wife to have them . . . My wife . . . Miranda . . ."

He broke off and started pacing the room as if the thought were too bitter to accommodate. Then he continued.

"I should never have given them to her. She was not worthy of them. My mother was a lady renowned for her virtue and integrity while *she* . . . I was foolish enough to tell her so once and she wore them every day after that. Morning, noon, and night she wore the damned things . . . I thought she had taken them with her when she left. I was glad. Though they had belonged to my mother, I never wanted to lay eyes on them again. And then I saw you wearing the brooch at Alicia's ball. Remember? I couldn't believe my eyes. It was as if she had come back to mock me for loving you. I wanted to rip it from your dress and crush it beneath my heel—as I would have liked to crush her. And then to see you wearing it again after you knew . . . after I'd told you how I felt about her . . . I just had to get away.

"I walked for miles, for hours, before I could see straight and realize what I had done. It broke my heart to think how I must have hurt you. I hurried back . . . longing for you . . . hoping you would understand . . . afraid you would not . . ."

"You came back—last night?"

"Yes. But you were so peacefully sleeping, I hadn't the heart to wake you."

"I wasn't asleep. I was awake all night."

"You were asleep when I saw you. And in a way I felt resentful—that you could sleep when—"

"I can't believe it, but if I was, it must have been only momentary, for I counted the hours as they chimed, waiting, hoping, longing for you . . . Oh, Charles."

I was in his arms. They were strong about me, his kisses warm and sweet.

"Oh, my dearest, my darling, forgive me," he whispered against my cheeks. "I love you so much. I would never deliberately cause you pain."

We clung together and this time there was no brooch to impede his ardor as he lifted me unresisting in his arms and carried me into the bedroom.

Chapter Sixteen

Paris!

City of dreams! City of lovers!

Charles and I loved and dreamed beneath the Parisian skies.

There had never been two people more in love than we, no two people happier.

Were we too happy? Was Fate waiting in the wings to snatch our happiness from us?

Such questions never crossed our minds.

Delighting in each other and the beauties of the city, by day we strolled down the Champs Elysees, walked in the Tuileries Gardens, ascended the dizzy heights of the Eiffel Tower. We sailed down the Seine and visited the Louvre Museum, marvelled at the great Cathedral of Notre Dame, and admired the startling white beauty of the Sacre Coeur. All was new to me if not to Charles, and I wanted to see everything. We spent our evenings at concerts, the Opera, and the Theatre and at night . . . At night we entered the realms of ecstasy.

Venice!

Nothing had prepared me for the magic that is Venice.

Jonathan had described it to me. I had seen his photographs of it. I had seen Canaletto paintings. I knew I was coming to a beautiful and exotic place. I did not expect to step into a fairyland of indescribable beauty. For Venice is a fairy tale. A haunting, mystical, magical place. Nothing can evoke the true quality of Venice but Venice herself.

Charles, for all his travels, had never reached this northern Italian shore, and we were able to discover and enjoy its many beauties together.

And so our honeymoon continued from delight to delight, from discovery to discovery—and so it would be, I thought, throughout our entire lives.

As the day for our departure drew near, I sighed deeply. "If only we didn't have to go back so soon. I love it here so. I love Venice. I love Italy. I love the Italian people."

A little after that Charles went out by himself, which surprised me for he never went anywhere without me. On his return he said with studied carelessness, "Oh, by the way, I've rented a villa in the Primavera Valley for a couple of months . . . What do you say to that?"

"Charles!" I threw myself at him. "Oh, my darling! How wonderful! Winter in the Dolomites," he swung me round in the air laughing at my enthusiasm, "with you."

Our lips met and clung. I was breathless when he put me down.

And so we sent a cable to Miss Selina—Aunt Selina, as I should call her now—telling her not to expect us back till the New Year, and settled down amidst the mountains gradually turning from gray to white as the snows fell, blissfully happy, growing closer as each day passed.

We made friends with the local inhabitants, a cheerful, volatile bunch who took us to their hearts and welcomed us into their homes. We skied and sledged beneath a deep blue sky over dazzling white sweeps of mountainside, where I expected every minute to meet Santa Claus himself with his reindeer and huge bag of toys.

But as Christmas gave way to the New Year, and January progressed, I began to long for home, for Rosemont, and the wide East Anglian skies. I began to feel a queasy kind of unease, grew edgy, and sometimes short-tempered. Charles diagnosed homesickness and booked passage back to England.

Rosemont. Rosemont. Rosemont. How I longed to be

there—hungered to be there. The Dolomites of Northern Italy were great and grand, the Primavera Valley beautiful, its people good and kind, the villa lovely and luxurious, but their charm palled now. It was Rosemont I yearned for and the East Anglian countryside, where no mountain soared to reach the wide open skies and the light was crystal clear.

I gazed out of the train window at the bleak wet sodden fields on the way to St Martinsbury and felt my spirits revive. And when Rosemont met my eyes through pouring rain I could not withhold my tears of joy.

Charles's arm went around me. "Home, my love," he said and I, turning to him in love, echoed, "Home."

Why, when I loved Rosemont so, did it harbor such disappointment for me? Lurking in the background was ever and always that something to cast a blight over my happiness. It was rising even now, though I did not know it as I entered the familiar stone-flagged hall, to ruin my homecoming. I was aware only of the pleasure of being greeted lovingly by my new aunt and sister-in-law.

"Come," said Aunt Selina turning to mount the stairs. "I've prepared your room. You'll wish to change before dinner and maybe rest a little. Take your time. I'll delay dinner till you are ready."

I had given little thought to the room Charles and I would occupy at Rosemont, thinking vaguely it might be either of the rooms we were used to occupying, and my heart turned over when she stopped outside the guarded door of the room that was always kept locked and threw it open.

For the first time I saw what lay behind that great oak door.

I stood on the threshhold transfixed. Everything was white. White carpet. White counterpane. White curtains. White furniture. Even the old oak panelling had been painted white. It was a cold snow-room and I started to shiver.

"Why has this room been opened up?" I heard Charles grate hoarsely above my ear. "I left no orders for it."

Miss Selina said softly, "I took it for granted you would wish the Master Bedroom . . ." but her explanation was cut short by an explosion of anger.

"You take too much for granted. You always have. I've excused it in the past, but this time you've gone too far. Things will change now that Deborah is mistress of Rosemont. Come, Deborah," he caught hold of my arm and began striding away with me down the corridor, "we'll use my room for the present. Later we'll choose together which room we will share."

"But I've had all your things packed ready to move in here," she called out after him.

"Then have them unpacked again," he growled, opening the door of his old room and thrusting me through it. "And let's have a fire in here. It's like an ice box."

He banged the door shut behind him and stalked across the room to stand with his hands gripping the mantelpiece, staring into the fireplace with its flameless logs supine in the hearth. He was in a foul temper, breathing heavily, shoulders tense — I had not seen him like this for weeks and I was frightened.

In an effort to calm him I went to place a hand on his arm and whisper, "Don't let it upset you so, Charles," and drew back, catching my breath as he turned to look at me with glazed eyes, as if for a moment he did not know who I was.

But then his eyes softened and he drew me to him with a little groan. "Oh, Deborah, my precious, precious darling. I wouldn't have inflicted that on you for the world. I don't know what can have induced my aunt to think I wish to use that room again . . . to share it with you . . ."

"It was the room you shared with Miranda, wasn't it?"

I had known it the moment I looked into it.

"Yes."

He tensed again as he spoke and let me go. He began pacing the room like a chained tiger. And continued.

"I gave orders for it to be striped bare and locked, never to be opened again. I thought my orders had been obeyed. I never checked. I never wanted to see it again. Then to see it suddenly like that . . . just as it had always been . . . cold, uninviting, heartless . . . and you trembling on the threshold . . . and Aunt Selina expecting you to enter . . . I saw red. I could have killed her."

He thrust his fist into his palm with a loud resounding smack. "Why did she do it? Why?"

Black despairing rage contorted his features, as it had done when he had been confronted by Miranda's portrait in the hall. I feared it, feared his hatred of Miranda, of the effect it had on him.

"Why did she disobey my orders? Why has she kept that room just as Miranda furnished it . . . and the portrait . . . even the brooch which she gave to you?"

"She didn't give me the brooch," I murmured. "Alicia did."

"What?" He gazed at me in disbelief. "She can't have."

"She did. I hesitated about accepting it. I could see it was valuable. But she became so upset when I refused it that I . . ."

"But how did it come to be in her possession?"

"I don't know. Perhaps Miranda gave it to her before she left."

"Yes, that could be it," he mused. "It's just the sort of thing that would appeal to her warped sense of humor. It would delight her to think of Alicia wearing it, reminding me of her."

"But Alicia never wore it. You never saw it till I came and she gave it to me."

"It could be she never wore it when I was around—knowing how I felt about anything connected with Miranda."

"Then why did she give it to me? I didn't know about you

280

feelings regarding Miranda then, and she must have known I would wear it—possibly at a time when you would see it, as indeed I did."

"Yes. It's strange. She's not usually so insensitive."

He caught me to him suddenly.

"Never wear it again," he said urgently. "Promise me you'll never wear it again."

"I won't," I promised. "I've worn it twice and each time it's brought us unhappiness. I shall never wear it again."

As he kissed me I made a mental note—for I knew when it was found under the bed at Denton House it would be returned to me—to sell it at the earliest opportunity and give the proceeds to charity—that way it would serve some useful purpose in the world.

Yet at the same time I could not help thinking it a shame to have to sell something that had belonged to his mother. If only he had not given it to Miranda. Miranda's portrait rose to my mind's eye with the periwinkle brooch glinting at her breast, the matching earrings . . .

Matching earrings!

"I wonder what happened to the matching earrings," I heard myself say.

He held me away from him. "Does it matter?"

"Was she wearing them when . . . when you . . . ?"

"No."

He turned from me abruptly. So that I should not see what was in his eyes?

What had put such a thought into my mind? All this talk about the periwinkle brooch? The portrait? Why had Miss Selina kept the portrait, Miranda's room as it was? Because she believed Miranda was still alive? She had hinted as much to me. Did she expect her to return one day?

Did Charles?

Was that why he reacted so strongly to everything reminding him of her?

No! No! Miranda was dead! She could not return!

But what if the girl they had buried down in Devon had not been Miranda? Charles had identified her as his wife, but he might have been mistaken. Her face had been unrecognizable. She could have been anybody.

Had he been mistaken? Or had he believed what he wanted to believe, burying a deep unsurety in the grave with the body? In which case he would harbor a fear she might return.

And if she did, what about me? Where would I stand?

I would cease to be his wife.

I felt myself sway under the onslaught of such desperate thoughts and heard Charles's voice dimly as he caught me in his arms.

"Darling! Darling! What's the matter? What is it?"

I was carried to the bed and gently set down upon it. His face came into focus. "Charles," I whimpered, wanting to say more, wanting to beg him to set my mind at ease, but he continued:

"My poor sweet. It's all that traveling. It's worn you out. We should have taken more time over the journey. You need rest. Why, you're trembling. You're cold. Why the devil haven't they come to light the fire? What's keeping them?"

He flung himself at the bell rope to summon someone, and as I watched him, concerned and angry on my behalf, I thought proudly, He loves me. He cares for me. He's my husband, not Miranda's. Miranda is dead and will never return. Yet I asked him, "Will Miranda come back?"

He turned and stared at me. *"What?"*

"If she'd been wearing the earrings there'd have been no doubt. It would be proof that . . ."

I broke off catching my breath. What was I saying?

"That she's dead? She is dead, Deborah. I've told you so."

"Yes, but . . ." Oh, stop it! Don't go on!

"But, what?"

"Oh, nothing." There, it was finished.

"Nothing," he said. "Just like that. Nothing. You imply

that I'm lying to you about Miranda and you call it nothing. Well, I call it very definitely something, and demand to know what you mean by it."

It was not finished. I heard myself reply, "Well, every time her name is mentioned or anything crops up to remind you of her, you . . . you . . ."

He crossed the room to me, eyes glinting blackly in a face carved out of granite.

"I, what?"

"You're always so . . . so . . ."

My heart was beating rapidly as he stood over me gimlet-eyed, and my voice shook as it trailed into silence.

"So, what?"

His voice was deadly cold. His face betrayed no emotion. I would rather he fumed and raged than retained this terrible icy calm.

Why was he so calm?

Once the question leapt to my mind others followed on in the same manner. Was it because he knew Miranda was dead—because he had killed her himself? He looked like a man who could kill. And his hatred was strong enough for it. Had Miss Selina suspected as much? Was that why she had tried to warn me against him and not, as I had thought, because of her desire to see me married to her favorite nephew, Jonathan?

"How can you be so sure she's dead?" I cried out in anguish.

His look knifed me. His icy calm cracked.

"What do you want me to say," he said, "that I'm not? If I told you the woman I identified as Miranda was not Miranda, would that satisfy you? I thought we'd had all this out before. I thought you trusted me."

"I do. I don't know what's got into me. It's not me saying all these things, it's someone else."

That was what I wanted to say. That is what I did say in my heart. But no words came out of my mouth. Instead, tears rolled down my cheeks.

He drew in a deep breath and said, "You'd better try to get some sleep. You're obviously overwrought," then went from the room.

"Charles!" I cried out at last, "I'm sorry! Don't leave me."

But he had gone and when I reached the door and looked out he was nowhere to be seen.

I went back to the bed and fell upon it weeping and wailing. What was the matter with me? Why was I thinking such terrible things about my husband. They weren't true. I knew they weren't true. Yet I had thought them and spoken them and hurt him in the process.

At last worn out by tears and travel I fell asleep.

When I awoke the room was bathed in shadowy firelight. Someone had been in while I slept to light the fire and draw the curtains. They had left the lamp burning low, but they had not left me anything to eat or drink, and I was parched.

I rose to tug at the bell pull and froze.

"Deborah."

Someone had called my name. Someone close by. Yet there was no one in the room besides myself. I stopped breathing and listened for my name to be called again. The only sound I heard was the crackle of the logs in the grate as the flames licked them.

I started to breathe again. The effort was painful. My heart knocked against my ribs in the effort and echoed loudly in my ears.

I reached for the bell pull again, and stiffened.

"Deborah."

Someone *had* called my name. There was no one in the room with me, so it must have come from outside.

I called out, "Come in."

No one entered.

"Deborah. Deborah."

It was a cry for help.

I ran to the door.

No one was there.

"Deborah-ah-ah-ah."

I ran along the corridor. Someone was in distress. I had to help.

At the door of the guarded white room I halted and turned the handle, slowly, as if in a dream. And like a dream I seemed to be standing outside myself, watching myself turning the handle of a room I did not wish to enter. In my mind I turned away from it and was already descending the stairs, but the knob continued to turn in my hand and the door swung inwards.

In a shaft of moonlight streaming through the darkened window she stood facing me, angelically lovely with her hair a golden halo about her head and a sweet smile curving her lips. Her blue gown matched her earrings and floated about her as if blown by a gentle breeze.

Miranda!

She raised a hand and beckoned to me.

From faraway came a long thin scream.

Charles was bending over me. I clutched at him convulsively.

"I've seen her," I cried. "She's alive!"

"Hush, don't talk. The doctor says . . ."

Hadn't he heard me? "She's alive!" I repeated. "Miranda! She's not dead! I saw her!"

"She's delirious," Miss Selina said as Charles drew back from me with a sharp intake of breath, and I saw her standing beside a tall bespectacled gentleman who was smiling benignly—Dr. Pinner. I wondered vaguely what he was doing here, but did not dwell on it. It was not important. I turned back to Charles.

"She beckoned to me."

"You imagined it."

"I heard her scream."

"That was you."

"Then it was because I saw Miranda."

"You didn't see her." He was getting very angry.

"I did! I did! She was in there! She's always been in there! She looks out of the window at me! She watches me! She's always watching me!"

"She's mad," Miss Selina said.

"No," Dr. Pinner contradicted her. "It's just a touch of hysteria. Quite common among women in her condition."

"My condition?"

Miranda, the locked room, were wiped from my mind as my heart began to beat faster.

"You're going to have a baby, Lady Denton." he beamed. "Early in September, I would hazard a guess."

I gaped at him. I had begun to suspect I might be pregnant while in Italy and had decided to consult a physician upon my return to England, but hearing it like this, out of the blue, I was stunned.

"A baby!" I breathed and turned to my husband, "Oh, darling! A baby! Our baby! Are you pleased? Say you're pleased! Tell me you're pleased!"

His face softened. "Do you need to ask?" he said, and as his arms enfolded me, I was consumed with joy. There was a child inside me. His child. An heir for Rosemont.

Miss Selina did not seem very pleased, however. When I was sick she gave me no sympathy, but said tartly, "What do you expect? It serves you right." When Charles had gone to London on business and we were sitting in front of a blazing fire together, I happened to mention that I hoped to have many more babies. "I suggest you get this one over first before you start thinking about more."

But then she sighed sadly and wagged her beautifully coiffeured head at me. "Oh, Deborah, you are so young. Hardly more than a baby yourself."

"I'm into my twentieth year," I reminded her.

"A great age," she responded sarcastically. "Why didn't

you give yourself a little more time, a few more months in which to enjoy your marriage before burdening yourself with—a *baby?*"

"You can't plan these things," I said. "And anyway I don't consider my baby a burden."

With a pitying glance she settled into silent contemplation.

I sat a few moments longer, then rose and went in search of Alicia. She was happy for me. She would be willing to listen to me talking about my new baby. How I wished she could do more than listen—squeeze my hand and smile and nod. How I would have loved to discuss my "interesting condition" with her. I could talk to her till I was blue in the face and she would listen, but it was not the same as having someone to discuss it with me.

I should also have liked to be able to discuss my sighting of Miranda with her, but I could not even talk to her about that. She would not listen, but shied away from me whenever I broached the subject.

Everyone pooh-poohed my "vision" as they called it. It was a product of my imagination, they said, brought about by my condition. It was a well-known fact that ladies suffered many disturbing things during pregnancy—some fancied strawberries and cream in mid-winter, others craved pickles and fried bananas—I saw visions.

I wished I could agree with them, but I could not. I *had* seen Miranda. *Had* seen her beckon to me. The knowledge made me tremble, but at least I accepted now that it was not a living creature I had seen, but a ghost. Miranda's ghost, which inhabited the cold white room and walked the silent corridors at night.

Miranda haunted Rosemont. Hers was the lurking presence I had sensed from the moment of my arrival. As evil in death as she had been in life, she had waited till the pinnacle of my happiness had been reached before presenting herself to me, dampening my joy with the knowledge that I should have to share Rosemont with her for the rest of my life. I would never be free of her.

Charles would never be free of her.

She would haunt us for the rest of our lives.

I felt again the cold breeze, as I reached the pilastered door, that had blown from nowhere and played with the gossamer stuff of her blue gown, lifted her golded curls into a halo round her head, revealed the conclusive proof of her identity—two sapphire earrings shaped like periwinkle flowers. She had looked as if she had just stepped out of the frame surrounding her portrait . . . But in the portrait she had been wearing the matching periwinkle brooch. When I had seen her standing in the middle of the white cold room, she had not. Why not?

My mouth dried as I answered my own question. She had not been wearing the periwinkle brooch because it was no longer in her possession, it was in mine.

Suddenly, I had to see it. Somehow, I knew it held a message for me, and I had to find out what it was before it was too late. Too late? For what? I did not know. But the periwinkle brooch held the clue. The periwinkle brooch held the clue to all the fears and anxieties that had plagued me since coming to Rosemont.

The brooch had been found and returned to me. I had pushed it to the back of a drawer under Doreen's watchful, questioning eye. In her sensitive understanding way she had not remarked on it, nor transferred it to my jewel case. Now I drew it forth and stared at it intently. I turned it over and over in my hands. It told me nothing. I pinned it to my bodice and looked at it in the mirror. The precious gems winked back at me inoffensively.

I sighed and took it off. It was only a brooch, an inanimate thing, how could it hold a message for me? I replaced it in the dim recesses of my drawer, telling myself I had been letting my imagination run away with me.

But I was far from satisfied and felt strangely uneasy.

288

What was the answer to the puzzle that foxed me? Did it even exist outside my own thoughts?

In sudden desperation I clawed a thick coat out from my wardrobe and fastened it round me, pulled on a woollen tam-o'-shanter and warm gloves and took myself out into the cold wintry air.

An icy wind carrying a hint of snow with it stung my cheeks and pinched my ears. I had to hold onto my hat lest it be blown away, and turning my back against the wind, was buffeted along hardly aware of where I was going till I reached the river and gazed out across the dark water to where the bare arms of trees bordering the estate lurched frantically to dislodge the white flakes of snow that were growing larger.

I walked further on by the river till I could see St. Martin's spire prodding the sky, as if trying to make a rent in the thick mantle of gray, and the village chimneys sending curling streams of smoke to add their little bit to the overall gloom. The waters of the river made a plaintive sound and struck a sympathetic chord in my heart. A sudden gust of wind wrenched my hat from my hands and sent it hurtling into the sad waters. I watched it grow heavy and wet — and sink.

And all the time I was pondering the periwinkle brooch and Miranda's appearance without it.

With the wind turning its attention to my hair and unlacing it from its pins, with the falling snow wetting my face and the light fading fast, I turned to go back.

The house appeared strange, mysterious, behind the thickening curtain of snow. It seemed to rise out of nothing and sway drunkenly as if it had no solid foundation. There was no warm rosy hue to Rosemont now, only the cold gray darkness of a tomb. Then as if to give the lie to my thoughts, a light appeared at an upstairs window, then another and another, till at last a whole army of lighted windows shone out into the gloom and the morbid impression of a graveyard disappeared.

I hurried forward, my thoughts turning from gloomy imaginings to happy thoughts of my husband's return from London. He was due home tonight, and it would not be long now before his train drew into the station and he would step into his white automobile waiting for him there and drive himself and Finch back to Rosemont.

He had been in London for over a week now attending to the business of his shipping company and seeing that the preparations for our impending arrival at Denton House were well under way. It had been decided that we would live in London till the baby was due to be born, for I wished as little separation from Charles as possible and he could not stay away from Lockhart's all the time. But just before the baby was due we would return to Rosemont for the birth. It would not do for the heir of Rosemont to be born elsewhere.

I smiled fondly to myself. How wonderful it would be when I held my baby in my arms. He would be called Charles after his father. It would be a boy. I knew it would. I had promised my husband it would. He had said he didn't care what it was, a girl would suit him very well, especially if she looked like me. How I loved him for it.

My heart gave a sudden lurch. A light was moving round the walls of the house towards the North Tower shrouded in darkness. Through the fall of snow I made out an indistinct figure carrying a lantern. Benson, perhaps, going about his duties, or Higgs, or even Newman. Anyway, whoever it was, there was no reason why I should be afraid. No prowler would advertise his presence with a light. Nevertheless . . .

I had come to a halt, but now I started walking again, not to the front door as I intended, but in the direction of the moving light — to investigate.

To investigate? I had just decided there was nothing to investigate.

But my footsteps were not guided by reason and I was drawn on inexorably till I came face to face with the holder of the lamp.

"Aunt Selina!" I was astonished to see she was wearing no warm coat over her dark silk gown. "What are you doing out here like this? You'll catch your death of cold."

"I was looking for you."

"Looking for me!"

"I saw you leave the house and saw my chance had come."

"You should have waited inside if you wished to talk to me."

"No. No. I couldn't do that. I couldn't let my chance go by."

There was that in Selina's voice that made me long for flight—but my feet still refused to obey my brain's commands.

"You couldn't leave it alone, could you?" Her voice, soft till now, sharpened and she spat out her words contemptuously. "Neither could she. You're all alike, you flibbertigibbets. Men. Sex. That's all you can think about. You're two of a kind, you and she." Now her voice became a whine. "No, that's not true. You're not like her. You're much nicer. I would have liked you to . . . Oh, why didn't you marry Jonathan? I pleaded with you to. I warned you not to marry Charles. You can't deny it. I did my best."

She was rambling. Perhaps sickening for something. She should not be out here in the cold.

"Let's go indoors," I said. "We can discuss all this in the warmth."

"No," she snapped. "We can't go indoors. *You* can never go indoors again."

My mouth dried and fear numbed my bones, but I managed to breathe, "Do let's go in, Aunt Selina. You're not yourself."

She took no notice and continued.

"I was very fond of you, Deborah. I still am. It will pain me to send you away. But there's no help for it. Now. I would have let you stay a bit longer. I was prepared to give you a few more weeks—but a *baby!* I can't have a baby at Rose-

291

mont. Not *his* baby."

Her voice had grown strained, high-pitched, and sent terror through me. I prayed someone would hear her and come out and put a stop to this—whatever it was.

"*She* was going to have a baby. She told me about it as she was preparing to leave. The little fool! If she'd kept quiet she might be here now, but she pranced and crowed and laughed in my face. She said it wasn't his, but she would pass it off as such. She would go to Witchet Towers and have the baby there. Everyone would believe it was Charles's baby. She would make them believe it. And she would bring the baby back to Rosemont with her. Having produced an heir Charles would not turn her out again. And so I had to see she never came back. And now you must join her."

Her voice grew calmer now. Too calm. I tried to edge away from her.

"Oh, my dear, I hope you're not going to be troublesome. She was troublesome. It didn't do her any good, only caused her more pain than it need. It will be much better for you if you cooperate. You won't be alone. I wouldn't wish you to be alone. She's waiting for you. You said she was beckoning to you. She wants you to join her. And you will, won't you? You won't keep her waiting?"

She was mad! Miss Selina was mad! Mad! Mad! Mad!

"Don't . . . don't send me to join Miranda," I begged, as the truth finally swept over me.

What else could I do? I did not know what else to do.

"I must. Anybody who poses a threat to my beloved Jonathan's inheritance must be disposed of—even Charles if needs be. But I don't think that will be necessary. Once you've gone, he'll never turn to anyone else, and if he does—he'll rear no sons. Rosemont belongs to me, and to my son, and to his sons after him."

She was insane. She imagined Jonathan was her son. What could I do? How could I reason with her? Attack the thing that was worrying her?

"I might not be carrying a boy!" I shrilled. "It might be a girl! A girl cannot inherit Rosemont!"

"I can't take the risk. You said you want many babies. You'd be bound to produce a boy sooner or later."

"No. I won't have any more. I . . ."

"Don't argue, Deborah. I can't let you stay. You must go. Miranda is waiting for you."

I felt rather than saw the movement she made towards me and screamed. Belatedly my feet sprang into action and I started to run. With surprising agility she caught me, her fingers curling round my arms like snakes.

I screamed and screamed and tried to shake myself free. But the snakes turned into bands of steel.

"Just one push," she cooed, "that's all it takes. Don't look at me like that. If you look at me like that, I shall feel sorry, and I don't want to feel sorry. You must go. You must."

She forced me backwards through the snow. The lamp which she had set down on a jutting stone cast a pool of light and I saw a gaping hole in the snow — a black, bottomless pit.

"No. No. No." I screamed in terror. But the cry was only in my head. I had no breath for screaming. All my strength, all my efforts were needed to counter the superhuman strength that was Selina Denton.

"Don't fight me, Deborah," she chastised me as if I were a naughty child, edging me nearer and nearer to the black gaping hole in the ground. "It has to be."

"God help me. God help me," I prayed and thought He had not heard me, as I felt myself slip and knew I should soon leave this world forever.

Chapter Seventeen

"He should be home sometime tomorrow. He's catching the next train down. I didn't tell him everything. Just enough to ensure his swift return."

Charles replaced the telephone receiver after speaking to his brother and went to stand by the fireplace. His eyes were dark and shadowed with grief. His shoulders sagged. He looked utterly exhausted.

"As soon as it's light I'll do something about that hole. I can't leave it as it is in spite of the weather. It's too dangerous."

"Yes. It must be very deep. I wonder how it came to be there? Your aunt couldn't have dug it herself."

But remembering her superhuman strength as she grappled with me, I was not so sure.

"It's always been there. It's an old well, I think — maybe something more gruesome — but it's always been covered by an iron grill. God knows how she managed to remove it, if indeed she did, it was welded into the ground by years of wind and weather."

"She had tremendous strength. It was like trying to wrestle with three strong men at once when she . . . when I . . ."

I could not go on. The memory of my fight for life on the edge of that awesome abyss was too much for me. Charles crossed the floor quickly and took me in his arms.

"Don't, my love. Try not to think about it. It's all over now. Forget it."

"That's easier said than done," I whispered, trying to smile.

How could I stop thinking about that yawning chasm that was waiting to drown me in its treacly depths? I thought I had drowned in it. But I had only fainted.

Newman, on one of his self-appointed rounds, had heard my screams and come running as fast as ageing legs would allow. He had surprised Selina, who had fled at his approach and disappeared from view. It was into his arms I had slid and not the pitiless depths of the gaping hole.

Charles arrived home just as Newman carried me into the house. He saw me safely installed before a blazing fire and left me with Alicia, Doreen, and Murkett in attendance to go in search of his aunt, returning an hour or so later leading her by the hand.

I had been stunned by her appearance. She was bedraggled and wet and minus one shoe, but she walked beside him like a dutiful child. I stared—we all stared—in dismay. Her glance, which had rested upon each one of us in so many different ways, warmly, icily, shrewdly, contemptuously, flickered over us carelessly, disinterestedly, as if she hardly saw us, and if she did, did not recognize us.

Charles led her with gentle concern up the grand oak staircase. I followed with Alicia, still clinging to my hand as if she would never let it go. Selina made no protest as Charles bade her to lie down on her bed, but curled herself up into a ball and with a breathed, "Goodnight . . . Papa," fell asleep at once.

His face stricken with grief, he pulled the covers over her.

"Stay with her, Lister," he said as his aunt's personal maid appeared, wondering what was going on. "Lock the door when we've gone and don't leave her alone for a second. Ring for anything you might require."

"But my lord, what's the matter with her? Is she ill?"

"Yes, Lister," he said brokenly. "She's very ill."

Rosemont was plunged in gloom. We walked about on tiptoe, spoke in hushed tones, going over and over all that had happened. It was unbelievable, incredible . . . But it was true. In a fit of madness Miss Selina had tried to murder me and was now locked away upstairs with only Lister for company.

Alicia would not leave my side, listening intently to all that was said, and I was never more aware of her need to express herself in words. I squeezed her hand to let her know I understood her concern for me.

"Do you think Aunt Selina really murdered Miranda? She implied she had."

"She was raving," said Charles.

"She said she was waiting for me to join her. If she had — murdered her, she must have followed her to Witchet Tower and . . ."

"She couldn't have done that. She never left Rosemont."

"Then . . . Are you absolutely positive the girl you identified was Miranda?"

"I was," said Charles, "till now. Now I don't know. Aunt Selina must have been mad for some time if . . . without our knowing . . . Can someone be mad without their nearest and dearest knowing? She exhibited no signs of madness . . ."

Lister interrupted us. She had heard the whole story of events from a servant who had answered her ring and had come flying down to cry she could not stay alone in a room with a murderess.

With a harshness unusual in him when dealing with servants Charles shouted, "Go back to your mistress at once. I told you not to leave her alone."

Fear made her bold. "I'm sorry, my lord, I can't. I'm afraid."

"There's nothing to be afraid of. She won't hurt you. She's not violent now."

"But she might be when she wakes up."

She was trembling and fearful.

Charles drew in his breath nosily then was silent for a moment. When he spoke again it was with more understanding.

"Very well. You may have another servant to sit with you."

But nothing would persuade her to return to Miss Selina's room. In the end she agreed to sit outside the door, listen for any sound her mistress might make, and to call his lordship at once if she heard anything.

And now, after many attempts, Charles had at last managed

reach his brother on the telephone and acquaint him with
the shattering news, not that his aunt was mad, but that she
was very, very ill.

But she was mad. Aunt Selina *was* mad.

It was a shocking, terrifying thing to have to admit and my
heart palpitated at the thought.

"She'll have to be put away, won't she?" I whispered huskily.

A spasm of pain crossed my husband's face. "I—think she
might."

"She will!" I cried, and more wildly, "She *will!* And it's all
my fault! I'm to blame! If I hadn't come here . . ."

His hold tightened round me. "No, no, my love, you're not
to blame. How could you be? Her mind became unhinged.
She didn't know what she was doing. It needn't have been you
. . . it could have been anybody . . . you just happened to be
here."

"I am to blame! I am! You don't know . . ."

"I know I still have you." His voice was rough with emotion.
"When I think what might have happened—I go cold."

"But, Charles, she said . . ."

"Never mind what she said. It's over. You've been through a
terrible ordeal, but you must try to put it behind you. It won't
be easy, but you must try. I'll help you all I can . . . and soon
there'll be the baby to help you forget."

The baby! The heir to Rosemont! The true heir? Aunt Selina had said . . .

"And now you must get some sleep," he continued. "And so
must you, Alicia."

Murkett was sent for and Charles raised Alicia from her
seat. She did not want to leave us, but he insisted, and used as
she was to being obedient, she left quietly with her nurse.

"I can't sleep," I said when they had gone.

He smiled and drew me down with him onto the sofa and in
his warm embrace with my head against his chest, I fell almost
immediately into a deep sleep, a blessed respite for my weary
soul.

It was light when I woke. A bright sun pierced the window from out of a cloudless blue sky. The window ledges were piled high with glistening snow. The fire was crackling merrily and a table was set in front of it.

I stirred in my husband's arms. He was wide awake. Had he slept at all? There were dark circles under his eyes and lines of strain round his mouth.

"What time is it?" I asked.

"Eight o'clock. Are you hungry?"

"No."

"Neither am I."

The dark cloud of misery and uncertainty still hung over us. Miss Selina was mad. She had tried to murder me. Something would have to be done about it.

"I think I'd better go and look in on Aunt Selina now you're awake, Deborah," Charles said.

"I'll come with you," I whispered.

He was facing an ordeal as great as mine had been, and he would need all my support.

We found her still asleep, curled up into a ball just as we had left her. As we looked down at her, she opened her eyes and sat up and smiled.

"Hello," she said and cold water trickled down my spine. Her voice was not Selina's voice—it was the high pipe of a child.

Charles's voice was a cracked whisper. "Good morning, Aunt Selina."

She giggled and looked vacant. He cleared his throat nervously.

"Would you like some breakfast?"

"Is it time to get up?" she piped.

His eyes flew to meet mine in despair and she followed his gaze.

She pouted like a spoilt child. "Who are you?" she said. "What are you doing here? Go away. I don't want you. I want Nanny. Where's Nanny? I want Nanny." Her face crumpled nd she started to cry like a baby.

I stared at her in bewilderment and Charles caught her in his
rms and tried to soothe her. I thought I had never loved him
o much as I did at this moment, when I saw him dealing so
ently with his poor witless old aunt. So old she was. Suddenly
o very old. And yet—a child. Last night she had been a fiend
:ady to kill. Now she could have harmed nobody.

She fought against Charles at first crying, "I don't want
ou. I want Nanny. Where's Nanny?" But under his calming
ifluence she quieted and eventually flung her arms around
is neck and kissed him.

Lister, who had been hovering in the background, came fur-
ier into the room. Her face was a study of mixed expressions.
Vonder, fear, anxiety, disbelief—love. Selina caught sight of
er and pushed Charles away.

"Nanny!" she cried with a radiant smile, and held out her
rms to Lister.

Lister clasped her mistress to her bosom. There were tears in
er eyes. She looked up at Charles.

"I'll look after her, my lord. She needs me. I'll take care of
er. I must bathe her and change her and give her something to
at . . ."

We left her fussing and fretting over her mistress, hardly
ble to believe this was the same Lister who had been too
fraid to stay in the room with her the night before. But there
as no doubting her concern now. She would indeed care for
Miss Selina.

Relieved in our minds to the extent of knowing Miss Selina
vas in capable hands, we found ourselves able to partake of
ie breakfast Croft had sent in to us.

We ate and drank in silence, each thinking the same
houghts, each contemplating the necessity of removing Miss
elina to an asylum with misgiving. But there was one thought
i my mind I was certain would not be in his. He had stopped
ie the last time I had attempted to broach it. Now I could
vithhold it no longer.

"Aunt Selina seemed to believe Jonathan was her son," said, and wished I had held my tongue at the look that cam over his face. I thought I had seen him at his lowest, his mos dejected, but now . . .

He looked at me as if he hated me. "He is her son," he sai harshly.

He stared at me broodingly, silently, morosely. I had un locked a skeleton in the cupboard and had forced him to look upon it. He looked as if he would never forgive me. Then h drained his cup and set it down.

"I'll tell you all about it," he said, rising and pacing the room as he often did when he was worried. "I should have told yo long ago. I tried to once, but . . . well . . . you turned me from it and I thought, it's been a secret so long, perhaps you nee never know, and I was glad to forget about it. But now yo have a right to know. I'll tell you the whole story—as I know it

"Years ago, when Aunt Selina was about twenty-five, sh had an affair with a married man. The inevitable happened She became pregnant. Her lover immediately removed himsel from the scene. I don't know what happened to him. It doesn matter. It's clear he wanted nothing more to do with her. Sh was stricken. Haunted by guilt and worry. Expecting a chil and unmarried she would be derided and ostracized by Soc ety. She couldn't face it. She tried to commit suicide. She threw herself into the river."

"Oh, Charles," I murmured, dumbfounded by what heard.

"It's a sordid story. I'm sorry to have to burden you with i but if you are to know anything you must know the whole. It' the only way you'll ever understand.

"She would have drowned had not my father, who had take his rod earlier in the day and gone fishing, heard the splash an gone to investigate. She was floundering upstream. He swar out to save her. He only just managed to reach her in time. was all hushed up. My parents took her on a protracted holi day abroad, and when they returned the newly born baby wit hem was easily accepted as my mother's own child."

"But . . . How do you know all this?"

"I found out by pure accident. Going through my father's
papers after his death I came across an old diary of his—it had
been a hobby of his, keeping diaries. He had drawers full of
hem dating back to when he was a boy. My mother said she
would like to keep them and I had had them sent to her room.
How this particular one came to be separated from the rest, I
don't know, but out of curiosity I flicked through the pages as I
took it along to my mother to add to the rest, and my eye fell
upon an entry made on the fifteenth of March. *Today, Selina
gave birth to a son. We have named him Jonathan.* I read
those words over and over again, unable to believe I read them
right. *Today, Selina gave birth to a son. We have named him
Jonathan.*

"I rushed to my mother demanding to know the truth of it—
badgered and bullied her into telling me the truth against her
will. She made me promise never to reveal a word of what she
old me to a living soul and to burn the diary. Stunned though I
was, I gave the promise gladly. I loved Aunt Selina like a second mother, and Jonathan—Jonathan was my brother. I
could never think of him as anything else. And I have kept my
promise—till now."

"Till I forced you into breaking it," I mumbled in self-con-
empt.

"If I had not wished to break it, I would not have done so,"
he said. "But you are my wife, and have been almost killed for
it. You have a right to know. And now I must extract from you
he same promise I made to my mother. Jonathan must never
know his true parentage. He is innocent of any blame and
nothing can be gained from telling him the truth. Only pain
and guilt can result . . ."

"I shall never tell him," I cried. "Never! You can rely on me."

"I know I can," he said and came to sit by me again.

"But why does she hate you so?" I asked. "After all your
parents did for her, you'd think . . ."

301

"She doesn't hate me. Not really. Not deep down. She just loves Jonathan more. It's natural enough. He's her son."

"She wanted Rosemont for Jonathan."

"The only way that could be would be on my death, if I died childless. He's in direct line. No one outside the family knows any different. When I married you, it must have been like thunderbolt to her. And when you became pregnant . . ."

"I was a threat. That's what she said I was. A threat."

He gave a groan and gathered me to him.

"She did shut me in that dungeon, you know," I whispered.

"I realize that now," he said. "I blame myself for it. I should have taken more care of you."

"Miranda was pregnant."

How I wished the words unsaid as he drew back from me. They were the echo of Miss Selina's and heavy with accusation.

"And you believe it was I who made her so," he said, his eyes like sea pebbles.

"I didn't say that," I cried quickly.

"No, but you thought it."

"No! Well, maybe, for a moment. Oh, darling, forgive me . . ." He sprang from my side and was pacing the room again. "It was a sudden jealousy, that's all."

"Jealousy!" He rounded on me furiously. "You can't still have that bee in your bonnet that I'm in love with Miranda! I am not. I never have been. Infatuated, briefly — but that is all not to be compared with what I feel for you." He stopped and stood looking down at me, breathing heavily. "I could shake you, Deborah," he said. "Now listen to me, for it's God's truth I'm telling you. If Miranda was pregnant, she was made so by another man, not me. I never touched her after the first few days of our marriage — and we were married for nearly a year. That's the truth. If you can't believe it, then I'm sorry, but you'll have to live with it, as I shall, for I tell you this, I shall never let you go. Never."

"Oh, Charles . . . Beloved . . . Forgive me."

"Forgive?" He fell on his knees and with infinite tenderness ook my hands in his. "There's no need for such a word to leave our tongue. I love you, more than I have ever loved another uuman being. Whatever you do, whatever you say, whatever ou think, I shall always love you. Nothing will alter that. I night argue with you, rail at you — you can be so aggravating t times . . ." His loving smile took the sting out of these vords. ". . . I might cause you pain by my thoughtlessness . ." "Never," I murmured. ". . . But I shall never cease to love ou. And nothing, *nothing*, will ever make me leave you. You an be absolutely sure of that. I'll never let you go."

Tears flowed down my cheeks and he took me in his arms. Tears of joy, tears of happiness. Never, never would I give him ause to regret his words. Yet in my heart I knew he never vould. Whatever I did, whatever I said, his love would remain teadfast. I felt secure at last and my heart almost burst with ove for him.

Sometime later we went out with our arms about each other rudging through the snow to the spot where the previous ight's terrible scene had been enacted. I went not without a ittle trepidation, but he was with me and my fear was sub- lued. I should come to no harm with him beside me. When we eached the gaping hole, black against the virgin snow, how- ver, I hung back at a distance while Charles, finding the iron grill a few feet away, started to drag it back into position.

"It's heavy," he grunted. "How on earth Aunt Selina . . . nanaged to . . . move it . . ."

"Do you think she had an accomplice?"

He paused for a moment, breathing hard from his efforts, und our eyes met in sudden contemplation of the frightening oossibility. If she had had an accomplice, that accomplice night still be about and perhaps I was not safe, after all. Then ie shook his head.

"No. Impossible. There's no one at Rosemont would do uch a thing. They would have to be as mad as . . . She *must* ave moved it. There's nothing else for it. You said yourself you were surprised by her strength."

"It was as if she were possessed of the devil."

He continued his efforts. "Her strength must certainly have come from outside herself. I can hardly move this thing, and I'm no weakling."

A rising wind moaned and tugged at my skirts, whipped the snow into little showers above the ground, dislodged thick chunks off tree branches, chimney stacks, and window ledges. Something tapped me on the shoulder—it might have been snow, but shaking all over I slewed round expecting to see Miss Selina standing behind me.

There was no one. Nothing but snow, snow, snow.

Charles was puffing and panting as he tugged and pulled the iron grill. "Just a bit further," he muttered, casting a swift glance at me, then, "Oh, my God!"

Terror renewed its grip on me. He was staring into the pit.

"What is it, Charles? What is it?"

But I think I knew even then.

He stopped me as I moved forward and rushed me back to the house ignoring my questions. Benson was waiting in the hall for him, but before he could state his business Charles took him to one side and spoke to him in undertones.

"I'll get a ladder, my lord," Benson said, as pale now as he had been ruddy before.

"There's one in the cellar," Charles said. "We'll need a lantern, too." He turned to me. "Stay in the house, Deborah."

"But I want to come with you."

"Do as I say," he said with all the authority of a captain at sea.

Nevertheless, when they left the house, I followed them.

He was angry and terse with me when he saw me.

"I told you to stay in the house."

"I couldn't, Charles."

"Well, stay back. Keep well away from the edge of the pit. And don't . . ." He didn't finish his sentence, just frowned and repeated, "Keep well away."

304

The ladder was really two in one and it had to be slid open to its full length it order to reach the bottom. Charles lowered himself over the edge and began the descent closely followed by Benson. Newman, the self-styled watchman to whom I would be eternally grateful for saving my life, had met us on the way and needed no invitation to join in the procession once he saw the ladder and the lantern, he had tagged along importantly, hung over the rim of the pit full-length on his stomach and held onto the ladder to keep it steady.

"Better not try that sort o' thing at my time o' life, mistress," he said. "A few years ago an' I woulda' be first down . . . 'Ere, what you doin'? You can't go down there . . ."

But I already had my foot on the ladder and was over the side.

I climbed down fearfully. The further down I went, the more I wished I had stayed above. But something stronger than myself drove me, a feeling of compulsion that would not be denied. Even the stench that rose to greet me and made me retch could not turn me back.

My feet touched the ground. I gave an involuntary cry.

"What the devil!" Charles rounded on me angrily. "I told you to stay aloft."

He moved swiftly to hide from me that which I had already seen. A skeleton, still covered in parts by ragged remnants of cloth, and the glint of diamonds and sapphires at each side of the skull.

Chapter Eighteen

Rosemont was abuzz.

The village constable had reported the incident to his superiors in King's Lynn, and in no time at all, cabs were disgorging uniformed policemen and officious detectives to besiege the place. We were asked countless questions which made us feel like criminals, till in the end Charles lost his temper and with a few well-chosen phrases put the questioners firmly in their places.

Looking aggrieved they accepted his chastisement. He was, after all, the Baron Denton — a peer of the realm whose influence ranged through the highest places. However, their expressions left us in no doubt that more enquiries would be forthcoming. It was only for the present they were silenced.

Other doctors were summoned to examine Miss Selina and they all supported Dr. Pinner's diagnosis that she was completely and certifiably mad. The police were all for taking her away at once to Bedlam. Charles refused to allow it, saying she would go into a privately run establishment nearby.

An undertaker arrived and placed Miranda's remains in a coffin which was then taken to bide in St. Martin's Church till burial could take place.

Jonathan arrived as the coffin was being carried out of the house.

"Aunt Selina?" he whispered, ashen-faced. "Is she . . . ? You didn't tell me it was as serious as . . ."

"It's not Aunt Selina," Charles said.

"Then who . . . ?"

"Come inside, Jon. I've a lot to tell you."

Jonathan listened in petrified silence while Charles recounted the events of the past hours—the true nature of his aunt's illness, the discovery of Miranda's body, the attempt on my life.

"Oh, God!" he moaned after hearing his brother out. "I was afraid of this."

"What do you mean?" cried Charles.

"I could have prevented the attack on Deborah."

"No one could have prevented it, Jon," I said. "Aunt Selina . . ."

"I could!" he shouted. "I knew she'd murdered Miranda!"

After a moment's absolute silence Charles breathed, "Impossible. No one knows for certain . . ."

"*I* know. I have proof."

"Proof?"

"Positive proof."

"You mean," Charles said quietly, "you've known all these years that Miranda's body was lying at the bottom of that pit, and you said nothing? You let me think . . . You let me identify that poor drowned woman as my wife . . ." his voice had risen and was ringing with contempt, ". . . and said nothing?"

"I didn't know then." Jonathan writhed beneath his scorn. "I believed she was Miranda, just as you did. It was only after I found that film and remembered those words . . ."

"What film? What words?" Charles demanded impatiently.

"It was while I was packing my equipment. Remember, Deborah, you helped me? I found that box of film and said I'd develop it when I got the chance. Well, I did—and wished I hadn't."

"What's all this got to do with—"

Jonathan turned back to Charles. "They turned out to be views of Rosemont and its environs. I was just thinking how good they were when I noticed, on one, something that had escaped me before. There were two female figures—one tall and dark, the other short and fair. They were partly obscured by bushes, but I knew who they were, even before looking at them through a magnifying glass. There was no mistaking that floaty kind of scarf Miranda used to like to wear, nor the little cape that was Aunt Selina's favorite. They appeared to be talking together. Or arguing. They were always arguing. But, enlarged, I could see Aunt Selina had the scarf in her hands and she was—tightening it round Miranda's throat."

The fire hissed and spluttered as a log collapsed in a shower of sparks. We all jumped and Charles moved quickly to prevent the log from tumbling out into the hearth.

"I tried to tell myself it wasn't what it seemed, but—I kept remembering her words."

"What words?" Charles asked impatiently again as he straightened.

"It was after you'd identified that woman as Miranda. Aunt Selina said to me, 'He's stupid. How can she be Miranda? Miranda never went to Devonshire.' 'But she did,' I said. 'You told us yourself she had gone to Witchet Towers.' 'Oh, yes, of course,' she said. 'How silly of me to forget that.' I put it down to a fit of absentmindedness, and thought no more about it. After all she was getting on and old people do tend to be forgetful. But together with the film . . ."

"It doesn't prove she murdered Miranda," Charles said.

But it did, and we all knew it did.

Jonathan continued, "The more I thought about it, the more uneasy I became. I imagined the same thing happening to Deborah. At last I decided to come home, give up my salon, and manage Rosemont again. I had the vague idea that if I could keep an eye on things . . . on Aunt Selina . . . But you'd given my job to Benson and told me I could go to hell."

Censure had crept into his voice and Charles responded angrily.

"That's not how it was, and you know it."

"That's how it appeared to me," Jonathan snapped. "Anyway, I stayed on for a while, but Aunt Selina appeared perfectly normal and seemed to adore Deborah, so I thought, What am I worrying about? and went back to my studio believing I must have been mistaken in the photograph, that some trick of the light must have made it look as if . . . Well, how could Aunt Selina have had the strength . . . ?"

"She had the strength," I murmured in heartfelt tones.

"You damn fool, Jon," Charles boomed. "Why didn't you say something instead of keeping it to yourself. I don't care about Miranda. She deserved to die. But Deborah's suffered greatly at Aunt Selina's hands, and her sufferings could have been averted if you'd spoken out."

"But what could I have said? That I thought I'd photographed our own aunt committing a murder — when I was not even sure I had?"

"You could have said something to put us on our guard. The cellar incident! Why didn't you say something then?"

"I almost did, but Aunt Selina came in and . . . Forgive me, Deborah. I should have spoken out. It's my fault you were attacked."

"No, Jon," I said, "don't blame yourself. I realize how hard it must have been for you . . ."

"Hard or not," Charles cut in, "he should have said something."

"Well, it's over now. There's nothing to be gained by recriminations," I said. "What puzzles me is how your aunt managed to live with the knowledge of what she'd done without giving herself away after you identified some unknown woman as Miranda."

"But she did give herself away, didn't she? To Jon —

though he didn't realize it at the time." He paused a moment, then continued. "I did believe it was Miranda. Her hair was the same color. I thought I recognized the clothes she was wearing. And all the time Aunt Selina knew . . ."

He broke off with a catch in his voice and I cried quickly, "It's no good worrying about it any more. We must just accept what has happened and put it behind us."

I was glad to see it made him smile—if somewhat wryly. "I seem to remember saying something like that to you."

"Yes, and it's good advice."

"She's right," Jonathan rallied to his normal self. "We'll all have to try and forget it."

"There's a deal to be done before we can do that," Charles said pessimistically. "There'll be the coroner's inquest, the funeral, the gossip . . . It will be a long time before . . ."

"A nine days' wonder," I said. "Then people will forget."

"I suppose I ought to go and see Aunt Selina," Jonathan said then, as if it were the last thing he wanted to do.

We went with him to her room. She was sitting up in bed and looked up disinterestedly at our entrance, but then her face lit up at sight of Jonathan. "Sammy!" she piped happily. "Have you asked Papa if we can go to the Fair? Did he say yes?"

Jonathan's face was working convulsively and he looked in great danger of breaking down.

"Answer me, Sammy!" she instructed him imperiously.

"Answer her," Charles whispered. "She thinks you're Father."

But Jonathan could not answer her.

She pouted and looked set to cry. "He said not, didn't he?"

With a gulping desperate cry Jonathan turned and staggered from the room.

"Where's my doll?" Miss Selina stared at me truculently. "Give her to me. I want her. I want. I want. I want."

She began beating her fists against the quilt and shouted

310

at Lister. "Tell her to fetch it, Nanny. Nanny, don't just stand there! Tell her to go and fetch it, or I'll have you dismissed."

"I'll fetch it," I said and stumbled out after Jonathan, almost blinded by tears. Miss Selina Denton, imperious mistress of Rosemont, had reverted to childhood and it was heartbreaking to see.

"I can't believe it, Deborah." Jonathan turned to me, stunned. "I can't believe that poor demented creature is Aunt Selina."

Rogers brought the carriage to the front door. He put on a brave face, as we all did. His mistress was to leave in as normal a manner as possible. She was going to Westways, an asylum for the insane run by nuns, where the inmates were cared for in as kindly and humane a way as one could wish. Though they were scrupulously guarded, they were never punished, but treated like backward children. If violence should erupt among the poor mad creatures, the culprit was immediately transferred to — another place. But we did not expect this to happen to Miss Selina.

Wrapped in furs and clasping a doll to her bosom — the one I had begged from Alicia and given to her — she stepped into the carriage ahead of her two nephews. She still referred to Jonathan as Sammy, her brother. She seemed to think Charles was her father. Everyone achieved a different personality in her eyes.

"Good-bye," she called out gaily. "I'll come back soon. Don't cry, Nanny. I wish you were coming with me, but Sammy says you need a holiday just as much as I do."

Gulping, Lister turned and fled to her room. She had begged to be allowed to go with her mistress, but the nuns had been adamant in their refusal.

The carriage pulled away. Selina's pale face looked back at me through the little window at the rear. My mind revolved dizzily and scurried back to the day I had painted in an unseen face at the window on my canvas. It had been Miss Selina's face, as I saw it now—little, pale, and pointed. With a twinge of discomfiture I realized that for a moment in time I must have been projected into the future and painted, in complete unawareness, that which was to come.

"We should be able to visit her often," I murmured chokily as I turned away with Alicia. "Westways isn't very far away and the nuns do not discourage visitors."

"It's a blessing she's lost her wits. It's saved her from prison."

"Yes. Who would have thought . . . Alicia!" I screamed her name, startling her. "You spoke!"

"Oh, Deborah," she breathed. "I did, didn't I?"

It is strange how sorrow can give way in an instant to joy. We flung our arms about each other and laughed and wept and laughed again till we were exhausted.

"How wonderful, how marvellous, to hear your voice," I cried ecstatically. "It's a miracle. A miracle."

"I hoped and prayed, but never really believed . . ."

"The last remnants of your illness gone. What a joyful surprise your brothers will have when they return."

"It wasn't illness that robbed me of my voice." Her quiet words sobered me. "It was fear. I was afraid, terribly afraid, of my aunt."

"I know. I guessed. I'm not surprised. She treated you abominably."

"It wasn't that. It was because I'd seen her murder Miranda and was afraid she would murder me because I'd seen . . . because I knew . . ."

"You saw . . . ? You couldn't have. You're blind. Or—are you?"

I had so often labored under the belief that she could see, in spite of all that pointed to the contrary, that I waited now for her to admit it.

"Yes. I've always been blind. I can't see in any way you could understand. But I can see, nevertheless. I can see what

I hear—and I heard Aunt Selina murder Miranda. I heard their voices, their struggle. I heard Miranda's scream. It was a long scream, high-pitched and thin—and terrifying to hear. Loud at first, it faded away gradually till there was nothing left but silence. Then I heard Aunt Selina chuckling to herself. 'Goodbye, Miranda,' she said. 'You'll never bring your baby to Rosemont now. It's dead. Like you.'

"I think I must have made a sound of some sort, trod on a twig or something, for she cried out, 'Who's that? Who's there?' I ran away then. I ran and ran and ran, bumping into things, falling . . . but I daren't stop. I thought she'd seen me and would kill me, too, if she caught me. Then I found myself at the old oak tree which Charles had taken me to see once. He told me he and Jonathan had both used it as children—as a refuge from parents and tutors. It became my refuge. I knew she'd never find me in the hollow of that old trunk.

"And she didn't. It was Charles who discovered me there.

"I'd been gone hours they said and demanded to know where I'd been. Aunt Selina was very angry with me and said I needed a good thrashing for all the trouble I'd caused. Charles said, 'She's only a baby, Aunt Selina. It was . . .' 'She's old enough to know better,' she snapped and started shaking me so hard, my teeth chattered. Charles told her to stop it, that bullying wouldn't help, and that I should be allowed to go to bed. Questions could wait till the morning.

"He picked me up in his arms and I clung to him, wanting to tell him everything, so that he would send Aunt Selina away, so that I would be safe, but . . . I couldn't speak. No words would come out of my mouth . . . I could make no sound at all."

I tried to mutter some sympathetic phrase, but was choked with emotion. It was a terrible tale she told, one she had carried with her through all the long years of silence. No wonder she had behaved oddly at times.

"I grew more and more afraid of my aunt. She was sharp

313

with me, said I was stupid and should be sent away. Shut away, she meant. I wished they would send me away, because I knew she would kill me if they didn't. Sometime, somewhere, she would get me alone and . . . In the end I suffered what they called a nervous breakdown and was sent away. I spent months, years, in one hospital after another. Charles took me to see specialist doctors abroad, hoping they would be able to bring my speech back — to no avail.

"At last I was allowed home again. Apart from my speech I was much improved. Away from Aunt Selina I was calm and happy. Aunt Selina welcomed me back lovingly, but I cowered away from her and she said, 'What's the matter with you, child? Am I an ogre that you cower from me?'

"Oh, yes, she was an ogre to me. Would always be. I could not pretend otherwise. I shivered and shook whenever in her presence. It irritated her — naturally, I suppose — and she started calling me stupid again, told people my illness had affected my brain and that I must be kept under constant supervision and looked after like a baby. It was too much for Nanny, who left saying she couldn't cope any longer with me now that I was dumb and daft as well as blind.

"So Murkett was put in charge of me and I grew to love her. She was like a mother to me and for the first time in years I began to feel safe and happy again. She knew I wasn't stupid and encouraged me to fend for myself. She gave me far more freedom than Aunt Selina realized and we both played the game of letting her believe she organized my life."

"And your tantrums," I said, "were they real — or faked?"

"Some were faked — it was the perfect way of being dismissed from Aunt Selina's presence — but mostly they were the results of sheer frustration at not being able to make myself understood."

"What about the sapphire brooch you gave me?" There were so many questions to ask her now she could answer me. "Did you know it had belonged to Miranda?"

314

"Yes. I found it quite by accident. I had strayed from Murkett's side when she stopped to flirt with one of the gardeners who, I think, was enamored of her, and was searching through the grass for daisies to pick when my fingers came into contact with something hard. I explored it and found I recognized it. It was the periwinkle brooch which had belonged to my mother and which Charles had given to Miranda. She loved it and always wore it — and the earrings that made up the set — and I knew she would never have lost it without making a fuss about it . . . So this must have been the spot where she had been murdered. As she had struggled with Aunt Selina the brooch must have become unpinned and dropped to the ground unnoticed by either of them, and had lain there ever since.

"As soon as I realized this I started to shake. I didn't know what to do with it. Should I take it to Murkett? She would give it to Aunt Selina, not knowing the significance of it. Should I give it to Charles when he came home? He might simply give it to Aunt Selina also. And Aunt Selina must never know I had found it. In the end I stuffed it into my pocket and later placed it in that little blue velvet box and hid it in my secret drawer. And there it stayed . . . for years . . . till you came."

"And you gave it to me." I experienced a moment's revulsion. "Why?"

"I had to warn you that you were in danger and it was the only thing I could do. I believed that if Aunt Selina saw you wearing it she would dismiss you, and as unhappy as that would have made me, it was preferable to what might happen to you if you stayed. I knew Jonathan was in love with you and wanted to marry you. I thought you were in love with him — you seemed to enjoy his company so much — and that you would accept him. I would dearly have loved you to be my sister-in-law, but I was afraid for you, for your safety. I kept thinking of what Aunt Selina had said about not wanting a baby at Rosemont. She killed Miranda because

315

she was going to have a baby. I was afraid she would kill you, too, if . . ."

"But she wanted me to marry Jonathan. She would have wanted me to bear his child. It was only . . ."

I stopped myself just in time from breaking my word to Charles and telling her the true facts about Jonathan's birth, but her head was cocked to one side questioningly and I had to add something. I added, "Only it was Charles I wanted to marry."

"No matter. Charles or Jonathan, the danger was there."

"Yes, I can see that now. I'm beginning to realize I've been in danger all the time I've been here. It's strange, but I sensed it from the moment I came. But I never dreamed it was Aunt Selina who threatened me. It was she who shut me up in that dungeon, you know. Everybody seemed so certain I had imagined it, and she was so kind to me, and so distressed I should accuse her of such a dreadful thing, that I began to believe I had imagined it."

"I knew it was Aunt Selina. I knew what she'd done to Miranda. When you were missing and couldn't be found I thought she'd killed you and somehow I would have to make my brothers see this. Then I thought, She never liked Miranda, but she liked you and wouldn't wish to hurt you for no reason. You were not expecting a baby. You were not even married yet. So maybe she just wanted to frighten you . . . into leaving Rosemont. But what had she done? Where had she taken you? Perhaps she'd locked you in the cellars? But the cellars had already been searched. Then I thought of the dungeons. Nobody would have considered them. They had been sealed off by my father before I was born. But supposing Aunt Selina had managed to break through? It seemed impossible, but I had to go and investigate."

"How glad I am you did. It was very brave of you. It was so dark and frightening down there."

"Dark or light," she said, "it's all the same to me."

I could have kicked myself. To be so insensitive after all

316

this time! It only went to prove how difficult it was to believe in her blindness.

"The door was bolted, but not locked . . ."

"It was locked. She had a key."

"She must have forgotten to lock it after her then. I made my way down the passages and heard you call out. I couldn't answer you, of course, so I made a scratching noise on the door . . ."

"I heard you . . ."

". . . and hurried back to find Charles."

"Oh, Alicia, I've so much to be grateful to you for. You saved me from a terrible fate. You gave me the periwinkle brooch to warn me of my danger. It always had a fascination for me, that brooch. As soon as I saw it nestling in its blue velvet box, I felt a strong pull towards it. It seemed to speak to me. It sounds farfetched, but I could have sworn I heard it say, 'Take me. Take me.' I think now, it might have been Miranda speaking to me through it, to find her through it. I think now, it was one of the ways she tried to contact me. Ever since I came to Rosemont I've had the feeling of being watched, of being wanted to do something. The first time I walked past that room — her room — I felt an irresistible urge to enter. She must have been in there then, waiting for the moment when . . ."

"You really believe you saw her in there?"

"I did see her."

After a moment's silence Alicia said, "Aunt Selina used to go in there."

I gaped at her in astonishment. "What?"

"She used to lock herself in there for hours. Sometimes she slept in there."

"Ho-how do you know?"

"Murkett told me."

"Murkett?"

"Murkett keeps nothing from me. She had to clean the room, wash the linen and everything. Aunt Selina forced her to do it and keep it secret. She told her if it ever got out, she would be dismissed and never allowed to see me again."

"And Murkett agreed because she couldn't bear to be separated from you."

"Yes."

"But why should she want to lock herself in there? I can understand her keeping the room as it was — for the same reason she kept the portrait — to spite Charles. But to sleep in there! In Miranda's bed! After what she'd done! It doesn't make sense!"

"She told Murkett it was because she missed Miranda so. Being in her room made her feel close to her again. Which was strange, all things considered."

"I think she refused to believe Miranda was dead."

"That's what Murkett said."

"And no one else suspected . . . guessed? Didn't any of the servants wonder why the door was always kept locked? Surely they must have seen Murkett laundering the bed sheets and asked questions?"

"They might have done. But Murkett's clever. She would have been able to give them a plausible explanation."

"So Aunt Selina went into that room," I mused. "It must have been she watching me from the window then. I knew someone was. No wonder she got so annoyed with me for insisting I saw somebody there. She must have been afraid I would find out her secret. And yet . . ."

I was not fully convinced that was the answer.

"Might it not have been Miranda trying to attract my attention? Mightn't she have been waiting in that room all these years for me . . . or someone . . . someone sensitive to atmosphere . . . to her presence? The very first day I sensed something about that room. An icy coldness seemed to emanate from it. A usual thing, I think, where ghosts are. I wanted to get into that room. Something propelled my hand to turn the knob . . . It was Miranda."

"It could have been your imagination," Alicia said, a nervous catch in her voice.

At any other time I would have respected it and said no more on a subject that obviously disturbed her, but now, "And the brooch," I continued musing. "It challenged me, too. It seemed to possess a life force of its own and terrified me at times. I believe Miranda prompted you to give it to me in another effort to . . ."

"Oh, stop it, Deborah. You mustn't think this way. It doesn't do . . ."

"And that night when someone came scratching at my bedroom door . . . I thought it was you." I went on to explain, for she knew nothing of this. "I thought I saw you going to that room and followed you, but by the time I reached it, you'd locked the door. I called out to you, but you didn't answer. I wasn't surprised. I'd called out to you before through that door and received no reply. I believed you used to lock yourself in there, to get away from everyone, but this was the first time I had *seen* you go in — though why you should wish to hide yourself away in the middle of the night perplexed me and I wondered if it had been you I'd seen. But of course it had been you, and to prove it to myself I went to your room and looked in, certain I would find it empty — but you were sleeping peacefully in your bed and I trembled to think who, or what, I had followed along the corridor."

"It must have been Aunt Selina," Alicia murmured unhappily.

"No, it was a ghost. Miranda's ghost. I thought so then and I'm certain of it now. She was trying to reach me. She'd been trying to reach me ever since I came to Rosemont, needing my help to bring her murderer to justice and release her from her earthbound existence . . . only the time wasn't right . . . I wasn't ready to believe. It wasn't till I came back from my honeymoon that I heeded her call . . . only to faint and fail her again. But she didn't give up. She called to me through the brooch, which drew me towards it and caused me such unease that I had to get out, even though it was a bitter cold night and such folly might put my unborn child at risk . . . and she led me to Miss Selina."

My breath caught in my throat as a new realization swept over me, and I clutched at Alicia in fear and trembling.

"She led me to Miss Selina who was waiting to kill me! She didn't want to be freed! She wanted me to join her! She wanted my death! As further revenge against Charles!"

"No, no." Alicia cried. "You're wrong. I'm sure you're wrong. But if Miranda was haunting Rosemont for the purpose of revenge, it wasn't against Charles, but against Aunt Selina, her murderer, and now that has been accomplished, she won't trouble us again. You've laid the ghost of Rosemont, Deborah."

She was right. The ghost was laid. Miranda was at rest.

"We'll get rid of the portrait," I said briskly, "as Charles wished. We'll strip that cold white room bare and refurnish it in a completely different style, though I doubt Charles and I will ever use it. The periwinkle brooch and earrings will go into a vault at the bank. I shall never wear them, heirlooms though they be. Maybe some future Lady Denton will — after all association with Miranda is forgotten. But I never want to set eyes on them again."

"Yes. Yes," Alicia agreed. "That's what we'll do."

We sat together in the window embrasure overlooking the courtyard, hands clasped, waiting for Charles and Jonathan to return. More snow had fallen and, with no wind to whip it into a turmoil, had settled into a clean white carpet over the sludge left by carriage wheels and boots.

The sun came out, parting the gray gloom of cloud and highlighting diamonds in the snow, and as the carriage bearing my husband and his brother appeared beyond the bridge, a great peace stole over me, for I knew we, too, would leave darkness and turmoil behind and emerge into a new and bright and shining day.